eyes on me

Also by Rachel Harris

FOR TEEN READERS

My Super Sweet Sixteenth Century
A Tale of Two Centuries
My Not So Super Sweet Life

FOR ADULT ROMANCE READERS

Taste the Heat
Seven Day Fiancé
Accidentally Married on Purpose
You're Still the One
The Nanny Arrangement

RACHEL HARRIS

Entangled Publishing, LLC
2614 South Timberline Road
Suite 105
Fort Collins, CO 80525
rights@entangledpublishing.com

Entangled Teen is an imprint of Entangled Publishing, LLC.

Visit our website at www.entangledpublishing.com.

Edited by Stacy Abrams and Judi Lauren
Cover design by Bree Archer
Cover images by
Getty Images/DaydreamsGirl
Getty Images/EricFerguson
Interior design by Heather Howland

Print ISBN 978-1-64063-526-5
Ebook ISBN 978-1-64063-527-2

Manufactured in the United States of America

First Edition March 2019

10 9 8 7 6 5 4 3 2 1

entangled teen
an imprint of Entangled Publishing LLC

For my beautiful girls, Jordan and Cali, who are growing up way too fast. Remember to enjoy every single moment of this crazy journey called life. We love you so much.

And for Holly and my real-life Viktória, who together helped bring ballroom into my life. Never stop being so fierce!

*"Dancing is like taking a mini vacation from the stress of the everyday.
You have to be in the moment."*

—Ofelia De La Valette

Chapter One

LILY

"Ms. Bailey, are you with us?"

Tearing my gaze away from my guidance counselor's creepy cat clock that was two minutes slow yet confirmed I was *at least* fifteen minutes late for AP English, I silently counted to three and then said, "I'm listening."

Mrs. Cooper gave me a quick, indulgent smile. "I'm sure it feels like we're ganging up on you, but I promise that's not our intention. Believe it or not, we're all on the same team."

Unfortunately, the smile on her face didn't match the worry in her eyes, so I figured I was screwed regardless.

Mrs. Cooper had gone above and beyond the call of duty to help me since Mom died. She was the kind of guidance counselor Hallmark made cards for, and it was tempting to hope she could pull out another miracle now. But as I watched her *tap-tap-tapping* her red-ink pen against the open file on her desk—a file that revealed the totality of my high school accomplishments and my near-stellar record, minus the freshman-year glitch—and scrunching her eyebrows in contemplation, I couldn't help feeling like the world as I knew it was about to be flipped.

Again.

For five long seconds, I inhaled oxygen, along with the sweet smell of jasmine from her diffuser. *AP and Dual Credit courses. Tied for highest GPA in the senior class. National Honor Society and Mu Alpha Theta.*

All that hard work.

Slowly, I let it out. *History Club. DECA. Key Club. Debate.*

Tutoring.

Crap. They'd better not take away tutoring.

Over the past seventy-two hours, I'd had strangers poke and prod my body and lecture me about my life choices. Up had become down, left had become right, and my workaholic, taciturn dad had started saying things like, "Getting into Harvard isn't absolutely essential," when he knew how much it meant to me…and when he hadn't really spoken to me otherwise in more than three years. At least not about anything important. Now he was here, at my school, keeping me from class and teaming up with my usually supportive, go-with-the-flow counselor, who was currently biting her lip and tiptoeing around the dreaded S-word.

Mrs. Cooper raised her eyes from my file and, after exchanging a glance with the imposing man seated in the stiff leather chair next to mine, said softly, "Your father and I are concerned about your stress level."

And there it was.

Honestly, this whole situation was ironic. When I'd woken up this morning, the only thing on my mind had been getting back to normal. Well, as normal as I could since Dad had found me puking blood. He'd vehemently refused to let me even so much as peek at my schoolwork since

Monday night, and I knew for a fact I'd missed a statistics quiz yesterday. Every minute I spent in this room was less time I could be spending in class catching up on the last three—going on four!—days I'd missed.

And they wanted to discuss my *stress level*?

"I'm fine," I assured her, assured them both, and forced a smile onto my face that hopefully said I was breezy. "I mean, I'm not gonna lie, this week has sucked. It's sucked huge. I took a couple of classes at the community college this summer to spruce up my applications, and it took a week or so to adjust to my advanced course load here this year. The combination of the two back-to-back, well, I guess they made me a little wonky, but I promise, Mrs. C, I've got everything under control now."

With my eyes, I pleaded for her to understand, and as she looked at me, I saw the softening. This woman knew me better than anyone else in Brighton High, other than my best friend, Sydney. I'd darkened her doorway too many times to count since I pulled myself out of the pit freshman year, asking for advice on the best ways to set myself up for success. She'd seen what I could handle; she knew what I could accomplish. What had happened on Monday was just a minor blip.

"I've got a hospital bill that says it's most certainly *not* under control," Dad contradicted with a grunt, and Mrs. Cooper flinched. The softness in her eyes dissipated, and her gaze darted back to the top sheet of my file, probably as much out of discomfort as to avoid the look on my father's face, and I slumped back against my chair. *So close.*

More than throwing up blood, it was the hospital that spooked him. Ever since Mom had gotten sick, neither of us could stand stepping through those chilling automatic doors, and I had to go and become a patient there for two days. Total overkill, in my opinion, but hey, no one listened to me. All it took for Dad was one look at me lying in the bed and clearly all those memories had come flooding back.

Mrs. Cooper cleared her throat. "Lily, I have to say, your father might have a point about your schedule. Looking over your transcript, it wouldn't be a horrible idea to drop a class or two. You already have more than enough credits to graduate come May, and what's important is for you not to be overly stre—"

"No," I interrupted, not wanting to hear that stupid word again until I was at least thirty. "I can't risk it. Harvard's not exactly a safety school, Mrs. C. Next semester, once I know for sure I've been admitted Early Action and won't need these grades on my transcript, *maybe* I can look into cutting back. But now's not the time to slack off. I need to focus."

I tried my best to appear accommodating, but the truth was, I had zero intention of cutting back or changing my schedule in January, either. My entire academic life had been carefully built and prepared over years of thought, and I couldn't let one tiny hiccup derail my plans.

Looking between them both, I fought the urge to fidget with my glasses and attempted to look as confident as possible while I said, "I can handle it."

Surprisingly, Dad caved first.

"All right, then. Keep your classes."

The concession was so abrupt and so completely out of left field that all I could do was blink. When his peculiarly neutral expression didn't morph or flinch after a few seconds of holding my stare, I added the ever-so-articulate, "Eh?"

He shrugged. "The courses are important. I understand that, and you're a bright student. You deserve to be challenged. I'm not on a mission to damage your future here, Lily, I just want you to find a balance."

That…well, that was awesome. It's what I'd been fighting for the last few days. A boulder-size weight floated off my shoulders and bounced, metaphorically speaking, against the cheap plastic frame guarding Mrs. C's poster on the wall.

Live today. Not yesterday. Not tomorrow. Just today.

It was a quote from Jerry Spinelli's *Love, Stargirl*, and my guidance counselor had an annoying habit of pointing to it whenever she felt I'd become too focused on the future.

I looked at that poster now, thought about the past week, and felt my eyes narrow.

The thing was, I appreciated the quote—heck, I loved the book—but I'd honestly never fully agreed with it, at least not for the day-to-day, in-the-trenches life of your everyday teenager. Every choice, every decision we made today affected and shaped our tomorrow. What college would we get into? What career path would we choose? Would the college we select be the best springboard for that career? As for our past mistakes, those bitches followed us forever on our transcripts.

Jerry Spinelli's sentiment was nice, but I wasn't so sure it applied in the real world.

Regardless, Dad had been preaching that same message for days now. Suddenly deciding my long-established plan of being valedictorian and getting into his alma mater, the same school where he'd met my mother and I'd planned on going my entire life, wasn't vital and harping on my, admittedly, tough school schedule.

I swung my gaze back toward his. "What's the catch?"

Dad shifted on his hip to face me, the stiff leather of the chair creaking under his solid weight. "I have an alternative proposal," he said, sounding every bit the high-end technology consultant he was, only this wasn't a board room, and it was my future we were discussing. "You can keep your full list of AP and Dual Credit courses, along with your tutoring duties"—I couldn't help it; I exhaled in relief and sagged against my chair—"*if* you take off on Saturdays and pick up a new activity. One that has nothing to do with books."

My head tilted in confusion. "What do you mean take off on Saturdays? I don't tutor on the weekends." Peer tutoring happened during lunch periods, and I worked with Liam on Tuesdays and Thursdays.

Something he'd know if he was ever around, but that was a topic for another day.

"Take off from studying," Dad clarified with a shrewd look. "No school projects, either. No books, no worrying, no stress. In fact, I don't want you doing anything at all, unless it's for fun."

My eyebrows scrunched together like an accordion. "*Fun*," I repeated. Not a word I'd associate with clubs or activities, unless you counted things like pep squad, which I most certainly didn't. "Er, Dad you might not realize this about me, but school spirit isn't exactly my thing."

Honestly, I wasn't trying to be a brat. But in my opinion, the whole high school experience outside of learning and a few key student activities was a huge waste of time. These four years were nothing but a stepping stone to bigger and better things, things just on the horizon if I could only get past this final hurdle. Who had time for pom-poms and drunken orgies?

I knew I should bite my tongue, take the extended olive branch, and run. It could've been a heck of a lot worse, and I didn't want to look a gift horse in the mouth. He was letting me keep my schedule, after all. But… "I can't write off an entire Saturday every weekend of my senior year. I'm gonna have papers and tests to study for."

"Things you always get done days or weeks in advance anyway," he told me with a strange spark in his eyes, and my entire body froze.

That spark was the first sign of life I'd seen in my father, other than fear and grief, in more than three years. I missed my dad, nearly as much as I missed my mom, and seeing that emotion was almost enough to stop me from pushing back. But *I needed my Saturdays*.

"I know you think I don't follow what's going on with you, kid, but I do. Your teachers say you could teach half your classes, you're so prepared. You turn in assignments before they're due, you accept every chance at extra credit, and you study more hours than should be humanly possible. One day off a week won't signal the end of the world."

I openly gaped at him, struck speechless that he knew all of this about me. Nevertheless, I wanted to argue that it could. You never knew what life might throw at you tomorrow. He and I understood that better than anyone. The only way to be prepared was to stay ahead of it, and the best way to do *that* was to keep on task. But before I could tell him that, Dad leaned forward and covered my hand on the arm rest.

He looked me in the eye, really looked at me, as if he could see the real me and not the version I pretended to be most days. As I looked back, it was easy to see the man *he* used to be, too, before salt infected his pepper hair and his shoulders weren't stooped with grief. Guilt, fear, and hope swirled in my stomach, almost making me dizzy, as I imagined what he could be thinking.

"I love you, Lily. I might not be the best at showing it, especially since your mom..." My eyes burned as his gruff voice broke, and I blinked rapidly. The muted *thud* of footsteps in the hall marked the time while he cleared his throat and visibly pulled himself together. "But I love you. More than that, I want what's best for you. Letting life pass you by as you make yourself sick over the future, sweet girl, isn't it."

My heart pounded in my chest. Dad hadn't called me *sweet girl* since Mom died. With one simple pet name, a rush of love, memories, and dreams flooded my veins, splintering all my protective barriers and sending electric sparks to my fingertips. The drama of the hospital was forgotten. The worry about class and my health didn't exist. All that mattered was my dad, looking at me the way he used to and telling me he loved me. My hand flipped over on the arm rest and linked with his.

Swallowing hard, my body swaying forward, I found myself asking, "What kind of activity?"

"*B*allroom dancing?"

At Sydney's shocked squeal, every eye in the crowded hallway turned in our direction. I flinched back against the wall, attempting to fade into the fresh cream paint while her fit of musical laughter ensured everyone got a good, long peek.

Nothing to see here, folks. Nothing to see.

For the record, I was aware of where I stood in the social hierarchy at Brighton High and, for that matter, the great big crazy world at large—and that was with the giraffes. Genetics had blessed me with long legs, skinny arms, and a neck I hoped would one day be classified as graceful but currently was anything but. In layman's terms, I was tall and awkward, and whenever possible, I preferred to fly under the radar of public scrutiny. Way, *way* under.

Tucking my chin against my chest, I kept my eyes low and grabbed hold of my pint-size friend's pointy elbow, steering her past the gawking underclassmen. "I didn't think it was *that* funny," I hissed, heading toward my locker and towing her tittering butt behind me.

Luckily, it was game day in southeast Texas, which meant everyone was obsessed with pigskin. Conversations quickly returned to the beatdown we were expected to give the Cypress Panthers, and as little as I cared about football—and that was to say very little—I was grateful. The last thing I needed on top of the spectacle that had become my life the past week was more questions from the peanut gallery.

As we pushed our way farther down a hall littered with bright blue posters for this afternoon's pep rally, I shuffled past two dance team members marking their routine. My steps slowed as I took in their smooth, synchronized moves. They were adorable, and they had rhythm along with that all-important quality known as ability, of which I had none. I released a sigh and picked up speed, sending Sydney into another round of hysterics.

"You'd think my best friend would *try* being supportive," I muttered, failing to fight off a small smile of my own. Objectively speaking, any feat involving me and expected agility was hilarious. But still. "Where's my pep talk and platitudes of solidarity?"

"Oh, please, you know I've got your back," she chided, elbowing me with a teasing smile. "You and me, we're like clownfish and sea anemone." At my blank look of *huh?*, she explained, "We go together. But let's be real for a minute. Ballroom dancing? Have you even seen *Dancing with the Stars*? That shit ain't easy, sweetheart, and you—"

"Have a tendency to trip on air," I finished for her,

gesturing toward today's tee of choice. Fittingly, it was emblazoned with a bright pink flamingo and the words "Majestically Awkward," and I'd paired it with one of Mom's flowy pink skirts and my comfy, worn-out Converse. It was eclectic and weird and about as close to a power outfit as I got, seeing as I'd guessed I would need the extra boost today. "Tell me about it."

I'd told Dad as much, once the initial shock of his suggestion had worn off, but he'd waved away the very real concern as it if was nothing more than a gnat. Mom had loved musicals and dancing, and apparently once upon a time she had even mentioned it was great for relieving stress. Who knows, for her it probably did. *She* glided through life like a graceful swan. I stumbled through it like a newborn colt.

We stopped in front of my locker, and I dialed the combination, my two-ton book bag falling at my feet. Despite the future chiropractic bills, I found comfort in the weight. School made sense to me. It was my happy place where two plus two equaled four, history was remembered, and scientific mysteries were explained. If only the rest of my life could've fallen in line so easily.

"Unfortunately, ballroom is the lesser of two evils," I explained over the sound of slamming metal echoing off scuffed tile. I exchanged my AP statistics book for government and surveyed the array of snacks I kept stashed inside. "It was either agree or drop something from my schedule, and you know I can't do that. Cameron's panting at my heels as it is, and after falling behind this week, I can't afford any more mistakes."

Cameron Montgomery had been my rival since freshman year, and she was just waiting for a chance to leapfrog me into the valedictorian spot. If everything went as planned,

I'd surge ahead by the end of the semester, but if I dropped a class like Dad had originally wanted, or even slacked off a smidge, it was game over. Cameron would win top spot, and I'd have nothing to show for the insane workload I'd carried for the last three years of my life.

I *needed* valedictorian.

"Don't worry, you've got it in the bag," Sydney said dutifully, calming the rising panic flooding my system, but I caught a strange, distracted twinge to her voice that set my bestie senses tingling. Ignoring the siren's call of chocolate inside my locker, I closed my door and turned to see her anxiously shifting her weight.

"What's up?"

"Nothing," she said, or rather grumbled, and I raised my left eyebrow. After everything we'd shared, I could see through her bull as easily as she saw through mine, and I was calling manure. Syd glanced at the ground. "It's just…I mean, you are okay, right?"

I winced, the worry in her voice making my stomach cramp.

She lifted her head, and her hazel eyes scanned my face. "I know you don't want to make a big deal about what happened or anything, but Lil…puking blood is pretty extreme."

I leaned against the cold metal locker. If it was anyone else, I'd have placated them or ignored the question altogether, but Sydney was my ride or die. We'd been glued at the hip ever since we were toddlers, and even with my insane schedule and her constant planning of world domination, we still made it work. She already knew about my previous struggle with anxiety; she'd seen me through it before. If anyone deserved answers, it was her.

"It sounds a lot worse than it is," I promised, slinking

farther down the metal. She walked over and slumped beside me. "I can't eat anything fun for a couple of weeks, and I've got to lay off caffeine even longer, which yeah, pretty much guarantees I'll be a grumpy cow"—Syd's face implied that wouldn't be different than the norm, and I playfully elbowed her in the side—"*but* I'm fine. The fast-paced summer sessions at the college were harder than I expected, you know that, and I guess with the new year starting and application deadlines looming, I let it all get to me. The doctor says I need to relax more, which is why Dad's all hot for this stupid hobby idea. But seriously, what is the man thinking? Mom was the one who lived for twirling around the living room. I inherited *his* coordination."

Sydney's mouth twitched at the corners. "Preaching to the choir, girl. If you recall, I was the unfortunate one standing next to you in the fourth-grade play." Her voice took on a faraway quality as she said, "Who'd have ever thought a shoe could fly that far?"

"Ah yes, another shining example of my infamous beauty and grace. Thank you so much for reminding me."

"It's what I'm here for," she said, knocking her head against my shoulder. She looped our arms and gave a gentle tug, her long blond braid flicking me on the back.

Near the bathrooms, Teagan Mitchell and Avery McCloud were entertaining the masses with their regularly scheduled mid-morning breakup, and we paused with the flow of traffic funneling on either side. For a second, the drama distracted me from my own impending doom.

Once we were clear of the chaos, Sydney asked, "So, what's the grand plan?"

I flashed a smile. "Let Dad think I'm playing this his way and stink it up," I replied. "Which shouldn't be hard with the two-left-feet thing. He'll realize the error of his ways, see what a huge waste of time and money it is, and then things will go back to normal. It's not like he'll be around to enforce the classes anyway. He leaves for Israel next Sunday. Two weeks this time."

Of course, even if I got him to back off on the dance class, that would only take care of the first half of Dad's "alternative proposal." I still had his moratorium on all school-related activities on Saturdays to deal with, but that was a problem for Future Lily.

"Sounds solid." Syd came to a stop outside marine bio, and her eyes brightened. This class was for her what English and European history were for me. The girl loved her some cuttlefish. "What about today? I mean, tomorrow you're stinking it up in a ballroom studio, but you want to come to the game with me tonight?"

I gasped. "And ruin my picture-perfect lack of attendance?" I shouldered my schoolbag higher and sidestepped a fresh surge of students. "Why on earth would I do a silly thing like that?"

"Gee, I don't know, maybe 'cause it's fun? Or because you only live once, and you barely even do that?" I mock-scowled at the truth, and she blew me an air-kiss. "Or how about because student council is manning concessions and you love the student council president more than life?" She combined the final bit with the patented eyelash bat and innocent smile that won her an election. Unfortunately for her, I was immune.

Obviously, if she needed help, I'd be there in a heartbeat, major pile of schoolwork be damned. But she really just wanted a wing-woman. Sydney had a huge crush on her vice president, Nick Bernhardt, but she'd die before she ever admitted it.

"*Fine*," she conceded with a huff when I failed to break.

"If appealing to your sense of loyalty and student duty won't work, how about tagging along because you've yet to see Stone Torres in his tight football pants? That's a travesty of epic proportions, Lil. I mean, I get that you're anti-establishment, but the boy is hot with a capital H. His goods deserve to be scoped at least once before you graduate, and time is a-ticking."

I wrinkled my nose. "I think I'll pass."

I appreciated a nice ass in tight pants as much as the next girl, but I refused to worship a guy just because he could throw a football. As for the sport itself, it was pointless. Sydney was right, time *was* ticking. We'd only had four years, seven hundred and twenty miniscule days to pad our applications and kick academic ass before an admissions committee decided our collegiate fate. A fate that then sealed our entire future. With three of those years already gone, I couldn't afford to waste even a second on anything trivial, and I didn't understand how anyone else could, either.

Besides, there'd be plenty of football games and parties in college.

"Whatever. You know, I could always dare you to come." A wicked gleam entered her eyes as she let the challenge hang. I tilted my head, curious if she'd pull the trigger, but a few short seconds later, she caved. "*But* I won't. I prefer to save those for the important things in life—like spotting me when I need to sit for the tiny terrors three nights in a row or making a Starbucks run when I'm fiending."

"Ugh. Don't tease the invalid with talk of caffeine," I whined. "As it is, my night's gonna be filled with catching up on makeup work and dreaming of peanut M&M's."

"At least dream candy is calorie-free," she replied helpfully, and I flipped her off with love. "Fine, be lame and responsible. See you at lunch?"

"I'll be the sad redhead eating rabbit food."

The warning bell rang, and I took off for the stairwell, determined not to miss another second of class. Dodging classmates, I hustled up the first flight and grabbed hold of the straps on my backpack, prepared to bolt once I cleared the landing.

With two stairs left to go, the path before me opened, and I surged ahead, already drafting my plan for tonight's study session. Visions of notecards and pink highlighters danced in my head…only to be thrown aside by the crushing reality of looming humiliation.

The toe of my right sneaker, followed quickly by my left, caught in the thin polyester lining of my flowy skirt. My body pitched forward, and I flung out my arms, accidentally cold-cocking a guy from my English class. Apologizing on autopilot, I let my blurry vision turn to the scuffed floor that was rushing to meet me, and as the concerning sensation of cool air hit my bare thighs, my tangled feet yanking my skirt impossibly lower, one lone thought crossed my mind: *This is how I die.*

A half second before my face hit the ground, two firm hands wrapped around my arms. "Whoa there. You okay?"

The world, much like my equilibrium, settled around me in waves.

First came sound in the chilling *rrriiiiippppp* of my mom's favorite skirt.

On its heels, the dawning horror that the world at large was currently perusing my sassy undies—the ones that say, *If you can read this, you are standing too close*, ironically enough—along with my inability to fix the near al fresco situation, thanks to the protective grip encircling my arms.

Next welled gratitude for the owner of those hands, the guy who'd saved me from a fate worse than ballroom dancing…namely, breaking my face on filthy, unforgiving tile.

Followed, finally, by a growing awareness of my hero himself.

Warm breath skimmed across the shell of my ear. A hint of Ivory soap mixed with wintergreen floated through my head. The deep register of his voice clicked, the last puzzle piece falling into place, and the fine hairs at the back of my neck prickled to life.

To be honest, I might've preferred eating tile.

Let me be perfectly clear. I stood by my conviction that my classmates' mindless worship of the football team was pathetic, and I'd have rather seen that enthusiasm shown toward the debate team or National Honor Society. But I wasn't a total social moron. I didn't eat lunch with a crowd of people, go to parties, or attend any sporting events, but I'd have had to live on the poor downgraded planet of Pluto not to recognize the smooth, rich voice that had whispered across my ear.

However, that didn't mean I had to acknowledge it. At least not yet.

Instead, I went with denial, choosing to keep my eyes firmly shut as my stomach churned and I unhooked my feet. The grip on my arms tentatively relaxed, and while I yanked my skirt back into place, clutching the gaping fabric to cover the taunting words, the squeak of rubber soles and hushed whispers hinted at movement. Hopefully away from me and not closer to gawk.

"You okay?" he repeated.

Everything inside me tightened. It was time to face the music.

"Mm-hmm," I muttered, hanging my head in defeat. "Just peachy."

Slowly, begrudgingly, I opened my eyes to a beat-up

pair of Nikes. Fairly innocuous as shoes went. Feeling brave, I drew my gaze farther north, taking in strong legs encased in denim, followed by a plain white tee that hinted at definition. Over that hung an open, long-sleeve blue button-down rolled up on thick golden forearms. My belly dipped. Moving faster now, wanting to get it over with in one big gulp, I glided across broad shoulders, a square jaw, and twin indentions for dimples (my personal kryptonite), then landed on a pair of dark eyes so rich and warm they were almost black, framed in inky lashes.

Ágoston "Stone" Torres. The wearer of tight football pants, Brighton High's all-star quarterback, the most popular guy in school, and now, my quick-thinking stairwell rescuer.

Of course.

"That could've been a nasty fall." Concern mixed with slight amusement in his eyes, and as the smooth tone of his voice rolled over me, I willed myself to speak.

I'd love to say I was the type of girl who could pull off a classic line and set the world to rights, but I was better suited for paper-and-pen situations. The kind where I could take my time searching for the perfect words—and then hide behind them. But if I couldn't be witty, I might as well go with its lesser-known cousin: awkward humor.

"That's what I get for trying to walk and think at the same time."

Stone's firm mouth twitched at the corners, his eyes sweeping over me, and then, *holy hell*, the famous grin broke free. My already-elevated heart rate skyrocketed, and my breath legit stuttered in my chest. Butterflies eloped, girls' hearts twittered, and unicorns sneezed rainbows over smiles like his. I'd seen it from a distance over the years but never once been on the receiving end. Let me tell you, it was every bit as magical as advertised.

Heat flooded my cheeks, no doubt matching the color of my hair, and I motioned toward the stairs—which would henceforth be known as *the steps of doom.* "Uh, so, yeah. Thanks for that. Obviously, I never quite got a handle on those gross motor skills. With luck, I hope to master stairway mechanics before graduation."

I plastered a hopeful smile on my face, eyebrows lifted sky-high, and Stone ran a hand through his spiky black hair, his own grin widening in degrees until a heart-stopping smile even more lethal than the last took its place. Wow. "I'll keep my fingers crossed for you."

A muted laugh erupted from my right, and looking around, I realized the rest of the stairwell had cleared out despite my embarrassing panty show. Only one other person remained. Chase Winters, aka Chasing Trouble, Brighton's wide receiver.

This day kept getting better.

Chase extended two fingers in a half wave, his green eyes glowing with mirth, and I took that as my cue to skedaddle. As it was, we were late for class, and since my ass was hanging out for all to see, I had to double back to my locker for my old gym shorts. Plus, conversing with hot guys clearly wasn't one of my strengths. It probably ranked right up there with dancing.

Willing my tingling legs to move, I gave them each a stilted nod, got head bobs in return, and then pivoted on my heel, being sure to lift my ripped hem this time to avoid a repeat performance.

Note to self: Tomorrow, do not wear a skirt. I could only imagine the carnage.

I quickened my steps, eager to forget the last few minutes ever happened, and heard Chase's amused voice trail behind me. "Bro, I wanna be you when I grow up."

Chapter Two

STONE

*I*lusiòn was dead. The last time I could remember the studio being this empty was right after it opened, thirteen years ago, and even then, it'd been midweek.

Normally, Saturdays were chaotic, with the bell on the door tinkling every two seconds. People came and went, and a mismatch of music played over the speakers as students rehearsed their various steps, all sharing the same crowded dance floor. Between solo lessons, group classes, and people scoping out the competition under the guise of practice, Ma's dance studio was always hopping.

Today the silence was deafening. It echoed off the gleaming hardwood floors and reflected from the spotless mirrors. Part of me appreciated the quiet after a long night of celebrating our win, but the larger part, the protective part that refused to let anything else bad happen to my family, was wigged the hell out. It made my paranoid assumptions real.

"I got my tile job back."

My out-of-the-blue announcement fell like an anvil.

Ma's head jerked up, and my twin sister looked at me like I'd lost my damn mind. Who knows, maybe I had, but I needed to do something. Granted, I could've waited until tonight to bring it up, or at least until they'd stopped talking about a member's program, but Ma hadn't stopped moving since I'd gotten there. Almost like if she kept busy enough she wouldn't notice the lack of students filling the space.

Also, I sucked at patience.

"No, you did not," Ma replied, her tone and expression implying the conversation was over when it was far from it. Chase, who'd been hanging out at the studio for years to avoid his own family drama, coughed to hide his laugh, but when he caught my glare, he went back to spinning aimlessly in the roller chair. I walked to where my mom and sister stood on the other side of the desk.

"Actually, Ma, I did. Mr. Hunt was at the game last night. He congratulated me on the win, and it might've come up that I don't have practice on Wednesdays or Saturdays. Turns out, they haven't filled my position from the summer, and he asked if I was interested in coming back." I flashed her an easy smile, the one that always got me out of trouble, and for some reason got a quick flash of the redhead on the stairs yesterday. Remembering her reaction to my usual grin made it turn more genuine. "It's perfect."

The narrowing of my mother's eyes said it was the opposite, but I failed to see the problem. Although my parents hadn't come right out and said money was tight, I wasn't an idiot. We'd been eating a lot more soups or rice and beans lately, and I'd heard the hushed conversations my parents had late at night. Something was going on, and the quiet studio today proved it.

My family couldn't lose Ilusiòn. It was Ma's dream, and Dad had worked two jobs to make it come true when

Angéla and I were kids. My sister grew up taking lessons here before becoming a junior instructor, and the wall behind the reception desk held a framed photo from her first performance. It hung next to one of Ma and her former partner at the Blackpool Dance Festival. Hell, there was even a picture of me from junior high, back when the studio hosted our school's Mother-Son dance.

Selfishly, *I* couldn't lose the studio, either. This was the only place outside my house where I could turn off the noise and not have someone constantly scrutinizing my every move. I didn't have to fake it at Ilusiòn. I could take a deep breath and just be.

"Ágoston, I need you here on the weekends," Ma said, her percussive Hungarian accent getting stronger. "Especially Saturday. It's our busiest day of the week, and now that it's fall, enrollment will start picking up."

Sidestepping the fact that it was currently Saturday and we were far from busy, I pointed to my sister. "Angéla has it covered."

We may've shared a womb for nine months, but my twin was considered the dancer, not me. Sure, I knew the steps. I loved letting loose on the floor, and I'd attended a few practice parties and even occasionally stood in when a student didn't have a partner. But as often as I came here to zone out, Ilusiòn was my sister's domain. My place was the football field and, as of this past summer, Hunt Construction and Remodeling, where, unfortunately, I'd made a shit-ton more laying tile than Ma could afford to pay me.

"Angéla assists with planning the programs and instruction," she said, planting her elbows on top of the counter. "I need you to answer phones, check in students, and schedule lessons."

My jaw dropped. "You mean be a *secretary*?"

For the record, I had nothing against desk jobs, and I wasn't a chauvinist asshole. But come on. I could work with my hands, lay tile, and earn fifteen dollars an hour with Hunt, or I could sit on my ass here for nothing.

It was really just about the math.

When Ma didn't argue, simply kept looking at me, I squeezed my forehead. A headache was coming on. "What happened to Tori?"

Her expressive dark green eyes flashed with emotion. "Tori will no longer be working with us." From the way Angéla's head swiveled in shock, I guessed my sister hadn't known that, either. Ma made a shooing gesture with her hands. "No worries. She was offered a position where she could earn more money, and we're happy for her."

She beamed a smile, the one she used to win over judges back when she competed. "But, my darling, you won't be a secretary. You shall be the face of the studio while I teach, yes?" Reaching over the counter, she grabbed my chin in her hand. "Such a handsome boy I have. After eleven hours of labor, it's time I capitalize on my son's heartthrob status."

As my best friend alternated between snickering and feigning vomiting behind me, and Ma patted my cheek, my evil twin jumped on board.

"Absolutely, Ma." Angéla waggled her eyebrows with a devious grin. "In fact, why stop at the door? We should make posters and graphics and spread those babies online. 'Come to Ilusiòn and Let a Football Stud Sweep You Off Your Feet.'" She ignored my death glare and added, "Now *that* would put us on the map."

As much as I wanted the studio to thrive, I had to draw the line somewhere—and stunts that made me sound like a prostitute or involved any type of social media was it.

I tried a different tactic. "You can't expect me to flake on

Mr. Hunt. The guy's a fair boss, and I'll make good money. Answering phones here won't bring in extra cash."

"No, you are right," she agreed, glancing at her splayed palms on the desk. "Helping here won't earn you a paycheck." I withheld my victorious grin, guessing more was coming. She looked at her hands and, after a moment, added in a soft voice, "But it saves me from paying someone else."

Angéla stopped fiddling with the program binders. Behind me, Chase stopped spinning.

My mother was a proud, strong woman. When she was a little girl in Hungary, she'd worked her ass off to become the best dancer she could, and when she'd turned nineteen, she followed her dream to Texas, where she enrolled as a dance major, met my dad at a salsa class, and continued to work. She didn't admit to weakness easily, so I knew that confession had cost her, and I felt like shit for it. But *finally*, we were getting somewhere.

Now if she'd only run the numbers, she'd realize how much more I could contribute working for Hunt. "But Ma, laying tile—"

"No." Her green eyes filled with love and steely determination. "You are the child. I'm the adult. You shouldn't be doing manual labor, especially not during the school year. Your father and I would rather you not work at all, but I need you and your sister until the season picks up. But your priority will always be school and football."

Chase wheeled the chair over. "He can always quit football."

I kicked out my foot, launching the chair backward, and he took off with a grin. I knew what he was doing. Playing the fool, saying stupid shit to break the tension like he always did. And, just like every other time, it worked.

He wheeled himself back, and Ma pulled a face,

leaning over the counter to ruffle his over-gelled hair, and remarkably, the air shifted. After reprimanding him for teasing her boy, she asked Chase about *his* family…a subject he'd sooner eat nails then dive into, but he kept the easy smile as he told her about his sister enrolling at UT, going pre-med, and how his parents were over the damn moon.

Having practically raised him the last ten years he'd avoided going home, Ma easily read between the lines. Chase would've gladly traded his family's wealth for even an ounce of love, but that was one thing my family had in excess. Her face softened as she tenderly put her hand on Chase's shoulder. "Tonight, we're having enchiladas!"

For those in the know, that was Viktória Torres for *you're coming over so I can spoil you*, and my boy wasn't dumb. Next to Hungarian goulash, enchiladas were Ma's best dish. It was my abuela's secret recipe, handed down when she married my dad, and our family's go-to comfort food. Which showed she understood how messed-up Chase's home life really was.

I hated his dad. But, I had to admit, I was grateful for a break from the constant soup.

"I'll be there," he replied, trying for his usual carefree smile and missing it by a mile. Lucky for him, the bell on the back of the door finally chimed, and Ma turned to greet the newcomers. Chase's shoulders sank with relief.

My best friend was a lot deeper than people gave him credit for, but that didn't mean he liked airing his dirty laundry. Especially in front of my sister. They'd grown up together, too, and in a lot of ways, Chase was Angéla's surrogate brother. But certain topics were off-limits even for her.

While Ma and her students headed onto the dance floor, Chase picked at the seam of his jeans, head down, feet still.

The lack of movement was more of a concern than anything else.

Angéla cleared her throat. "You know, if my brother did quit, the Tigers would suck. He's the only half-decent player we've got."

Chase staggered in the chair, making a production out of grabbing at his chest, and I shot my sister a look that said, *What the actual hell?*

"Damn, girl." His mouth twitched with a smile. This time, a genuine one. "Next time tell me how you really feel."

She bounced on her toes, fighting a grin. "I call it like I see it."

He wheeled forward again. "You do realize that without me, your brother would have no one to catch those perfect spirals, right?" He wiggled his fingers in the air. "Recruiters have called these babies the best hands in the nation. Some people have even called them magic."

Chase's cocky grin left no misunderstanding of who those people were, or their gender, and my sister's lighthearted smile fell right off her face. There one minute, gone the next. It was enough to give me whiplash.

The muscles in her jaw clenched. As her lips pinched, she shook her head. "I bet they do."

He visibly flinched at the cold sound of her voice, and while she started stacking the program binders, Chase looked at me in befuddlement.

I shrugged, just as confused. But I did look at her closer.

Maybe I was biased, but Angéla was beautiful inside and out. She was the kind of girl who bent over backward to make others happy, which unfortunately made her an easy target for people who liked to take advantage. It was one of the many reasons I was so protective of her. It also made her abrupt mood shift so bizarre.

My sister wasn't rude. Ever. I wasn't the most observant guy in the world, but that meant something was eating at her. But what? Worry over Ilusiòn? Or was it something else?

A guy, maybe?

My hands clenched into fists. Angéla never talked boys with me—one time, Chase and I set a guy straight for making her cry, and she stopped telling me stuff—but I'd keep my ears open from here on out.

She huffed a breath and rocked back on her heels. When she lifted her dark brown eyes, she looked at us both and then rolled them, trying to play off her moodiness.

"Fine, I *guess* you're both half decent. The entire program's screwed when we graduate, so neither of you can quit, okay?" She shoved a chunk of glossy black hair behind her ear and hugged the binders to her chest. "I should get back to work. These lessons won't plan themselves." She bit the corner of her lip. "If Ma needs me, tell her I'm in the office, okay?"

I nodded, and she sent us a quick smile before spinning on her heel and disappearing behind the office door.

"That was weird," I muttered. Which said a lot, because I'd seen a lot of weird shit.

The usual reason for weird shit nodded beside me, staring at the blank space where my sister had stood. Regardless of what was up with her, Angéla had accomplished one thing: Chase was clearly no longer thinking about his dad.

Music rolled over the speakers, and more students trickled in. He sighed and kicked back in the chair, putting his feet on the counter. "So, what was that with your mom?"

I groaned and scrubbed a hand across my face. "Man, I don't even know. Things have been off lately. Money was tight after Dad's car accident, but he's back on the job now. I figured it'd gotten better, but obviously it hasn't." I glanced at the closed door and lowered my voice. "It actually reminds me of when Angel got sick."

Chase's body turned to stone, and his eyes flicked to mine. "She's not…?"

I quickly shook my head. "No. No way. She would've told me."

Seven years ago, when Angéla first got diagnosed with leukemia, my entire world came to a halt. She was my twin, my other half, and as much as she drove me nuts, she was the best part of me. I called her Angel for a reason. I'd gotten lost for a while, not knowing how to deal while my parents shuttled her back and forth to MD Anderson. That was when Chase's dad signed us up for peewee football.

To this day, it remained possibly the one solid thing the man ever did for his son. Thankfully, it helped me, too. Football had given me a much-needed outlet for the storm that had raged inside, and it even gave me my nickname because of how hard I could take a hit. It brought me attention of my own…something I still felt guilty about.

What kind of asshole got jealous of his sick sister? A twisted one, obviously.

Angéla deserved every drop of love and support she'd gotten that god-awful year. Hell, she still deserved it. But those fourteen months had defined us both. Apart from the studio, she continued to struggle with where she fit in the world, while I'd found my place on the field. For better or worse.

"No, Angel's fine, but something *is* going on. That's why I jumped on Mr. Hunt's offer." I watched Ma talk with her students, looking as happy as I'd ever seen her. "I need to keep that job, man. Laying tile will bring in way more cash than they'll save by me working here, and it's clear we need it. Desperately."

Chase blew out a breath. "Well, it goes without saying, but if there's anything I can do…"

He left the offer hanging, knowing I'd never touch his family's money, and I nodded in appreciation. It was enough that he had my back.

The bell on the door jingled again, and I got out the clipboard for the group class sign-in. Today, Ma was teaching an advanced salsa combination. Ilusiòn offered the full array of expected American and international ballroom dances, along with a few nontraditional ones, but she preferred teaching the Latin styles. It's what had drawn her to my abuela's studio all those years ago, and eventually what led to her meeting my dad.

As I greeted the regulars, a few couples who'd been taking lessons since my peewee days, talk turned to last night's game. While the older men gave us pointers for next week, subtly and sometimes *not* so subtly questioning my decisions, Chase and I exchanged knowing looks. These guys considered themselves family and felt they had a vested interest in my success, so I didn't really mind their weighing in with their opinions. But it went to show that even here I wasn't completely free of the field. Even here I needed to be on guard.

As I nodded along to their collective take on my ability to read defenses, my eyes shifted to the window, and I muttered a quiet curse.

Chase pushed to his feet. "What's wrong?" When he caught sight of who'd pulled into the parking lot, his face twisted, and he fell back into the chair. "Damn, she doesn't give up, huh? I'll give her one thing, the girl's persistent."

"More like delusional." I forced a smile for the gathered crowd and politely excused myself before turning my back to the door. "She needs to get it through her thick skull that we're done and move on. I'm tired of this shit."

Back when Cameron and I were together, I thought it was awesome that she took lessons. It helped improve her cheerleading, and it gave me a chance to see her even when football took up most of my time. Hell, I'd actually thought it was sweet that she could bond with my mom and sister over dance. Now her coming around was just pathetic. What made it worse was there was no pattern to predict when she'd stop by, so my options were to sit here and hope today wouldn't be one of those days or avoid the studio altogether.

How was that fair? This was supposed to be *my* space. My one drama-free zone. Somehow, Cameron got it in her head that if she spent enough time around me, I'd take her back. As if my disinterest was because of some secret need to spend more time with her. Wrong—it sprang from revulsion. No matter how many times she swung by and re-spun her apology, it wouldn't erase what she did.

Cammie's twisted delusions were just one more reason laying tile was better than manning the front desk.

A silver Altima jolted to a stop next to the parked green Prius, and Cameron slid out of her car, tossing her wavy brown hair over her shoulder as she greeted her best friend, Ashley.

Chase shook his head. "Giving up isn't Cammie's style. Girl knows she fucked up, but now she wants you back."

Yeah, I'd say getting caught on Snapchat making out with a guy who wasn't her boyfriend counted as screwing up. I pushed off the desk. "Well, too bad. Been there, done that, and I'm over it. Hell, I'm over drama, period. I'm not messing with girls at all this year." Chase shot me serious side-eye as I glanced longingly at the closed office door. "I don't need this right now…"

"Get out of here," he told me, nudging my ribs with

an elbow. "Go work out your new monk philosophy with Angéla, and I'll deal with Cameron and Ashley before heading home." When I hesitated, he put his hand on my arm and shoved. "Go. I won't even make it obvious. I'll get her signed in, stonewall her questions, and work the desk until class starts and Marcus takes over."

The bell on the door chimed, and I nodded gratefully. I should check on Angéla anyway. See if I could figure out what was bothering her, and after that, I'd let her put me to work doing whatever she wanted. Making copies, planning lessons, killing bugs. I'd even join a class if they needed me, as long as I didn't have to dance with Cameron. I'd do everything I could for Ilusiòn. Including going back to work for Mr. Hunt.

A surge of adrenaline hit my blood. It was the same rush of energy I got whenever I stormed the field. We'd find a way to save the studio. *I'd* figure out a way, and in the end, that was what mattered. Not Cameron and her twisted delusions. Hell, she did me a favor when she cheated on me. She might've made me look like a fool, but, thanks to her, my senior year was gonna be drama-free. Now I could focus on what was important.

My family and my game. In that order.

Chapter Three

LILY

From the reception area, Ilusiòn appeared exactly how I'd pictured it, right down to the friendly, professional smile on the man seated behind the desk. Beyond the cozy couches and plush chairs of the lobby area lay an expanse of honeyed hardwood floors that *click*ed when you walked, wall-to-wall shiny mirrors that didn't miss a thing, and a dance space currently teeming with skilled students. My basic nightmare brought to life.

Yep, this hour is going to suck.

Technically speaking, the dozen or so people taking part in the class already in session probably didn't count as a crowd, but it was a heck ton more than the empty room of my best-case scenario. Even if they were too caught up in their own steps to notice my clunky ones, I'd assume they were watching, and the anxiety alone would make it worse. God, I hated failing. Especially with an audience.

Maybe they had a separate room for the private lessons?

Dad's firm hand on my lower back ushered me ahead, and I inched away from the door. Whatever spell had fallen between us in Mrs. Cooper's office yesterday had been broken by the time I'd gotten home from school. He'd spent the night locked in his office again, hiding until about an hour before it was time to come here. As for me, I'd spent the night as I'd planned, tackling my mountain of makeup work, and this afternoon bored out of my mind.

I could've studied. Dad wouldn't have known behind that thick oak door of his, and I wouldn't have had to spend a good part of the morning reorganizing my crammed bookshelves. But I couldn't bring myself to do it. Maybe it was premature guilt over my plan to throw today's lesson. Whenever I'd thought about picking up a textbook, my hands shook and my stomach would cramp. I figured it wouldn't kill me to honor one of his wishes. At least until he left town again.

The reception desk was tall and imposing, despite the man with the smooth brown skin and easy smile chatting on the phone. As we came to a stop in front of him, and I set my folded hands on the cool marble surface, he caught my eye and winked. I glanced down at my choice of tee, wondering if perhaps it *was* a tad overkill. Dad certainly hadn't been amused.

Hanging up the phone, he pushed to his feet and said, "Welcome to Ilusiòn. How can I help you?"

Dad held out his hand. "I'm Steven Bailey. We're here for my daughter's first private lesson."

First and hopefully last. I snagged a red and white striped peppermint from the bowl on the counter, then popped it in my mouth as I surveyed the room, searching for a secondary private space where the other students wouldn't watch me fall on my face. Bistro tables lined the dance floor in groups, allowing further observation. Twinkle lights wrapped a black-painted column near the monster stereo system, and a high, industrial-looking ceiling illuminated the space in bright light. From what I could see, that was it. In other words, there'd be no hiding here.

A flashback of yesterday's stairwell disaster flittered through my mind. The true beauty of today's plan was, spectator or not, I wouldn't even have to *do* anything to stink up the place. I was a natural. With that thought, my *Don't Follow in my Footsteps, I Run into Walls* T-shirt was really a simple public service announcement.

"Okay, my darlings!" A loud voice broke through my musings.

At the center of the dance floor stood a slender woman dressed in black from the tips of her heels to the buttons on her silk blouse. Her dark hair was cut short in a pixie style, accenting high cheekbones, a swanlike neck, and eyes that sparkled with an intensity bordering on magnetic. In short, she was striking.

"From here, you're going to go back with the left," she explained, demonstrating the step. Her warm, musical accent sounded central European, and I found myself inexplicably drawing closer to the dance floor, wanting to hear more. "Replace your weight onto the right, and then you're going to do half a turn to the right, going side with the left."

I was lost just hearing the directions, but I couldn't deny I was captivated.

My gaze swung to the students, curious to see if they could replicate the step. I smiled as a cute older couple executed it flawlessly, thinking for just a second that *maybe* I could do this after all. I moved on to observe the couple beside them...and the blood drained from my face.

Oh, holy crap.

Cameron Montgomery. I blinked, but she was still there. Even worse, she wasn't alone. Ashley Thompson stood to her right. As if being my rival for valedictorian wasn't bad enough, now Cameron, of *all* people, was here to witness my shame…and of course, she was awesome. I groaned, watching her execute a pattern of fancy footwork. Her presence was just too strange a coincidence to be anything less than a sign. Clearly, the universe hated me.

My heart palpitated. This wasn't happening. Ilusiòn was supposed to have retirees trapped in the 1940s, like the cute old couple, or housewives with too much time on their hands. People my own age weren't supposed to be here, especially not ones I'd ever have to see again. Or rivals already looking for signs of weakness.

The walls started closing in, and as my vision tunneled, I leaned my back against the tall cherry-wood desk, letting the chill of the marble top ground me in the here and now as a familiar prickle traveled up my spine. Closing my eyes, I focused on my breathing.

The mild anxiety attacks had started after Mom was diagnosed. I couldn't handle seeing her in pain. Then, after she'd died and I became the girl everyone stared at and pitied, well, they decided to stick around. For the first few months, I fell into a deep, dark hole, and I hadn't cared much about anyone or anything. All I could see was grief. It wasn't until the second semester of freshman year that I'd fought my way back out, kicking and screaming, and threw myself into school, focusing on all the promises I'd made my mom for the future. Ever since then, I'd worked hard to deal with my anxiety, not letting it win, and after a year and a half with no more attacks, I was able to wean off medication and handle any minor flare-ups on my own. One way I'd done that was by keeping a low profile.

Essentially, the opposite of being in the spotlight—or taking a dance class surrounded by a bunch of strangers and one major rival, like I was now.

Breaths leveled, I opened my eyes and immediately searched for the closest door, spotting it about six yards away. That was doable. Now for an exit strategy. Feigning illness was always an option, but after my recent hospital stay it wouldn't be cool. Plus, Dad wouldn't buy it anyway. He was expecting me to bolt.

Maybe I could hide in the bathroom, or say I was having ladies' issues?

"Ah yes, here you are, Mr. Bailey," the man behind the counter said as I unsteadily pushed to my feet, ready to run. "It's been quite a while since your last lesson. Will you and your wife be returning as well?"

My head snapped forward, all sense of self-preservation abandoned.

What did he just say?

My father winced.

"No," he said quietly. Shakily. "Just Lily this time."

The sharp pain in my chest gave way to an aching sadness, and my body swayed with the sudden shift of emotion. My system wasn't built for this level of adrenaline.

I shook my head in confusion. My dad didn't dance. Ever. Weddings were the bane of his existence because Mom had always tried to drag him out onto the floor. He'd become a master at hiding in bathrooms, waiting in buffet lines, and talking with obscure relatives, all to escape the horror of dancing...and now I discovered he'd taken actual *lessons*?

Dad looked at me and pulled at the collar of his shirt. "We started coming here after…" He swallowed hard and pressed his lips together. "After your mom was diagnosed."

A memory clicked into place. "Date night," I whispered.

He nodded, and it felt as if I'd been sucker punched.

For six months, from the time right after Mom was

diagnosed with stage-four pancreatic cancer until she got too weak to do much of anything, my parents snuck away for twice-a-week date nights. I never knew where they went— I'd been too wrapped up in my own misery and grateful to hide out at Sydney's to ask—but it had always been Mom's dream to dance like the actresses in her favorite musicals. Of course, Dad had made that happen. He'd have given her the world if he could.

"Is this why…?" I glanced at the floor in a daze then raised my head as the pieces came together. "But you said this relieved *stress*."

Clearing his throat, Dad blinked, and the hint of stark grief vanished. "It does."

A combination of love and pain squeezed my throat. *This* was why Dad wanted this so much. He wasn't punishing me for trying to get into a good school, which was how it had honestly felt. He was trying to take care of me the best way he knew how. By giving me back a piece of my mother.

I couldn't throw the lesson. Not anymore. It would disrespect Mom's memory. I didn't need to have seen her dance here to know she'd loved every second. In fact, looking around now, the entire room appeared to glow brighter, as if I was seeing it with new eyes. *Her* eyes.

"Steven!" The dazzling instructor had spotted us and was striding across the floor with a smile that could've lighted up Manhattan. The lithe way she moved exuded confidence and grace even as her feet ate up the ground. "It's so good to see you!"

I had a half second to realize what was happening before she'd swooped me into a hug. "Hello, love, I am Viktória." A clean, fresh scent lingered in the air as she turned to embrace my father. Dad accepted it with one arm, looking only slightly uncomfortable, and when she pulled back again, she clasped my hand, staring straight into my eyes. "Isa was one of my dearest students. She had so much potential. I was very sad to hear of her passing."

I smiled stiffly and tried not to fidget under her warm gaze. I never knew how to respond when people offered their sympathy.

"Usually, I only teach the advanced classes while Marcus instructs our new students," Viktória explained, nodding toward the man who'd greeted us. Marcus pushed to his feet. "But I'd very much like to lead your first lesson, if that is all right with you."

The spirit dancing in her green eyes was infectious, and I doubted it mattered who led my lesson. I was going to suck regardless. I nodded nervously and bit my lip, already counting the minutes until the lesson would end.

Marcus took over leading the group practicing the hammerlock turn with hair drape finish...whatever that meant...and as I very purposefully ignored looking—hoping against hope that Cameron and Ashley hadn't spotted me, despite their teacher's enthusiastic greeting—Viktória surveyed my appearance, biting back a grin at my tee before frowning at my shoes. I lifted a purple Converse in confusion.

"I couldn't find Isabella's shoes," Dad murmured in apology.

"Not a problem." Waving her hand in the air, she marched toward a display case lined with CDs, DVDs, books, and, on the bottom two shelves, shoes. Dread curled my stomach. Her dainty hand slid across a row in contemplation before stopping in front of a pair of tan pumps. "Size ten, right?"

My mouth tumbled open. How had she guessed that just looking at me? Viktória must've taken my stunned fish-face as confirmation, because the next thing I knew, she'd snatched up the pair and was presenting them with a flourish.

"Oh, no, I couldn't—"

"I insist," she replied, wiggling the potential death traps until I accepted them. "Sneakers make it almost impossible to dance. Your feet cannot slide properly, and you could get hurt. No, these shoes have a suede bottom, so they glide."

To illustrate, Viktória glided across the floor in her own shiny heels, executing a dazzling pattern of steps I found impressive and intimidating. I hugged the shoes to my chest.

"Come, put these on and then we can get started!"

Unable to tell the perky woman no, I let her lead me to the black leather sofa to change. This was such a bad idea. On so many levels. As I tugged off my Converse, Viktória explained that going forward, my lessons would be in the morning. Apparently, Dad had had a business call this morning, and she'd rearranged the schedule to accommodate him.

I shook my head. I was beyond used to work coming before me, but this time it stung. Because of that stupid phone call, unless some magical secondary private room was hiding somewhere, I'd soon have two girls from school watching me fail, in heels no less.

I pushed down the flutter of anxiety threatening to rise.

Once I was buckled and back on my feet, Viktória turned to my dad and asked, "Steven, would you like to be Lily's partner today? It has been a few years, but the steps will come right back. The body is a marvelous thing."

Dad glanced at me. It'd be hella awkward for sure. We barely spoke anymore, much less shared any sort of physical contact. But part of me wondered what it'd be like, dancing with my father. Maybe if we did something together that Mom had loved so much, it could lead to talking about her more, too. Or even growing closer ourselves.

He shook his head. "No, I'm just here to watch. My

dancing shoes are too rusty, I'm afraid, and I leave soon on business. It'd be best if Lily starts as she intends to go on."

In other words, without him.

Hiding the hurt behind a smile was easy by this point.

"Guess it's just me."

Viktória nodded. "Not a problem." Then her eyes lit with excitement. "Actually, it would be good, just this once, for you to feel and see the movement from both sides. But do not worry, I have the perfect partner for you. If you'll excuse me, I'll go get him and then we can begin!"

She disappeared behind a closed door in a rush of excited energy, presumably to scrounge up the poor guy doomed to be my partner, and I threw my head back with a groan.

Mom, if you're watching, please help me not make too big an idiot of myself. And while you're at it, if you can, maybe find a way for this to not be completely awful?

The air-conditioning kicked on, and a chill danced down my arms. The door Viktória had vanished behind opened again, and I took a fortifying breath, prepared to meet my new partner with as much grace and dignity as I could.

That went right out the damn window when Stone Torres waltzed into the room.

Chapter Four

STONE

Well, I'll be damned.

"*You?* You're the perfect dance partner?" Lily Bailey, the redhead from yesterday, made a choking sound in her throat. She threw her head back and glared at the tall black ceiling. "You're so not funny right now."

I raised my eyes and glanced at the exposed beams. Who was she talking to? A spider?

"You two know each other?" Ma looked between us, and I shrugged a shoulder. I guessed you could call passing each other in the halls for years and our run-in in the stairwell yesterday *knowing each other*. Her smile stretched wider. "Wonderful! This will be even better than I expected."

Eyes glowing, she ushered us toward the open end of the dance floor. I didn't want to rain on my mother's parade, especially when she was in teacher mode, but I had a hunch this wouldn't be her easiest lesson. More likely than not, I'd be spending the next hour as more of a stepping stone than a dance partner, but that had to be more productive than trying to get my suddenly tight-lipped sister to spill whatever was bothering her. Besides, my steel toes could take it. Centers weighed almost twice this girl, and they did more damage on a Friday night than she ever could. And it sure as hell beat being stuck in the group class with Cameron.

"Since when are quarterbacks fluent in ballroom?" Lily hissed quietly, glancing at Ma before shooting me a suspicious look like I somehow skulked around dance studios, preying on innocent girls for nefarious reasons.

Was this girl always strung this tight? Unable to stop myself from teasing her, I leaned in and asked, "Oh, you didn't know?" Her gaze shot to mine. "Football players have *all* the moves."

The cheesy line, coupled with the waggled eyebrows, produced the desired effect—Lily rolled her eyes and huffed, a bit of the starch leaving her rigid shoulders as she picked up the pace behind my mom. I fell back a step, letting her walk ahead of me, and smiled at the ground.

As we neared the other side of the room, I felt eyes tracking us. Cameron and Ashley had no doubt been watching ever since I stepped foot out of Ma's office, but I refused to acknowledge them. I did, however, feel bad for this poor girl. First the embarrassing scene yesterday, then the extraordinary bad luck of being my dance partner on a day Cameron had shown up. I wanted to believe she wouldn't make a scene, but then again, I also once believed she'd never cheat.

Once Ma had us standing a few feet apart and facing each other, she explained her approach to teaching. "We will take it easy for this lesson. First, we'll learn the steps, then we'll add the music, later we'll worry about the technique. Okay?" Lily nodded, fiddling with her glasses, and Ma gestured to her shirt. "And don't worry. No one will be following you here. It is your partner's job to do the leading."

I could hear the feminist dissertation undoubtedly running through Lily's head as I dropped my gaze to read the words printed on her black tee: *Don't Follow in My Footsteps, I Run into Walls.* I smirked at the high probability of that but wisely kept my comments to myself.

"So, Lily, your parents liked the smooth dances, like the waltz and foxtrot. But my younger students tend to prefer the rhythmic styles, like cha-cha, rumba, and salsa." Ma shimmied her shoulders with a playful grin. "The choice is yours. What would you like to learn? Would you like to try a waltz, or would you rather one of the rhythmic styles? Say, the salsa?"

Lily's big blue eyes widened behind her lenses. "Um, honestly? I have zero rhythm. Like, think of your favorite dancer, subtract every ounce of talent they have…take a little more, and then you'll have me." She wrinkled her nose. "Then again, I can also barely walk smoothly, much less dance, so…sure. Let's go with option two. What can it hurt?"

I snorted. I swear, I'd tried to hold it in. I didn't want to hurt her feelings, and Ma clearly needed every student she could get. But I kept seeing Connor Davis's face as she clocked him upside the head yesterday trying to catch her balance.

Her gaze jerked to mine, and I grinned, hoping she was at the point where we could laugh about it. "You sure you're not tempting fate asking that?"

Lily's eyes narrowed. I guessed she wasn't ready to laugh about it yet.

Ma frowned at me before turning to her student. "None of this nonsense about not having rhythm," she scolded with a *tsk*ing sound. "Everyone has rhythm. You just haven't had the right teacher yet." She shot her a wink. "That is where I come in. You just focus on the steps."

The heavy bass of a salsa beat kicked on for the group lesson, and my body naturally shifted with the rhythm. Ma had me dancing since I could walk. Everyone in my family danced, on both sides of the genealogical tree, and the groove of the music was in my blood. As much a part of me as my need to protect those I cared about.

As Shakira sang about climbing the Andes, I bobbed my head, eager to release some of the tension of the day. When the music flowed, and I lost myself in the movement, the weight of expectations floated away.

"We'll start with the two-handed salsa basic," Ma declared and came to stand beside Lily. "The footwork is the most important part. To begin, you step back on your right foot, rock with your left, and then, step together. Good! Now switch feet. Come forward with your left…rock…then together. Not so big of steps. Think delicate and sexy. Okay, now back, together. Forward and together. Excellent!"

Lily squirmed under my mother's praise, and her cheeks went positively pink at the word *sexy*. Her forehead was scrunched in concentration, and her lips were pressed together so tight they were nearly invisible. I tilted my head and watched in fascination as she continued to hesitatingly pick up her foot, then place it back on the floor.

The girl was shockingly uncoordinated. Seriously, she couldn't seem to find the beat to save her life, and that was with Ma calling it out. Forget about trying to follow music. Hell, I supposed we were lucky she was still upright at this point, but from her intense expression it was clear Lily Bailey was a fighter. I'd bet she was the type to either get the step right or die trying.

I liked that about her.

Over her head, I glimpsed a flash of movement and looked out of habit. Cameron was actively ignoring her partner and the step they were learning, choosing instead to watch me dance with Lily. Even from across the room, I could see her brown eyes swimming with hurt and even jealousy, an emotion that made no sense, considering I wasn't hers. A fact I'd told her multiple times, but Cameron never did accept defeat easily. She always fearlessly went after what she wanted, a trait I once respected until the night when what she wanted was to make out with another guy.

I heaved a sigh. Now I sounded bitter. *This* was why I needed my drama-free space back. Shoving that unpleasant memory back in the recesses of my mind, I tuned in to my partner.

Ma smiled encouragingly. "You are doing very well. With practice, it'll be just like breathing. Now, after our feet, our frame is vitally important. It is how we hold ourselves and connect with our partner." She exaggerated pulling to her full five-six height. "We want to stand tall, with our spine strong, and our weight over the balls of our toes. Our feet are turned out in a V shape, with our left foot facing ten o'clock, and right foot facing two."

Lily nodded and tried to replicate the position, straightening her spine and widening her stance, and wobbled a bit for balance. Instinctively, I reached out to steady her, expecting the worst even for the simple move, and my hand closed around the soft skin of her arm. Clear blue eyes shot to mine, wide and surprised as if she'd forgotten I was here. Huh. That was a first.

Fighting a smile, I released her arm and rubbed the back of my neck.

Ma made a few minor adjustments, then signaled her approval. The final part of the two-handed basic was, of course, adding the hands. Lily bit the corner of her lip as she placed her fingertips in my waiting palms, and I held them loosely, not missing the fact they were slick with sweat. She released a nervous breath, and a small yet sharp pang of protectiveness hit my chest. I gripped her hand more firmly, trying to infuse her with confidence.

We started to move, doing the same basic step she'd learned before, and I squeezed her fingers to the beat. "One, two, three, four," I murmured softly. "Five, six, seven, eight."

Muscle memory guided my feet as I focused completely on Lily. Willing her along as I danced in the opposite direction. As I watched the light bounce off her red hair—her eyes, of course, were focused on the floor—I realized how different it was, dancing with someone almost as tall as me. The women in my family were all on the average to shorter side, five-six or less, and Cameron was a full foot shorter than my six-two. Lily, on the other hand, had to be close to five-ten. When I leaned in, her temple grazed the tip of my nose.

A citrusy scent floated from her hair, and with her so fixated on her feet, I let my gaze drift down her body. No skirt today. She was in jeans, a safe choice considering yesterday, and the form-fitting denim showed off her long legs. I'd always been a leg guy, so I could admit I enjoyed the view.

Too bad she couldn't control them, though.

Once she'd mastered the two-handed basic...or gotten close enough...Ma moved on to the closed frame position and trying the steps with music. This new arrangement had us standing closer together with my right arm wrapped around her back and left hand holding her right. Standing that close, I realized just how long it had been since I'd held a girl in my arms. Thanks to Cameron, I'd been flying solo since May.

I blamed that for my quick glance at her lips.

Lily's face flushed as she rested her arm on mine. "Nothing like getting up close and personal, huh?" she asked, grinning sheepishly. Darting her gaze past my right ear, she blew a strand of hair off her face, and the sweet scent of peppermint hit my nose. "I, uh, feel like I should apologize in advance for tripping or crunching your toes. I assure you it won't be intentional. My feet have a tendency to go rogue."

I laughed. "I'm sure I'll be fine."

"No, seriously," she said, glancing back at me with a wry smile. "You think yesterday was bad? You ain't seen nothing yet. I'm like a newborn colt, all skinny legs and no rhythm."

"Well then, lucky for you, I've got that in spades." I raised my eyebrows with a haughty grin, trying to get her to loosen up, and Lily rolled her eyes.

Mission accomplished.

The music poured through the speakers—"Muevete" by D.L.G.—and after finding the beat, I began murmuring the count for her to follow. "Quick, quick. Slow. Quick, quick. Slow. One, two, three, four. Five, six, seven, eight."

Dancing with music was harder. Even doing the same steps you'd mastered a second ago, the extra stimulus could jumble your feet. That's where a strong partner came in handy. At least in theory.

"You're ahead of the beat," Ma said, modeling the steps alongside her. "Stop watching your feet and lift your head. Listen to the count. Trust that Ágoston will guide you when it's time to move."

The muscles in Lily's back twitched under my arm, and her jaw turned to granite. Sensing control was a bit of an issue for her, I tried teasing again. "Yeah, unlike you, I *don't* walk into walls. It's okay to follow me."

Her head jerked up, her gaze leaving the ground long enough to stare at me with a mixed expression of self-deprecation and annoyance. I grinned.

"You really can let go," I told her seriously. "I've got you. And hey, if you make a mistake, it's no big deal. Play it off or make it part of the dance." I shook our linked hands. "Believe it or not, this is supposed to be *fun*."

Lily exhaled heavily and darted a glance to the side. "I don't like attention," she murmured quietly, her blush deepening with the admission. "The mirrors in this room... they make it feel like everyone's watching us."

I couldn't promise they weren't—in fact, I knew of at least two who were, seated at one of the small tables to the side now that group class was over. But, I could help her forget about them. "Then keep your eyes on me," I told her. "No one else here matters anyway. It's just you and me and the music, okay?"

Lily's eyes drifted across my face, and she released a shaky breath. When she inhaled again, the muscles in her back and arms slowly relaxed, and the tension in her face smoothed away. Blood rushed back into my hands as her Hulk-like grip turned less frantic.

I winked. "Good. Now, let's dance."

I couldn't say she rocked it from there. The girl was far from a natural, and she was never quite sure of her feet. But she did get better, and more importantly, she started having fun. I doubted she'd admit it, she seemed stubborn like that, but when Ma had us try a variation where we didn't hold hands, instead asking us to add our own flair, Lily wrinkled her nose and went with a duck face.

It was kind of adorable.

This quirky girl who tripped over air and held herself so rigidly finally let loose, and when she went so far as to add a hint of a shoulder shake, I had to smile. As luck would have it, she looked up right at that moment and a flash of insecurity crossed her face, so I immediately busted out a ridiculous face of my own and shook my shoulders in an exaggerated shimmy.

Lily threw her head back in a laugh. It was loud and genuine and so completely free that I joined in. A fiery look entered her eyes, and she shimmied again. This time with a playful grin.

I had to admit, this hadn't been the worst hour of my life. If things were different, it could even be fun making this a regular thing, helping students, if that's what Ma wanted. Unfortunately, what our family *needed* was cash.

With the latest song trailing into its final counts, Lily got more into it. Her feet grew steadier, and from the look on her face, you'd have thought she'd mastered the vortex turn or death drop instead of a basic beginner move. But she'd worked for it. She'd earned every bit of that confidence. In a weird sort of way, I was proud of her.

The music ended, along with the lesson, and to Lily's clear chagrin, light applause erupted. Looking around, I saw most of the room had cleared out, but a few people remained. Marcus came over with a smile, and while he and Ma congratulated Lily on a successful first lesson, Lily became oddly fascinated with the floor.

It was strange how so averse she was to attention, considering she was always up for academic awards, but for her sake, I was glad she was preoccupied. With her eyes on the ground, she didn't notice the targeted looks Cameron and Ashley threw our way.

Or the even stranger one from the man I assumed was her father.

*A*few hours later, the sun was setting through the windows, and I was entering the day's totals in the computer. Ma had left to pick up ingredients for Chase's enchiladas, and Angéla was watching the bakery at the end of the strip while the owner grabbed a smoke. I was in a hurry, wanting to beat Ma home and talk to Dad about my plan, so when the bell on the door went off, I didn't bother looking up.

"Sorry, we're closed."

Footsteps sounded on the floor, coming closer instead of out the door. "I won't bother you long." I raised my head at the gruff voice, and Lily's dad shoved his hands in his pockets. "I'll only take a moment of your time."

"My mom's not here," I replied. I looked around the dark, silent room, subtly pointing out we were closed for the day. "Ilusiòn isn't open tomorrow, but if you want, you can leave a message and she'll call you back on Monday."

Mr. Bailey shook his head. "No, no message."

He pressed his lips together, and as he watched me with appraising eyes, I tried not to react. This was a parent of one of Mom's students. Evidently, a former student himself. I couldn't flinch even if the guy did make me uncomfortable. Then he said, "Actually, I came by to talk to you."

My eyebrows lifted. Was he here to give me "helpful" advice, too? I didn't get the sense the man was a football fan. Lily's dad was built like a linebacker, tall and solid, but he had a commanding energy fit for a boardroom that seemed better suited for a golf course than a football field. But other than the game, what else could we possibly have to discuss? Ma was the instructor.

"I noticed you and my daughter seemed to know each other."

Okay. "Yes, sir," I replied, somewhat hesitantly. "I mean, we go to school together, but we have a big class. Lily and I don't really hang out in the same circles."

He nodded, as if he'd expected that. He took a step closer and spread his hands on the marble counter. "Then I'm guessing you didn't hear about her recent health issue due to stress."

My eyes widened. Now that, I hadn't heard. Or expected. Lily and I had shared a couple classes over the years, and she'd always been the girl with all the answers, the one teachers called on to make the rest of us look dumb. I'd have bet money she had her shit together. Then again, she did seem wound pretty tight.

"The doctors say it's important for her to relax," her dad explained, his thick eyebrows drawing together, "and a hobby could help with that. I have fond memories of taking lessons here with my wife, which is why I suggested Lily try dancing."

That explained at least one question I'd had. There was no way this had been Lily's idea. I shook my head. "Why are you telling me this?"

Mr. Bailey sighed, and the wrinkles in his forehead grew deeper. "I'm not an idiot. Lily doesn't want to take lessons. The only reason she agreed to come was because she hoped she'd be so bad at it that I'd let her out of our deal. When I leave in a week for work, there's not a thing I can do to force her to come back. But I believe this can help her, that it'd be good for her to do things other than study and worry about college." His eyes grew sharp as he leaned against the desk. "It'd help if someone had her back when I wasn't here."

I shifted in my chair. I didn't know her well, but I doubted Lily would want her dad telling me such personal details of her life, and I didn't see how I could do anything to help either way. "Like I said, we really don't know each other like that—"

He put up a hand, cutting me off. "All I'm asking is for you to help make this a fun experience for her. Just for a month or two."

This guy took helicopter parenting to unhealthy levels. "Look, I respect that you care about your daughter, but I'm not sure how much I can do. I might not even be working here much longer. Maybe you should try talking to Lily about this."

And let me shut this place down so I can get home.

Mr. Bailey stood back and reached into his pocket. "I think you're missing my intent, so let me be clear with what I'm asking. I'd like for you to be Lily's permanent partner while she is a student at Ilusiòn. If you can get her to stay in lessons, maybe even add an extra class or two throughout the week, I'll pay you for your time. Generously."

My mouth fell open, sure I'd misunderstood. This kind of thing only happened in TV shows. Then he took out a wallet fat with cash, and I sat up in the chair.

"I've already paid upfront for the first month of lessons," he said. "The ultimate package that lets Lily take unlimited classes, in case you can convince her to sign up for more."

I almost laughed out loud. *No one* signed up for the ultimate package. It was ridiculously priced, as a class cost a hundred dollars a pop, and that package equaled taking three lessons a week. No one had time for that.

"If I didn't have to travel so much, maybe I'd eventually take the lessons with her…" He trailed off, his face tightening, but he quickly cleared his throat and said, "And if so, I'd have to pay double that amount anyway."

Any words I would've said lodged in my throat as he started setting bills on the counter. Benjamins. A whole lot of them.

"I know my daughter, Mr. Torres, and she'll bail if she doesn't see the value in the lessons or enjoy them."

We were up to eleven bills now, eleven hundred dollars. He dropped one more onto the pile, and my heart started pounding.

Laying tile on Saturdays would pay fifteen dollars an hour. I'd make half the amount he was offering in a month. A bit more if I worked Wednesday afternoons, but the jobs were slower during the week. Plus, if I could convince Lily to keep taking lessons beyond this month, that'd be additional income for the studio.

That'd be better than working for Hunt.

My stomach knotted as I stared blankly at the cash. Ma would be pissed if I said yes. She'd say it was my job to help students, which was true. If Lily needed me to dance with her, she'd work it so that I could be available during her lessons for free. Ma was too proud to admit we could use the additional income. Lily probably wouldn't be too thrilled, either. I really did think in his own warped way the man meant well, but it felt like he was trying to buy his daughter a friend. Or thought she needed a babysitter.

I pressed my hands together in front of my mouth and exhaled. "Listen," I said with a slight laugh. "I'm not gonna lie. I could use the money. Your offer is crazy temping, but the truth is, my mom wouldn't like it. It's sort of my job to help wherever I'm needed, at least until I go back to my old job, so I'll be around for the next week or so if Lily needs me. After that, Marcus will be here. He's taking over her lessons, and the girls really like him. She'll be in great hands." My chest grew tight as I eyed the cash. Swallowing thickly, I forced myself to say, "So, while I appreciate the offer, I'm afraid I have to say no."

Mr. Bailey bit the inside of his cheek and picked up the

stack. My shoulders hunched.

"I'm sure Marcus is a great teacher." He tapped the bills against the counter. "He seemed friendly enough, and I watched him lead the group class. He handled it well. But Lily doesn't know him, and he's not her age. She also wouldn't be his sole focus while she is here. You remember, I've taken lessons before. Instructors come and go, and they can switch out for various reasons. There'd be no assured continuity."

He had me there. Instructors loved working at Ilusiòn because Ma was a great boss and she made the environment fun, but it was a commission-based system. Not everyone was hungry enough to see it through.

"Besides, I watched you today," Mr. Bailey said with a small smile that softened the hard lines of his face. "You made her laugh."

Damn, this was hard.

Objectively speaking, this could be the best solution for both our problems. Ma would get what she wanted—I'd stay at Ilusiòn—and I could bring in extra cash. Mr. Bailey would get what *he* wanted—Lily would stay in lessons—and I'd make sure she had a good time while she was here.

The only problem was, Ma would never agree.

Mr. Bailey held out the money and leveled me with a look. "I'd consider it a personal favor if you agreed. That said, I'd rather my daughter didn't hear about this arrangement, and I suspect you'd prefer it to stay quiet, too." He raised a questioning eyebrow, and I gave a reluctant nod. "This can stay between us. A gentleman's agreement. I won't tell your mom, and you won't tell Lily."

Looking at the money in his hand, all I could see was the stress in my mom's green eyes. This could make it go away. I'd said I would find a way to help save the studio, to do my part to contribute, and this man was literally handing me a solution. Not a long-term solution, but a start. I'd be a fool to turn him away.

The pressure in my chest loosened as I pushed to my feet. This could stay between us. No one else had to know. I'd figure out a way to slip my parents the extra money, and in the meantime, Lily would have the best experience possible. I'd see to it. Remembering how I'd actually gotten her to loosen up earlier made me think this could even be a good thing for her.

With a shaky breath, I met Mr. Bailey's eyes, nodded, and took the money.

Chapter Five

STONE

"Come on, one more. You got it, you got it. Push! Awesome job."

Grunting, I heaved the metal bar onto the rack, and Chase grabbed hold to help. His floating head leaned over the bench to stare at me upside down. "Feeling extra aggressive today, are we?" he asked with a smirk. "How's that whole monk thing working for you?"

I flipped him off with a shaky exhale and sat up, reaching for my towel. "Laugh it up, pretty boy. You won't be smiling so much when it's your turn." I scrubbed the sweat off my face, then hung the towel around my neck. "God, I love conditioning."

A perk of the team was our regular P.E. classes were replaced with daily workouts in the team gym. That, along with before-school practice, left us with only needing to stay after school two days a week for film and weight training, along with the Thursday-night family meal.

My stomach rumbled thinking about the lasagna on tonight's menu.

Next to my station, our running back Aidan finished a deadlift set and dropped the weight with a metallic *clang*. He looked over as he wiped down the bar, his lips quirked in amusement. "Any idea who pissed in Cameron's Cheerios? I swear the girl's been acting bitchier than normal this week."

I grunted and hauled my ass up on burning legs so Chase could switch places with me. He nudged me in the ribs. "I think you can thank Lover Boy here for that."

Aidan shot me a look. "She's *still* trying to win you back?"

"You know Cammie," Chase answered for me, sliding under the bar. "Defeat isn't in her vocabulary."

As I walked over so I could spot him, my mind snagged on the text she sent me Saturday after she left the studio, asking *again* when we could talk and repeating how much she missed me. Why couldn't she have put this much effort into our relationship when we'd actually had one?

"She seems to think if she wears me down, I'm gonna crawl right back, but the girl's got another think coming."

Chase blew out a breath as he grabbed hold of the weight. "Yeah, our QB here has it all figured out." I shook my head as Aidan walked over, leaning his shoulder against the wall. "He's becoming a monk. Giving up girls and sex all because of one bad egg. Can you believe that? See, I told him what he needs to do is be more like me. Stick to straight hookups. That way you avoid all the drama."

Aidan busted out laughing. He bent over at the waist and put his hands on his knees while Chase lifted the weight with a frown. "Dude," he said, wiping at his eyes, "you mean like the girl who egged your car last spring?"

"Or the one who TPed your house?" asked our kicker Robbie, chiming in from the treadmill.

"Or how about the one who broke into your locker and trashed it," I added, causing Chase to pause mid-rep with the bar on his chest.

He thought about it for a second and shrugged. "Obviously, it's not a perfect plan." Then he pursed his lips. "And why bitches always gotta mess with my shit?"

The room erupted into laughter, and Chase lifted the weight from his chest.

Aidan pushed off the wall, still shaking his head, and looked at me. "I'm grabbing a water before heading to the locker room. You guys want anything?"

I nodded, holding up two fingers, and reached out to spot when Chase's arms shook. "Look," I said, "I know not every girl is gonna be another Cameron. That's not what it's about. Take Saturday, for example. I danced with a girl who, given the option, would've probably rather spent the afternoon studying calculus than be in my arms, and would be more likely to run from drama than bring it. I'm just not interested in any of it right now. I've got too much else going on."

That was the damn truth, too. While Mr. Bailey's offer potentially solved one of my problems, finding a way to contribute, two new ones had cropped up in its place. I might have extra cash for my parents, but I still had no clue how I'd give it to them without spilling the details about our agreement. Then on top of that, I still had to win over Lily. According to her old man, she had no interest in dancing and had every intention of quitting after Saturday's lesson. I couldn't let that happen.

I'd thought about it all week, and with time running out, there was only one resource left to tap.

"Hey, what do you know about Lily Bailey?"

Chase looked up in confusion. "The redhead from the stairs?" I nodded with a grunt. "Not much. She hangs out with Sydney Greene a lot."

"Who, Lily?" Aidan asked, handing Robbie a water

before turning to us. I accepted mine with a grateful chin lift, and he set down Chase's near his feet. "Nice girl. Smart, too. I've had her in a couple of classes. I'm pretty sure she's battling it out with Cammie for valedictorian."

That helped explain Cameron's reaction Saturday. While she'd made it abundantly clear she wanted me to give her another chance, I'd thought the look she'd shot us at the end of class was a bit much. I'm guessing watching me dance with her class rival hadn't been fun.

"Well, I'm off to hit the showers." Aidan waved and disappeared into the locker room.

Chase looked up at me. "Why the questions about Lily?"

I took a long pull of the ice-cold water and considered telling him about the deal. Unfortunately, my best friend couldn't keep a secret to save his life, and this was one I might take to the grave. But he did have eyes and ears all over the place, and his love of gossip could help my cause.

"Her dad signed her up for a month of lessons," I said instead, going with a version of the truth. "After what happened last week, I wouldn't have expected her to be a dancer."

Chase seemed to accept my reasoning and went back to lifting. As he pushed up the bar, his face tightened in a grimace. He exhaled and muttered, "Iron Stomach."

I chuckled. "Okay. Good to know your self-esteem's not suffering, man."

He rolled his eyes and dropped the weight to his chest. "No, dumbass. Lily is Iron Stomach."

"Say what now?"

Chase took a deep breath and released it. "Seriously, man, don't you remember seventh grade? I used to dare you to eat stupid shit at lunch." I raised my eyebrow, not seeing where he was going with this. "One day, Lily and Sydney were at the other end of our table, and she called you out for refusing to do it. She used to be kinda scrappy, now that I think about it. Anyway, you turned it back around, daring *her* to eat my stupid concoction, and she did it." He laughed at the memory. "It was disgusting, too, dude. My best one yet. Mashed potatoes mixed with Salisbury steak and gravy, tuna fish and olives from the salad bar, pineapple chunks, and chocolate milk."

I gagged thinking how that must have tasted. No wonder I'd turned him down.

But Lily hadn't. Huh.

"We called her Iron Stomach for the rest of the day," he said, pushing up the bar again.

Robbie shrugged, looking mildly impressed, and slipped his earbud back in as his feet thumped on the treadmill. And I did an inner fist-pump.

Jackpot, baby! Lily Bailey, Ms. Control Freak herself, couldn't say no to a challenge.

I'd found my way in.

Chapter Six

LILY

*I*t was a tale of two studios as I walked into Ilusiòn one week later. I did a double take at the door. Unlike the chaos and excitement of last Saturday, the large room was as empty as the school parking lot ten minutes after final bell.

Granted, I *was* fifteen minutes early, and it was nine-thirty in the morning. It was possible the other students preferred sleeping in. I could never do that. Sydney liked to tease that I woke with the birds, but it'd been a habit ingrained in me since birth. Mom had been an early riser, and mornings had been our special time to cuddle up on the sofa, watching old movies on the weekend or talking about life before school.

A pang of loneliness hit my chest. Three years without her and it never got any easier. Every time I blinked it felt like another memory slipped further away. Mom's voice got fainter. Her rosewater scent faded. It'd been a pleasant surprise, coming here and discovering something new about her. Adding a different colored thread to the tapestry I'd created in my mind.

Even if it had involved embarrassment to get it.

Letting the door close, I tiptoed to the reception desk and looked around. Seriously, where was everyone? Oldies music bounced off an empty dance floor, and without a dozen or so bodies crowding the room, the air-conditioning felt practically arctic. Not that I was complaining. It was September in Texas, in other words hot as Hades, and the short walk from the parking lot had felt like a brisk swim through water. A welcome shiver swept down my arms as I leaned my back against the cool counter.

Well, one thing was working in my favor. If it stayed this deserted, hopefully my anxiety would stay at bay, too. And, if no other dancers showed, then maybe Cameron wouldn't, either. Which meant maybe, *just maybe*, things could go back to normal at school.

Her reaction seriously boggled my brain.

Clearly, she was the superior dancer between us. Granted, it didn't take much to be better than me, but there was no way she felt threatened. In the land of dance, she was the obvious victor.

As far as our rivalry for valedictorian, we were pretty evenly matched, but we'd always done a good job of keeping it on the down low. Other than a slight competitiveness in our few shared classes, we stuck to our own corners. She had cheer, yearbook, and newspaper, while I took debate, Key Club, and DECA.

We tolerated each other's presence in NHS and ignored each other in the cafeteria. The sides had been chosen, the lines drawn, and we'd kept it that way for over three years. That left only one possible explanation for why Cameron was so angry—because I'd danced with Stone. But she couldn't actually be jealous, could she? I mean, I knew they dated last year, but *come on*. Had she looked in a mirror recently?

Of course, with all the confusing glares shot my way during lunch, my best friend was bound to notice, which led to me sharing my theories, including the fact that we were both students at Ilusiòn... Oh, right, and that Stone Torres had been my dance partner.

Yeah, I don't think Syd heard anything I'd said after that.

It hadn't mattered that I was quitting once Dad left. Or that even if I *did* stick with the lessons, which I wouldn't, I wouldn't see Stone again. Partnering with him had been a one-time deal. No, all my bestie cared about was that I'd danced with a hottie, and in the world of my uneventful romantic life, that was equivalent to a marriage proposal.

Okay, fine. So Sydney hadn't been the *only* one fixated on the guy. As it turned out, I wasn't entirely immune to the Torres charm, either. The white knight act on the stairwell had been ridiculously attractive—especially when I was able to replay it in the quiet of my room without the embarrassment of my near-nakedness weighing me down—and, admittedly, the Magic Mike moves during our lesson had been a turn-on. Not that I'd admit it aloud.

Sure, Stone was the stereotypical, obvious choice for a crush—hot, popular, and a bit full of himself—and I prided myself on going against the grain. But he'd also helped calm my nerves during the lesson and even made me laugh.

And did I mention the boy could *move*?

As if she sensed my thoughts, Sydney's text tone chirped out from my phone. I chuckled, already guessing the gist of the message, and pulled it from my back pocket.

Has the football god been spotted yet?

I shook my head with a smile, then glanced around for

good measure. Still not a soul.

Nope, the whole place is deserted. I told you last week was a random event. It won't happen again.

The office door behind me opened with a pop of air, scaring the crap out of me, and I juggled my phone. Laughter poured into the lobby, and while I attempted to calm my racing heart, my phone buzzed once more in my hand.

You say random, I say FATE! Knock 'em dead, Ginger! xoxo

I snickered. Ginger Rogers I was not, and as far as fate went, well, that fickle bitch did have an interesting sense of humor when it came to me. Returning my phone to my pocket, I smiled as Marcus and Angéla walked through the door. Stone's twin waved before setting up shop behind the computer, and I covertly cast a glance back at the office, curious if another dark head would stroll through.

"Good morning," Marcus greeted, joining me on the other side of the desk. "You're here early. I like it. Eager students mean they're ready to get out there and kill it."

More like they were ready to get it over with, but I let the nice man keep his delusions.

"So, what's the game plan for today?" I asked.

He grabbed a thin black binder from the shelf. "I thought we'd build on what you learned last week. We'll review the basic salsa move, then add two new elements we can build into a pattern. After practicing those for a bit, getting you confident, we can go over the program I put together for you."

I inwardly cringed. That program would never get used, and I hated that he'd wasted his time, but I couldn't afford to come clean yet. Dad didn't leave for Israel until tomorrow morning. Until then, I had to continue acting like the perfect student. Or as close to perfect as I could get. Really, I was aiming for mediocre.

Following him toward the dance floor, I made a mental note to get Marcus a gift card to Starbucks. High-calorie caffeinated drinks made everything better, right?

I was in the middle of deciding the best way to sneak it over here without getting suckered into another lesson when a second door, one I hadn't yet noticed, opened from a short hallway. A tall figure exited in shadow, and before I even saw his face, my ridiculous heart did a pitter-pat.

Stone was dressed in jeans again with a slim-fitted blue T-shirt that stretched at the shoulders and showed off his muscular arms. His black hair was styled in a messy fauxhawk I wanted to poke, and his dark chocolate eyes appeared to glow as he walked to where I stood, wearing a smirk.

"What? No sarcastic shirt today?"

I glanced at my plain green tee and sighed. "I own other things, you know. I just happen to think the T-shirts are funny."

Stone shot me a wink. "I do, too." He turned to Marcus and clapped. "Hey, man, listen. Lily and I are friends from school. Think it'd be cool if I continue helping with her lessons?"

A sharp squeak issued from my throat—both at the claim of friendship and the even crazier request for a second round.

Marcus glanced at me with a frown. "I don't have a problem with it, but ultimately it's Lily's call to make."

Stone raised an eyebrow, as if daring me to say no, and Marcus crossed his arms over his wide chest, watching us curiously. Me? I huffed out a laugh and searched the room for hidden cameras.

Was this some new, weird, teen-geek reality show? Or was Stone in need of service hours, and I was this week's attempt at klutzy outreach? What other reason could he possibly have for wanting to push this?

"Haven't your poor toes been crushed enough?"

Stone's shoulders shook with silent laughter before he said, "I think they can handle it."

My head felt dizzy, and it was like someone had suddenly kicked up the heat to ninety. But, as confused as I was, I couldn't deny my insides were doing the cha-cha. Or, more appropriately, the *salsa*.

A hot guy wanted to dance with me. *Me*, Lily Bailey. Was I really standing here trying to argue with him? For some reason I'd yet to understand, my anxiety didn't flare up around Stone, and after the complete and utter craziness my life had been the last two weeks, didn't I deserve a little treat in the form of man candy?

Answer: yes. Yes, I did.

"Fine," I said, forcing myself to look blasé. "It's your funeral."

Stone let loose his smile, and my stomach went into a tiny free fall. Swallowing a squeal, I turned on my heel and followed the instructor onto the dance floor.

"Okay, so last week you learned a few variations of the salsa basic," Marcus instructed after he had us face each other. "But Viktória kept the movement going forward and back. Today, we'll add in a few side-breaks, or cucarachas."

"Oh, goodie," I muttered under my breath.

From the corner of my eye, I saw Stone's lips quirk, and my insides squished.

Holding hands, an action that made my giddy heart pulse

in time with the drumbeat playing over the speakers, we reviewed the same basic step over and over until I thought I'd go insane—of course, it didn't help that I struggled to find the beat and kept taking too large of steps. But it wasn't like I was *trying* to mess up. I had long legs, dang it! One of my steps equaled two of Sydney's. Thus, the curse of being tall.

Not helping matters was the faint hint of wintergreen wafting off Stone's skin, or the slightly roughened texture of his palm sliding against mine. Every brush had my stomach fluttering. My insides were vibrating, my skin felt hot and itchy, and if the slight smirk still lingering around his lips was any clue, the boy was all too aware of his effect on me.

Finally, after several rounds with moderate success, both with the steps and with me swallowing down the giddy giggle bubbling in my throat, Marcus declared us ready to move on.

Thank God.

"Now, for the side-breaks," he said, coming to stand alongside me. "It's essentially the same move. You're just traveling in a different direction. Lily, starting with your right foot, I want you to step to the side on one, then step in place with your left for two, and then bring your right foot back to close for three. Yep, just like that. Now on the other side, you do the exact same thing, only in the opposite direction. Step left, then in place, and close together. Good! But, remember, take smaller steps."

My back teeth clicked as my hand clenched around Stone's.

I'd thought those *were* smaller steps.

"Try not to anticipate what's coming next," Marcus advised a few minutes later. "And don't worry so much about your feet, either. Look at your partner instead and let him and the beat be what leads you."

I snorted under my breath. That was easy for him to say.

Marcus was a guy. They didn't have to depend on someone else to get the moves right. It's what drove me so crazy. Unlike in school, it didn't matter if I knew what came next, or if I was the best salsa dancer this side of the Rio Grande. I still had to wait for Stone.

What if *he* messed up? What if he forgot the step, huh? Then we were both screwed.

Who decided on this archaic, patriarchal system anyway?

Stone squeezed my hand, and I grudgingly raised my head. "You've got a thing for control, don't you?"

I growled in annoyance, because cute or not, he was making my patience run low. He widened his eyes with a laugh.

"Whoa, down girl, I'm not judging. Quarterback, remember? I need to be in control of what happens on the field. But that need is what's messing you up. You're so worried about what step comes next that you're sabotaging yourself. You're too in your head." His dimple flashed as he ducked down and looked me straight in the eyes. "I know it sounds wrong, but to dance well, you have to give up control."

Sucking my teeth, I drilled him with my stare. The hot guy was officially starting to crunch my toes—and *not* in the way I'd been crushing his. The thing was, Stone didn't know me. We'd spent one hour together—*one*—a week ago, and we'd spent most of it dancing, not talking. Now he was some sort of expert on my headspace? *Please.*

Of course, the fact that he was probably spot-on in his assessment was irrelevant. He wasn't the instructor here; Marcus was.

As if he were reading my thoughts, the man in question snapped his fingers. "I've got an idea. Lily, close your eyes."

I stopped dancing altogether. "I'm sorry, what?"

"Close your eyes," Marcus repeated, a hint of humor sparking in his own, and I shook my head incredulously.

"Yeah…see, I don't think that's such a good idea. I'm already a klutz with my eyes *open*."

His full lips quirked. "Trust me. Or rather, trust *him*. I think Stone's onto something. Rhythm isn't the problem here. You're ahead of the beat because you're too in your head. Closing your eyes will force you to use your other senses, like the feel of his hand guiding you, to know when to move. It's a trust exercise."

I hung my head. If there were a white flag around, I'd wave it, too. I failed to see how losing the sense of sight would miraculously make my feet find the beat, but at this point, I was willing to try anything. Especially if it got them both to stop staring at me.

Only thirty more minutes.

With a tired sigh, I shut my eyes…and immediately felt stupid. "Okay, now what?"

"Now we dance," Stone said, his rich voice somehow sounding deeper in the dark. He lightly squeezed my left hand, guiding me, and I hesitatingly stepped in that direction. He repeated the action on my right, and I followed suit, avoiding his toes and further mention of my King Kong–sized feet.

So far so good, I guessed.

He cleared his throat. "What did you think of last night's game?"

My eyes opened so I could roll them. "What could that possibly have to do with salsa?"

"Nothing," he replied with a smile. "Close your eyes."

I blew out a breath of annoyance and shut them as instructed.

"It's called distraction, Miss Control Freak, and besides,

I'm genuinely curious. What did you think of the final play?"

I shrugged, rocking my body to the right. "I wouldn't know. I didn't see it."

"Didn't you go to the game?"

"Nope, I was home studying."

Stone grunted, like he was shocked I hadn't been in the stands with the rest of the town, watching him in the tight pants Sydney loved so much, and I chuckled. "No, it's cool. It's just the Knights are one of our bigger rivals. I figured everyone was there. You have a big test on Monday?"

I snorted. "Uh, actually, I do, but that's not why I didn't go. Believe it or not, QB, not everyone is obsessed with pigskin. To be honest, I haven't been to a game since the first one freshman year."

The pressure on my hand went slack for two whole seconds. My feet froze, and Stone retightened his grip, his voice sounding utterly confused. "The Tigers are state champions. Friday night lights are like a high school rite of passage, especially in Texas. Do you have a job or something?"

I cracked open an eye. "I tutor during the week, if that's what you mean, but not at night. I study and do homework."

"Both eyes closed," he reminded me, distracted now and no longer smiling.

I fell into darkness with a huff.

Stone was quiet for a few more counts, letting my revelation sink in. Then he asked, "Do you ever just let loose? Like at all? Do you ever go to parties, or dances, or anything?"

"I'm not a freaking robot," I replied, feeling my skin grow hot for a new reason. "I read, I hang out. But mostly, yeah, I focus on school. That's what these years are *supposed* to be about. Parties and football games would just distract me."

Rocking in place, I scowled and frostily added, "If it makes you feel better, I'll be sure to attend a few ragers at Harvard."

When he didn't reply or say anything else, I assumed I'd stunned him into silence. Or pissed him off with the "rager" comment. For that, I felt a bit guilty, but he was the one judging me for not fitting his standard. I mean, in a way, I understood. Stone Torres was the king of Brighton High. It was no surprise we didn't see eye to eye. The things I thought were trite and silly were probably a big deal for him, and hey, more power to him. Football could be a ticket to college, and he should grab hold of that with both hands held tight.

But what Mr. High School didn't grasp was it wasn't like I was missed at all those events anyway. Other than Sydney, no one cared if I was there, and I wouldn't begin to know how to act at a party. At the games, Syd mostly worked concessions. What was I supposed to do, sit in the stands by myself? No, thank you.

Tension in my right hand had me propelling my foot in that direction, and my breathing grew heavy. This was the same argument I'd been having with Dad, only it was none of Stone's business.

Then he said, "Life is about a hell of a lot more than books and tests. I mean, seriously…do you ever just have *fun*?"

I threw my hands in the air with a growl of frustration. "Can't you tell?" I snapped. "I'm having a total blast right now!"

My voice echoing off the hardwood floor acted like an old-school record player scratch. With a mental *skrrrp*, I winced and peeled my eyelids open. Stone stared back, his dark peepers blown wide in shock, and we held each other's gaze for two solid beats…then we busted out laughing.

"Well," Marcus said with a chuckle, shocking me once

again. I'd completely forgotten he was here. "I'd call that a success. A bit off topic, perhaps, but at least we got your mind off your feet."

My lips parted in surprise. *Huh.* He was right. The entire time Stone and I had been arguing, I hadn't once thought about the beat or what step came next. Miracle of miracles, I hadn't stumbled, either.

Stone grinned, both dimples on display, and as much as I hated myself for wanting his approval, I basked in the feeling of it. Warm and fuzzy across my skin like one of my bath bombs. Hot-boy scented.

After calling it a day, Marcus quickly shared his plans for the next few lessons, and I nodded along, feigning excitement. When he headed back to the office, Stone and I were left alone at one of the bistro tables around the dance floor, drinking much-needed bottles of water.

"You did good today," he told me, stretching his long legs out.

I fiddled with the peeling label. "Thanks. And, uh, thanks for being my partner again. You must be a masochist, subjecting yourself to my feet a second time, but I'm glad you did. That last exercise helped." Lifting my eyes, I added with a grin, "I even had *fun.*"

Stone smiled and said, "Surprisingly, I did, too. Even with the crushed toes."

"I didn't step on you once!" Glancing back at the shiny dance floor, a few particularly stellar moments came to mind, and I winced. "Okay, so I trampled you a *couple* times. It wasn't half as bad as last week," I argued, my cheeks growing hot.

"I'm teasing you." He kicked the bottom of my chair. "I meant what I told Marcus. I wouldn't mind making this a regular thing. I'm here helping my mom anyway. Might as well let out some aggression and dance while I'm at it." His smile softened as he focused on me and asked, "What do you say? Would it be cool if we partner up while you take lessons?"

Er. Here was where it got sticky. Technically, Stone was the owner's son. If I told him the truth, that I was quitting, he could tell his mom, who I was sure would call Dad. That would mess up everything I had planned. But for some reason, I trusted him.

I blamed that silly exercise.

"To be honest…" I shifted forward in my chair. "I don't really plan on staying a student much longer."

"Oh?" Stone put his elbows on the table. "But Marcus has your program set for a month."

I nodded and shoved a section of hair behind my ear. "Yeah, see, my dad's actually the one who wants me in lessons. This is his deal. But he leaves tomorrow, and that's when I'm gonna get my life back. I don't have time for dance classes right now. As you know, progress reports went home yesterday, and I'm nowhere near as solid as I'd like to be."

Watching me, Stone picked up his bottle of water and took a good, long pull. The thick knot in his throat bobbed, and I glanced away, biting my lip. "I thought you got straight A's."

"I-I do," I admitted, turning back as he set the bottle on the table. "But that's beside the point. Being valedictorian means being the best, and Cameron aced a history test when I was in…er, when I was home sick last week," I covered quickly, ignoring his sharp, inquisitive look. "That's just an example. I'm making the test up Monday. But there's more pressure than ever to make sure I take the top spot. I can't afford to fall behind."

He rubbed the back of his neck. "I've got to say, I think

you're making a mistake. It's senior year. This is our last shot before we head off to college and are expected to act like adults. You should spend at least some of it doing more than just studying."

"Oh, I *should*, huh?" I said, rolling my eyes. "Strange, I don't recall asking your opinion." At his pursed lips, I laughed and pushed up from my chair. It was time to head home. "Listen, I get that you mean well, and I appreciate it. Somewhat. But this is my life, okay? I get to choose how I live it."

Tucking in my chair, I threw a wave over my shoulder and headed for the door.

Halfway across the floor, he called out, "I dare you not to quit."

My feet stumbled as my mouth fell open. *She wouldn't have...*

Slowly, I turned around, realizing my best friend oh so definitely would, and narrowed my eyes. "You talked to Sydney."

Stone pushed to his feet. The right side of his mouth kicked up in a crooked grin as he covered the distance between us. "I didn't talk to anyone. I remember you, Lily Bailey. The girl who used to be scrappy as hell and never backed down from a challenge."

My breath caught audibly, and his gaze drifted across my face. "She's still in there, too," he murmured. "Buried under a mountain of textbooks. I've seen glimpses"—he nodded to the dance floor behind us—"quick flashes that show she's busting to get out of the cage you've put her in. But you're too stubborn to let that happen. So I'm daring you."

I blinked silently, still lost on him remembering me, and he reached out, sliding a strand of hair behind my ear. The skin on my cheek tingled.

"Give me one month," he urged, eyes pleading. "Stick with the lessons Marcus planned and let me prove to you that life is for living, not waiting."

My stomach fluttered, and I whispered in confusion, "Why do you even care?"

A muscle ticked in his jaw. "You remind me of my sister," he said, glancing away. "If Angéla was this lost, I'd want someone to help her, too."

So I *was* a charity case. Tucking my arms across my chest, I hid the hurt behind a mask of indifference. "And if you can't convince me? What do I get out of it?"

Stone smiled. "If I can't prove I'm right after one month, then you can quit the lessons, and I'll cover for you with our parents."

Blood rushed in my ears. A spark worked its way through my chest, gaining speed as it zipped up my spine and exploded in my belly. Adrenaline. An intoxicating rush I hadn't felt in a long time. Three years, if I wanted to get picky about it.

Him handling our parents would resolve a major issue; Dad intended for me to stay in lessons indefinitely, but if Stone helped keep him in the dark once I quit, he'd stay off my back. Plus, if I was honest, a month wasn't that big a deal. Yeah, I'd bitched about it, but it had never been so much about the lessons as what they represented—a constraint on my time, and my dad's inability to understand me. I didn't need another thing on my massive to-do list, and he should've known that. But even I could admit it wouldn't be hard to make up one hour of study time once a week. And it wasn't as if Stone would last an entire month anyway.

Clearly, the guy was bluffing. Stone Torres lived a life filled with football and popularity. He didn't have time to walk me through the finer points of Teenager 101 any more than I had time to listen. As for convincing me high school was more than a stepping stone? He'd have better luck selling ice cream to a penguin.

What was tempting, though, was knocking him down a peg or two in the meantime. God, he was cocky. Acting like his approach to life was the only way to live. And assuming he knew me after only a week. It'd be nice showing Stone he wasn't as infallible as this town made him out to be. Then, soon enough, he'd grow bored…and I would win. *And* be done with lessons.

Rolling back my shoulders, I met his smug look with a confident grin of my own and said, "Okay, twinkle toes, you're on."

"Good." Stone's eyes lit with triumph as he put his hand on my shoulder. "We start tomorrow."

Chapter Seven

LILY

I *don't belong here.*

A group of giggling girls jumped out of the idling car and took off across the steaming blacktop. Ponytails streamed behind them as they waved at friends like giddy extras in a CW show, completely carefree, and I swallowed down a mini-wave of panic.

Ducking behind a sapling, I walked backward and pressed my back against a lamppost holding a banner welcoming everyone to the Festival at the Lake. The heat from the metal pole singed past my shirt while a series of flashbacks fired in rapid succession.

Mom, cheering on a dance troupe as they marched past us in the parade and eating her weight in popcorn.

Dad, buying three huge hot dogs slathered in mustard and ketchup and promptly spilling the condiments on his shirt.

Me, laughing as Jolly Ranchers beaned me in the head from the Lions Club eyeglass float.

My chest pinched as those memories, and a dozen others

just like them, washed over me. That laughing girl who'd looked forward to coming to the annual festival would've never believed I'd be here a few short years later, hiding behind a stupid sapling.

I closed my eyes. God, I used to live for this event. What kid didn't love a festival, much less one kicked off with a candy-tossing parade filled with themed floats and loud music?

Twelve-year-old me would've so kicked my ass.

My phone buzzed in my pocket, and I grabbed it like the lifeline it was. Sydney had planned to meet me behind Handyman Hardware five minutes ago but had called when I was already on my way to say she was running late. She'd promised she wouldn't make me do this alone, though, and would give me a heads-up as soon as she was en route.

Seeing this first part of Stone's dare through was imperative. I couldn't let him win. Being my best friend, Sydney understood this challenge was important, even if she thought I was being silly about attending a simple parade.

Blowing out a breath, I read the message.

So sorry! Stuck with the rug rats. Someone called in sick and Mom got guilted into working a double. At least try to have fun, k? Tell me EVERYTHING tonight! xoxo

Ugh! I'd known this would happen. The second she'd said her mom hadn't gotten home yet, I'd smelled trouble. That was the way my life worked. Still, I'd hoped for the best, and now here I was, alone in a sea of semi-familiar faces. I threw my head back and groaned.

The noonday sun sat straight overhead, roasting my shoulders and making my eyes water. Somewhere, a school band was warming up, which meant the parade would start rolling soon. I still needed to find Stone's float.

So I was alone. Big deal. I'd make an appearance as promised, let Stone show me some of the so-called "fun" I'd been missing, and then duck back out. It might even be better this way. Without Sydney tugging my arm, wanting to see and sample everything, I could be back home and studying before lunch.

With a new pep in my step, I set off to find my new nemesis.

The parking lot was packed. Over the years, the town's parade had combined with our old homecoming one, creating one giant party celebrating the entire town of Cypress Lake along with the high school. Ducking around the 4H float, I meandered past the Knights of Columbus flatbed and headed toward the towering papier-mâché tiger I spotted in the back. Brighton's football team and cheerleading squad had a joint float every year. It didn't take a genius to guess their design.

My shoulders hunched as I got closer. Tons of people were circling the blue, white, and black float, and I didn't know any of them. Sure, we'd gone to the same schools for roughly twelve years, but forced birthday invites stopped in elementary school. It was a well-established fact I didn't frequent the current party circuit. Stone's friends were gonna take one look at me and wonder what in the heck I was doing here.

What would he say? Would he tell them about the dare? How embarrassing would that be? But if he didn't, how else would he explain my presence? This was a total no-win situation.

Gah, me and my stupid dares!

Stone was hanging beads on the giant tissue-paper goalpost, so he didn't see me when I made it to the float.

I flirted with the idea of leaving despite the dare, but then his number five jersey lifted, exposing the smooth dip of his lower back…along with the strip of golden skin above his low-hanging jeans.

Man, what a view. I was in *so* far over my head.

Curving a hand over my eyes, I called out, "You've convinced me!"

Stone turned, looking confused, and I waited until he found me standing a few feet away. He grinned as I held up my hands.

"You were right. This is what's been missing in my life— chicken wire and tissue paper. Who needs college when I can have all this?"

He laughed, a rich, deep rumbling sound that made my insides happy, and jumped off the truck, landing in front of me. He lifted a chin at my shirt. "*Boys in Books Are Better*, huh?"

"Duh-doy," I replied, discreetly drying my palms on my shorts. He shook his head with another laugh. "So, yeah, um, you know I was kidding about the float, right? It looks great, and there's a huge crowd gathering out there, too." I needlessly threw my thumb over my shoulder—as if he didn't realize where the town was—and bounced on my toes. "I heard people saying this year will be the best parade yet."

Awesome. Maybe he'd like a weather report, too, while I was at it. I rocked at small talk.

Stone went with it anyway. "Thanks. We added a few things this year," he said, pointing to the giant tiger, goalpost, and football helmet. "Wanted to end our reign on a high note."

I smiled with a nod, not having much else to contribute. Thankfully, I didn't have to. Some of his teammates—Chase, Robbie, Aidan, and Kurt—came over with bags of candy to throw at the crowd, and Stone casually put his hand on my shoulder. A swarm of butterflies dipped in my stomach as he squeezed, but I tried extremely hard not to react.

"Guys, Lily's gonna ride with us today," he announced, before going around and basically introducing me, as if we hadn't gone to school together for years. What made it sadder was the intro was probably needed. Well, with everyone but one.

Aidan had never said if it was a stigma thing or if he was simply embarrassed, but he didn't want his friends knowing I tutored him. I didn't mind either way. Whenever I saw him in the halls, we'd smile and be friendly, but we generally acted like we didn't know each other, which, honestly, wasn't that big a stretch. We didn't talk about our personal lives during peer tutoring. We always kept it focused on school.

Shifting my feet, I exchanged a friendly smile with Aidan, realizing next time we met we'd actually have a shared experience to discuss, then felt my eyes widen as Chase ran right for me. He plucked me off my feet and, as I squealed, spun me in a dizzying circle before plopping me back on the ground.

"Welcome to the party, Iron Stomach."

My hand flew to my thundering chest. I couldn't believe he'd remembered, too. Or that he'd just tossed me around like a rag doll. Blushing at the old nickname—and the weight of five pairs of eyes solely fixed on my person—I shoved my glasses against my face and breathed, "Th-thanks, Chase."

"I thought only the team and squad were allowed on the float."

I turned to where Cameron was kicking her feet on the edge of the flatbed. Gnawing on the corner of her lip, she transferred her gaze between Stone and me, and I could've sworn I saw a hint of panic in her eyes. "I mean, that's what

Coach said, wasn't it?"

Like a ping-pong match, the collective group's eyes bounced back to where I stood with Stone, and I shrank away from the weight of attention. "Oh, well, that's okay then. No big deal, I just—"

"It is a big deal," Stone declared, shooting her a look before fixing his focus on me. "You're riding with us, Lily. It's the whole reason I invited you here. Who in the hell cares who rides on the damn float?"

He glanced pointedly at each of his teammates, who all shook their heads and lifted their hands in the air. Then he turned his attention to the cheerleaders, most of whom widened their eyes and stepped back, while a couple glanced at Cameron.

Ashley shrugged a shoulder. "Rules are rules."

A siren sounded, followed by a rush of activity. The parade was about to begin. As the other floats and groups circled up, preparing to ride, Stone's teammates shifted on their feet, waiting for direction. He gripped the back of his neck and engaged in a standoff with my academic rival.

With each confused stare that swung my way, I cringed back another step. I didn't belong here. I wasn't a cheerleader, and I certainly wasn't on the team. I didn't want to rock the boat. Or the float, in this case. The only one who cared if I stayed was Stone, and he was too consumed in his staring match to notice me slowly slipping into the crowd. I took a final, stealthy step backward, ready to bolt—and felt the spongy give of toes beneath my shoe, followed by a soft gasp at my shoulder.

Crap. I was busted.

I turned to apologize to the latest recipient of my wayward feet, and Angéla waved away the toe-crushing with only a slight wince.

"Hey, bro, it's no biggie." Stepping up, she linked her arm through mine. "Lily can watch with me. Trust me, it's more fun in the crowd anyway. Plus, we get candy." Her eyes widened like a little kid at the word *candy*, and her bright smile was as potent as her brother's.

The muscles in Stone's jaw clenched, and his biceps flexed as he tightened the grip on his neck and scowled at the ground. Finally, he focused his attention on me. The rest of the group quickly followed. "Are *you* okay with that?"

I swallowed, then licked my lips. I couldn't cower under the unwanted attention. I gave a small nod, and he watched me carefully before releasing his neck with an exhale.

"Fine. But we'll hang out after the parade is over, okay?"

Everyone was watching us. I couldn't say no, even as I felt my study plans slip further away. "Sounds good," I lied, and Angéla immediately started pulling me backward. I stumbled a bit, then waved with my free hand at Chase and Aidan and the rest of the guys. "Y'all have fun out there. Uh, go Tigers!"

Angéla snickered, and I fell in step beside her with a groan.

"School spirit not really your thing, huh?"

I sighed as we walked past a family eager for the parade. The parents were seated in matching black-and-yellow lawn chairs, and the kids were practically vibrating on the curb. The girl in pigtails reminded me of a young me. "What gave it away?" I asked drily.

"Like calls to like," she replied with a grin. "Now churros, on the other hand? That's something I can get spirited about, and I'm pretty sure I spied a stand about a block away. You in?"

Oh, the dilemma. Doctors' orders said I was supposed to stay away from fried foods while my stomach healed, but I'd been crazy good for almost two whole weeks, I'd religiously taken my medicine, and I hadn't had a churro in years. Technically, I *should* wait two more days before breaking my bland as hell rabbit-food diet, but after the showdown at the float, drowning my worries in sugar sounded beyond awesome.

"I'm so very, very in."

Just to be safe, I'd pop a couple Prilosec when I got home.

Cypress Lake had turned out en masse, and as many people lined the street for the parade, an equal number were strolling the cracked sidewalks, hopping in and out of stores nestled under striped awnings, and browsing the various pop-up tents. A reporter was interviewing the mayor in front of Missy's Antiques, and as I ducked my head to pass behind them, Angéla stood up straight and waved into the camera.

We got in line at the churro stand, and she pointed to my chest. "Love the shirt. Book boyfriends, man. Why can't they be real, huh?" After a second, she said, "Actually, why can't *any* fictional boytoys be real? It's a conspiracy, I'm telling you. The media gets our romantic hopes up only for reality to dash them to tiny bits."

She heaved a dramatic sigh, her dark eyes twinkling, and the couple ahead of us moved forward. Angéla jumped to cover the distance. "Mmmm, smell that? That's quality grease right there. My taste buds are already tingling!"

I inhaled the naughty scent with a grin. I'd give my weight in peanut M&M's to have a sliver of this girl's energy. Clearly, the Torres charm extended across genders.

While we'd had a few classes together over the years, Angéla and I didn't really know each other. That being said, I'd always liked her, and I assumed she had a large group of friends around here waiting for her. It wasn't fair she got stuck babysitting me.

The line moved again, we placed our orders, and after grabbing a handful of napkins, I said, "Hey, I appreciate you rescuing me back there, but please don't feel like you have to hang out with me. You can go find your friends if you want." The guy behind the window held out my churro, and I took it eagerly. "I'm cool with people-watching on my own."

It sounded pathetic, but it was the truth. I was used to doing the solo thing, and for the most part, I didn't mind. Taking a big bite of deliciously fried goodness, I glanced at Angéla and stilled at the contemplative expression on her face.

"What?" I mumbled around a mouthful of dough. *Classy.*

Her lips curved with a slight smile. "You're a Beca," she declared as if I should know what she was talking about, then turned back toward the parade route.

Taking another bite, I furrowed my eyebrows.

"From *Pitch Perfect*," she explained, looking over at me. "Anna Kendrick's character is Beca. That's you. See, I've got a theory. All life's answers can be found in a movie."

Angéla wiggled her fingers at a passing couple with a baby, then took a bite of her churro. "Beca was a loner," she said around her own mouthful. "She didn't think she fit in or had a place in college, until she found the Bellas." She glanced at me again from the corner of her eyes. "Sound familiar? I mean, I get it. I'm a Beca, too."

My mouth fell open, thankfully after swallowing this time, and I openly gawked.

First, the girl nailed me in two seconds flat, then she implied she was a misfit, too, when I'd seen her at school surrounded by people tons of times.

No way. Uh-uh. I wasn't buying it.

She chuckled under her breath. "Don't give me that

look. I feel stuck a lot, trust me. People like to assume they know me and where I fit, and everyone thinks I should act a certain way because of who my brother is." She ducked her chin with a sigh. "Hell, I'm waiting for them to realize I'm seventeen and not still a fragile ten-year-old kid. It's kind of like once people see you a certain way, that's it. You're locked in forever."

The pain in her voice was unmistakable, and of course I knew what she was talking about. I'd been in that assembly along with everyone else in fifth grade when people from the hospital came to explain about leukemia and how Angéla shouldn't be treated any differently when she returned to school. But once she did and life returned to normal, I guess I never really thought much about it. It went to show how self-centered I could be that I'd never considered how hard it must've been to stay on schedule with our class. I'd spent two whopping days in the hospital. I had zero room to complain.

Further, Angéla was gorgeous and petite and popular in the sense she was well-liked by everyone, but, now that I thought about it, she didn't exactly hang in the same circles as her brother. She didn't join the cheer squad or the dance team, even though she was a killer dancer. No, Angéla was a floater. I'd assumed she was on top of the world based on her happy smile and last name alone, but I guess you never really knew how someone else really felt.

I'd judged her, unfairly. That sucked.

"Anyways," she said, bumping me with her elbow. "For what it's worth, I think you fit in fine. I don't know if Ilusiòn will be your Bellas, or if you already have one, but you don't need to throw up that tough, loner-girl exterior with me. I'm a kindred spirit." She smiled. "Plus, you had me from the moment you slid under Cameron's skin. That girl is all fired up about you, and I'm loving every snarling minute of it."

At her wide-eyed look of happiness, I grinned…a grin that broke into a laugh when she dinked her churro against mine and took a massive bite.

Kindred spirit indeed.

We made it back to the street where the parade was rolling amid laughter and applause. The elementary school's float had a superhero theme, and the kiddos were dressed like tiny Avengers. The sides of the flatbed were decorated with bright, neon posters of *BANG*, *POP*, and *CRASH* while the kids waved from a Metropolitan cityscape. I couldn't help grinning at the mini-Hulk jumping up and down, excitedly tossing beads at the crowd. He was the happiest little angry green man I'd ever seen.

Up next was Cypress Junior High with their colorful Candy Land concept. A sea of gumdrops and fluffy clouds housed children dressed like princesses, kings, gingerbread, and strange woodland creatures. Their throw of choice was naturally candy, which under normal circumstances, I'd be more than happy to accept. Trying to be good, especially after my delicious churro, I dutifully handed over my loot to Angéla and watched in envy as she popped a Hershey's Kiss in her mouth. *Two more days.*

While Brighton High's dance team strutted their stuff to our band's rendition of "Eye of the Tiger," Angéla wiggled her hips beside me. She bobbed her head, sending me serious side-eye to join in, and I bit my lip. The song was catchy, and this wasn't Ilusiòn. Everyone else was already laughing and having fun. They wouldn't care if I looked stupid, right?

My stomach fluttered as I rocked my shoulders. Angéla grinned, silently encouraging me, and I looked at the ground, gently bringing the rock to a full-on shimmy. She let out a *whoop* and took my hands, spinning me in a tight circle on the crowded sidewalk, then bumped my hip with hers, making a goofy face. I laughed and bumped her back, adding a curled lip à la Elvis. Then I threw my hands in the air and bounced to the beat. No one was watching us anyway.

Behind the dance team came a row of convertibles. Each one carried a different nominee for Homecoming queen, all decked out in sparkly dresses. Of course, they weren't *all* represented in the procession, as Angéla pointed out. Apparently, Cameron and Ashley had fashioned themselves sashes to wear on the float, so no one would forget they'd been included.

We looked at each other and rolled our eyes.

The guys couldn't care less about nominations. Stone and Chase were both up for king and neither wore anything over their uniforms, or they weren't last I saw them. Going on tiptoe, I tried to catch a glimpse of their float beyond the red Mercedes.

The parade moved forward, and my eyes fell on Stone at the center of the truck.

It was strange. I'd always known who Stone Torres was. You couldn't go to Brighton, or live in Cypress Lake the last few years, and not know his name. But I'd never paid attention beyond the obvious. The good looks, the popularity. The crazy stats. Watching him now, though, was like watching the eye of a hurricane. Everyone on the float seemed to move around him. They reacted to his moods. They noticed what he did, and they sparked from that.

A soft breeze tousled my hair, and I tucked it behind my ears. The float stopped near the bleachers across from city hall, and the emcee announced, "Give it up for your State Champions, the Fighting Tigers!" The entire crowd went berserk.

My eyes went back to Stone. His full mouth quirked as

his hand went up, waving at the adoring fans. He played the part, nodding to everyone, going through the motions—but it was as if a wall had been built around him. The QB smiling for the crowd wasn't the same guy who danced and teased me at Ilusiòn. It wasn't even the guy who'd rescued me on the stairs. This version was tighter at the edges. His smile didn't crinkle his eyes, and his dimples didn't come out to play. Watching him, I didn't get the sense he thought he was better than anyone else. He wasn't cocky, like I'd originally assumed him to be. It was more like he held himself back, on guard for some reason.

It made me sad to see.

Not to be upstaged, Chasing Trouble stuck out his butt and started shaking it for the crowd. People hooted, Chase flirted, and the little girl on her daddy's shoulders behind me yelled, "He's cute, Mama!"

Laughing, I glanced back to see her parents' reaction, and when I did, I caught Angéla wistfully gazing up at the float. *Interesting.* Figuring she wasn't mooning over her brother, her obvious interest narrowed to a few hot candidates. My gaze darted back, focusing on Chase, and my eyebrows popped in surprise.

She sighed softly, and her gaze drifted toward me. The dreamy expression fell in an instant. A light and easy smile replaced it, with only a hint of panic around the edges, and I turned back to the parade, letting my new friend have her secrets.

"Lily!" From the float, Stone grinned at me mischievously, beckoning me closer. Wary, I shuffled forward, and he bent to riffle through the boxes at his feet. When he popped back up, his arms were dripping with beads. "Incoming!"

I yelped as blue, white, and black trinkets fell over my head, Angéla's head, and the young family behind us, much to the little girl's delight, if her contagious giggles were any clue.

When the onslaught was over, I raised my head to see Stone looking mighty pleased with himself. Holding onto the goalpost, his lips quirked in smug satisfaction. "Having fun yet?" he called out while the truck rolled down the street. I shook my head in amused exasperation.

A few minutes later, the fire truck's siren ended the party. After doling out beads and uneaten candy to the kids around us, Angéla and I headed for the grocery store parking lot where the floats were gathering.

Heat from the blacktop seeped through the soles of my shoes. My ears rang from the noise of the parade, and my stomach was still happily digesting my delicious churro. I couldn't swipe the smile from my face.

We passed a stand selling deep-fried Oreos, and Angéla's eyes widened with longing.

"Girl!" I laughed, pulling her away. "You can't be serious. You're like a bottomless pit."

"Eh, fat and happy ain't the worst way to live."

I grinned at the truth of her words. "You got a little drool," I teased, wiping at the corner of my mouth. "Right there." She stuck out her tongue, and I shook my head. "All I can say is thank God you're a dancer. If you weren't, we'd have to roll you down the street."

Angéla opened her mouth, presumably prepared with a witty comeback, but her eyes darted beyond my shoulder. A deep voice rumbled near my ear, "Don't look now, but someone's enjoying herself."

A shiver that defied the weather swept over me, and I turned to find Stone's arrogant smirk in full force.

"I can admit I'm having fun." The confident grin widened, so of course I had to shoot it down. "But I hate to tell you, the festival has nothing to do with high school. It's simply part of living in Cypress Lake."

I held out my arms, indicating the familiar colors, sounds, and smells around us, and felt the truth in my words settle over me. This *was* a part of living here—or at least it had been until Mom died.

A wave of homesickness rolled over me, and my hands fell to my sides. Stone's smile dimmed. His eyebrows knitted together, and I blinked away the memories, shoving them back in the drawer with the others.

"So, what's the plan now?" Chase asked, sliding up next to Angéla. Aidan and Robbie came over, too, with Cameron and Ashley hot on their heels. Oh joy. "Hit up rides or stuff our faces?"

The sweat dampening my hair trickled down my back. More than the heat, I felt claustrophobic standing in the middle of a group consisting of one guy I sort of knew, two I didn't, one girl I'd kind of befriended, two others who hated me, and Stone. The complicated guy who equally challenged and confused me. My face flushed as my pulse drummed in my ears, my breathing started to spike, and a dreaded tingle danced along my spine.

Oh God. Please not here.

I closed my eyes as a familiar emotion tightened my chest…and then, someone took my hand. Glancing down, I saw Stone's long, tanned fingers wrapped around mine. It wasn't romantic. He didn't graze his thumb over my palm, or gaze into my eyes and declare undying love. He simply held my hand, giving me a bit of his strength, whether he'd known I needed it or not.

My heart rate calmed in my chest, and the rushing wave of panic subsided.

"I don't know about you losers," he said, grinning to

show he was teasing, "but Lily and I are gonna explore the festival. We'll catch up with you later."

The looks of surprise from the group almost matched my own.

Angéla's eyes widened, and her lips stretched in a smile so wide it was a wonder her cheeks didn't hurt. Ashley looked like she'd smelled something foul, and Cameron just stared at our hands, her eyes slightly narrowed as if she could make them fly apart simply by wishing it. As for Chase and Robbie, they quickly recovered and started talking about where they were headed next, and Aidan's forehead wrinkled in concern as he watched Stone tug me away.

Me? I was still trying to catch up.

"So, what do you want to do?" Stone asked, releasing my hand to grab a discarded water bottle. I curled my fingers into my tingling palm as he tossed it in the trash and gestured toward the festival. "Hit the rides, or are you more of a gaming girl?"

"Er…" I motioned behind me. "You sure you don't want to hang with your friends? I wouldn't mind."

That was technically a lie. I'd mind a whole lot if I was expected to hang out with the group, too, but it was perfectly okay if he wanted to ditch me for the others. In fact, it was preferable.

"Nah. I can see them anytime." He waved at a little boy who called his name. "I invited you out here, and we didn't get to hang on the float." Stone slid a playful look my way. "I bet you're the type who plans everything, right? You probably had a schedule mapped out with studying or something today, huh?"

I scowled, neither confirming nor denying, and his eyes crinkled in amusement.

"Well, if you could pencil me in for a couple hours, I'd

like to check out the festival with my new dance partner."

"You mean try to convince her you're right about the dare," I countered drily, and he smiled.

"That, too." Stone laughed, a light, happy sound that unleashed his dimples with a two-ton punch.

The guy from Ilusiòn was back. The QB mask was gone, left on the float, and although I *did* have a schedule planned, just then I couldn't think of a single thing on it more important than figuring out why he was different with me.

Was I so unattractive he didn't feel the need to impress me? Or was it because he'd seen my stupid underwear and horrid dance moves, so he figured I had no room to judge? Maybe it was because I knew squat about sports. Whatever the reason, Stone Torres, invincible football god, chose to relax with me. Just for this afternoon, I'd accept that like the gift he may or may not have intended.

A bright red balloon slipped from a festival sign, and I lifted my eyes as it floated lazily into the sky. An idea came to me, and I grinned.

"Hope you didn't eat recently," I said, already increasing my pace and leaving him in the dust. "Because I believe the Tilt-a-Whirl has our names written all over it."

Chapter Eight

STONE

The metal stairs were unsteady beneath my feet as I gingerly exited Lily's favorite ride. The nickname Iron Stomach had taken on a whole new meaning.

"You," I said, pausing to hold a fist over my mouth. I closed my eyes and breathed through a wave of nausea, then slowly dropped my hand. "You were messing with me back there, weren't you?"

She grinned and wiggled her eyebrows devilishly. "Maybe." Dancing down the steps like she hadn't just done everything in her power to make our steel death trap spin like a damn top, she taunted, "Aw, don't tell me the big, tough football man can't handle a little ride. It wasn't spinning *that* fast."

I shot her a look that called bullshit and swallowed down another wave of bile.

Lily bumped my shoulder. "My dad used to get sick, too. Mom and I would lean from side to side, trying to make it go faster and faster, and he'd fuss and complain the entire time." Her slender shoulders shook with a small laugh. "Didn't stop him from riding it with us, though."

At the mention of her dad, I looked away, feigning interest in the crowd. Earlier this week, Ma finally told me about Mrs. Bailey. How she'd loved dancing at the studio, even while battling fatigue from chemo and radiation, and how she'd worn colorful scarves on her head and bright, flowy skirts that contrasted with her pale skin and gaunt features. She said she'd never seen a woman more beautiful or strong.

Lily's mom's cancer explained a lot. It explained why her dad was so protective and why she was so closed-off. I couldn't imagine losing one of my parents. The fear I'd felt when Angéla had been sick still knotted my stomach, and remembering that, I reached out to take Lily's hand.

She looked at me, curious, and I asked, "What else did you like doing?"

"At the festival?" I nodded, and her forehead wrinkled in thought. "We were total dorks," she said, lifting her shoulder before a playful smile twisted her lips. "Clearly, Dad and I still are, but back then we rode the typical silly rides you'd expect—the Ferris wheel, the merry-go-round… I always rode the mermaid," she confided with a serious expression. "Dad rode the frog because he knew they freaked me out and he loved hearing me squeal. After that, he'd hit up the hot dog eating contest."

The imposing image of the man I'd met didn't compute with a fun-loving guy riding frogs and eating his weight in pork products. But I was glad to hear not all of Lily's memories revolved around throw-up rides.

Wanting to keep the playful look on her face, I lifted my shirt to expose my flat stomach. "Can't do the hot dogs, I'm afraid. I'm in training." Her eyes fell to my abs and stayed there. Unable to help myself, I slowly dropped my shirt back in place, grinning when her eyes drifted back to mine. "But I'm man enough to handle a frog. Especially if you hold my hand through it."

Lily rolled her eyes, waving the hand I still held. "Kinda already doing that, bud." She scrunched her nose. "Speaking of which, you realize people are gonna get the wrong idea if you keep touching me."

I looked around, wondering who was watching me now, and didn't see anyone. "We're just hanging out." Though, now that she mentioned it, I did grab her hand or touch her arm a lot. I'd done it back at the float, too. I wasn't hitting on her. Lily was a pretty girl, but I was officially on a break. My family had always been touchy-feely, and now that we'd danced together a couple times, it was probably normal for me to be this comfortable around her. I shoved the thought away. "Besides, no one's paying attention."

Lily made a face, as if she didn't quite believe that, but then her attention shifted to the side, and her big blue eyes lit up behind her lenses. I turned to see what was so fascinating, and when I spotted the Quarterback Toss, my own smile broke free.

"Oh, hell yeah," I said, tugging her toward the stand. "You're on."

She pulled back on my hand, dragging her feet. "Who said I wanted to play?"

"Your Katy Perry eyes sold you out," I told her, weaving around a mom with five kids. They each had their faces painted like demons and held a bag of cotton candy. The woman was either insane or a saint. "Don't try to act like you're not chomping at the bit to kick my ass at something, either. You're as competitive as I am."

Lily craned an eyebrow, not denying it, and let me lead her to the game.

A folk band was on the main stage, and as the twang of dueling banjos washed over the crowd, I couldn't help feeling smug. So far, everything was going to plan. Lily had agreed to stay in lessons for a month, *and* I'd caught her having fun several times already. This was only day one. Who knew what I could accomplish in the next thirty.

"Next player," called the carnie, and we stepped forward in line. The guy appraised us from under a Gone Fishin' trucker hat pulled low over wispy, graying hair. He sucked his teeth over the pinch of chew in his rounded cheek, turned to me, and said, "Three tickets."

"Uh, excuse me," Lily huffed. "Why did you assume he was the one playing? We're having a friendly competition here, and I'm about to settle it. My dad used to love this game." She bumped me out of the way with her hip and handed over her tickets. "Ladies first, right?"

I waved her on, biting back a smile. "Be my guest. Though, I feel I should remind you this is the Quarterback Toss." At her blank stare of *and your point is*, I added, "I don't exactly suck at that."

"Or maybe you simply have really good catchers," she replied saucily, and the guy behind me coughed to cover his laugh.

"Receivers," I corrected with an amused grin. Folding my arms, I leaned back and looked at her, trying to figure out if she was messing with me. "Last year I had three hundred and twenty completions and threw for over forty-six hundred yards."

The carnie whistled, and I lifted my chin in recognition.

Lily looked between us. "Is that good?"

I laughed out loud and handed over a football. Well, we'd proven one thing: Lily couldn't care less about my stats and didn't know jack about the game. It was actually refreshing. Also, annoying.

Lily squeezed the ball between her hands and eyed up the target. The cartoonish image on the background showed a receiver in the red zone with his arms extended and a defensive back closing in. A net cut into the fabric above his hands waited for the ball.

Gripping the football in her right hand, she slid her index finger on the nose. I winced. "You should really—"

She silenced me with a look, and I sighed, taking a step back with my hands lifted.

Walking right up to the line, Lily palmed the ball and raised it to her ear. Elbow down, eyes narrowed, she planted her feet and twisted her hips. It physically hurt to watch. Exhaling her breath with what could only be described as a *kiai!*, she slung the ball forward, mouth open and face snarling, releasing it way too late and dropping her arm with absolutely no follow-through.

The wounded duck jackhammered into the ground. Lily jumped back, slamming into my ribs with her pointy elbow while her hands slapped against her mouth in surprise.

"Oops," she muttered between splayed fingers.

I buried my face in her hair to stop from laughing.

Damn, what was it about this girl? Every time I saw her, she cracked me up. Seriously, I hadn't laughed this much in years, and that was saying something, since my best friend was a buffoon. I guessed I'd grown immune to Chase's antics over the years, but Lily…she surprised me.

"It's harder than it looks," I assured her, or at least, I tried to assure her. The chuckle I couldn't keep from escaping probably didn't help. I cleared my throat. "You sure you don't want any pointers?"

Lily craned her neck to look at me. Cheeks flushed, she slid her hands down to her chin, revealing a self-deprecating grin. "I think I found something I'm worse at than dancing."

"Nah." I smiled and squeezed her shoulders. "Your dancing is coming along, and like I said, throwing a football is harder than it looks. It's not as simple as lobbing it across a field. It's all in how you hold it, how you position your feet, where you point your elbow, and when and how you release it. If anyone could do it, the NFL wouldn't be a multibillion-dollar organization. And it wouldn't be my potential ticket to college."

"Touché," she said with a begrudging smile. Sighing, she glanced at the line forming and wrinkled her nose. "But I, uh, think you can save the throwing lesson for another day. The natives are getting restless. Besides, I'm willing to concede defeat on this one." She bent and picked up a second football, then tossed it at me. "It's our dare I'm focused on winning."

"Dream on, sweet cheeks," I replied, positioning my fingers in between the laces. "You're going down on both counts."

Falling back a few steps, I dropped into position, keeping my grip firm and in my fingertips. The noise of the crowd, the tantalizing smell of funnel cake, and the solid earth beneath my feet disappeared as I zeroed in on the target. This was my home. It was what I was good at.

Two throws and two perfectly placed spirals later, I handed Lily a pair of purple fuzzy dice amid enthusiastic applause. "For being a good sport," I said, walking away from the stand and nodding at the people gathered. In hindsight, it probably looked douchey throwing a football at a kid's game, especially while wearing my jersey. Oh well. "And because Chase would give me shit if I rolled up with those things hanging from my rearview mirror."

She laughed. "Well, we can't let that happen now, can

we?" She swung the dice like a lasso and grinned. "Thank you, kind sir, I accept your generous gift. It so happens purple is my favorite color, and these will look awesome in Debbie."

I shot her a look. "Debbie?"

"My car," she explained. Right. Because everyone named their car. "Actually, Debbie is my mom's car that I inherited. It's a vintage-red Camry she used to say was classic, bubbly, and spunky, just like her favorite actress, Debbie Reynolds." Lily smiled at the ground. "God, my mom loved musicals. She used to dance in the kitchen, pretending to be Ginger Rogers, and we always jammed out to 'I Ain't Down Yet' while driving around."

"I'm guessing that's a song title?" I asked, and she nodded distractedly.

She kicked at a tuft of grass, and her eyebrows drew together. "She's been acting up lately. The car, I mean. More than usual. The ALT warning light came up on the dashboard this morning, and it's been getting iffy about starting. I'll have to take it in to get looked at, but I couldn't say anything to my dad before he left. He's wanted to trade in Debbie for a while, and this would only tip him over the edge." Glassy eyes met mine, and she bit her lip. "I can't lose another part of my mom."

Heaviness tightened my chest. I couldn't imagine going through something like that, and seeing her so upset made me feel helpless. I wasn't great with words, and I couldn't bring her mom back. What I could do was let her know she wasn't alone. Reaching out, I offered what little I could and took her hand again, sliding my thumb across her satiny skin. Her long, thin fingers clamped around mine, and I pulsed a squeeze.

We walked in silence after that, people-watching and

checking out the various tents filled with jewelry, lawn signs, and homemade jam. Lily nodded politely as the craftsmen tried to entice her with random trinkets, but a touch of sadness clung to her, stooping her shoulders and dimming her smile. I didn't know what to say. This wasn't the mood I'd wanted for today.

"Tell me something real," she said softly a little while later. We'd looped back around to the rides and were in line for the Ferris wheel. I was still searching for a way to lift the mood.

"What do you mean?"

She leaned her back against the temporary gate. "I don't know. It's just…do you ever feel like the world can be all flash and no substance?" She pursed her lips and glanced back toward the tents. "Ever since Mom died, I've noticed how rare it is for people to be honest anymore. To be real. So many people act like those vendors out there, pasting on sunny smiles and only showing the best parts of themselves, except instead of trinkets and snacks, they sell filtered images and edited statuses."

My eyebrows rose as a surprised rush of air escaped my lips. Seriously, who was this girl? People rarely wanted the truth. At least not in my experience. Sure, they *said* they did, but they didn't really. They just wanted to hear something funny or cute or with enough detail they could pretend the conversation was a two-way street before diving back in with their own stories. Not that I was complaining. Canned, superficial answers were a hell of a lot easier than cutting myself open and giving the world even more of me. Most days it felt like the entire city knew my business. I didn't need to share my every thought, too.

But, as I was quickly learning, Lily wasn't like most people.

Releasing a heavy sigh, she turned back, and her mouth

curved in a gentle half-smile. "I feel like I've been doing all the talking today. What about you? What are some of *your* favorite memories of the festival?"

Crossing my arms, I thought back over seventeen years of family outings and smiled when it came to me. Brushing it aside, I scratched a phantom itch on my elbow and looked up at the swinging blue cars suspended in the air. "The same things you mentioned, I guess. Riding the rides with my parents. Eating churros with Angéla."

"Stone…" She huffed a breath. "I asked you to be real."

"What makes you think I'm not?" I peered at her curiously. "My sister and I used to live for those churros. In fact, training be damned, I'm grabbing one of those suckers when we get off this ride."

Lily pushed off the gate. "Yeah, I'm well acquainted with Angéla's love of the churro, but see, that's not really a memory. And it wasn't the first thing you thought of, either." My eyes widened before I could stop it, and she waved a finger at my face. "When I asked about your favorite memories, you smiled for real, then you dropped it and did that QB thing."

"QB thing?"

"You know, where you fake a smile, but it doesn't crinkle your eyes or activate your dimples," she replied matter-of-factly. "Your guard goes up. You did it during the parade today, too. I mean, I get it. I can't imagine what it's like being a minor celebrity and always having people watching. But right now, it's just me." She shrugged. "I'm nobody. You can be honest with me, right?"

I stared at her. The cloak of sadness from before was gone, replaced with a frankness that made me feel like I was back on the Tilt-a-Whirl. And even more on display than usual.

She was right, of course; not that I didn't love churros, but I had thought of a different memory first. The real answer, though, was personal and silly, and I made it a practice not to expose myself to possible criticism. Still, Lily had spent the afternoon sharing real things with me. She deserved for me to do the same. Especially since there were other things I was hiding.

"We, uh, we were five," I said, briefly glancing at the ride before meeting her eyes. I slid my hand around the back of my neck. "Dad had taken me to see the horses while Ma waited with Angéla to get her face painted. She wanted a rainbow across her entire forehead that went into her eyes." I shook my head. "I told her later she looked like a multicolored alien. Anyway, when we got back, they weren't at the stand anymore. Dad's phone was dead, he never keeps it charged, and I could tell he was getting nervous we wouldn't find them. His hand got tighter on mine, and his face got real tense, you know? He started walking faster, and with my short legs, I was almost running to keep up. Then I heard her. Giggling like crazy."

I laughed at the memory and moved forward in line. Lily smiled and shifted closer to me.

"Angéla was in the pirate ship—the obstacle course thing for little kids? She refused to come out when Ma called, so the guy finally let our mom in to get her. Angéla thought it was a game. She made Ma chase her all over that stupid ship, shooting up the rope wall and ducking around inflatable boulders. Ma got all twisted up in the rope, and I thought for sure Dad would jump in to help her...but he just started laughing. This huge belly laugh that shook his shoulders and almost had him crying. Of course, I joined in. My old man never lost it like that, plus Angéla was laughing, too. My sister's giggles still set me off, but back then? She was an angelic terror.'"

"Oh, I can imagine." Lily's smile widened as she leaned toward me like she wanted to hear more, and a knot in my chest loosened.

"So Ma looked over at us, still holding onto that damn rope, and glared for at least thirty seconds before she started cracking up, too." I shook my head with a laugh. "Angéla came out of hiding then, all smiles like she hadn't just driven our mom batshit crazy, and skipped out the damn door like a happy little multicolored alien."

The carnie motioned us forward, and I gave him six tickets before waving Lily ahead to the waiting car. We pulled down the bar, and I put my arms over it, testing it for good measure.

"That's a nice memory," she said, smiling at me with a wistful expression. "I'm an only child so I never had anyone to help me terrorize my parents. I had to do it on my own." She laughed and tucked a strand of hair behind her ear. "You and Angéla seem close."

I nodded, watching the world drop as the ride carried us higher. "I'd do anything for her."

Lily studied the side of my face for a moment. "She's lucky to have you."

I stopped myself from saying I was the lucky one. I'd shared enough already with the pirate ship story, and today was about proving a point, not baring our souls. "So, about the dare," I said, clapping my hands and rubbing them together. "I think we need to set some ground rules."

She craned an eyebrow, looking suspicious. "What kind of ground rules?"

"Nothing major. Just to make sure we're on the same page and the parameters are clear. Otherwise, how will you know when I win?"

"You mean when *I* win," she clarified with a haughty grin, "but I see what you mean. All right, you may proceed with the commencement of the rules."

I shifted my back against the car's side to face her. "Number one: no talk about studying or college when we're together. You do that enough on your own, I'm sure, and this dare is about proving there's fun to be had now. So we live in the moment whenever we're hanging out or at lessons. No talk of the future."

"Easy enough." Lily shot me a wary look. "Rule number two?"

"You only get to veto one of my suggestions or you forfeit the dare." Her eyes widened and then narrowed, and I quickly raised my hands. "*But* I promise not to suggest anything too over-the-top that will negatively impact your grades, either. I get how you are about that."

She seemed to consider this, a frown tugging the left side of her mouth, creating the tiniest divot in her cheek. My gaze traced it, along with the smoothness of her skin and the way her cherry lips parted when she finally nodded and asked, "Anything else?"

"Uh, one more." I cleared my throat and looked away. *Holy shit, what was that?* "It's, uh, one you already agreed to anyway," I stammered, shifting in my seat, "but I think it bears repeating." I glanced back, keeping my eyes firmly on hers. "You have to take at least one dance lesson a week for the rest of the month."

"Oh, *at least*," she repeated, those blue eyes shining like the thought of anything more than one was completely ludicrous. "Fine. I agree to these rules, as long as you agree that when *I* win, and/or you get bored and drop this whole charade, you can't renege on your end of the deal."

"I'll handle our parents if it comes to that, trust me,"

I told her with a small grin, shaking off the last bit of weirdness…and keeping my thoughts off her lips.

Lily scooted back in her seat, a triumphant tilt to her chin as she took in Cypress Lake from the sky, which meant I obviously had to knock her back down to reality.

"You realize I've won this first round, right?" Her eyes shot back to mine. "You said earlier that the festival has nothing to do with high school, but that's not entirely true. Almost the entire parade was about Brighton, and I'd wager half the crowd down there either goes to our school, went there, or will be going soon. Even if not, the point of the dare was never so much about the high school experience as it is about not waiting until college to have fun."

Lily blinked rapidly, her mouth opening and closing like a fish, and I grinned.

"The way I see it, since you're not holding a textbook, and you even admitted—near witnesses, mind you—that you had fun today, this round goes to me."

I leaned back in the seat, ankles crossed, a triumphant tilt to *my* head now. As the world went by outside our car, Lily remained upright, her calculating thoughts so loud I was sure the people in the car next to ours could hear them. After a moment, she exhaled and crossed her arms in defeat.

"Yeah, well, don't get used to winning, pretty boy," she muttered, raising her eyebrow and giving me serious side-eye. "Because I'm on to you now."

Chapter Nine

STONE

*I*n my next life, I planned to be rich enough to hire people to do my yard work. If not that, I'd at least follow Dad's model and have a few kids to do it for me. Lifting the hem of my soiled tee, I swiped at my face, marveling at how the sun was setting and I was still dripping with sweat.

Originally, the plan for today had been to make my appearance at the parade, shake a few hands, let some of the more outspoken "fans" let me know what I could do better on the field, then make my escape so I could catch up on the yard work I'd been putting off. Then Lily happened. Cameron throwing a wrench in my plans for her to ride with us didn't help, so I'd had to improvise. Granted, I didn't have to hang out with her as long as I did, but surprisingly, I'd had fun. More importantly, so had she. Victory was practically mine.

With the lawn cut and gardens groomed, I was bagging up the last pile of weeds when a familiar green Prius pulled to a stop at the end of the driveway. *Shit.* Here was what my already exhausted brain needed: a visit from the ex.

Cameron rolled down her passenger window. "Hey there, hot stuff. Need a hand?"

Her smile was wide and hopeful as she leaned across the console, and I returned it with a forced, inauthentic one. A quick survey of the street proved there were no neighbors within earshot, but you could never be too careful. Small towns thrived on gossip. Tying off the bag with a bit more force than required, I shook my head. "Nope. Just finished."

Of course, that meant I had to carry the bag to the curb with the others, a fact she must've figured out, since she cut the engine and hopped out of the car. She leaned back against the hood and watched as I dropped the trash at her feet. "Perfect timing, then. I was hoping we could talk."

A sigh that had been building for six months heaved out of me, and my shoulders sank with the weight of it. When Cameron first cheated—well, no, when I first caught her cheating; who knew if that had been the first time?—I'd been angry. Hell, I'd been hurt. I'd poured almost a year into this girl, and I'd thought she was loyal. When I learned how wrong I'd been, I'd wanted nothing more than to make her pay for making me look like an idiot in front of the whole school—hell, in front of the entire town—but I'd swallowed it back and took it all with a canned smile and a shrug. *Never let them see you sweat* became more than just my approach to the field, thanks to Cameron, but now? Now I was over it. I'd gotten hopeful when she'd stopped coming to lessons over the summer, thinking it meant she was willing to let it go, too, but obviously I'd been mistaken.

My jaws ached from how tightly they were clenched. I blew out a breath, praying she heard me this time and walked away. "Listen, Cammie, I'm not trying to be a dick about this. I'm really not. But there's nothing left for us to say."

"I disagree," she replied stubbornly, and I huffed a humorless laugh. "I know I messed up, okay? And I know I've apologized a hundred times, but I'll try a hundred and one if it'll make a difference. There's no excuse for what I did. I was lonely, and Noah was there, but it was stupid and wrong, and I made a mistake. Just…let me prove it to you. Let me show you how sorry I am. All I want is another chance."

I'd give Cameron this, she was a great actress. For almost a year I'd had a first-row seat to her putting on a show for the school and her Instagram followers, so I knew how easily she could turn on the waterworks or the megawatt smile, whatever emotion the situation warranted. But looking into her warm brown eyes now, I saw the hurt and hope, and for the first time in a long time, I actually believed it.

Still didn't matter.

"Your apology is noted, Cammie, but it doesn't change anything. We're over. I don't know how much clearer to say it, and frankly, I don't understand why you're fighting this so hard again. It's been six months. Don't you think it's time to call it?"

Her lips tightened, and the hurt I saw quickly shifted to irritation. "Is this about Lily?"

My head jerked back at the switch, and I felt my eyebrows squish together. "Is *what* about Lily? Me not wanting to take you back? Cameron, you cheated. And we weren't even that happy before Noah. *That* is why I don't want to get back together. Why would it have anything to do with Lily?"

"I saw you with her yesterday," she said, having the audacity to look jealous. "I've been coming to the studio for weeks, and you choose to dance with a girl who has two left feet. Why not me? Don't you remember how well we moved together?"

I shook my head in wonder. Was she serious right now? "Sorry, I must've hidden that memory behind the one of you sucking face with Ruckert."

A sharp look entered her eyes, and I instantly regretted my words. Now *I* sounded jealous.

I sighed again, suddenly feeling like I'd been awake for a hundred years. Cameron didn't deserve an explanation, but the last thing I wanted was for her to start targeting Lily. That girl had enough problems. She didn't need my ex sniffing after her.

"Look, Lily is a new student at the studio, and I was just helping out," I told her. "We're friends now. Sort of. But nothing's going on there."

Cammie opened her mouth, like she wanted to push back, but she must've thought better of it. Instead, she reached back to scrape her hair into a loose ponytail and twisted it over her shoulder, her lips pinched like she was trying to decide her next move. Behind me, I heard the front door to the house open, and I glanced back to see Angéla lean her hip against the outdoor brick, a hard look in her eyes.

To say my sister wasn't a fan of my ex-girlfriend was putting it mildly. Very mildly. I fought back a laugh and shifted my focus to Cameron.

The irritated lines on her face softened with a smile. "I'm sorry. I didn't come here to argue with you—I just wanted to remind you that I'm here. That I'm always here. And whenever you decide you're ready to forgive me, I'll be waiting, okay?" She bit the edge of her lip and stared into my eyes. "I still love you, Stone."

With that final declaration, she turned around on her heel and got back into her car.

The garbage disposal rumbled with a flick of the switch, draining the water with a sucking gurgle. Staring at the sink, I related to that sound. After a very long, strange, drama-filled day, I was officially dead on my feet. Canned laughter floated from the living room, where our parents were watching an old sitcom on Netflix while Angéla and I finished cleaning the kitchen.

"I think the mayor should declare the day after the festival a holiday," I said, pushing up onto the squeaky-clean counter as Angéla scrubbed at dried sauce on the stove. "No one's gonna be productive tomorrow anyway. Almost the entire town was at the parade."

"You wouldn't hear me complain." Angéla tossed the sponge in the sink and hung her head. "I have a test in Advanced Math first period. The universe is out to get me."

Snorting at her theatrics, I snagged a red apple from the bowl. We'd eaten dinner a half hour ago, but I was still hungry. Ma liked to say I'd eat her out of house and home one day, so clearly, she's where my sister inherited her flair for the dramatic.

"Hey, I didn't get to thank you for jumping in with the Lily situation this morning," I told her, polishing the fruit on my shirt.

"No thanks required," she replied, reaching over and popping the back of my hand. The apple flew from my grip, and she snatched it from the air. Angéla grinned as she took a bite. "Lily's awesome," she mumbled around her mouthful. "I liked hanging out with her."

Chuckling, I snagged a second apple, a Golden Delicious this time—which happened to be my favorite—and waggled my eyebrows. You learned to be sneaky with a sister like mine.

Angéla pushed up to sit on the island opposite me. "You know people were talking after the parade."

"What people?"

She shot me a look that said I was being dense. "Your ex for one. Cameron's feathers were all kinds of ruffled, and Robbie kept asking when you started dating another smart chick."

Damn. People were always in my business. "We're not dating," I muttered, tipping my head back against the cabinet—and trying not to think about that weird moment on the Ferris wheel. "Lily and I are friends. She's a sweet girl who's way too serious, and I'm trying to help her loosen up. That's all."

"Well I like her," Angéla declared, swinging her feet. "We're both Becas, which means we're destined to be besties. Hate to say it, but you're gonna have to share her, bro."

My smile spread. Luckily, I was well versed in Angéla's movie-speak, so I understood the reference. Even more, I liked the idea of Lily and my sister being friends. Angéla always seemed to attract girls who either wanted to use her to get closer to me or were passive-aggressive in their jealousy of her. She'd never had a solid friend like I had in Chase.

Lily could be good for her, and Angéla could probably get her to lighten up, too. All afternoon I'd been thinking about her slip about being sick and her dad mentioning a recent stress issue. After seeing Lily at the festival, relaxed and having fun, I liked the idea of this dare even more. If I could help her not be so stressed, it'd go a long way in making me feel less guilty about hiding the truth. Especially after all her talk about being real.

"She'd be lucky to have you," I told my sister, jumping down. I kissed the top of her head and said, "Night, Angel."

"Night, Captain. Love you."

She made a heart with her hands, and I returned it as I walked away, shaking my head at the reference.

As I maneuvered down the short hallway, I couldn't help wondering if Captain America would've taken twelve-hundred dollars to be Lily's dance partner. I wanted to think he would, given the circumstances. Angéla said he was the ultimate leader, strong, protective, and loyal, which is why she'd given me the nickname years ago. She always said I was *her* hero, and in the end, that's all I wanted. To be her hero, the studio's hero, and if I could swing it, even Lily's hero, because that girl deserved a break. But a part of me couldn't help feeling like this whole thing was kind of shady.

I peeked my head around the corner to the living room, wanting to tell my parents good night before crashing. The television was on, but they weren't watching it. They were seated close together on the sofa, Ma with her legs tucked under her, Dad with a hand on her knee and the other clenched in his black hair. A stack of bills was on the coffee table.

Dad rubbed his forehead. "We'll find a way to make it work, Vik. I'll ask the chief for extra shifts and take on more security jobs. Brighton put in a request for police presence around the school and games anyway. That'll let me take care of my family double time." He wrapped an arm around her shoulders and hugged her close. "We won't lose Ilusiòn."

Ma exhaled shakily. "After thirteen years, I got complacent," she said with a slight sniffle. "The old owners only raised the rent a handful of times. But this?" She grabbed the bill on top of the pile and studied it. "I don't know if we can make it past the holidays."

"We've got enough in savings to cover this month and next," he told her, rubbing her shoulder. "As for after that…" Dad kissed her temple and closed his eyes. "We'll figure it out. I promise."

My heart pounded as I slumped against the wall out of sight. I'd guessed things were tight, but I had no idea they were this bad. Not make it past the holidays? It was already mid-September.

Gathering myself, I shook my head to clear it and washed my face of all emotion before entering the room. Ma sat up instantly, discreetly wiping under her eyes, and Dad took the bill from her hand and set it facedown on the table.

"Just wanted to say good night."

Ma gave me a quivery smile. "My handsome boy. Did you have a good time at the festival?"

"Yeah." I shoved my hands in my pockets and tried not to stare at the stack of papers threatening my family. "I, uh, actually ran into Lily Bailey while I was there."

"Oh?"

I nodded, flexing the muscles in my jaw. "Yeah, I didn't get to tell you yesterday, but I spoke with Marcus before her lesson. I'm gonna be Lily's permanent partner." Ma's eyes widened in surprise, and Dad looked between us. "Angéla already agreed to cover the phones for the hour class, so it's all good."

A slow smile transformed my mother's face, chasing away the sadness and replacing it with pride. I swallowed another wave of guilt. "That is wonderful. Isa would be so happy to see her daughter flourishing in dance. You can help make that happen." Her smile quivered again, and her gaze darted to the bills. "It's good to have you at Ilusiòn with us."

I heard what she hadn't said—*before we lose everything*—and raised my gaze above her head, focusing on the framed picture of the Virgin Mary. "I'll always do what I can to help you, Ma. Never doubt that." Forcing a smile, I reined in my emotions and glanced at my parents. "I'm turning in."

Ma beamed with lingering pride, but Dad's dark eyes were narrowed. I didn't have a doubt in my mind his cop intuition was going off. I could never keep a secret from him, although I'd never had a reason to until now.

As I retreated, he leaned forward with his elbows on his knees and his mouth set in contemplation. "Night, son," he called out, suspicion lacing his tone, and I muttered a good night as I slunk to my room.

The shoebox was at the top of my closet. I didn't know how much they'd raised the rent, but the amount inside had to cover the difference for at least a couple of months. Hopefully that'd be enough time for enrollment to pick back up and we could get through the holidays. New Year Resolutions always brought a fresh wave of students.

My mind raced as I grabbed the box and sank onto my mattress. All the possibilities of how to explain where the money had come from bounced in my head. Unable to decide on anything remotely believable, I inhaled a long, deep breath and raised my head. My eyes landed on my bookshelf.

Trophies cluttered the four dusty shelves, along with various awards and accolades all given to me because I could throw a decent spiral. My fingers drummed across the lid of the box as a rock settled in my stomach. I'd trade the whole damn bookshelf of trophies to save my mother's dream. Helping my family meant more than any stupid achievement I'd made on the field. This was real life. This was what mattered—not some meaningless, entertaining skillset, here today and possibly gone just as fast tomorrow. Forgotten in the rubble of past hotshots who were once somebody in high school.

My knuckles blanched as I brought the shoebox closer. Shady or not, this deal with Lily's dad was a way to help my family. My *only* way. Lily would understand if she knew the whole truth.

After counting the total inside, needing the reassurance, I surged to my feet. My knees popped in the quiet. I carried Mr. Bailey's money back to the closet, then hid it under my baby blanket on the top shelf where no one would see it. Dad had said they had September and October covered, which meant I had at least a month before they needed extra cash. My parents weren't desperate for my help just yet.

Hopefully by the time they did, I'd have figured out a way to explain where it came from.

Chapter Ten

LILY

"Come on, girl, you can do it." I leaned over the steering wheel, stroking the dash as I willed my car to start. My eyes burned with unshed tears, and I cursed myself for not getting her looked at sooner. "Please start. Please, please, start."

Holding my breath, I flicked my wrist again. A series of empty clicks met my ears, and I banged my head against the wheel.

The school parking lot was a ghost town. A couple cars remained, but there wasn't a soul inside them. I'd hung back after final bell to discuss my upcoming AP European history paper with Ms. Kat, and now because of that, I was stuck.

Groaning, I shoved my door open. I popped the latch for the hood and walked around to peer inside, not because I had a single clue what to look for but because it seemed like the thing to do. Yup, lots of stuff to see. Black boxes. Hose-looking things. Couple of jiggambobs. It all appeared normal to me.

Male voices floated in the air, shooting hope through

my chest. I leaned against the bumper, hoping whoever it was had a pair of jumper cables in their car, and watched as Stone and Aidan turned the corner of the main building. I sighed. Poor guy. He seemed forever destined to save me.

My designated white knight held a football in his right hand while Aidan gestured at an open binder, animatedly saying words like *Open 236 Belly G.*

These guys spoke a whole other language.

"Uh, hey there!"

They instantly froze at my awkward call, and I waved with a slight wince. I hadn't seen Stone in three days, ever since I lost Battle One of our dare on Sunday, and here I was, a damsel in distress. Feminists everywhere were groaning in sympathy.

Shoving my glasses higher on my nose, I pushed away from my opened hood and said, "Any chance either of you can give me a jump?"

Aidan's eyebrows shot sky-high, and I swear Stone snorted. Playing back my words, along with its juvenile implications, I lowered my head and groaned.

Gah, just shoot me now.

"Sorry, Lily." Aidan tucked the binder under his arm and grimaced. "I don't have a car here. I only live a couple blocks away, so it's easier to walk."

I nodded, raking my teeth over my bottom lip, and swung my gaze to Stone. His mouth turned down at the corners as he shoved his hands in his pockets. "I can look in the truck, but I'm pretty sure I lent them to Chase this summer and never got them back."

I nodded again because that figured. It'd be too easy if he had them, though truth be told, I doubted a jump would do the trick anyway. While I knew squat about cars, I did rock at research, and from the little I'd done I'd discovered if the alternator was wonky, a fully charged battery didn't necessarily make a difference. I had a hunch that was the issue. This time, at least.

Stone walked over, giving the engine and other jiggambobs a glance. He lifted his head with a sheepish expression. "I have no clue what I'm looking at. I mean, I know the basics, but that's about it. My cousin owns the best shop in Cypress Lake, though. I can give him a call and have him pick it up while I give you a ride home."

I rocked back on my feet. Debbie had to be looked at, but part of me was worried about what they'd find. An alternator and battery issue should only cost around five hundred dollars, at least according to Google, but what if it was more? I had just over a thousand in my checking account. I could use Dad's credit card, but then he'd see the bill and push to replace her again. She was thirteen years old and had over two hundred thousand miles. I was already fighting a losing battle.

Plus, I didn't want to put Stone out. Every time he looked around these days, there I was. Falling down staircases, tripping over my feet in the studio. Now he had to drive me home?

"Look, if it's the money you're worried about, the shop's not too far," he told me. "If my cousin waits until tonight to come get it, he probably won't even charge you for the tow."

"That would certainly help," I admitted. "But are you sure you don't mind giving me a ride? I can call Sydney and see if she can pick me up…" Although she watched her siblings after school and it'd be a huge hassle to schlep them all over here.

Stone's mouth did this slow twitching thing as he glanced at Aidan. "How many stupid stunts have girls pulled over the years, trying to get in one of our cars, and this one fights me over it."

He shook his head, and while Aidan frowned, Stone's smile stretched into the unicorn-sneezing-rainbows variety that made my stomach flip. He needed to put that thing away.

"I have to bring you home now, on principle," Stone declared, pointing to a green truck parked two rows over. "Get your stuff. I'll call my cousin and drop you off on my way to Ilusiòn."

I bristled a bit at his bossiness, but it wasn't like I had a ton of options. Plus, he *was* doing me a huge favor, and by this point, I'd almost gotten used to Stone being pushy. In a weird way, it was part of his charm.

After grabbing my bag and snatching a few other necessities from the trunk, I locked the car and handed the keys to Stone, who'd already made plans to drop them off with his cousin. I waved goodbye to Aidan, wondering why he still had a weird look on his face, and followed Stone to his truck.

"Thanks for this," I said, hopping into the muggy cab. My shirt was plastered to my back just from standing outside. Technically fall started next week, but you'd never know it. "And thanks for calling your cousin. Have him get in touch with me once they figure out what's wrong, and I'll take care of it from there."

Stone nodded, and with a flick of his wrist, his engine roared to life. I sighed in envy. That's what was supposed to happen when *I* did it, too. "Have you figured out how you'll get to school tomorrow?" he asked.

"The bus picks up at the front of my neighborhood." I shifted the A/C vents so they'd hit me full-blast when he turned it on, and Stone rolled down the windows, letting the stupid-hot air escape. I glanced over with a grin. "Looks like I'm riding with the freshmen."

"I can pick you up, if you want," he offered. "I've got practice at six fifteen, but if you don't mind getting here early—"

"Oh, I don't mind," I cut in, not even ashamed at how quickly I latched on to his offer. Never mind the underclassmen, the bus driver was an old bat, and the whole thing smelled like tuna. "It'll give me more time to study."

Stone smiled, like he'd expected I'd say that, and reversed out of his parking spot.

After putting my address into his GPS and stuffing the books from my trunk into my overstuffed bag, we drove in comfortable silence, listening to the radio while pretending I wasn't checking out his inner sanctum. Other than a receipt for Foot Locker and an empty water bottle, I got nothing. We were at the red light on Maple and I'd just shoved my face in the delightful stream of cool air pouring from the A/C when I noticed Stone frown at my backpack like it had offended him.

I leaned back and kicked at the enormous bag at my feet. "What?"

Guilty eyes, like he'd been caught, raised to mine. They coasted over my face as his firm mouth twisted back and forth, as if he wanted to say something but at the same time didn't.

Yeah, that didn't make me suspicious at all.

"The other day…you mentioned you'd been sick and missed a test."

I narrowed my eyes, wondering where he was going.

He glanced back at the road. "You don't seem like the type to skip over a cold or anything. I was curious what happened."

The red light switched to green, and Stone accelerated past the intersection. I shoved my hands under my thighs, unsticking them from the warm vinyl.

I'd known the guy for twelve days—minus the twelve years of shallow acquaintance prior to that, of course—and I'd already shared a ton. Stone knew about my approach to school, my focus on the future, and a couple key memories from my past. That was more than my old therapist had gotten out of me. He'd been shockingly easy to talk to so far, but this…this was kind of heavy. I hadn't even told Sydney the whole story yet.

Then again, if Stone knew the truth, maybe he'd better understand the way my mind worked. And why he was never going to win the dare.

Inhaling a breath filled with Clean Linen air freshener, I focused on the St. Christopher medal hooked to the visor. "This summer, I took a couple classes at Cypress College. Basic pre-reqs to beef up my Harvard application, nothing too big, but the pace was faster than I expected. They squeeze an entire semester's amount of material into a shorter session, and I guess the classes stressed me out more than usual."

Luckily, it'd been nowhere near as bad as freshman year—no panic attacks, only a disgusting byproduct—which was good, because the side effects of my anti-anxiety meds sucked. So far, Dad was allowing me to stick with just the Prilosec…along with the prescription for ballroom dancing, of course.

Stone fiddled with the radio, turning down the music so I didn't have to fight with Drake to be heard, and I fidgeted with my school ring. This was where it got sticky. Going with the Band-Aid method, I decided to throw it out there in one big ramble.

"The first time I threw up blood, I didn't think anything of it. I figured I'd eaten something red and funky, and since

I'm addicted to peanut M&M's, I wrote it off as that. But then I kept getting sick. Dad was traveling when it started, and I didn't want to call him over nothing…but then he came home, and he found me in the bathroom where I'd thrown up what looked like a bucket of blood. It nearly filled the sink."

Stone's hands clenched on the wheel as I cringed at the memory.

"I never saw my dad look like that. Not even with Mom. Looking back, he was probably thinking the same thing I feared at first—that it was cancer. Then I was in the hospital for two days, which brought its own haunted memories." My chest tightened at those memories now, but I pushed them back down again. "Apparently, I burst capillaries in my duodenum by throwing up so violently, and it was all stress related. The acids in my stomach built up because I wasn't handling it well, which made me sick enough to throw up. The doctors said I could've caused permanent damage to my GI tract with scarring and a bunch of other scary-sounding stuff…"

Stone inhaled a sharp breath as I trailed off, and I turned my head. The concern in his eyes was so sweet and unexpected, it made *me* want to comfort *him*. I reached over and touched his knee. "It wasn't life threatening," I assured him with a small smile. "Just scary. They put me on meds, took away my caffeine, and told me I needed to find a hobby, which is how Dad came up with the dancing idea." I smiled to lighten the mood. "It's ironic if you think about it. The lessons are his attempt to get me to relax, when really, all they do is stress me out more."

Stone's eyebrows drew together in confusion. "Why do they stress you out?"

I rolled my eyes. Was he serious? "Because I *suck*," I

said, laughing a little. "I'm not used to sucking, or not being the best at something. Books, school, you work hard, study enough, you get the grades. But you can't make up talent where there isn't any."

A low noise, almost like a growl, came from the driver's side of the truck. "You've already gotten better after two lessons," Stone said, looking at me like he could will me to believe him using only the power of his stare. "You've got potential, Lily. I see it. You should, too."

The mood was suddenly way too serious, and I had to work not to fidget with the way he kept glancing at me. Having Stone Torres's full attention was intense. It made my chest feel light and my stomach all fluttery. I wasn't sure anyone would be immune.

Figuring that was enough of that, I discreetly wiped my palms on my shorts and said, "There you go again, telling me what I should do. It's got to be hard walking around with that giant head of yours weighing you down."

Stone's lips twitched, not looking offended in the slightest, and his huge shoulders bounced in silent laughter. "Damn, you're stubborn."

I shrugged because it was true. But it did shut him up.

Or so I thought. "You know what I think?" he asked a few seconds later, turning into my subdivision. "I think you like picking apart what I say just so you can ignore me when you know I'm right." He shot me a smug look, and I made a face. Stone laughed under his breath. "I also think you do it to change the subject."

My eyes widened. "Now why would I do that? You've heard my entire life story by this point. Let's keep it going. Is there anything else you could possibly want to know?"

Stone stayed silent as he pulled into my empty driveway and put the truck in park. He kept the engine running but turned to me, the skin around his eyes pinched in apology. "Honestly? There is something I'd like to ask, but I'm not sure how to do it."

I tilted my head, curious in spite of myself, and unhooked my seatbelt. "I have a feeling I'm gonna regret saying this, but ask away."

He still seemed hesitant, but he unhooked his seatbelt, too, and leaned his back against the door, like he planned on staying awhile. After a moment, he gave me a small, sympathetic smile. "I was wondering…well, hoping actually, you'd tell me about your mom. You don't have to. Ma told me the basics. I just thought I'd get the full story from you."

Outside my window, my neighbor Mrs. Tracy stepped out to get her kids from the bus stop. She did it every day, rain or shine, and she often had her dog Riley on a leash. They were a beautiful, perfect family who had pool parties in the summer, barbecue tailgates in the fall, and decorated their house every Christmas. Kind of like we used to do.

I swallowed the lump in my throat and pressed my face against the window. "You mean how she died?" I asked, my voice barely above a whisper.

Stone hesitated, then mumbled a, "Yes," and I watched Mrs. Tracy walk away.

"She was diagnosed with Stage Four pancreatic cancer," I told him softly, "around the end of eighth grade. I sometimes wonder what would've happened if we'd caught it any sooner. If we would've had more time. She tried chemo for a while, enough to lose her beautiful red hair and feel even weaker, but ultimately decided to live her life as fully as she could until the end. I guess that's where Ilusiòn came in." I smiled sadly. "You were right before. I'm not normally the type to skip school over a cold, or anything else, really. I've always liked learning. But I didn't have a perfect attendance record before this year. First semester of freshman year? Total disaster."

I shook my head with a dark laugh, and Stone sat quietly, waiting for me to string together a cohesive story out of a past filled with blurred edges.

"In the beginning, my priorities were Mom first, school second, and everything else way after that," I said, waving my hand through the air. "I didn't go to social events, except for the one football game because Mom made me, and I lost touch with all my friends except for Sydney. We were in crisis mode, and everything happened so fast—Mom died before Halloween."

My voice broke, and Stone stiffened, his eyes tightening before he hesitantly reached out and took my hand. I squeezed it tightly, letting his strength anchor me. "Everything after that is a blur until we came back from Christmas break. That's when Mrs. C got hold of me. I escaped into schoolwork, and the teachers let me retake tests and basically redo our first semester. But by the time I was caught up, life had gone on without me."

Stone slowly brushed his thumb over the back of my hand and asked quietly, "What do you mean?"

I stared at his perfectly neat, squared-off nail as a slight shiver swept up my arm. "Sydney was busy taking care of her siblings. Everyone else was occupied with clubs and activities, and new cliques had formed. Dad couldn't handle losing his best friend, so he kept taking more and more consulting jobs." I lifted a shoulder and dropped it. "It seemed easier to continue burying myself in schoolwork, too."

It was as if my life had been divided into two sections: With Mom and After Mom.

With Mom, people had known me as the fun girl who never backed down from a challenge. Attention hadn't bothered me, and I'd had a lot of friends.

After Mom, I was the girl whose mom had gotten sick, and people pitied or sent me uncomfortable looks—until they stopped looking altogether. Dad was rarely around, and when he was, we never talked. It was like he'd stopped seeing me, too.

"Sometimes, I wonder if people would notice if I wasn't here," I mused aloud, and Stone's hand turned into a tourniquet around my fingers. I sent him a look. "First off, *ow*. Secondly, calm down. I'm not depressed or anything. I just mean, if a tornado swept me up to Oz tomorrow, would anyone notice, or would life simply go on as usual?" My head fell back against the seat. "Sydney's great, but she's got her family and student council. Dad's always traveling. Other than that, the rest of the school barely knows my name. I'm like a ghost walking the halls. People see right through me. In a way, it's how I like it. The me who liked attention feels like a whole other girl...but I'm not immune to loneliness, either."

When I chanced a glance at Stone, he had a strange expression on his face, lips pursed and eyes gazing off into space.

"What are you thinking?" I asked, torn between worrying it was about me or something else entirely. He shook his head, going for the fake-smile thing, and I released his hand with an incredulous look. "Seriously? You're *really* gonna try that mess with me, after I sat here and told you all that?"

He winced. "Good point."

"You think?"

Stone blew out a breath. "I was just thinking, it's the exact opposite for me. People pay too much attention." He drummed his hands on the steering wheel. "It's like they have to know what I'm doing or what I'm thinking every second. They talk about what girl I'm seeing, what college I want to go to. When I'll enter the draft once I get there. Everything's discussed, with or without me even being there, but at the same time, they don't really care about the answer, either. They just want me to say what they want to hear. I guess that's why I do the '*QB thing.*'" He made air quotes as his cell phone chimed in the cupholder. "It's easier to play the part and be who they want me to be."

Seizing the phone, Stone looked at the display, gave me a panicked look, then quickly hit accept. "Hey, Ma."

Viktória's animated voice reached me all the way on the other side of the cab. I couldn't decipher what she was saying, but I fought a smile as Stone cringed and his ears turned pink.

"No, Ma, I'm not dead in a ditch somewhere. I had to take Lily home." He paused for more spirited words, which seemed only slightly less frazzled. "No, look, her car wouldn't start, so I brought her home, and Gabriel's gonna swing by and pick up her keys tonight. I'm heading to the studio now."

He sent me an apologetic look, and I grabbed the strap of my enormous book bag, heaving it up onto the seat. Stone rolled his eyes and nodded, reaching around to put on his seatbelt. "Okay, Ma, I promise, next time Lily gets stranded and I bring her home like the nice guy you raised, I'll be sure to call or text."

I snorted under my breath, and he shot me a wink.

"Ma says hello," he said after hanging up, and I smiled as I closed my hand around the latch. Instead of bolting, though, like I would've expected to do after such a revealing conversation, I felt the desire to linger. To keep talking and see what else came out. Weird.

Not wanting to risk the ire of Viktória, however, I tugged

open the door and mused aloud, "Maybe you and I aren't so different, after all."

Stone's hand snagged the strap of my bag, stopping me. "What do you mean?"

"I don't know." I slipped out of the truck, biting my lip, and turned to lean into the open door. "It's kind of like we're both hiding in our own ways. Me behind my books. You behind your QB smiles."

A wrinkle settled over his brow as he let the strap go, and I tugged my school bag toward me, hiking the heavy weight over my shoulders. "Thanks again for the ride."

Chapter Eleven

STONE

Five thirty in the morning.

The sky was pitch-black, the neighboring houses were dark, and I was still half asleep, sitting in Lily's driveway with the truck idling and coffee on standby in the holder. I got why Coach scheduled practices early. In Texas, it was the only time the heat wasn't completely unbearable, and once we got out there, I was ready to go. Right now, though, I just wanted two more minutes of sleep...

Slam. My eyes snapped open as my heart jumped in my chest. I blinked rapidly, searching the yard for World War III, and saw Lily marching across the lawn, the front door shut behind her. I exhaled a heavy breath, sagging against my seat, and choked out a laugh. Thank God Chase wasn't here. I'd have never lived that shit down.

I slapped my face to wake up and reached for my cup. Warmth filled my hands while scented steam rose upward, chasing the mental cobwebs away. The truck's headlights illuminated Lily's shirt as she rounded the hood, and I bit back a laugh as I read the snarky words she'd chosen for the day: *I'm Silently Correcting Your Grammar.*

This girl was something else.

"Morning!" she exclaimed, hopping up into the cab with a smile. I grunted at her perkiness. Shit, she was a morning person. Lily laughed as she set her book bag on the floorboard, but when she took in the second cup in the holder and the brown bag on the seat between us, her forehead crinkled in confusion. "Uh, is…is that for me?"

I gave another grunt and took my first sip of caffeine, enjoying the heat as it poured down my throat and ignoring the sting on my tongue. Everything worth having comes with a sacrifice. After another bracing sip, I took a deep breath, feeling a bit more human, and glanced at her.

"Breakfast," I mumbled.

Lily's jaw dropped, and her hand flew to her chest. As she stared at me in awe, I shifted uncomfortably in the seat. "I didn't make it myself or anything," I muttered, returning my cup to the holder. "It's just a breakfast sandwich and strawberry smoothie. I would've gotten you coffee, but I remembered what you said about no caffeine."

Instead of helping, that seemed to make everything worse. Lily's blue eyes widened almost comically behind her lenses, and if the dim lighting inside my truck wasn't playing tricks on me, they even looked shiny. What the hell? My face flared hot, and I turned back to the windshield, putting the truck in reverse.

Lily's hand closed around my forearm, and my entire body stilled. "Thank you, Stone. It's just, it's been a while since someone took care of me." She gave a short laugh and fidgeted with her seatbelt. "Not like you're taking care of me, or even think of it that way." She bit her lip. "You're probably thinking I'm gonna go stalker-level clinger on you over stupid Starbucks, huh?"

She shook her head, staring at my hands on the steering wheel. "I know I'm being ridiculous. Maybe it's because it's so early and I'm tired..." She trailed off, and while I sat there thinking this was her *tired*, she finally raised her eyes, soft and filled with gratitude. A warmth that had nothing to do with coffee spread over me as she said, "It...it means a lot. Thank you."

I swallowed hard. Hell, I'd just been hungry this morning. When I got to Starbucks, I'd figured she would be, too. I hadn't thought much beyond that, other than not wanting to get her sick again with caffeine. But the way Lily was staring at me reminded me of how Angéla looked whenever I did both our chores or brought her a snack when she was studying.

All because of a damn four-dollar sandwich and a smoothie.

"You're welcome," I said, hating how rough my voice sounded. I cleared my throat and took my foot off the brake, reversing out of her driveway while the heat in my face spread to my neck.

We were quiet for a full minute while I drove through her subdivision. My pulse thundered in my throat, and it was strangely difficult to catch my breath. When I got to the main road, I chanced a glance over to see Lily hesitantly reach into the brown bag and withdraw the wrapped bacon and gouda sandwich. Mine had been inhaled the moment I left the drive-thru.

She peeled back the paper and whispered, "Oh, *yum*."

A shifting feeling clenched my chest. Eager to change the subject, even if that had been cute as hell, I asked, "So, uh, what is it your dad does, anyway? You said he travels a lot?"

Lily nodded as she took a big bite, and after swallowing

it said, "Dad's a tech genius. He created software major corporations use, and they fly him around the world teaching their employees how to implement and use it." Her head fell back against the seat with a contented sigh. "Mom used to go as his assistant sometimes, and if it was in the summer, they'd take me, too. We went to some incredible places."

The way her smile went plastic implied it'd been a while since that happened, but then she took another bite and true happiness returned. Not wanting to see her sad again, I switched to a safer topic.

"Do you have plans after school?" She raised her eyebrows curiously, still chewing, and I explained, "I figured you might need another ride. Today the team has our family meal, but it's not until five. I can swing you back home before that if you want."

She pursed her lips. "If you don't mind, that'd actually be great. Our librarian, Ms. Joice, was friends with my mom, and I normally tutor her son every Tuesday and Thursday, but Liam's got a doctor's appointment today. My plans now involve homework and a date with my latest book boyfriend."

I grinned, remembering her shirt from the festival. "How many books would you say you read a year?" I guessed it was something crazy like fifty or a hundred.

"Oh, I don't know." Lily tilted her head back and forth, did some counting on her fingers. "I'd say at least two hundred."

My eyes popped wide. I did a double take, certain I'd misheard her, and she busted out laughing.

"You recall I don't have a social life, right?" she asked with a wide grin. "Besides, I love reading. Exploring another world, trying on a different skin. It's my favorite way to escape. Sydney and I like to buddy read, and we always text each other, freaking out and swooning over what's happening. Even when we're both swamped with school or busy with life, books are something we can share, and it's almost like we're in the same room."

I stopped at the intersection, fighting to keep my smile while I waited for the fancy BMW to make its turn. This girl broke my fucking heart. First, she was over the moon because I'd picked up breakfast, and now she was stoked because she exchanged texts with her closest friend over fictional worlds. To be clear, there was nothing wrong with reading. Angéla was a proud book nerd, and I wasn't afraid to admit I'd swiped a few books from her shelves over the years. But nothing compared to actually living life.

"I see you over there judging me, Mr. McJudgey." She thrust her pointer finger into my biceps but didn't look offended. "Tell me, then, what do *you* like to do that's so riveting?"

I accelerated past the four-way stop and repeated the question with a laugh. When she blinked at me, I shrugged a shoulder. "Football," I replied, like it should've been obvious.

"No. Football is the sport you play that's almost like a job. I want to know what you do to unwind and have fun, *away* from the field, and don't give me one of your canned responses, either. I want the real, unfiltered Stone Torres. Hit me with the truth, QB."

I frowned at the road. What did I like to do, other than football? What the hell did she want to hear? If this had been an interview for the school paper, I'd have said I liked helping with the peewee league during the summer and hanging out with friends, going to parties.

But did I genuinely like that stuff?

The truth was, the kids were cute, and it was fun watching the one or two who showed promise, but the hero worship wore thin by the end of the season. As for parties, the monotony was getting old there, too. It was all about hooking up, which I was on a break from, and rehashing the previous game or looking forward to the next. I couldn't relax. Everyone watched my every move. It felt like I was on a stage. Other than that, though, I drove around with Chase, played video games, or worked.

When I didn't say anything, Lily changed tactics. "How about this, then? What do you want to be, like after college? Have you thought about what you want to major in?"

I shot her a side-eye. "I'm not falling for that. It's a blatant attempt to get me to break a rule, and it's not gonna happen."

She rolled her eyes. "I believe that rule is more for *me* than you," she replied, and I laughed because she wasn't wrong. "Please?"

I took the turn onto Winchester and sighed. To tell the truth or not to tell the truth. Finally, I admitted quietly, "I don't know."

I waited for the inevitable gasp of shock from the girl who mapped out her entire life, but it never came. When I looked over, Lily merely looked curious, and maybe a bit sympathetic.

"Do you want to play in the NFL?" she asked, and I shrugged again. "Be a dancer?"

I laughed out loud. "Uh, definitely not."

"What's wrong with being a dancer?"

"It's not that there's anything wrong with it," I explained, turning into the mostly empty lot of Brighton High. Only football players dared to arrive this early. I drove down the line of recently painted senior spots, feeling her watching me, and pulled into my designated slot. I put the truck in park, sliding her a look.

"Listen, dancing's in my blood, but other than my family and the regulars at Ilusiòn, the only people who even know I dance are you, Chase, Cameron, and Ashley. Mambo King doesn't exactly fit with the vision most people have in mind for their football captain."

Even *if* my classmates were cool about it—which, other than a few idiots, they probably would be—other people wouldn't. This was Texas, after all. Land of the cowboy. Old-school Boosters wouldn't think twice about commenting on a Twinkle Toes quarterback, and reporters and DJs would do the same for ratings. They'd all shown their colors when I dated Cameron last year, questioning my focus and implying my priorities were split just because I had a girl. My entire life was dissected for sport. If they got wind of me *dancing*? Hell, I'd never hear the end of it.

After a few beats of silence, I threw off my seatbelt, and Lily sighed as she released hers. "Well, that's just sad."

My jaw ticked. Balling the empty wrapper from her sandwich, I asked, "What is?"

"That you don't think you can be who you really are," she replied softly, her words and tone compelling me to look across the cab. Again, I waited for judgment that never came. Instead, her eyes filled with understanding and compassion. Somehow it was almost worse.

More cars were pulling into the lot, and I glanced out my window in time to see Aidan walk by. He tapped his fist against the glass, and I waved a hand to say I was coming.

Turning back to Lily, wanting *her* to be on the hot seat again, I asked, "What about you? What does our future valedictorian plan to do with her life? Run for president? Take over Apple? Solve world hunger?"

She smiled, amusement on her face as she grabbed her book bag and popped open the passenger-side door.

"Nice try, bud, but that *is* a rule violation." She waggled her eyebrows and hopped out of the truck, a lilting laugh floating through the slight crack in the window as she strolled away. Even though she'd bested me at my own game, I found myself laughing, too.

Damn. That girl loved a good exit.

Chapter Twelve

LILY

"I'm *so* not meant to be a doctor," I whined, writing the term *abdominopelvic cavity* onto a notecard as lunch trays slammed and chairs scraped around me. As vocabulary terms went, it was a relatively easy one, but my brain was too clouded with words like *parietal pleura*, *chondroblasts*, and figuring out the difference between afferent and efferent neurons, to make heads or tails of it. Why couldn't every subject be English or history?

Sydney thrust her hand across the table and set it over my open textbook. "You realize if you didn't work so far ahead, and took things slower like they were actually intended, it might make more sense, right?"

I stuck out my tongue. "The day I *don't* work ahead is the day you should worry about me," I said, grabbing a blank notecard from the stack between us. "Besides, you're one to talk. I bet you the new Sarah Dessen you've already memorized the textbook."

"Ah, but see, I *like* science," she replied, knowing she had me there. I grumbled and went back to writing, and she watched me while a group seated at the table behind us got into a heated debate over the Mandela Effect. She sighed. "Fine, even though it's a *total* waste of a night free of babysitting, I'll help you study tomorrow if you want."

My face lit up in a giddy grin, and I batted my eyelashes gratefully. My best friend rolled her eyes. "Good Lord, you can stop the theatrics, I already said I'd come over." Sydney stole a carrot stick from my plate. "Of course, I'd *rather* study Sunday night, since I'm off then, too, but it's an away game tomorrow and you refuse to go with me, so I've got nothing else to do."

Beyond her head, the entire back wall of the cafeteria was plastered in posters about Homecoming. Banners for various court nominees and reminders to purchase tickets were scattered everywhere. We still had two weeks until the dance, and unlike me, Sydney wanted to go. While she'd worked the event a few times in the past, she'd never gone with a date.

I picked up a cucumber slice and dunked it in ranch. If I was gonna eat more rabbit food like the doctors wanted, it was at least gonna taste good. "You know, as much as I want you to study with me, you could always ask Nick to the game."

Sydney's panicked gaze flew to the neighboring tables to see if he was around.

"He's your vice president," I continued, ignoring the sharp kick under the table, "which means he's off concession stand duty, too. I bet if you asked him, he'd love to go."

Her hazel eyes narrowed, but before she could issue the excuse already forming on her lips, Angéla Torres plopped down in the empty chair beside her. A bright orange tray filled with French fries, a slice of pizza, and a chocolate-glazed brownie landed next, and I blinked in a mix of awe and food envy.

While I repressed the desire to dive headfirst into her tray, Angéla plucked up her carton of chocolate milk and took a good long pull, eyes closed in bliss. Sydney watched in confused fascination. "Uh, hi there."

Angéla smacked her lips with a satisfying *ahh*. "Sorry, I was positively parched. Speech class always gets me going." She wiggled happily in her seat and twisted her glossy black hair in a thick rope before sliding it over her shoulder. "I'm Angéla, by the way. You're Sydney Green, best friend of my future bestie, which makes us future besties, too. What are we talking about?"

Sydney glanced at me, as if seeking confirmation this was really happening, and answered somewhat distractedly, "We're making plans for the weekend."

"Oh, good!" Angéla sat up tall and reached over to grab my hand. "That's one of the things I wanted to ask you. You'll come to the game with me tomorrow, won't you? Both of you? I hate going to those things alone, and I'll drive the whole way, so don't worry about that. My brother told me about your car."

She grinned widely and flipped her hand over her brow. "*Sa-woon*, by the way. Very *One Tree Hill*-ish." When she caught my and Sydney's dual looks of bewilderment, she said, "Nathan? Haley? Lucas?" She sighed. "It's on Hulu. Watch it. Trust me, you'll thank me later."

"I'll be sure to check it out," I replied, trying hard not to laugh. If Angéla planned on hanging around, I'd seriously need to up my television and movie game.

A warm feeling floated through my chest, and I grinned at my stack of notecards. Then I remembered her proposal for tomorrow.

"Yeah, about the game…"

Angéla's pretty face lit with a beam like she was incandescent, and I winced, hating to be the reason she faded. Sydney, the evil girl she was, grabbed hold of my weakness and ran. "Yeah, we were *just* talking about that, weren't we, Lil? I was telling her I could drop by her house *Sunday* to help with her index-card-a-thon, so she could go to the game with me tomorrow night, and now you're offering us a ride. It's like fate or something."

I shook my head with a grin. *Point: Sydney.* Clearly, she was on board with Angéla's new bestie plan—not a surprise, since Sydney always made friends quickly. It was one of the things I both loved and hated about her. Glancing at her attempt at sappy puppy dog eyes that held the tiniest hint of wicked glee, and knowing I was outvoted, I decided arguing was futile.

"Fine, I'll go," I conceded, laughing when Angéla did a fist pump. "But I seriously need to get this anatomy straight at some point."

"Don't worry, I'll help on Sunday," Sydney promised, dancing a little in her chair. "This is gonna be so much fun! It's been forever since we had a real girl's night."

Angéla twirled a French fry in ketchup. "Me, too. In fact, why don't we go the full nine and have a sleepover? Ooh, that'll be perfect. 'Chasing Trouble's' having one of his infamous parties after the game," she said with an exaggerated eye roll, "so we'll have the house to ourselves. We can do the whole retro, teen movie, pillow fight/spa routine. It'll be great!"

I tapped my pen, studying her. She looked genuinely excited, but I could've sworn I'd picked up a crushing vibe at the parade. Sneaking a covert glance across the room to where Chase and Stone held court, I glanced back at my newly declared bestie. "You're sure you don't want to go to the party?"

Angéla wrinkled her nose in disgust. "God, no. I'm over that scene." She pushed away her half-eaten tray, and that, more than anything else, shocked the heck out of me. "It's the same silliness every time. People drink too much, they hook up, someone gets thrown into a pool, and it's all documented on Snapchat or Insta. It's like the entire student body is stuck in reruns and no one even notices."

Sydney seemed to consider that, as unfamiliar with the party scene as I was, then swung her gaze to mine. "So... sleepover?"

You'd have to have known her as well as I did to catch the slight flare of desperation in her eyes. As anti-stereotype as I was when it came to the high school experience, Sydney lived for it. It was even more of an issue for her because she had so little free time between schoolwork, Student Council, and watching her siblings.

I pressed my lips together and looked at my growing stack of notecards. I really *should* study at some point tomorrow, even if it wasn't Anatomy and Physiology. But I also couldn't deny it felt nice to make plans and feel included.

A fleeting thought entered my mind that Dad would go bananas if he learned I'd slept at a house with a teenage guy down the hall, but then, he hadn't been in town to ask. Problem solved.

Plus, it wasn't like Stone was interested in me like *that* anyway.

Raising my head, I took in their matching, hopeful expressions and laughed out loud. At first glance, Sydney and Angéla were total opposites. One was blond, a fierce Type-A, and made my own aspirations for the future look like child's play. The other had dark hair the color of licorice, was bubbly and fun, and evidently saw the world through a Hollywood lens. But they both had huge hearts, an even bigger zest for life, and for some strange reason, wanted to be friends with me. How could I deny them?

"I'll bring the face masks and cucumber slices," I muttered, and they squealed in sync before turning to give each other a high five. Ah, crap. These two were gonna be the death of me.

Chapter Thirteen

LILY

Stone laughed as he barreled down Main Street, fingers tapping the steering wheel to the local variety station's drive-time hits. It was the only channel we halfway agreed on. We were headed home after a long-ass day of academic learning mixed with a healthy dose of teenage angst, and I'd just divulged Angéla's lunchtime declaration of bestie-hood.

"Yeah, she can be a force of nature when she wants to be," he said, affection clear in his tone. "But my sister has a huge heart, and she wears it on her sleeve." He glanced over, and the loving grin turned down slightly at the edges. "People can sometimes take advantage."

It didn't seem like he thought *I'd* take advantage but was doing his brotherly duty in warning me, and an unexpected rush of protectiveness flooded my chest. I hated that the funny, affectionate girl who'd welcomed me with open arms wasn't always treated the same way, and it made me appreciate her spunky brand of friendship even more.

"She invited us to sleep over after the game," I told him,

curious as to how he'd react.

Would he find it weird, me being in his house, around his personal things? Or would he be glad to hang out again in a non-dance, non-damsel-like situation?

What would happen if we, say, accidently bumped into each other in the middle of the night, like on the way to the bathroom? Would he linger and talk and reveal more of his secrets…or would he slide past me and go on to do his business?

And what did Stone look like, first thing in the morning? Was he the type of guy who woke up perfect, or did he suffer from bedhead like the rest of us mere mortals?

Gah! When did I become such a head case?

"Oh yeah?" he said, snapping me out of my crazy thoughts. We rolled to a stop at the traffic light, and he pursed his lips. "You know, I should drag you to Chase's party. You still haven't been to one, and his are particularly legendary."

"I'd use my veto if you tried…"

"*But*, I'm kind of over the scene myself," he said with a smirk. "Besides, I'm glad you'll be hanging out with Angéla. Just do me a favor and try to rein her in if she goes too wild…and whatever you do, *don't* let her watch the BBC version of *Pride and Prejudice* unless you want a shot by shot breakdown of why it's brilliant and how it compares to the book."

I laughed and shifted on the seat to face him. "I take it that's her favorite movie?"

"It at least makes the top five," he replied, his face a mask of feigned exasperation, but the sparkle in his eyes betrayed how much he adored her. "She discovered it the summer after we were freshmen, back when it was on our suggested reading list. It's been Darcy fever ever since."

I smiled as the song on the radio ended with a boom and a perky voice rolled through the truck's speakers. "That was 'Thunder' by Imagine Dragons, here on KSBY 96.5, but you want to know where there won't be thunder this weekend, Chris?"

"Where's that, Kasey?" a second voice, just as peppy only slightly deeper, chimed in.

"Over in Fairwood City, where our beloved Tigers are taking on the Hokies! I'm not a meteorologist, Chris, but I predict a major butt-whooping tomorrow, led by none other than local legend Stone Torres. It's gonna be a great night of football."

"That might be true," the second DJ chimed in, "but the real game on everyone's mind is the matchup against Morton in a few weeks. Sure, Torres can easily handle the Hokies, and after next week's bye, the Wildcats should be easy picking. But can number five hold up against the Mustangs' top-ranked defense? When it counts, and the game is on the line against a true contender, can he keep his composure in the clutch? *That's* what everyone wants to know."

"Very true, Chris, and only time will tell. Now, don't go anywhere, friends, because we'll be back kicking off another commercial-free hour of hits from the eighties, nineties, and today after this word from our sponsor."

A somber mood fell over the cab as a jingle for a car dealership blathered on, and Stone's jaw turned to granite. As surreal as the last few seconds had been, what made it even crazier was that it was only a tiny glimpse of what he dealt with every day. A second wave of protectiveness washed over me, this one even stronger than the last.

While I struggled with what to say, Stone sighed, then turned his attention to the shopping center outside my window. His eyebrows lifted as he scanned the lot, and the affectionate smile he'd worn when he'd talked about Angéla returned.

"Hey, you mind if we make a stop before I bring you home?"

"Not at all," I told him, curious as to what he could be thinking. "You're saving me from smelling like tuna on the bus. We can make as many stops as you want."

Stone flicked his turn signal, and when the red light switched to green, he pulled into the lot. It was surprisingly filled for a Thursday afternoon, and people were streaming in and out of the various stores. Bath & Body Works, an H-E-B grocery store, Hobby Lobby, and One More Chapter, a local bookstore.

I surveyed each, wondering which could've caught his fancy, while he navigated around shoppers and discarded carts. He selected a space closest to the bookstore, and I grinned, unable to resist teasing. "Ahh, all that talk of Mr. Darcy got you hot for your own copy, huh?"

Stone unbuckled his seat belt, the slightest twitch of his lips the only indication he'd heard me. He gazed up at the building and said, "Sunday marks five years Angel's been cancer free."

My playful smile fell from my face.

"Normally, I take her to dinner and give her a gift card," he went on while I slowly released my seatbelt. "But, I don't know, I guess after hearing you go on this morning about the books you read, and then talking about *Pride and Prejudice*, I thought maybe I should do something different this year."

I bit my lip, tucking my legs up beneath me. "Angéla's a fellow booklover?"

Stone laughed, making me remember her strong reaction to my book boyfriend shirt at the festival. I wasn't surprised when he said, "Yeah, you could say that." He glanced at me.

"Of course, her first love will always be movies, but in the hospital, we didn't always have access to a DVD player. Or a huge selection of cable channels. Books were easy to carry around, though. In the beginning...man, she must've gone through four or five a week. Minimum." He shook his head and then cleared his throat, his smile dulling at the edges. "Later on, when she got too tired to read, I made it my job to do it for her."

Stone's broad shoulders seemed to shrink in size. His thick, dark eyebrows drew together as if he were in pain, and my heart throbbed at the rare show of emotion. I pressed a hand against my chest as my own memories rushed back.

"It was the only thing I could do for her, you know?" His hands clenched the steering wheel. "I wasn't a doctor. I wasn't a nurse. I didn't even have my license yet, so I couldn't drive her to appointments or make an ice cream run to make her smile. The only thing I could do was read to her when she couldn't." He leaned back with a huff of exasperation and splayed his hands wide. "For a while there, it became our thing. Twin-time, she used to call it."

Stone shook his head, then laughed softly, glancing at me with a small, almost shy smile. It transformed his usually rugged face, making him look more innocent, more vulnerable. It hadn't escaped my attention that he was opening up and being real, like I'd asked him to do at the festival, and wanting to comfort him—but also not wanting to scare him off—I scooted closer on the bench, lifting and then dropping my hand before setting it on his thigh.

"It sounds like you did everything you could," I told him honestly, my words strained because my throat was tight. "More than enough."

Stone inhaled a deep breath. The thin press of his lips said he didn't believe me. Regardless, he said, "Maybe. But after Angéla got better, life kicked back into high gear. We both got busy. Between school and football and her dancing at the studio…" He trailed off, and his mouth twisted ruefully. "I don't know, maybe the book idea is stupid. She's got an e-reader thing now anyway."

"No." I shook my head earnestly and leaned down, needing to catch his eyes. "I don't think it's stupid at all. I think it's very thoughtful, and your sister's gonna love it."

His eyes tracked over my face. "Yeah?"

I nodded, my heart melting over the vinyl seat. "Yeah. And as for the e-reader thing, take it from a dyed-in-the-wool book nerd, nothing compares to the feel and smell of a real live book."

At his slow, relieved smile, I squeezed his thigh—and nearly dropped my jaw at the rock-hard muscle beneath my hand. Holy crap on a biscuit. The guy was built like…well, like a stone. For a second, I physically forgot how to breathe, and I fought to not swallow my tongue.

Focus, Lily. Now's not the time to lust over the guy.

"I, uh, like seeing this side of you," I said, reluctantly removing my hand. My fingertips tingled, protesting the absence of warmth, and I mentally told them to shush.

"What side?" Stone asked quietly, and I smiled at how uncertain he sounded. What a change from the normal confident front he portrayed.

"The protective brother side," I murmured. "The guy who'd do anything to take care of his sister and make her smile. Listening to you, it's obvious how much you care about her. I admire that."

I also couldn't help wondering if he was so fiercely protective of *everyone* he cared about, and if he was, what it would feel like to be on the receiving end of that kind of loyalty.

The tips of Stone's ears turned pink, but when he looked at me again, there was a new, haunted look in his eyes that made my stomach clench. He hesitated for a minute, the muscles around his jaw flexing and releasing, then he said, "I was scared I was gonna lose her."

His eyes closed at the admission, and he slid a hand behind his neck. "Hell, Lily, I'm still scared. It's been five years in remission, so everything points to the cancer not coming back. But I can't help worrying it will. Every ache. Every fever. Every random bruise, they all scare the shit out of me."

"Oh, I get it, trust me," I said, thinking back to the awful days of chemo and trips to MD Anderson with Mom. "When I got sick a few weeks ago, that was immediately where my head went. My dad's, too."

The hand around Stone's neck fell to his lap, and he muttered a soft curse, but I pointed at him before he could even begin to apologize.

"Don't you dare. Yeah, I lost my mom, but that doesn't make what you and your family went through—what you're *still* going through—any different. We all have our own struggles, and they're all valid. I just meant I understand how scary it can be, dealing with the unknown, and how you can feel completely powerless to do anything."

Stone and I shared a look, and on the radio, an artist started singing about hanging by a moment. As I listened to the words, staring into the eyes of a football legend in the making, I realized that in *this* moment, I finally felt understood.

God, I'd forgotten what that was like.

With Stone, I didn't feel anxious or worried. I wasn't scrambling to hide what I felt or trying to project an aura of control. Stone looked at me like he saw the *real* me, warts and all, but he didn't pity me or judge me, and he wasn't trying to fix me.

He just got me.

Slowly, I inched back onto my side of the cab. The last thing he probably wanted right now was me jumping in his lap and tackle-hugging him, though it was suddenly all I could think about doing. When I deemed myself a safe enough distance away, I shoved my hands beneath my thighs for good measure and said, "Thank you."

A wrinkle creased his forehead. "I believe that's my line."

I snorted a laugh, which made my already-warm cheeks flare hot. "I meant for telling me about Angéla. I know you don't like talking about yourself, but…" I raked my teeth over my bottom lip. "I appreciate you sharing that with me."

Stone's mouth kicked up in a crooked grin, and his gaze traveled over my face. "You make it surprisingly easy, Lily Bailey." He laughed softly, like he was a bit bewildered by that, and our eyes held as he turned off the engine with a flip of his wrist.

The radio fell silent, the A/C went still, and I sucked in a breath as my heart started pounding in a strange, confused rhythm.

What in the heck is happening?

Stone shifted slightly, his chest turned toward mine, and I adjusted, too, my body drawn to his like two magnets across the cab. Seconds ticked as my insides vibrated with awareness. I didn't know what was about to happen, but I knew it would be monumental.

His gaze fell to my lips…

Then, as if I'd imagined the whole thing, he smiled brightly and popped open the driver-side door.

"Ready to do this thing?" he asked, glancing back at the bookstore, and I quickly shook my head to defog it.

"Mm-hmm," I replied, swiping my palms across my shorts while I tried to unstick my tongue from the roof of my mouth. "Yep. Right behind you."

On spaghetti legs, I, too, got out of the truck and walked through the doors of One More Chapter, dazedly leading Stone toward a center display under the words Teen Romance. Draped with a red silk cloth, it held a variety of classics and new releases, and having snagged a basket at the entrance, he proceeded to add them to his collection, the slightest hint of a vulnerable smile reemerging on his lips.

Occasionally, I offered my own suggestions, including my favorite time-travel romance, and when he took it and our fingertips brushed, the strangest sensation jolted my stomach. I whisked it away as hunger pains.

But it was when we headed farther into the store, stopping to point out books we liked along the way—Stone lingered near graphic novels and mysteries, while I perused fantasy, history, and romance—that a sexy cover with a kissing couple caught my eye, and the truth hit like a final exam I hadn't prepared for.

The inexplicable twitch in my stomach?

The runaway tingle tiptoeing down my spine?

The vibrating insides and Sahara-like mouth?

They were symptoms of an ill-timed, all-consuming, and completely inconvenient *crush*.

I was crushing on Stone Torres. Hard. And I was so very, very screwed.

Chapter Fourteen

LILY

"So your topic is…what exactly?"

Aidan deflated across from me in the back of the library. "The Renaissance and how it compares and contrasts to modern-day society," he said, his voice pitched almost like he was asking a question, and he dropped his head to the table. I bit back a laugh at his antics, and he looked up with a pained expression. "I take it that's not obvious?"

"Well…no. But it's got good bones," I offered with a weak smile, and he dropped his head again. This time, I couldn't stop the soft laugh. Reaching out, I shoved his shoulder. "Hey, we've been over this. You're a great writer. Seriously. It's just your organization that's a little off. We'll figure it out, though, that's why I'm here. Have I ever steered you wrong?"

"No," he said with a sigh, sitting up with a defeated look still on his face. "But what's gonna happen next year when you're off at Harvard and I'm at A&M, still struggling in English 101?" He peered at his paper and muttered, "If they even take me."

I rolled my eyes skyward.

Aidan was smart. Any college he applied to would accept him. The problem was he needed a scholarship. Money was tight, and unlike Stone, he didn't think he was a strong enough player to get in on athletics. He was aiming for an academic ride, and lucky for him, his high GPA should make it possible.

Unfortunately, writing papers was a bit of a weakness, at least when it came to organizing his thoughts, which is why we'd worked together for the past two years. Undercover, of course.

Scanning his rough draft again, I found a jumping-off point and slid the paper back across the table. We had the entire back room to ourselves (well, other than the dust mites), and the only sound besides Aidan's frustrated sighs was the loud ticking of the clock, so I didn't bother lowering my voice as I pointed at the first paragraph.

"You're gonna be fine wherever you go, Drama King, because this introduction is strong." I flipped a few pages to the end and put a star next to a sentence buried in the middle of his conclusion. "It all comes down to putting things in the right order. I think *this* is your topic sentence. If you move it to the top, your paper will flow from there."

Aidan sat up straight and reread his final paragraph, his mouth moving with the words as his eyebrows drew together. When he was finished, they shot straight to his hairline, and he flipped back to the beginning, reread his intro, and grinned when his eyes came to mine. "Damn, you're right. That'd be so much better."

"Hey, you're the one who wrote it," I said, leaning back as he made chicken-scratch notes across the page. Thank goodness the final would be typed, or we'd have a whole other issue to tackle. "And if it makes you feel any better, you're already doing better than I am. I haven't even started my paper yet."

I sighed as the crushing weight of how behind I was pressed down on my chest, and mentally added "history paper" to my mile-long to-do list for the weekend. Which, of course, got me thinking about *other* things I'd be doing the next three days, too. Namely, sleeping over at the Torres house.

Tiny jackrabbits bouncing in my stomach replaced my previous stress, and a warm, gooey sensation oozed through my veins. A slow grin spread across my face. It had rarely left since yesterday's excursion to the bookstore.

Aidan cleared his throat, and I blinked to see him no longer writing on his paper. "You haven't started yet?"

By the way he'd asked that question, you'd have sworn I'd said *Harry Potter* was simply a mediocre book. "Nope," I said, tilting my head in confusion. Why did he care about my history paper? The only reason he'd started *his* was so that we could have time to workshop it.

"Huh. Then let me guess, you're pulling an all-nighter tonight?"

"Actually…" I said, drawing out the word. "No. I'm going to Fairwood for the game."

I smiled, recalling the many times the running back had gotten on me for missing his games the last few years, and was rewarded by Aidan gaping at me. I shifted in my chair uncomfortably.

"So, yeah. Guess you'll have to find something new to tease me about," I said, my smile dimming to a half-smile/half-wince situation the more he gaped. "My reign as Official Stick in the Mud is coming to an end."

Instead of laughing at my admittedly unfunny joke,

Aidan narrowed his eyes. Pushing to his feet, he quickly scanned the neighboring rows of dusty reference books and empty desks, then, satisfied we were alone, sat back down and said, "Tell me you've heard the rumors."

My forehead wrinkled. "Say what now?"

He sighed. "Lily, you have to have noticed people staring. Ever since you showed up at the festival with Stone, it's all anyone is talking about. The quarterback secretly hooking up with the nerd—their words, not mine. Seriously, has no one asked you about it?"

A familiar feeling of dread built in my chest, and I shook my head. "N-no. I mean, I guess a couple people stared during lunch yesterday…but I figured that was because Angéla sat with us." I swallowed down a slight wave of panic and said, "The rest of the week I ate back here."

I scanned my memory for anything else that could've jumped out. Any weird interactions or strange whispers, and came up short. Truthfully, I *had* been preoccupied this week, wanting to get my life back on track, and then there was my car breaking down, Angéla's sudden declaration of friendship, and yesterday's discovery.

But surely, I would've noticed people staring at me, right?

I dropped my head in my hands. I hadn't been the source of gossip since Mom had gotten sick, and thinking about that time had the old feelings of anxiety swirling in my gut. Closing my eyes, I took a deep breath of stale, musty air as memories of whispers, pitying looks, and awkward questions washed over me. Unwanted attention made my skin itch like I had hives—but, unlike freshman year, this was something I could control. At least in theory.

"Stone and I didn't *go* to the festival together," I argued, forcibly relaxing my shoulders. "We just hung out there. You know that. And no hooking up is happening. We're friends."

Heck, even *that* might've been an overstatement.

Despite my recent crush revelation and that nanosecond of a moment in his truck, I was no closer to figuring out Stone's real motives than I was two weeks ago. Did he consider me an actual friend, or was I just a challenge of sorts? I didn't know. Yeah, he'd shared with me about Angéla, and he'd told me that sweet story at the festival about his family, and he seemed to show me a different side than the one everyone else saw. But I was the school ghost. His secrets were safe with me.

It's more than that, my inner romantic asserted, and I dropped my hands to the table. Was it, though? Or had I built up a bunch of tiny moments inside my head, wanting them to mean something when they didn't?

I raised my head and found Aidan studying me. "Since when are you friends?" he asked, pushing his paper aside. My eyes widened, pretty sure I'd been insulted, and he held up a hand. "I'm serious. A week ago, Stone asked about you in the team gym like he barely knew who you were. Then, a few days later, he's going toe-to-toe with Cameron about you riding on the float? It doesn't add up."

"Hold on. Stone asked about me in the gym?"

Aidan gave a stiff nod, and I drummed my fingers on the tabletop. That had to have been before Stone came up with the dare. But why?

My head swam with possibilities, and I quietly murmured, "No, it doesn't add up."

He snorted skeptically, and I ground my teeth, refocusing on the current problem.

As I leaned forward on my elbows, my confused anxiety floated away, and annoyance surged to take its place. "Two weeks ago, I started taking lessons at Viktória Torres's studio, and the twins decided to adopt me. Don't ask me why, I don't know myself. But Stone and I aren't hooking up. That's the truth. We couldn't be more different if we tried. But if we were, it *still* wouldn't be any of your business because my social life, or lack thereof, has nothing to do with your paper, peer tutoring, or European history."

Throughout my outburst, Aidan's eyes had slowly widened, and by the end of it, he was leaned back in his seat, mouth agape. I lifted my chin and discreetly let out a shaky breath, feeling a bit surprised myself.

Old Lily would've thought nothing of standing up for herself if the situation warranted it, but that fearless girl was long gone, or so I'd thought. The slight tremor in my hands indicated she was at least partially still on vacay, but the thrum in my blood felt a heck of a lot like my old friend adrenaline.

Silence fell over our table, made more noticeable by the utter stillness of our hidden alcove, and Aidan hung his head, blowing out a steady breath before looking at me.

"You're right," he said, and I craned an eyebrow. "Partly. Who you date has nothing to do with history, but I'd like to think it's somewhat my business because we're friends." I snorted, and he had the decency to look guilty. "Okay, I deserve that. I know we don't hang out, and I'm weird about the guys finding out you tutor me, but, Lily, that's about me and my issues. Believe it or not, I *do* consider you a friend, just like I consider Stone a friend, and because of that, I'm trying to look out for you. I don't want to see you get hurt."

I rubbed my forehead, feeling a tension headache coming on. "Okay, say we *were* together…in this fantasy world scenario, why assume I'd get hurt? You said you're friends with Stone. Do you make a habit of being friends with assholes?"

He sighed like I was being purposefully dense. "Actually, I like to think I'm a pretty good judge of character," he replied, jabbing his pen against the table for emphasis. "And seriously, do you not remember what happened with him and Cameron last spring?"

Frowning, I let my fingers fall from my face. "Not exactly," I admitted, suddenly feeling nervous for a whole new reason. "I mean, I know they broke up, and I remember there was some sort of drama around it, but I didn't really pay attention to the details. That sort of stuff always seems so stupid."

My lack of interest in the constant soap opera surrounding me was one of the things that drove Sydney nuts. The players changed so frequently that it wasn't worth the effort to keep up. For the first time in my life, I found myself wishing I'd clued in more.

"What happened?"

Aidan pressed his lips together, hesitating. Somewhere in the library, a throat cleared, and a cell phone pinged. Another series of loud *ticks* of the clock went by, and when he still hadn't opened his mouth and didn't appear as if he would, I sighed, mentally exhausted with this entire conversation.

"Good talk. Glad we got that cleared up."

Cursing, he reached out and stopped me from leaving. "Look, it's pretty much public knowledge now anyway, so I guess it's not a big deal if I tell you. Just…for obvious reasons, we try not to talk about it around Stone." He looked around again, then lowered his voice to a whisper. "Cameron cheated."

My eyes widened as I plopped back on the chair, my mouth tumbling open.

What a stupid girl.

"It was the weekend of Spring Break. Ashley had a party, and Stone didn't show. We found out later his dad had gotten in a car accident and was at the hospital, but at the time, no one knew where he was. Cameron swears she was drunk, but from what I saw, and what everyone else said, she wasn't acting like it. She was just being typical Cameron, needing to be the center of attention like always, and flirting with the hottest guy around."

He leaned across the table. "Do you remember Noah Ruckert? Star wide-out, graduated last year?" I shook my head. "Well, trust me, he was a big deal. Almost as big as Stone. Everyone expected him to kill it at LSU, and they were already placing bets on what NFL team would snag him someday." He laughed darkly, his mouth twisting in a cruel smirk. "Poor Noah's stinking it up in Baton Rouge these days, though. A bad camp followed by two wildly disappointing games. Turns out, karma's a bitch."

"Aidan," I prompted, tapping the tabletop. "Focus. What happened at the party?"

"Right, sorry." He shook his head. "Obviously, Cameron and Noah hooked up, and *someone*…no one knows exactly who because the girl who owns the account swears she was hacked and out of town, but that's a whole other mess… posted a video of them making out in a story on Snapchat. A lot of people saw it, the rest heard about it or watched a recording of it later, and by the end of the night, so had Stone."

My heart physically hurt. I wanted to storm out of the library and find Stone, then hug him and apologize on behalf of all womankind for Cameron and anyone else who'd ever cheated. Cheating was just another face for dishonesty, and that was one thing I'd always said I couldn't forgive. Life was too short to hurt or betray the people you loved.

"Stone acts like he's tough," Aidan said, "but that shit messes with your head. He laid low all summer and then came back saying he's out. He's given up on girls and the drama that comes with them. Chase calls it his '*monk philosophy*.'" His fingers made air quotes as sympathy filled his eyes. "Lily, Stone said he's not looking to date *anyone* right now, and you're a sweetheart. I just don't want to see you get hurt thinking this is more than it really is."

Ouch. That stung, having my own fears spit back by a guy who, claim of friendship or not, barely knew me. Clearly, I was so out of my league that he naturally assumed I'd get my heart broken from spending time with Stone. Because it wasn't possible I could simply have friendly feelings for the guy—or that Stone could ever have real feelings for me.

What made it sadder was he was pretty much right on the money.

Tossing my hair over my shoulder, I fought to keep my emotions in check and grabbed my notebook. "Listen, I appreciate you looking out for me, but it's not necessary. I'm allergic to drama, which is probably why Stone likes hanging out with me."

Honestly, it seemed as likely as any other reason, which left a bitter taste in my mouth.

Pasting on a smile, however, I yanked my bag closed with a sharp *zziiippp* and threw the straps around my shoulders as I declared, "I'm the anti-Cameron."

That sounded as sexy and appealing as a worn-out pair of pajamas. Accurate, but sad.

As luck would have it, the bell rang for fifth period, and I shot to my feet. Aidan lumbered to his, too, looking concerned, and I waved it away with a reminder about his introduction, then booked it down the hall.

Gratitude chased the hurt tightening my chest. Now

that I'd had a second to process, I was glad Aidan had butted in. Yesterday my heart and hormones had formed an unholy alliance, and in the hours since, they'd run away with themselves. Playing out silly fantasies, linking my name with Stone's in pink neon. Imagining heat where there'd just been pathetic unrequited yearning. So dumb.

Friends and dance partners, that's what we were, and that's what we'd stay. In the long run, that was better than hooking up and kissing anyway. Less mess and more innocent fun.

My inner romantic snorted in my head. *Yeah, keep telling yourself that, lover-girl.*

My inner romantic was an unhelpful witch.

Chapter Fifteen

STONE

"Go, fight, win!" The clichéd cheer rang through Cameron's megaphone, and the crowd in the stands echoed their excitement. The rustle of pom-poms mixed with the scent of damp grass, and a tangible pulse of energy electrified the entire stadium.

It was game night.

Unfortunately, my head wasn't in it with everyone else currently going crazy under the bright lights. The team we were playing, Fairfield Academy, was known for its killer baseball team, but they had a craptacular football program. The freaking Hokies. They were an insult to anyone who'd ever played at Virginia Tech, and maybe that was the problem. Knowing we could hand these guys a beatdown in our sleep, a fact the radio announcers were so quick to point out the other day, made it hard to care, especially when Ma was hosting a practice party at Ilusiòn tonight. Probably scared it could be one of her last.

"All right, you know what to do," Cameron called, signaling the elongated ending to the chant that wouldn't quit. Kickoff was moments away. Even though the Hokies had elected to receive, I grabbed my helmet, figuring our defense would shut them down quick.

"Go!" the crowd screamed, and my shoulder bumped against Chase while I jumped up and down, trying to psych myself up. I could already hear the announcer's reaction if I didn't: "*Well, Kasey, we'd thought this matchup would be a breeze, but turns out, number five totally choked.*"

A hard shove knocked me out of my head, and I glanced over to see Chase staring back with a big, stupid grin. Not wanting to mess with his game, too, I feigned a replica in reply.

"Fight!"

I inwardly groaned. And here it came, the ridiculously extra-long pause that—

"*Win!*"

A lone, high-pitched voice reached my ear, awkward and obviously unfamiliar with the weird pause Cameron had added to the chant at the beginning of last year. I turned around on instinct.

First row, middle of the bleachers, directly behind the fifty-yard line, Lily sat surrounded by Angéla and Sydney, wearing an expression of complete mortification when three full beats later than her own yell, the rest of the fans chimed in, "*Win!*"

Sydney cracked up, grabbing onto Lily's arm as she turned an alarming shade of red.

My sister covered her mouth, her slim shoulders shaking but at least trying to hide her amusement at her new *bestie's* predicament.

And then there was Lily...ah, Lily. My surprisingly funny, annoyingly controlling, and most definitely out-of-her-element dance partner...who winced as her big blue eyes shot to mine.

I swear, I couldn't have stopped the smile stretching my face if Tom Brady or Drew Brees had come down and asked me to.

Choking back a laugh, I lifted my hands to the sides, indicating the electric stadium going nutso around us, and cocked an eyebrow, silently suggesting this was, in fact, pretty damn awesome. Even from the sideline I could see the roll of her eyes, and I laughed out loud, stoked she was having fun. Even if it was somewhat at her own expense.

With the static of the announcers forgotten, and even Ilusiòn's troubles on the backburner, I turned back to watch the kickoff with a wide smile, my eyes landing on Aidan standing near the end of the bench. I raised my chin, still laughing, then focused on the game.

Finally, I was ready to do this.

As expected, our defense dominated the series. With each failed play, my pulse rate kicked higher. The prickle of the lights seeped beneath my skin, and I breathed in the familiar earthy scents of game night. The whistle blew, three-and-out, and our punt return team stormed the field.

With the marching band playing the opening riff from "Eye of the Tiger," the remaining guys strutted back to the sideline, showboating like only true defenders can, and I joined in, yelling and slapping their backs, feeling the hard kick of the drumbeat in my stomach.

Chase slammed his helmet on his head and shoved me. I pushed him back, bouncing on my feet. After a huge return, it was our turn to take the field, and I thrust my helmet on, ready to kick some Hokie ass. Normally, I'd hold back for a series or two. With a team like Fairfield, Coach might've even suggested taking it easy the entire first half. But tonight, I had a girl to impress.

I wasn't holding anything back.

Chapter Sixteen

LILY

"**F**udge stick!"

Shaking my hand, I glared at the evil pushpin that had bit me back, then shoved it into the wall, this time with more zeal. Taking my pain out on an inanimate object seemed healthier than cursing a blue streak, and a heck of a lot more productive. Once it was firmly in place, I smirked to show it who was boss and leaned back to admire my handiwork.

A huge sign declaring *Survivor: 5 Years and Counting!* in bright orange bubble letters carried the theme of the night, along with the bowls of neon orange Cheetos, nacho cheese Doritos, and golden, delicious Funyuns, which, admittedly, weren't orange, but they were tasty. So were the Tostitos and Ruffles, which further messed with the whole motif, but this was a sleepover, which meant if it was salty and yummy and in chip form, it had to be included. Rule number one in the sleepover handbook, at least according to my mom, and lucky for me, I could even partake guilt-free. Bring on the carbs!

Grinning at the room, I sucked my throbbing thumb into my mouth and carefully stepped over the coffee table... only to trip on the upraised corner of the Torres's geometric area rug.

A loud cackle followed my sprightly *thump*, and Sydney's voice floated from down the hall. "Hey, Grace! Is it safe to come out yet?"

I flipped off the air, even though she couldn't see me, then said excitedly, "Come on in!"

Angéla was the first to enter, being not-so-gently pushed by Sydney from behind. She gazed in confusion at the multicolored balloons I'd taped to the edges of various photos of family vacations and dance competitions, and, strangely enough, to the frame around the Virgin Mary, which I was 99.9% sure wasn't sacrilegious. I mean, biblical people had parties, too, right?

Second-guessing that decision, I winced and watched Angéla grab an orange party hat from the entertainment center. Her sweet face was a mask of bewilderment—then she noticed the sign.

Dark chocolate eyes, the exact replica of her brother's, met mine, and her mouth formed one word. "How?"

"Stone," I answered, hoping I hadn't overstepped a boundary. "He told me about your upcoming milestone. I know we haven't known each other long, and I understand it can be hard knowing how to celebrate, or even if you *should*...but coming from the other side of the story, I've seen how easily it could've gone another way."

With a cautious smile, I walked over, hoping the shine in her eyes was from happiness and not pain. "I think it's awesome and inspiring you're a survivor, and we should honor that. So I hope you don't mind, but..." I reached into the duffel bag at my feet and plucked up a sparkly boa, wrapping it around her neck. "We decided to throw you a little surprise party."

While Sydney grabbed the gift box we'd stashed behind the sofa, a present wrapped with pristine orange paper and topped with a huge white bow that could've been done by professionals—Syd never did anything halfway—I reached into my bag and pulled out two more boas.

"You guys." Angéla stared wide-eyed at the box in her hand, gently touching the paper like it held the greatest gift in the world, and she hadn't even opened it yet. "You didn't have to do this. I don't know what to say right now."

"Well, maybe you can start by opening it," Sydney teased, although her hazel eyes looked awfully misty, too. She blinked a couple of times and waved a hand in front of her face, then quickly grabbed a boa from me, looking away as she threw it around her neck.

The old softie.

Angéla released a breath and gently flipped over the box, studying the precise lines of the wrapping for an entry point. Delicately, she slid her finger beneath the seam, tugging the tape up to not rip the paper. It was so cute that my heart hurt a little. When it was finally uncovered, she took another breath, then opened the box and stared at its contents.

"I found a website online," I explained. "Not Another Bunch of Flowers. It specializes in survivor gifts, and the woman who owns it had breast cancer. She donates a portion of her profits to different charities."

A small smile tugged Angéla's lips as she removed the colorful "*I Kicked Cancer's Ass*" pin, and she promptly set down the box so she could pin it to her pajama top.

A hard knot lodged in my throat, wishing I could've had this moment with my mom, but I swallowed it down, wanting tonight to be about Angéla and her story.

With slightly shaky hands, I reached over and removed the second part of the gift. "I discovered 'touch wood' is the English equivalent of 'knock on wood.' Soldiers in WWI used to wear 'touch wood' charms for good luck, and since wood is a traditional gift for five-year anniversaries, and this is your fifth year being cancer-free, we thought it was fitting."

I pulled out the necklace, and the delicate shine in Angéla's eyes swelled to full-on tears. One fell down her cheek as she turned and held up her hair, silently asking me to put it on her. Fighting my own tears, both for Angéla and Mom, I carefully slid the charm around her neck and clasped it.

Angéla turned, her fingers touching the charm. Her voice was soft when she said, "I love it," and after a moment, she raised her head and looked around the decorated room. More tears fell, and she let them go, not even trying to stop them. "I-I love everything. You…you don't understand… what this means."

She drew a breath, looking at us both with eyes holding so much gratitude and surprise and naked vulnerability that my own tears gave up the fight as I grieved my mom and celebrated the sweet life in front of me. A choked sound came from Sydney, and she dragged her hands under her eyes with a watery smile.

Angéla blubbered a laugh. "I'm trying to talk, but I have no words. Seriously, you should mark this down because this never happens to me."

I laughed, too, a half-sob/half-snotty whimper that was disgusting and real and heartfelt, and the next thing I knew, I was wrapped in a three-way hug of tears and new friendship.

From the outside looking in, this moment probably looked weird—three girls blubbering together, one of them practically a stranger. But it didn't feel that way. My heart expanded to hold all the emotion until I felt like how I supposed the Grinch did on Christmas morning. Cool air-conditioning ghosted over my skin, and suddenly, Mom was with us, too.

We were still one big puppy pile when a *beep beep* in the kitchen broke us apart, and I sucked in a ragged breath, dragging my hands over my wet face and feeling twenty pounds lighter than I had that morning. I'd had just enough time to somewhat collect myself when one of the most gorgeous men I'd ever seen waltzed into the room carrying a tall stack of pizza boxes.

A beautiful man and cheesy carbs. Now *that* was what romance novels were made of.

Sydney and I exchanged dual looks of awe as he swept into the room, scooting the chips aside to make room for the pizza. Next to me, my best friend muttered under her breath, "*DILF*," and I stifled a snort, elbowing her in the ribs.

"I hope you're hungry," said the man, who was obviously Angéla's dad. He smiled at us, flashing the same set of dimples made popular by his son. "I'm Mike, or Mr. Mike, if you prefer. I'll answer to either, you're practically adults."

His smile grew curious as he took in our red, puffy eyes, and he transferred his attention to the rest of the room, finally noticing the decorations. Walking over to the wall, he read our homemade sign and placed a hand on his chest. He bowed his head and briefly closed his eyes, and when they opened again, they immediately found his daughter. Angéla flew into his arms.

Sydney shifted uncomfortably next to me, but I couldn't look away from the father-daughter moment. Mr. Mike whispered something in Angéla's ear, and as she nodded, I forced my gaze away, wiping my eyes when a fresh batch of tears sprang free.

"Thank you," he said a few moments later, and I glanced back to see Angéla smiling the sweet smile of a girl who knew she was loved. I quickly bounced my eyes to her dad. He was already watching me. "I appreciate you doing this for my daughter. Lily, is it?"

I nodded, shoving my own family drama in the closet of my mind, and smiled at the man who'd brought me food. That old saying about the stomach being the way to a man's heart? I was here to say that stuff worked on women, too.

"It's a pleasure to finally meet you," he said, a strange note in his voice making me wonder what he meant. Had Angéla talked about me? His wife, Viktória? Or could it have been Stone?

Mr. Mike grinned at the collection of snackage on the coffee table and nodded in approval. "I was gonna say help yourselves to anything in the kitchen, but I think you've already got that covered." He winked to show he was teasing, and twin surges of heat ignited my cheeks.

Sydney simply continued to gawk.

He chuckled, shoving his hands into his pockets. "I'll get out of your hair now. If you girls need anything, I'll be down the hall, and Viktória should be here shortly. And don't forget to save some pizza for your brother."

With a final grin, he wished us good night and headed back to where the bedrooms were. Not five seconds later, and not bothering to lower her voice, Sydney announced to the room at large, "Angéla, your dad is freaking *hot!*"

A masculine chuckle floated from the hall, and Angéla groaned.

Chapter Seventeen

STONE

Casa Winters was a madhouse.

From my vantage point behind the kitchen island, its granite surface covered with liquor bottles and mixers, I surveyed the crowded living room. Wall-to-wall bodies were packed so densely you couldn't see the hardwood. The oppressive body heat battled with the air-conditioning. In one corner of the room, a girl looked like she was crying—not in the sad way that'd make me go over and check on her; more like the psycho, angry way that made my balls shrivel up. In another corner, two couples were huddled in a circle, all four of them with their heads buried in their phones. I fought a wave of disgust. It brought back unwanted memories.

When people stopped to congratulate me, I nodded. Teammates clasped my shoulder; I smiled. I even laughed when a drunk Kurt mounted the antique dining table for an ill-advised striptease to what I was pretty sure was Britney Spears circa 1999. Admittedly, seeing my massive center gyrating to bubblegum pop made me almost hope someone was recording so I could rib him for it later, but I kept myself in the kitchen. I had less than zero interest in joining the chaos.

Something was off. I'd gotten my head out of my ass in time for the game, but now that it was over, I was right back to feeling like a stranger in my skin. Normally, it took a couple of hours for the walls to start closing in, especially after a big win. Tonight, I'd been struggling to breathe since I arrived. I couldn't stop thinking about what Lily had said the other day, about me hiding behind my smiles.

Was that what I'd been doing?

Britney turned into "Pony" by Ginuwine, and as the song that made Channing Tatum a household name blared over the state-of-the-art sound system, I glanced back at the table. Kurt was down to his undershirt, boxers, and tube socks. While the words "*I'm just a bachelor…*" rolled across the room, my normally reserved teammate thrust his hands in the waistband of his shorts.

"Ah, hell." He was going to regret this in the morning.

Before I could even think about stopping him, Kurt spun around. His sports socks slipped on the mahogany table, but he caught himself…and then proceeded to flash the room his huge white ass.

The crowd *whooped* in appreciation. A few girls yelled for him to take it all off. I turned the hell away, shaking my head with a tired laugh.

Maybe I needed a drink. It'd been a long week, and if nothing else, it would get my mind off the troubles with Ilusiòn. Scanning the options, I decided to go with a Crown and Seven, and as I uncapped the bottle and filled the red plastic cup with amber liquid, I found myself wondering what Lily would have chosen.

Was she more of a wine cooler girl, or a salt-of-the-earth, beer-from-the-keg chica? Knowing her, she'd probably stick to water.

Smiling to myself, I grabbed the soda and added it to my cup.

The crazy thing was, if I was home right now, I could've asked her. I also could've found out what she'd thought about the game, if she'd had fun, and if she'd seen me make the impossible throw in the third quarter that put us up forty-nine to three. I smirked as I dropped a couple of ice cubes in the mix. Holy shit. It was a good thing Fairfield's baseball team was nationally ranked because, *damn*.

"Already smiling into your cup, huh?"

Aidan sauntered into the kitchen, brushing past me on his way to the keg. He glanced over his shoulder with a wide smile, but it seemed off. "You deserve to get tanked. I can't even fathom your stats after that performance."

"Hey, I didn't do it alone," I replied, not bothering to correct him about the drink. This would be the first of the night, and I barely even wanted it. "Four of those TDs were yours."

Aidan snagged a Solo cup and pumped the keg. "I didn't see your sister out there," he said, gesturing toward the general bedlam beyond the kitchen. "Where is she tonight?"

I leaned my hip against the granite. "Home. She asked a couple of girls to sleep over."

"Oh yeah?" His cup filled to the brim, he took a long pull, then licked his lips. "Same girls from the game?"

"Yup."

After watching him take another sip, I glanced at my own cup. The sound of glass breaking rose over the cacophony of loud music, obnoxious chatter, drunken hooting, and phones chirping behind me.

Flipping on the faucet, I dumped my untouched drink down the drain. Standing back up, I already felt lighter. "Hey, man, I'm gonna bail." I tossed my cup in the trash and threw up deuces. "See you Monday."

As I turned, I could've sworn I saw him shake his head. When I glanced back at the doorway, Aidan waved and took another sip of his beer, going back to scanning the room. I scrubbed a hand over my face. I was officially losing it. Rolling back my shoulders, I left to look for Chase.

Five minutes later, I found him, past the congested hallway filled with discarded cups and bottles and beyond the massive line outside the bathroom, where someone was definitely puking up their guts. He was in the den, seated on the sofa with a girl wearing a short skirt and a bright pink tank top in his lap and a couple making out next to him.

That wasn't what caught my attention.

What made me pause, halfway across the room, was Chase didn't even seem to notice the brunette rubbing her boobs on his arm. He was leaned in talking to Robbie, who was parked on the coffee table in front of him, and completely ignoring the girl.

"Yo." I stepped over the legs of the guy rounding third on the couch and took a knee so Chase could hear me over the music. "I'm out of here."

He raised his eyebrows in surprise. "You want me to come with ya?"

I shifted back, studying his eyes to see if he was high. They were clear as ever, though they did look bored as shit. "Dude, it's your party."

"The guys will shut it down." He glanced at Robbie, who nodded in the affirmative. "A service is coming in the morning to clean anyway. I can jet if you want."

Shit, now I was gonna look like a dick. My oldest friend had a hot girl on his lap, in the middle of a party of his own making, and he was asking to leave with me. Clearly, the answer I should've given was yes.

"Nah, man." I shifted my gaze to the French doors leading outside. "I promised Angel an empty house for her sleepover. I'm just gonna sneak in, duck into my room, and call it an early night."

Chase's shoulders drooped, and I wrapped a hand around the back of my neck. I almost relented, but I really did promise my sister a quiet house. Plus, a pair of pretty blue eyes swam in my head. Remembering that charged moment in my truck, I leaned in and added, "Besides, they're tearing apart your house, man. Something broke a few minutes ago, and Kurt did a striptease on old Louis."

An amused glint entered his eyes, and I smirked. It'd serve Mrs. Winters right if her cherished Louis XVI dining table got scuffed. Neither she nor her husband could be bothered to attend any of her son's games, which was why I couldn't have been bothered to tell Kurt to get down earlier. Still, someone at least somewhat responsible should hang around to make sure the place didn't burn down.

Plus, I wanted to go home alone.

Chase sprawled back on the couch. "Yeah, that's cool. I better stay anyway. A Fairfield cheerleader said she'd meet me in the pool house in twenty," he told me...still failing to notice the brunette already perched on his lap.

The girl squawked—legit squawked, like a bird—and Robbie fell over laughing.

As Chase winced, his body already shifting forward to protect his junk, I clapped him on the shoulder. "Good luck, man."

Pushing to my feet, I headed straight for the French doors. I didn't even pause to acknowledge the girls who called my name or the guys who slapped my back as I shot past.

I was going home.

Chapter Eighteen

LILY

Carefully stepping around the prone bodies of my friends, navigating the cushy pallet of blankets, sleeping bags, and pillows on the living room floor, I presented the tray of freshly baked cookies with a flourish. "Voila!"

Angéla cheered, as the occasion clearly called for, while Sydney shook her head like I was a dork. Good thing I wore the banner proudly. I could admit, though, that tonight I felt different. I didn't know if it was watching the game, throwing the impromptu party, or just something in the air, but I felt more like myself than I had in a long time—and, since my true self was a major dork, that was what they were getting.

"How long are we supposed to leave these on again?" I asked, gingerly touching the mostly dried green goop on my face. My nails were freshly painted, and I was wearing those weird rubber dividers between my toes. All in all, my mom would've been proud.

"I think this one said twenty minutes," Angéla replied, finishing the polka-dot art on her fingernails. Nail art was on her list of Teen Movie Sleepover Musts, as were the other spa treatments we'd experimented with tonight. A huge pile of DVDs lay scattered across the entertainment center—only a tiny fraction of her massive collection—but so far, we hadn't touched a single one.

Sydney sighed happily. "This reminds me of the sleepovers we had when we were kids, Lil."

I nodded in agreement, and Angéla perked up. "Really? I thought most of these things were Hollywood clichés. I didn't know real, actual people did them." She curled her lip and said, "Man, I had sucky friends."

Sydney sat up and peeled the cucumbers off her eyes. Taking a bite out of one, she said, "We mostly just had each other, Lil and me, but Mrs. Isa would pull us into her bathroom for 'spa time,' and she always had the best junk food."

"Don't forget about the dirt, either," I added. "No sleepover was complete without talking about the latest gossip: who was crushing on who, who had gotten in a fight that week." I shook my head at the memory. In a lot of ways, my mom had been a big kid, and she'd always been my best friend. "The best part, though, was her words of wisdom."

"Definitely," Syd agreed.

"What do you mean?"

"Mom never let a sleepover end without handing out sage life advice," I told her.

Sydney cleared her throat and, affecting my mom's Boston accent so perfectly it made goose bumps dance down my arms, she recited, "Girls, always remember to be the heroine in your own story. You don't need a prince to rescue you."

"*But*, if one does come along," I added with a grin, "snatch him up something fierce and remember to treat him right, because a good man deserves to know he's wanted."

After the words fell, we both sighed, and Sydney crawled over from her side of the pallet to lay her left ear on my shoulder, carefully avoiding the green goop on her cheek. Angéla snuggled up to my other side, doing the same. "I would've liked to have met her," she said softly, and I ran my fingers down her glossy hair.

"She would've loved you," I told her with confidence, and Angéla smiled up at me.

Quiet descended again for about thirty whole seconds, then Angéla sat back up and spun to face me. "I still can't believe you're not going," she complained, picking back up the argument we'd been having since lunch. "It's *senior* Homecoming, Lily. This is it. Our last one ever!"

I shrugged, bouncing Syd's head on my shoulder. "I just don't see what the big deal is. I've never done the school-dance thing. No one's asked me, but even if they had, I probably would've said no. I was always studying."

"Homecoming falls the weekend *after* first quarter exams," Sydney piped in unhelpfully, and I pinched under her ribs. My best friend yelped, totally ticklish, and I sat back victorious. She was supposed to be on *my* side.

"What if my brother asked you?" Angéla challenged, and every muscle in my body chose that moment to jolt. Since they were both practically sitting on top of me, there was no hiding it.

"Th-there's no point in speculating about that," I sputtered. "It would never happen."

Sydney rolled forward to face me, grabbing a pillow to hold in her lap. Plucking the decorative strings, she said, "It'd be awesome, though. I could finally see the two of you dance."

Angéla eyes lit with enthusiasm. "*Girl*, they've got

serious chemistry, let me tell you."

Scoffing loudly—even as my heart did a funny little flip in my chest—I looked at both girls like they were nuts. "The only thing remotely chemistry-related between your brother and me is when I step on his toes and he reacts in pain."

"So you're telling us you don't have any fun at all when you're dancing?" Angéla asked with a scrappy look that said not only was she not giving this up, but she also saw straight through me. I deflated against the couch with a grunt. *Fine.*

"I didn't say I didn't have fun," I muttered, studying my siren-red-painted nails—a bold color I would've never selected on my own. "Surprisingly, I'm actually looking forward to tomorrow's lesson. And I feel closer to Mom when I'm there."

To tell the truth, it was more than that. Despite my best efforts to compartmentalize the lessons to one hour a week, I found myself dancing around the house, practicing the steps I'd learned and even going so far as to search out tutorials on YouTube. I still sucked at them, of course, but they were fun to watch.

"Yeah, yeah, that's great and all," Sydney said, sitting up on her knees. "But I want to know if you're *feeling* Stone there."

I rolled my eyes at her merciless grin. Ugh, this was so embarrassing.

"I guess…" I blew a strand of hair off my face. "I guess he's different than I expected."

Sydney tossed her throw pillow at me. Laughing, I ducked my head and grabbed a second pillow, chucking it back.

"Okay, okay. Yes, I *might* have a slight crush on the boy. Are you two happy now?"

Angéla started squealing and stomping her feet on

the ground, which I took as a yes. Sydney lay back on her section of the pallet with a wide smile. Thinking back to my conversation with Aidan, I felt it necessary to add, "But everyone has a crush on Stone Torres. It doesn't mean anything. It's not like I'm sitting around doodling our names together or planning a wedding. We're friends, and he's hot. That's all."

The lack of any sort of facial change or recognition of my words assured me neither of them was buying what I was selling. I made a distressed sound in my throat. Angéla handed me a cookie, winking as she turned her attention to Sydney.

"Now that we've got *that* out of the way, I want to hear about cuttlefish boy."

The blush that tinted my best friend's ears almost made up for the trauma of the last few minutes. Finally, Sydney had gotten her man, and the way Nick had asked her to Homecoming had been particularly fabulous. He'd met her at the door to AP Bio with a sign that said, "I want to Cuttle with you at the dance." A seriously cheesy line, not to mention a huge stretch of the word, but it'd been perfect for Sydney. She'd absolutely loved it.

Of course, Nick could've grunted and said, "Will you?" and she would've agreed wholeheartedly, too, but it helped that he went the extra mile. He got my seal of approval.

"I've been waiting years for those two to get together," I said, and Angéla turned to me, seeing that Sydney was suddenly Fort Knox. Funny how that happened when *you* were the one on the chopping block.

"Why did it take so long?" she asked, and I raised a questioning eyebrow at Syd, wondering if she wanted to take this one.

She blew out a breath. "I've really only had two

relationships," she said, poking a finger in the mask drying on her cheek. "Both short. Which is fine, because I don't really have time for them. I'm always busy babysitting or doing something for student council. It's just…whenever I do date, I'm always the one to break it off. I always find something wrong with the guy. Some flaw that becomes impossible to ignore. A habit I suddenly find annoying. I'm actually starting to worry there's something wrong with *me*, since I can't seem to stay interested longer than a couple of weeks."

Sydney gnawed at her bottom lip, lost in thought for a second before she looked at us, genuine worry in her eyes. "I really like Nick. He's smart and funny and so damn cute. I've been crushing on him for forever. I want *this* one to work. But what if it doesn't? What if we go out for a couple of weeks and then it just…fizzles? Am I doomed to be single like my mom forever?"

I reached out and put my hand on her foot, squeezing it in a hug. Sydney's mom was a serial dater. She had married Sydney's father, but that only lasted long enough to have Sydney. Her relationships since had resulted in two additional children and a string of broken hearts.

This wasn't the first time Sydney had expressed her worry over her romantic future, so I knew enough not to comment. Her questions were rhetorical, and giving advice would only shut her down.

Angéla, obviously sensing that, too, laid back down. Her black hair spread across her pillow like a dark halo. "I'm definitely not the one to ask," she muttered. "I'm like the opposite of Dr. Phil. A guy has to have balls of steel to show up at my door, what with Ágoston and Chase guarding me, which means my dating history is pathetic."

I took my place between them, scooting back until my

head landed on my pillow. "Does that mean Sean has steel balls?" I asked with a grin. "Because he did ask you to Homecoming."

Angéla scoffed. "Sean's harmless. Trust me, if Ágoston thought for one second I was genuinely interested, it would be a totally different story. He's crazy protective. Even though we're twins, and I'm actually seventeen minutes *older* than him, it doesn't matter. Somewhere along the way, he decided to take on the role of big brother."

Unconscious or not, her hand fell to her touch-wood charm. It was clear why he'd taken on that job.

The moment lingered, and I opened my mouth and closed it several times, wondering if I should push. It really wasn't any of my business, and she deserved to have her secrets. But then, we were friends now, right? And she'd had no qualms about grilling me.

"Angéla…" I scrunched my nose, trying to figure out how to word it. "Could it be there's someone else you would've preferred had asked you to the dance, instead of Sean?"

She rolled her head to the side, and I lifted my eyebrows with a slight smile, hoping she'd spill.

"Ugh." Making a face, she wiggled in her spot on the floor, shaking her shoulders and scissoring her legs like she had a sudden excess of energy she needed to get rid of. I bit back a smile, not wanting to scare her away, but unable to hold it in. She was just so *dramatic*.

"Obviously you've already figured it out," she said, adding an almost comedic sigh while she pushed herself up until she was sitting. "Which is funny because I've officially known you for, what, a *week*, and yet my brother remains utterly clueless. He's such a guy. But yes, given the choice, I would've loved for Chase to have asked me to the dance… or to the movies, or to dinner, or to just about anything that involves being alone with him, because I've been in love with the stupid boy since forever. And while we're at it, I also wouldn't mind having his beautiful babies one day, either. Years from now, like after I'm ruling E! and he's the king of ESPN."

When she saw my lips twitch, Angéla blew a raspberry. "It doesn't matter, though, because Chase thinks of me as a sister. When he looks at me, he sees the tomboy who followed them around when we were kids and the fragile girl who was sick once. Chase visited me in the hospital almost as much as Stone did, and at times, he fusses over me more than my own brother. It's like he thinks I can keel over from exhaustion or a simple allergy attack. When he's not trying to wrap me up in bubble wrap, he's got blinders on. I doubt the guy even knows I have breasts!"

As she grabbed her admittedly impressive rack, I sat up again, and then so did Sydney, and we exchanged a wordless look. "You could always ask him," I said sympathetically. "Show him you're all grown up?"

Angéla huffed a laugh. "*Riiiight.* Look, I'm all for women's lib, but could you imagine how that would go over? Even if my brother would be chill about it—which he wouldn't—I'm telling you, Chase isn't interested. Despite Ágoston's total cluelessness, I'm almost certain Chase knows how I feel, how I've always felt, and he's never once made a move. Or even acted like he wanted to. Hell, he's probably over at his party right now with his tongue down some girl's throat." Her pretty face twisted in a snarl before it dropped, leaving behind an expression of complete heartbreak. "Actually, he's probably doing a lot more than kissing."

Having already watched this beautiful girl cry once tonight, I was in no hurry to repeat the performance, especially when they weren't happy tears. Grabbing the bowl of Doritos from the table, I quickly handed it over, and Angéla accepted it with a watery, grateful smile.

This was why she hadn't wanted to go to the party. I rubbed her back, imagining how many times she'd had to watch the guy she was in love with hook up with someone else. It made me want to grab that invisible bubble wrap Chase supposedly wrapped her in, beat him to within an inch of his life with it, and then wrap her up myself so she never had to feel that kind of heartbreak again.

Staring into a giant bowl of nacho cheese, Angéla took a breath. "I need to move on. I can't keep hoping for a future that's never gonna happen. It's beyond time I got over him, and that's exactly what I'm gonna do."

Lifting her head, she looked around the room, taking in the orange party hats and homemade sign on the wall. "If leukemia taught me anything, it's that tomorrow's not guaranteed. I can't live scared about what could happen... or worse, put my life on hold. Not when today can slip away so quickly."

She popped a chip into her mouth, like she hadn't just challenged my entire outlook on life in thirty seconds, then grabbed the remote for the television. As the colorful box art on Netflix scrolled by, I laid back on the pallet, my mind in a tailspin.

Chapter Nineteen

STONE

Standing outside the back door of my house, I toed off my shoes. I didn't know if the girls were asleep or not. I hoped they weren't, because I wanted to talk to Lily, but if they were, I didn't want to wake them. I grabbed my Nikes and carefully slid open the door—completely forgetting about the warning from the alarm system whenever a door opened.

Beep beep beep.

Well, so much for that plan.

Shaking my head with a soft laugh, I shut the door behind me and continued padding through the kitchen. The scent of vanilla hung heavy in the air. My stomach rumbled, and I followed my nose to the living room, hoping whatever it was they'd baked hadn't been completely devoured. The sound of whispered giggles made me smile.

"Y'all better have saved me some," I called out, turning the corner with a playful smile...and then abruptly did a double take.

Our living room looked like a twelve-year-old's birthday

party had exploded on it. Balloons were taped to the walls, random feathers dotted the floor, and the coffee table and sofas had been pushed back to make room for a pool of blankets and pillows housing an entire chip section of the grocery store, along with three girls who looked like rejects from *The Mask*. All of whom were frozen in place…and staring at me like I was Ghostface from *Scream*.

"What are you doing here?" Angéla asked, at the same time I said, "What in the hell?"

I scanned the room again, this time spying a handwritten sign posted on the wall. I read the words, and my head snapped back to find Lily already watching me.

"Um, yeah, about that." Sitting up, she shoved a section of red hair behind her ear. A nervous smile twitched her lips. "We sort of celebrated a little early."

The soft look in her eyes was apologetic, like she legit thought I'd be mad that she threw my sister a party, when all I could think was how grateful I was. And how incredible this girl truly was.

My chest expanded as I turned to Angéla. I wasn't sure if it was the mask on her face, the atmosphere of the room, or the happiness in her eyes, but she looked younger than usual. Almost like I could see the kid she'd been before life got so totally screwed up.

"Does this mean I can give you my gift early, too?" I asked, and she nodded eagerly. Her beautiful smile cracked the dried green goop on her face, and I choked back a laugh. "Wait right here. I'll be back."

I hustled down the hall to my bedroom, dropped my shoes at the door, and snatched the gift bag from the bottom of my closet. I sucked at wrapping, and this was better anyway. Quicker to get to the good stuff. I hurried back, my palms growing sweaty as I wondered how Angéla would react to what I'd gotten her, but I refused to second-guess myself now. Lily had promised she'd like this. I trusted her judgment.

When I returned to the living room, Angéla's eyes immediately landed on the bright yellow gift bag in my hand and widened in surprise.

"Yeah, I decided to go a different route this year," I said, sneaking a glance at Lily. She gave me a small nod of encouragement, and I handed the present to my sister. "I thought we could reinstate Twin-time. You know, if you wanted to."

Angéla's eyes instantly swam with tears, and as her hands clutched the bag, pure panic rose in my chest.

"We don't have to," I rushed to say, again seeking out Lily for confirmation. She wasn't supposed to cry, dammit! "I just thought—"

"*Shhh!*" Angéla threw up a hand, effectively shutting me up, and dropped to the ground.

She didn't say anything after that—she was too busy plucking tissue paper out of the bag. When she got to the tall stack of books hidden beneath it, she squealed so loud I was afraid she'd woken our parents.

"We, uh, tried to get a mix of everything," I explained, wrapping a hand around the back of my neck. No way was I taking all the credit. None of this would be happening if it wasn't for a certain redhead. "Lily came with me to the bookstore. She knows a hell of a lot more about this stuff than I do."

Angéla held up a book, and my dance partner chimed in. "That's one of my favorites. It's a romance where a girl from the sixteenth century time-travels to modern-day Beverly Hills and discovers the joys of flushing toilets and an American high school while falling for a hot surfer." Lily exchanged a grin with Sydney and said, "We're both Team Austin."

Grinning, Angéla clutched the book to her chest, then dug some more. Each new discovery got a smile and a reverent stroke of the cover. Paranormal, fantasy, sci-fi, contemporary, it didn't matter. When she got to the nonfiction one I'd picked out, written by the screenwriter of *The Princess Bride*, her eyes tripled in size and she proceeded to dive right in, sitting in a pool of purple and white tissue paper.

Lily clasped her hands under her chin, joy radiating from her eyes. The smile she sent me could only be described as ethereal. I swallowed hard, feeling grateful and lucky and confused—and everything in between. Overwhelmed, I turned back to my sister.

"I love them!" Angéla declared, hugging the final book to her chest before pushing to her feet. She rushed toward me, and I had half a second to open my arms before she threw herself into them, smearing bits of cracked green crap from her face all over my shirt. I tightened my hold around her, not giving a damn.

"You promise?" I asked, low and against her ear. "If you don't, or there's something else you'd prefer, we'll go tomorrow and return them. It's not a problem."

She punched me in the stomach, shutting me up again, and squeezed me tighter. "I couldn't love them more," she vowed, and a boulder-sized weight lifted from my shoulders.

Over my sister's head, I caught Lily's eyes and mouthed, *Thank you.*

Her lips parted. Somehow, next to the bright green mask, they looked pinker than usual, softer, and she shook her head, downplaying her part in all this. It was something I'd learned quickly about her. Lily didn't do things for accolades or attention. She wasn't Cameron. Lily was the type of girl who'd throw my sister a party and help me buy her a thoughtful gift, then act like it was just another day of the week. Maybe for her it was. Her heart was just that big.

A rush of warmth flooded my chest, followed by a nudge of guilt prodding my skull. This girl…this girl contradicted everything I thought I knew about relationships. There was no drama with Lily. No gameplay. She was sweet and real, and she challenged me more than the most infuriating sports reporter on a slow news day—yet somehow, I only wanted more.

Angéla stepped back, and I forcibly dragged my gaze to my smiling sister.

Reeling like I'd just been blindsided by a three-hundred-pound lineman.

"You're the best brother in the world. You realize that, right?"

Thoughts scattered, brain scrambling, I scratched a phantom itch on my arm, my ears growing hot. "Nah, you're just easy to spoil." Reaching out, I rubbed her head, needing to do something to release the sudden rush of energy, and she knocked my hand away with a groan. But her smile remained, and the look that said I was her hero was back in her eyes. Focusing on that, my rapid pulse calmed. In a quiet voice, I told her, "Love you, Angel."

"I love you, too."

Shifting on my feet again, I surveyed the room. Three different stares were trained on me. One was filled with sisterly affection. Another held curiosity and amusement, with just enough intensity to make me feel like a bug trapped under a microscope. The last one had me wanting to run from the room, even as my fingers twitched to touch.

Lily's eyes swam with open adoration and naked fear.

It was a toss-up which one affected me more.

I rocked back on my heels, the need to escape winning out. "Sorry for invading girls' night," I said, taking a step closer to the hall. I opened my mouth to say good night, then spied the tray of cookies on the makeshift bed. My stomach growled. Loudly.

High-stepping it over the pile of pillows, I bent to grab a few cookies for my room, and my eyes locked with Lily's again. Subtle rays of white were shot through the crystal blue, like thin bolts of electricity. I hadn't noticed that before.

For a second, I hovered there, staring into the pair of eyes I'd spent way too much time thinking about lately. Without her glasses on, they seemed bigger, bluer. And so damn honest.

A delicate throat cleared behind me, and my head snapped up. Lily blushed, and I proceeded to grab a handful of cookies from the tray, hoisting them in the air like they were a goddamn treasure.

My sister snorted, and when I shot her a pointed look, she grinned back, looking annoyingly pleased. It was definitely time to call it a night.

Backtracking to the hall, I snagged one of the pizza boxes from the table and announced, "Night, everyone."

"Night, Captain," Angéla replied in a singsong voice, a soft giggle trailing her words.

Clenching my jaw, I fled to my room.

A creak sounded outside my door. My phone said it was a quarter past three, which meant I'd been locked in my room for two and a half hours, beating my head against the pillow. A hundred and fifty minutes later and I still didn't have an answer.

Since when did *Lily Bailey* have me tied up in knots?

This was my awkward dance partner. A girl who got hot studying for the ACTs. Why was I acting like an insecure virgin with a crush? This was supposed to be my year *off* from girls. I was going to focus on football, get my ticket out of here, and help my parents with the studio. The last thing I needed was to get all twisted up in relationship drama again, but that's exactly what I'd get if I gave in to this need to make her mine. Because while *Lily* might be theatrics-free, the shoebox filled with money in my closet screamed Greek tragedy.

Another sound came, this time a slight shuffle on the carpet in the hall, and I sat up. That one I hadn't imagined. Someone was out there, and while it could've been Dad or Angéla or even Sydney, I knew who I wanted it to be. Even if it did complicate things.

I pulled open my door and stuck my head out. No one was there.

Disappointed, I glanced down the hall. Yellow light glowed from beneath the closed bathroom door. With my hand clenched around the doorknob, I contemplated going back to bed. It was late, and I had a long day tomorrow. But I was up, and my brilliant plan to snag food hadn't included anything to wash it down.

That was the story I was going with, anyway.

As I padded down the hall, I listened for whispers or giggles, a sign the girls were still awake, other than the bathroom light. All I heard was silence. When I made it to the living room, I could make out two bundles curled on the floor but couldn't tell who was missing.

I lingered for a second, then continued into the kitchen

with soft steps. Grabbing a water from the refrigerator, I removed the cap and took a long pull while I stood there to quench my thirst. And to waste time.

Yup, I was an idiot.

Wiping my mouth with the back of my hand, my disgusted gaze landed on my parents' darkened office. Since I was already an idiot, I might as well be a useful one.

On quiet feet, I slipped in, closed the door, then switched on a lamp. Dim amber light revealed a cabinet, short bookshelf, and two full-size desks crammed into the tiny space. One held a large calendar, marked with Dad's work schedule, my games, and Angéla's upcoming dance competition, as well as a crystal 2015 Officer of the Year trophy in the corner. The other was meticulously organized. A magazine holder corralled the latest copies of *American Dancer*, a variety of rose-gold bins held accessories, and to the right of the laptop, a file sorter displayed colored folders.

Inside the one labeled "Unpaid Bills," I found what I needed.

Due to consistently rising maintenance costs, it has become necessary to increase your rent.

I grit my teeth, doubting costs had risen much, and found the new amount typed in black ink a few lines down. Beside it, written in red, was a lower number, along with the difference between them.

Five hundred dollars. That was how much they'd raised the monthly rent. Coming out of the slow summer season, and on the tail-end of Dad's hospital bills from the accident, that was a small fortune my family didn't have.

Anger consumed me. It was tempting to crumple the paper in my fist or take it to my parents, demanding they stop shutting me out. That they let me help. But Dad would just say he had it handled, and Ma would tell me not to worry. That was like asking the Pope not to pray.

I closed my eyes as a feeling of powerlessness washed over me. My parents had put their lives on hold when Angéla was sick, and they'd scrimped and sacrificed to send me to the best football camps every summer. After everything they'd done, I needed to do my part and help fix this for *them*.

With a frustrated sigh, I found when the rent was due — the fifteenth — and returned the notice to the file before stalking out of the room.

Thanks to Mr. Bailey, I had enough to cover almost two and a half months of the increased rent. It was just a patch, but it'd be enough to get us over the hurdle come November when our savings ran out — especially if Lily stuck with the lessons and a few more students enrolled. Just a handful should be enough to at least keep us afloat. But I still had no explanation for how I'd scored the cash.

The other problem was Lily. The closer we got, the more it felt like her dad's money was a bribe, or at least a dirty secret. I'd shaken the man's hand and promised not to tell his daughter about our deal, so coming clean wasn't an option. Neither was giving it back.

Lost in my head, trying to decide the right course, I didn't see the figure in the hallway until I was almost on top of her.

Lily was dancing outside my bedroom, her weight shifting from foot to foot as she peeked inside my open door and then backed away. Even as the guilt ate another hole in my chest, I couldn't fight a smile. Seeing her eased the tension threatening to strangle me. It was selfish, but I needed more of that calm.

I crept closer and a shot of citrus hit my nose. Leaning in close, I whispered, "Boo."

"Oh, shit!"

Lily jumped and spun around, her hand slapping the wall outside my room. I clamped my lips shut to keep from laughing, not wanting to wake anyone up, and her hand flew to her heaving chest. Amused, I folded my arms and leaned a shoulder against my doorjamb.

I'd never heard her curse before. How in the hell was *that* adorable?

Lily blew out a breath. "You scared me."

I wanted to point out she was skulking outside *my* room, but I didn't. Smiling, I took in her fresh face, her skin pink and glowing—presumably a byproduct of the atrocious green mask—and noticed the blue of her eyes seemed deeper than usual. She still wasn't wearing her glasses, and I zeroed in on the bolts of white I'd recently discovered.

Playing nervously with her fingers, she glanced at the floor. "I, uh, thought you might've gone back to Chase's."

Uncertainty, laced with what sounded like relief, underscored her tone, and my eyebrows drew together. On impulse, I slid a section of reddish-gold hair behind her ear. "No, sweetheart, I'm still here."

An inner voice mocked me. *Way to go, Captain Obvious.*

I swear, I was normally better at this.

Girls had always come easily to me. When I wanted to turn on the charm, it was usually second nature. With *this* girl, though, I could never find my footing.

Lily slowly raised her eyes back to mine, and as my hand trailed down her soft cheek, the natural pinkish hue turned brighter. Swallowing hard, I stepped back.

"You wanna come in?" I asked, gesturing toward my room. She glanced inside, and I followed her gaze to the unmade bed. Then further, to the opened closet door across from it. On second thought... "Actually, I have a better idea."

Taking her hand, I led her back down the hallway. We walked through the quiet living room and across the noiseless kitchen, out through the back door. The stupid chime went off again, and I quickly shut it, sending up a silent prayer that no one followed us.

Out on the deck, I plugged in the lights strung across the ceiling. They gave off just enough glow we could see where we were going without wrecking the mood. I paused near the fire pit. The temperature had fallen to the mid-sixties, which wasn't cold to anyone living above the Mason–Dixon, but this was Texas. For some people, that was downright chilly. I turned to Lily, and she shook her head, so I grabbed a picnic blanket from the storage box just in case, and she followed me to the patio set. I'd never been more nervous in my life.

Tonight felt pivotal. Like we were perched on an old-school teeter-totter. If I pushed up and took a chance, everything would change—we'd be in a relationship, because there was no going halfway with a girl like Lily, and my plan for the year would be toast. If I chose to stay still, senior year would be a breeze—I'd keep my priorities, focus on my family and my game, and the Boosters would be happy. Without a doubt, inaction was the choice everyone in our town would want me to make…well, everyone other than my romance-obsessed twin.

But what did *I* want?

The answer to that question hesitated a moment before sliding back on the two-cushioned love seat. When I sat beside her, my leg brushed against her smooth, soft skin, and I stifled a groan. A jolt of electricity skittered across my thigh, and my fingers flexed with the need to touch. Instead, I scraped them through my hair and focused on the backyard.

Only a thin thumbnail of moon was visible, leaving most of Ma's prized garden in shadow. Her angel fountain gurgled faintly in the corner. A gentle breeze sent the wind chime swaying above us with a musical *cling*. Over near the tree line, a low *tweep tweep* made me smile.

If a fiberglass carousel frog made Lily squeal, what would she do if she knew a Rio Grande Chirping Frog was squatting less than fifty feet away? Would she scream…or crawl into my lap?

She sighed beside me, relaxing against the cushions, and I put my foot on the low table, trying like hell to do the same. My knee bounced while I breathed in her fruity, tropical scent, and I willed my racing thoughts to chill.

Minutes passed. Night sounds swelled between us. It was nice, in a way, not feeling the need to talk. Everyone in my life seemed to hate silence. Get Angéla going, and she could give a dissertation on anything. Chase constantly quoted stats or broke down games. He called it practice for his future broadcasting career. Even my parents were talkers.

Sometimes, though, I craved quiet. I liked turning off the noise and just being still. When the world went crazy around me—like it was now with Ilusiòn in trouble and Mr. Bailey's money in my closet, or when announcers and *helpful* citizens chimed in with their thoughts on my performance—sitting in silence was the only way I could think.

After a few more minutes, my restless tapping slowed, and my head was finally clear enough to tease her. "So…did you have *fun* tonight?"

Lily laughed. "Sleepovers aren't exclusive to high school, you know. In fact, they primarily rule elementary, and they'll be even more fun in college. No adults or rules to worry about." She wiggled her eyebrows. "Think about it."

What made it cute was she wasn't flirting, at least I didn't think she was, or insinuating anything, either. She was simply being her. I shook my head with a begrudging grin. "I guess

I can give you that. Round two goes to you."

"Yay!" Eyes wide, she held up her hands for spirit fingers, and we both laughed. The comforting scent of my mom's flowers floated on the wind.

After another minute, Lily rested her head on the cushion. "Can you believe our lesson is in six hours? Ugh. I should warn you, my clumsiness is amplified when I'm tired."

"I'll be sure to wear steel-toe boots," I replied, smirking when she sent me a mock glare. She shifted again, bringing her knees up to tuck them inside her oversize red-and-white T-shirt, and I reached over to drape the picnic blanket around her shoulders. She smiled in thanks, and I nodded to her shirt. "So, why Harvard?"

Lily pursed her lips. "Is this an off-the-challenge-record question, or are you trying to win another point?"

I laughed and held up my hands. "All rules are suspended for the night," I promised. "I seriously want to know. Why the obsession with the Ivy League?"

"Why not?" she tossed back with a grin. "It's where my parents met, it's a great school, and getting in Early Action will ensure I've got a spot."

I didn't buy it. "There's got to be more to it," I said, and she shrugged a shoulder.

"It's what I've always planned to do."

When she rested her head again, hair falling across the worn cushions, the decorative lights—Angéla called them fairy lights—illuminated her face. A small smile curved her mouth, and as her eyes seemed to shift into a memory, a kick of attraction hit my gut.

Damn, she was pretty.

"Mom was from Boston," she said, the gentle smile widening. "She loved growing up there and said she'd planned on staying a Yankee for life—*until a cowboy stole her heart.*" The last part was said with an accent, and from her wistful tone, she'd obviously been quoting her mom. "After they graduated, she followed Dad to Texas, which is why she said college was where her real life began. It was the catalyst for her happy ending."

Lily sighed, and her mouth turned down at the corners. "Harvard was where she found her place in the world," she murmured, almost like she was talking to herself. "It's where I hope to find mine, too."

I took her hand, losing the fight not to touch her and wanting to erase the lost look in her eyes. She squeezed my fingers, and her expression cleared. "When Mom was dying, we talked a lot about the future. She hated that she wouldn't be able to see me go to college, but I told her she'd always be with me and that it was okay because she already knew what my future held. I'd make valedictorian and then go on to Harvard, the same way she did. The same way we'd planned since I was a kid."

A cloud passed, shifting the dim moonlight across the ground. Listening to her talk about her mom, I understood why she pushed herself so hard. I also thought her reasoning was skewed, but I was in no place to judge. I was more lost than she was.

Lily released a slow, steady breath, then rolled her head along the cushion to face me. "What about you, QB? Why the fixation on high school?"

Shit. I should've known she'd turn the tables. Looking away, I focused on the tree house I'd built with Dad when I was eight, hoping I could wait her out.

"Please, Stone?" Her voice was soft and sweet, and there was no way I could deny her.

Sliding my hand out of her grip, I swiped my palms down the length of my basketball shorts and sank back into the

lumpy cushion. My foot started tapping again. Damn. I was
really going to admit this out loud.

"This might be it for me." I paused, letting the words
settle. They hadn't been as hard as I'd expected. "People talk
about high school being their glory days. That could very
well be my story. Right now, I'm king. Football is my ticket
to college, but no one knows what'll happen once I get there.
And after that, I'm not playing professionally. Everyone
expects it, but it's not what I want to do. The thing is, I don't
know *what* I want. It's not like I'm good for much else."

Sensing she was about to argue, I held up a hand,
needing to get it out now that I'd started. "Lily, if I fizzle
out in college, these could be the best years of my life. So
for you to say they don't even matter…when it's the only
thing I have going for me?" I blew out a harsh breath. "What
does that say about me?"

Her mouth fell open. Blinking incredulously, she shook
her head as she slowly slid her knees out from beneath her
shirt and scooted over until our shoulders touched. Placing
her warm hand on my leg, right where my skin and the hem
of my shorts met, she said, "Stone, you are so much more
than football."

My teeth clenched. I didn't need her blowing smoke up
my ass. I'd had enough hero-worship to last a damn lifetime.

"I'm serious," she said, squeezing my thigh, and sparks
of energy crackled over my skin. "You're incredible. The
way you are with Angéla…the way you are with *me*. How
protective you are. Anyone can see you're a natural leader,
and I've been in enough classes with you to know you're
smart. Maybe you haven't figured out what you want to do
right now, but that's okay. You've got plenty of time."

Tightening my jaw, I traced a path across the back of
her hand. Pale white skin against my golden brown. Our

skin tones were one of the many examples of how we were different. But listening to her, it felt like maybe Lily got me in a way other people didn't. A strange feeling worked its way through my chest. A blend of hope and relief trailed by guilt.

"I *see* you, Stone. I see how you set yourself apart, even when you're the center of the crowd. Even now, in the middle of the night, I can see you're struggling. You take life on like it's your job to fix everything, and you refuse to share the burden." She squeezed my leg again, urging me to look at her. "Talk to me. Please. I want to help you handle whatever it is. You just have to let me."

God. The emotion in my chest constricted, making it hard to breathe. How did she do it? Lily knocked down every wall I put up, saw through every front. A part of me wanted to take a chance. Tell her about Ilusiòn and, hell, screw my promise and even tell her about the deal I made with her dad. The other part wanted to change the topic and avoid this conversation altogether.

I lifted my eyes and found hers already on me, waiting. The hand on my thigh pulsed with a final squeeze…and I surrendered. At least partially. Drawing a deep breath, feeling the oxygen fill my parched lungs, I put my hand on top of hers. "Ilusiòn's in trouble."

Those three words set off an avalanche.

For the next five minutes, I unloaded on her—I told her how the studio had been Ma's dream, how Dad had helped make it happen, and how I'd do almost anything to make sure they kept it. I told her everything. Everything *except* how far I'd already gone. Staring into Lily's kind, compassionate eyes, I couldn't find the courage to admit the full truth, but I silently begged her to understand. It was possibly the closest I'd get to the apology she deserved.

When I was done, the entire mess laid at her feet, Lily flipped her hand over, threading our fingers together. "I wish I had answers for you. I promise I'll do whatever I can to help, though. Ilusiòn's important to more than just your family. It means a lot to mine, too."

"I know," I told her, my voice rough from overuse. "And talking about it took some of the weight off. Not feeling alone…" I released a breath. "It helps."

Her entire face lit up in a relieved smile, and she laid her head on my shoulder.

A sense of peace I'd never felt before rushed through my body. This girl got me. She cared, and she believed in me. More than anything else, that hit home. Her honest faith meant more than any backslap or praise I'd ever gotten on a field.

I never knew it could be like this. Girls, relationships, they'd always been so superficial. I'd taken it because I thought that was all there was, even though I'd seen my parents' relationship firsthand. Lily made me realize their connection wasn't a fluke. It was *real*.

I looked at her head on my shoulder, the fairy lights setting the red-gold strands on fire like toasted cinnamon, and my heart lodged in my throat. Swallowing it down, I asked, "Why couldn't you have taken lessons years ago?"

She made a pleased sound, and her body curved against mine. After a moment, she lifted her head and peered up at me from beneath her lashes. "You weren't ready for me yet."

She smiled—not quite flirtatiously, but damn close—and her gaze fell to my mouth.

My pulse drummed in my ears. I recognized the heat in her eyes, and an answering one was already building within me. It'd been building all night. Lily's pink tongue swiped across her parted lips, leaving them wet and glistening, and my entire world boiled down to one thought: *Do they taste as good as they look?*

Slowly, I raised my eyes and made my choice.

"Maybe not," I admitted. I'd been a clueless idiot, and the truth was, I probably hadn't been ready before. The increased pant of Lily's sweet breath coasted across my chin, and I waited until those big blue eyes were locked on mine again before saying, "But I'm ready now."

Her whole body went still.

Not looking away, not wanting to read this wrong, I lowered my head and watched as Lily's eyelids drooped. She tilted her chin, offering me her mouth…and I took it.

The first brush was easy. Sweet, like her, and so damn soft. Twisting on the seat, I brought my hands up to cradle the sides of her face, and she made a low noise in the back of her throat. She grabbed hold of my wrists and pressed harder against me.

I smiled, triumphant. Then, I deepened the kiss.

Lily tasted like mint and vanilla. Groaning, I swept my tongue into her warm mouth, and she responded with a tiny, tentative flick. I felt it in my toes. Sliding a hand around her head, I knotted my fingers in the silkiness of her hair, tugging her even closer, and she sighed.

I could get addicted to that sound.

My free hand dropped to her hip. Wanting to explore but also not wanting to push, I kneaded the soft flesh through her oversize T-shirt. Lily wasn't so cautious. Her hot skin on my stomach was like a brand, and I hissed a breath. She raked her nails across my abdomen, flinging her long leg over my lap, and I gripped her hips, yanking her higher.

With shy hands, Lily traced every line of my abs. As she did, little whimpers escaped her lips, and I sent up a silent shout of thanks to every coach who'd ever made me do a sit-up. If it kept her hot hands on me and those sexy noises in her throat, I'd do two hundred of them a day.

When air became a necessity, I broke away, sliding openmouthed kisses down her throat. Her citrus scent surrounded me. At the sensitive hollow where neck and shoulder met, I lowered my forehead, breathing her in, and wrapped my arms around her. Lily slid her hand between us and placed it over my heart, where it pounded beneath her fingertips.

My hands were shaking. My entire body felt like it'd been electrocuted. Alive and tingling and like fireballs were zinging through my veins. More than lust, this felt *right*. We already had a connection that was stronger and deeper than anything I'd ever experienced. Staying still may've been the safe choice, but I'd never taken the easy road before, and I wasn't about to start now.

A niggle of guilt prodded my skull, reminding me of the things left unsaid, but I shoved it aside for later.

Lily shivered in my arms. Pressing a kiss at the base of her neck, I lifted my head. Her eyes were dazed, her hair a tangled mess from my fingers, and her lips were red and kiss-swollen. She was beyond beautiful.

"Wow." Gingerly, she touched her mouth, like she was making sure it was still there. Her shoulders rose and fell on a breath, and her gaze intensified on mine. "Give me a few minutes, and then we are *so* doing that again."

I busted out laughing. God, this girl. A sensation of lightness floated through my chest, and I yanked her on top of me, twisting my body as I lay us down on the cramped love seat. I'd get her back to the living room before my parents woke up.

For now, though? She was mine.

Chapter Twenty

LILY

Exhaling a short breath of confidence, I popped open Debbie's door. Stone's cousin Gabriel had dropped her off last night, freshly detailed, after fixing her up and pretty much cleaning out my bank account. It was totally worth it. My girl was back and running great—or as good as she'd been before the alternator issue, anyway—and now I could turn my focus to other things. Namely, impressing my boyfriend's parents at their family barbecue.

Gah! That word still boggled my mind. *Boyfriend.* Stone Torres was my boyfriend.

What the actual hey?

It was so incomprehensible that when he'd casually dropped the term while asking me to Homecoming last night—yep, I was officially going to the dance, and with the hottest guy *ever* to boot!—I'd actually asked him to repeat himself twice. Ever since, I'd made a habit out of whispering it to myself every thirty minutes, hoping it'd sink in. With only thirty-two hours having passed since he kissed me (eep!!!), thus kicking off our new status, I was cautiously optimistic I'd believe it eventually.

Shaking out my hands, I turned back to grab the chocolate cake I'd picked up at the bakery—because everyone liked chocolate, right?—then walked to the front door. The lively beats of a Spanish song floated on the wind, and I bopped my head to the rhythm. After knocking a couple times with no answer, I tried the bell, and when I got the same result, I figured they'd already moved things outside. Following the delicious scent of charred meat and the music that was quickly becoming my life's soundtrack, I made my way to the backyard.

At the gate, I hesitated. Would it be rude to let myself in? After all, I'd only known this family a couple weeks. Then again, they *had* invited me, and after getting *this close* to whatever was on that grill, there was a high probability my stomach would revolt if I left.

Deciding to fake a confidence I didn't feel, I rolled back my shoulders. Putting on a smile, I lifted the latch and entered the loud, boisterous backyard.

Three steps in, my feet froze.

The entire Torres family was laughing. Big belly laughs, quiet giggles, and every happy noise in between. Mr. Mike and a woman I assumed was his mother were spinning and twirling across the yard, maneuvering around a large dining table and past rosebushes as air shimmered above the grill. Angéla and Viktória—*I should probably call her Mrs. Viktória*—stood with their heads together, watching the mother-son dance, and Stone observed from the love seat...the same love seat where he'd kissed me two nights ago...with a small smile on his lips.

For a second, the memories were overwhelming. Dad working the grill while Mom flitted among the neighbors, making sure everyone was comfortable. Replace the Latin beat with classic rock, and a similar scene once played out in my own backyard—but that felt like forever ago. Closing my eyes, I took a deep breath and whisked away the vision.

Today was not a day to be sad. Today was a day of new beginnings.

With that in mind, I relaxed my shoulders and wiped my free hand on my denim skirt. I'd found it in the back of my closet and paired it with a cute white top Sydney had forced me to buy last year. I'd had to take the tags off, but luckily it still fit. I was hoping the outfit said, "*nice girl totally worthy of your incredible son.*"

Admittedly, I was expecting a lot.

"Strange, right?"

Before my eyes, two drinks materialized—a water bottle dripping with condensation and an equally cold can of Sprite. The drinks were attached to Chase's hands, and as he wiggled them in offering, I smiled awkwardly and took the bottle, shivering as a drop of icy water slid down my wrist.

Chase nodded, sliding the cake box from my hand and setting it on a chair. Then he turned back to people watch beside me.

"Uh, what's strange?" I asked, sneaking a look at him. After my heart-to-heart with Angéla, I wasn't sure how I should act around Stone's best friend anymore. Not that I'd known how to act around him before our talk, either. Chase and I belonged to two different worlds.

"Them," he answered, lifting the Sprite toward the general backyard. "If I hadn't grown up with the twins, I'd swear this was all for show."

"What do you mean?"

"Well, I don't know about you, but my house isn't like this. My family's closer to the Kardashians than the Bradys, minus the reality show and with more passive-aggression."

"Ah." I nodded with understanding, uncapping my water bottle. "Yeah, this isn't my life, either."

Not anymore.

He slid me a tight-lipped grin and tapped his drink against mine. We both took a sip. I found it interesting he'd used a pop culture reference to explain his family's dynamic, which was something Angéla would've done.

"Are you the family disappointment, too?" he asked, quirking an eyebrow. He pointed to himself. "See, my parents think I'm a screw-up, though it doesn't help I plan to major in sports broadcasting." He wiggled his fingers, like the profession was equal to satanic worship, then said in a snide, booming voice I assumed represented his dad, "Every self-respecting Winters goes to medical school."

He took another sip and turned back to watch the dancing. I watched him.

"Chase, why are you telling me this?" He shot me a guarded look, and I said, "I don't mean to be rude, it's just... we don't know each other very well. Why tell me something so personal?"

Caution softened into a small smile. "We're not that different, you and me. We're both outsiders with our faces pressed against the glass, wanting in, and these people"—he waved his drink toward the picture-perfect family—"they're good. Every single one of them. They don't judge or expect anything. Once you're in, you're in." Chase dropped his gaze to the hand fidgeting at my side. "You don't need to be nervous here. You're already accepted."

My hand stilled, and he shot me a wink. After taking another sip of his soda, he walked away whistling, and I released a shaky breath. "Okay, don't be nervous. Just be yourself. Except, maybe not so klutzy."

I sighed at the unlikelihood of *that*, grabbed my cake

box, and waltzed into the yard. Angéla was the first to spot me. "Girl, it's about time you got your butt here. I'm freaking starving!"

And just like that, my nerves flittered away.

Mrs. Viktória swept me up in a welcoming yet slightly awkward hug, considering I was still holding the cake, and Mr. Mike appeared behind her shoulder to whisk it away with a grin. When he returned, he introduced me to his mom, who insisted I call her Abuela.

"Everyone does," she announced, pulling me into a warm, floral-scented embrace.

Other than Angéla, and I assumed Chase, I wasn't sure if anyone knew I was now Stone's girlfriend or if they simply saw me as Angéla's friend or even an overeager student. I had a hunch that to them, the title didn't matter. I was welcome here. Period, end of story. And standing in the middle of this group of enthusiastic, loving people, I felt exactly as Chase had said I would—accepted. There was no room for anxious flare-ups or nervous energy. At least not the familiar, dreaded kind. There was a whole *other* kind of nervous, excited energy still running through my veins, though.

Dark chocolate eyes were watching me. I'd lost track of Stone when his family surrounded me, but I felt him close. It made my belly cramp and my pulse skip a beat.

When his grandmother stepped back, I discreetly searched the yard. My breath caught when I found him. A few feet away, he was standing with his bottom lip trapped between his teeth and a look on his face that said he wanted me in his arms every bit as much as I wanted to be there.

Holy Hades, the boy was *hot*.

Wearing camo-printed cargo shorts, a black V-neck tee, and black leather flip-flops revealing the tops of his feet and long, slender toes, he made me want to pour the bottle of ice-cold water over my head. Never once had I found toes sexy before, but after getting a glimpse of Stone's…yep, they totally were.

Mrs. Viktória clapped. "All right, my darlings, make a plate!"

After swallowing the excess saliva in my mouth—and trying *not* to swallow my tongue in the process—I followed Angéla to the pop-up table loaded with food. It almost looked as mouthwatering as Stone.

Again, I felt his eyes tracking my every step, and when a shadow fell over my arm, followed by the intoxicating scent of Ivory soap mixed with wintergreen, I grinned in anticipation.

"You look beautiful," he whispered, snagging my pinkie finger with his as he stopped beside me.

A jolt of excitement traveled up my arm and pinged low in my belly.

"So do you," I whispered back, then promptly blushed. "I mean, manly. Er, sexy. Hot?"

Behind me, Angéla snickered, and the warm blush deepened into a forest fire.

Curse you, pale skin!

"You look nice, too," I finally muttered, closing my eyes and hiding my face against his rock-hard arm. I could just stay here for the rest of the day. No need to make eye contact or say anything else ridiculous. This was safer.

Stone's body shook with silent laughter, and he pressed a quick kiss to my head. "My favorite was sexy," he admitted, and I playfully slugged him in the ribs. He hunched over, pretending it had hurt, and I rolled my eyes, focusing back on the table.

We each filled our plates to overflowing with

deliciousness, then everyone took a seat around the large table. I kicked off my sandals and tucked in with gusto.

Everything was incredible. The salsa was spicy, the meat tender, the barbecue sauce sweet and tangy. Of course, it didn't take long before I dropped some of it on my cute white top—this was *me*, after all—but Mrs. Viktória brought out club soda, which helped with the stain. It also left me with a wet boob. *Sigh*.

Throughout the meal, I kept sneaking glances at Chase and Angéla. They were a puzzle. He never stopped trying to engage her in conversation, asking questions and making comments, but she, sticking to her sleepover vow, always kept her responses short. The flashes of hurt on Chase's face were unmistakable, and I couldn't help feeling sorry for the guy, especially after the surprising pep talk he'd given me earlier. Then I'd remember Angéla's face Friday night, and I was confused.

All in all, wet boob and confusion aside, the meal was amazing. Seated next to Stone, with his left hand drawing tiny circles on my knee, the kiss of the sun against my skin, and the prickle of grass on my bare feet, I felt like I was in the middle of one of Angéla's rom-coms. Even dancing at the studio yesterday had felt different. Being in Stone's arms and seeing the smile he seemed to reserve just for me had made me feel special, even though I'd been half asleep from our late night of stolen kisses. And most likely resembled an extra from *The Walking Dead*.

It wasn't just him, either. The lesson itself meant more now that I understood the studio's history and its troubles. Stone wasn't alone in his worry; *I* needed Ilusiòn to stay open. Not only because I cared about his family, but because it was a connection to Mom.

It was halfway through my second helping of rice when

Angéla, evidently, had enough.

"Ugh, I can't take it anymore! Can we *please* talk about Homecoming?"

Mrs. Viktória pursed her lips in confusion. "What do you mean, loves?"

"Ágoston asked Lily to the dance last night," she announced to the table at large, "and he refused to tell me the whole story. I'm sorry, I tried to be patient, but you guys know I suck at that."

One by one, almost as if they'd planned it, the entire group turned to me. Varying shades of interest colored their faces, and my own, which had only just returned to its near-Casper-like quality, instantly flamed. Stone shifted beside me, and Angéla made a puppy dog face.

"Please, Lily? I got to see the *before* when I snuck into the garage and found him working on it, and later, after I hounded him, he confirmed you said yes. But I need to know the *middle*." In an instant, her imploring look transformed into a grin, and she turned to her mom. "The way he asked her was so *cute*."

Stone looked affronted. "It wasn't cute. It was romantic," he grumbled, and a flash of insecurity hit his face. I covered the hand on my knee and squeezed. As he looked at me, the uncertainty slowly faded from his eyes, and he sighed. "You can tell them if you want."

I searched his face, and when he nodded with a small smile, a huge grin took over mine. The whole thing *had* been magical, and I hadn't gotten to squeal about it with anyone yet.

I set my napkin on the table, suddenly eager to spill.

"Okay, so last night, I was studying for statistics when I got a text," I explained, fighting back a laugh at Angéla's animated expression. She set her elbows on the table and leaned in. "It said, 'knock, knock,' which I thought was kind of odd, especially when he didn't say anything after I replied, 'who's there?' So, I went to the front door. When I opened it"—I glanced at Stone—"he was standing there with gold spray-painted fingers, holding a homemade Snitch and a sign that said, 'I'm Seeking a homecoming date…and I think you're a Keeper. P.S. Long Live Gryffindor.'"

I fell back in my seat with a dreamy smile, and matching ones lit up the faces of his sister, mother, and grandmother. As the women collectively *aww*ed, proving how romantic it had been, and his dad nodded with pride, I heard a faint snort come from Stone's other side.

Under the table, away from Abuela's keen eyes, my man flipped off his best friend, and Chase laughed, putting his hand on Stone's shoulder. "I'm teasing, dude. The first trick to women is knowing your audience, and clearly, you nailed that. Awesome job."

Angéla made a face, and I quickly corrected, "More like *excellent* job."

Despite my bluster about school dances, I'd been downright giddy. I still was. Stone's invite hadn't been public like Sydney's or Angéla's, and the entire school wasn't gossiping about it, but I liked this better. The moment had been just between us, private and perfect—especially since it had ended with another earth-shattering kiss.

I squirmed in my seat, and Stone smirked like he knew where my thoughts had gone. "Homecoming is a milestone high school experience," he teased, leaning over to kiss my cheek. Against my ear, he whispered, "I can't wait to see you in a dress."

Hell's bells. Would it have been considered rude if I'd dumped the entire ice chest over my head?

A short while later, my feet were still barely touching

the floor. I was traipsing through the house on my way back from the bathroom, gliding my fingertips across the cool countertop in the kitchen, when I noticed a large photo album on the island. I leaned in, curious, and gasped.

A young Viktória stared back at me. She couldn't have been older than twelve, and she stood proud and beautiful in a jaw-dropping costume next to an enormous trophy. Just looking at the fierce expression on her face, it was obvious she was born to dance.

Entranced, I tugged the book closer, flipping the page to see more.

"That was back in Hungary," a voice said from behind me, and I winced at being caught snooping. Mrs. Viktória put her slender arm around me. "This was my first big competition. I had been in others, but this one was against some of the best dancers I had ever seen. It was the first time I let myself believe I had a future in dance."

She turned another page and pointed at a large family standing in front of a water fountain. A mom and dad were surrounded by one, two, three…*six* children. Wow.

"When I first started dancing," she said with a small smile, "I did it for all the wrong reasons. My parents pushed me into it, then I wanted to stand out from my siblings. But eventually, I found myself and what I was meant to do." She looked at me. "Now, I dance for me and no one else."

My hand shook on the counter. She couldn't have possibly known what those words meant, or that I'd been searching for where *I* fit in the world and what *I* was meant to do. But her green eyes stared into mine like she was conveying some sort of message.

"You know, I, too, lost my mother young," she said, her intense eyes warming. My breath caught. "Dancing helped me deal with the pain of her passing. I danced my heartache.

I danced my anger. I found peace in the movement."

I lowered my head, and the old photos blurred with unshed tears. Mrs. Viktória gently smoothed her hand down my hair. "Ah, Lily. You remind me so much of myself when I was younger."

I sniffed with a nod. "We both lost our moms."

"It is more than that," she said softly, resting her head against me. "I see myself in the way you dance."

I couldn't help but scoff, which turned into a blubbery, snotty mess, since I was already fighting tears. Mrs. Viktória handed me a napkin, and as I wiped my face, I flipped back to the photo of her standing next to a trophy almost as tall as she was.

"Look at you," I argued. "Even when you were a kid you were winning awards. I'm lucky if I don't trample your son's feet. How can you possibly see yourself in me?"

She smoothed a hand over my hair again, meeting my eyes with a gentle smile. "You show promise," she told me. "Especially when you stop fighting and just dance."

Her green-eyed gaze sharpened with an astute expression. Then, with a comforting squeeze of my shoulders, she walked back outside.

I swallowed hard and returned to the album.

It wasn't the first time I'd been told I got in my own way. My intensity, my drive, tended to overcomplicate things. During my second dance lesson, both Stone and Marcus had told me I was too in my head, and yesterday, I'd even tried to stay in the moment. I'd been moderately successful. There were a few times when I'd started thinking about the steps to come and my feet had gotten jumbled in the present, but luckily, those moments were growing fewer and further between.

Whenever I *had* turned off the world, though, something

truly amazing happened.

I'd lost myself in the music. For those short moments, there'd been no worrying about Harvard or Early Action. No thinking about Cameron or our race for valedictorian. Even my dad had fled my mind. My entire life had shrunk down to the beat of the music and the steady pressure of Stone's hand guiding me.

A young girl with green eyes stared back from the album, and I realized that for the last three weeks, I'd done exactly what she had. I'd taken lessons for my dad, I'd put in effort for my mom, and I'd continued dancing for Stone. Not once had I considered doing it for me. Mrs. Viktória was right, I *had* been fighting it, scared of really trying and then failing, terrified of letting go. There was comfort in control. Because of that, though, I'd never fully committed.

Looking into the elated eyes of that young girl, I made us both a promise.

For the rest of the dare, I was all in. From now on, I was dancing for me.

Chapter Twenty-One

STONE

A flash of lightning streaked the sky, followed by a decisive *crack*. As a loud boom rent the air, I slammed the kitchen door closed and set the last of the covered plates on the counter. I shook my wet head like a dog, sprinkling Lily with rain, and she shrieked before throwing her head back in surprised, delighted laughter.

It was quickly becoming my favorite sound.

"Holy crap," she said, sliding a hand down her wet arm and flinging off the collected water. "That storm came out of nowhere."

"That's what we get for not checking the weather before a barbecue," I said, grabbing the roll of paper towels. I tore off a section and handed it to her, then ripped off more to dry myself. "At least we got to eat before the downpour."

And man, did we eat. I was stuffed full of beef, refried beans with chorizo, Abuela's *chiles rellenos*, and *arroz verde*. I couldn't fit one more bite in my stomach, and believe me, I'd tried before the skies opened. Chucking the crumpled towels in the trash, I took Lily's hand and said, "Let's go find the others."

Abuela had snuck off to take a nap about an hour ago, and my parents had brought in most of the other dishes shortly after. Even Chase and Angéla had disappeared. Only Lily and I had lingered outside, talking about anything and everything, not noticing the clouds moving overhead until it was too late. In hindsight—nah, I'd do it all over again, even with the storm.

We found the others in the living room, my parents on one sofa, and Angéla and Chase stationed on either end of the other. Individual servings of Lily's chocolate cake were on each of their laps, and as I led her to the large cushion between my best friend and sister, a chorus of contented sighs reached my ears. My stomach perked up.

Maybe I had room for more, after all.

Lily sat, looking pleased as I cut a thick slice, then she glanced around the room. A puff of air escaped her lips. "Oh! I was looking at that earlier. Angéla, I swear, you look just like your mom when she was younger."

A photo album was opened on the coffee table. Lifting my plate, I breathed in the rich scent of chocolate, calculating the number of crunches I'd have to do to compensate for today, and said, "Yeah, they're the real twins in the house. Ma loves breaking out old photos and reliving her glory days," I teased.

Secretly, I loved it when she did. Getting out albums and watching old performances made her happy. She'd given up a lot when she decided to focus on teaching, so if she wanted to show off sometimes, even if it was just to us, I figured she'd earned it.

Having a new victim—er, *guest*—to impress must've inspired today's walk down memory lane, and from the way my sister's eyes suddenly widened, I assumed she'd drawn the same conclusion.

"Ooh, Ma, Lily's never seen any of your performances," Angéla said eagerly. "We should show her the one from Blackpool. Or maybe the World Pro Salsa Championship?"

Ma bit back a smile. "No, no one wants to see that," she said, trying to downplay her excitement. "We should watch a movie. The latest Marvel is on Amazon…"

Whether Lily picked up on my mother's pathetically veiled eagerness, or she was genuinely interested, I didn't know. But her eyes lit with enthusiasm. "Are you *kidding*? I'd love to see you dance. I mean, technically I've watched you at Ilusiòn, but it'd be awesome to see it done with costumes and makeup and the whole shebang."

"Well, if you're sure," Ma said modestly, casually playing with the strings on her favorite throw pillow. Her lips twitched at the corners, and my sister and I shared a glance as we started mouthing the countdown: *three…two…*

The battle didn't even make it to one. Ma's smile flew free as she bounced out of her seat, rushing to the cabinet where she kept her prized collection. Dad coughed to hide his amusement, Chase chuckled quietly, and I stuffed my mouth with a forkful of chocolate frosting. The woman was in charge of my meals. I wasn't about to piss her off.

A minute later, the familiar horns from "Salsa" by Yuri Buenaventura filled the room, and onscreen, a couple pranced out onto a wide-open dance floor. Ma dove back onto the sofa, everything but her physical body already reliving the 2002 World Championship. Lily leaned forward, her feet planted on the ground, already mesmerized by the performance.

Since I'd seen this routine more times than I could count, I chose to watch Lily's face instead, cataloging her expressions as she experienced the intricate steps, high-energy twirls, crazy tricks, and sheer attitude that was my mom in the zone. If I had to pick one word to describe her reaction, it'd be wonder.

"She's breathtaking," she whispered with a slight shake of her head. "*This* is salsa?"

"This is salsa," I confirmed, setting down my plate. I smiled and pressed close to her ear. "Look at their feet," I murmured quietly. "It's the same basic moves you've already learned. They just added a few you haven't."

Lily's body began subtly moving to the rhythm, and I pointed out the steps I recognized. "Cross-body lead...the hammerlock. That's the copa, straight into a barrel roll."

With every step, every kick, every dip, Lily swayed beside me, almost as if she were dancing vicariously through my mother. Her breathing sped, her cheeks flushed, and her eyes darted across the screen.

When the final horn section kicked in, signaling the end, Lily clutched my hand. Her nails dug moon-shaped crescents into my skin while she watched my mom climb on top of her partner, rising until she was straddling his shoulders...and as the last notes rang out, Lily's entire body went still, totally entranced as Ma flipped around, dipped straight back, and hung upside down while the song faded to a close.

Lily's mouth tumbled open and stayed there.

Grinning proudly, Angéla picked up the remote and hit pause. "So...what did you think?"

Lily blinked. "What did I think?" she repeated incredulously. She pressed her lips together, and her shoulders vibrated with a small laugh before she shook her head in amazement. "I think it was incredible...and I couldn't pull off any of it in a million years, *especially* that killer ending."

"Eh, sure you could," Ma replied, waving a hand

dismissively. From her spot snuggled up against my dad, her green eyes glowed with contentment. "It takes practice and confidence, as some of the moves are advanced. But they are nothing you couldn't handle. Even the ending."

Lily snorted. "I doubt there's enough hours in the day for me to earn *that* level of confidence."

My mother didn't reply, but her gaze was warm and knowing. I had the strangest feeling she was up to something. While we continued visiting her favorite performances of years past, she kept sneaking glances at Lily, at Angéla, and at me, making my suspicions grow. By the time she turned off the television and the room fell quiet, I was officially on high alert.

The sofa creaked as Ma shifted. She licked her lips, and my pulse began pounding in time with the rain hitting the windows. Angéla and I exchanged another look. Were they finally gonna tell us about the rent problems? Or was something else going on now, too?

One by one, empty plates dotted with cake crumbs hit the coffee table, and the air grew thick with anticipation. Other than the rain, no one made a sound, not even Chase, which by itself was noteworthy.

Lily scooted closer on the sofa, her fingers fidgeting with the hem of her shirt…and then Abuela's sonorous snore cut through the tension like a nasal chainsaw. The entire room took a collective breath, then chuckled lightly.

"Ma, what is it?" I asked. "What's going on?"

Dad smiled encouragingly, and she exhaled. "I've decided to hold a showcase," she announced. My eyebrows lifted in surprise. "Some old friends at Cypress Performing Arts Center have generously donated the space, and in one month, Ilusiòn is going to show this town what it really means to dance!"

The last line was delivered with a dramatic, over-the-top flourish, clearly orchestrated to make us smile, but she'd failed to hide the slight tremor in her hand.

I leaned forward. There was more to this than a simple recital. While she'd trained couples for various competitions over the years, she'd never once held one herself. Not anything larger than an in-house exhibition, anyway. Doing so now, when her childhood dream was in trouble, seemed like an odd choice.

As if reading my mind, Angéla asked, "Why now?"

Ma cleared her throat delicately. "We believe it will bring attention to the studio. If enough people come to watch the performances, they might decide to sign up for lessons, too. And if not, well, it will still be fun."

While the words, "*Then we'll end things on a bang*," never left her mouth, they might as well have.

Angéla, who still didn't know the full extent of our money issues, smiled cautiously, and my best friend sent me a curious look. It was Lily's reaction, though, that made my heart clench.

Gently biting her lip, she turned to me with wide eyes shining with hope. I wasn't alone in my worry anymore. The studio wasn't just important to me. But even as her optimism acted like a balm to my soul, it made the tight knot in my gut grow thicker.

I'd started feeling guilty when we were friends. Now that we were more, it was almost overwhelming. Every time she slid me her sweet, trusting smile, I wanted to believe I deserved it. That I was the guy she thought I was. But how could I be when I was keeping a secret?

"*Ever since Mom died, I've noticed how rare it is for people to be honest anymore. To be real.*"

Lily's words from the carnival raced through my mind

as self-loathing joined the toxic sludge of anxiety already churning in my stomach. The box of cash in my closet whispered from down the hall.

"Who's going to perform?" Angéla asked, bringing me back to the current problem. She tucked her legs under her, apparently over her previous shock. She practically vibrated with excitement. "I have a couple students who'd love to show off what they've learned."

Ma's shoulders relaxed, looking relieved my sister hadn't pushed the issue. As she shifted forward, a bit of that old sparkle returned to her eyes. "I want a variety of styles represented," she told us. "Smooth and rhythmic. Couples and individuals. A group of ladies and then a group of couples, dancing to the same song. High-energy and unique. Some of the students will be obvious." She winked at Angéla before turning her attention to Chase. "And I have the perfect MC in mind."

Up until now, my best friend had quietly observed the conversation from his side of the sofa. Almost like he didn't want to intrude on a private family moment. He still hadn't grasped that he *was* family. "Me?" he asked, sounding dumbfounded.

"Of course. I want to charm the town into taking lessons," she told him with a smile. "You will have them eating out of the palm of your hand."

"I'll do anything I can, Mrs. V," he said humbly, and Ma nodded, struggling with emotion.

Next, she shifted her gaze to the center of the sofa, and Lily's eyes went comically wide. "What? Not *me*." She gestured to her chest with her free hand while the one around mine clamped down. "I mean, Stone, I get. Absolutely. He'll have people jumping to sign up for lessons. But *me*? Mrs. Viktória, I'll have them running for the exits."

I nudged her in the ribs, even if I understood her concern. Lily had come a long way in three short weeks, but this event was taking place in only four more. She was a beginner. A baby one at that.

Ma reached across the coffee table, setting her hand on Lily's knee. "My darling, you have a beautiful dancer body with long lines and graceful arms. When you let go and have fun, you positively shine." Then, she glanced between us, a knowing, happy smile twitching her lips as she added, "Besides, I'd like to showcase a youthful couple. The two of you are perfect."

"But what if I mess up?" Lily pressed, her voice rising with concern. "All those people watching? I'll tank the performance and ruin the whole event."

"Sweet girl, you will not be the only couple performing. Even if you were, you must stop fighting so hard. Don't worry about what *could* happen. Live in the moment. If you mess up or stumble, just make it part of the dance."

Looking between them, it was obvious my mom's words had struck a chord. Lily nodded slowly, but her eyes kept darting around the room. "But you said the event is in a month. Will four more lessons be enough?"

I wasn't the best at reading women. My sister confused me on the regular, my mom was a mystery most of the time, and my abuela? She was an enigma, wrapped in a puzzle, coated in a riddle. But I was already growing fluent in Lily Bailey. I knew what made her tick. And while I still didn't understand why Ma was pushing for this now, and I wasn't thrilled with the idea of dancing in public myself, or the inevitable comments from a few of the more outspoken Boosters, I recognized that for whatever reason, this meant something to Ma.

Lowering my gaze, I focused on our linked hands. I

couldn't see the trust in Lily's eyes when I played my ace card. "Did you know Harvard has a Ballroom Club?"

The acid in my gut gurgled.

When she didn't respond, I licked my lips. "If you added another lesson during the week, you'd be better prepared for the dance, and it'll help pad your application. Round it out a little more." I swallowed past the knot lodged in my throat. "You don't tutor on Wednesdays, and I'll be working at the studio anyway. It'd be a perfect time for a second class."

I forced myself to look up. Lily stared at me in guarded bewilderment. Next, I turned to Ma, and she smiled at me gratefully. Hope warred with sadness in her eyes, and as Dad put his arm around her, I finally understood.

This was the studio's swan song. That was what she believed. It was why she was so nervous, and it explained why she was pushing so hard. She wanted her family involved in her last hurrah, along with every other person she truly cared about. Evidently, that list now included Lily.

Focusing back on my girlfriend, I squeezed her hand, needing help once again. I was asking a lot. We hadn't even been officially together a full weekend, and here I was pushing for more, adding to a debt I doubted I could ever repay.

Blue eyes held mine for a long, tense moment, and in their depths, I could see her weakening. She knew I was right about Harvard liking ballroom lessons on her application, and even more, she wanted to help. Even if it took more time away from schoolwork.

A fresh batch of guilt piled on the steaming mixture.

Finally, she whispered, "Okay," and I released the breath I'd been holding. "Let's do it."

A cheer rose across the room. Ma and Angéla jumped up from the sofas, yanking her into a three-way hug. As

Lily laughed, already getting swept up in their enthusiasm, I shoved down the emotions threatening to choke me.

A few hours later, Chase found me in my room. "There you are. I thought you'd decided to follow Lily home."

I looked up from the hole I was staring into my wall. "Nope."

He lifted his eyebrows. "I see hooking up with a brainiac has expanded your vocabulary. Good for you." I flipped him off, and with a smartass grin, he shut the door and walked over to where I sat on the bed. He dropped like a rock onto the mattress. "Watching paint dry?"

I sighed heavily. I wasn't in the mood for his jokes. "Just thinking, man."

"Ouch. Don't hurt yourself."

I didn't respond. We sat there quietly for about a minute. Chase looked around my room, staring at the same furniture, same books, same trophies he'd seen a thousand times. His knee bounced and then he pushed to his feet, headed to my opened closet.

"You know, despite what you might've heard, I'm not just a pretty face," he quipped as I dropped my head into my hands. I listened to him dig through my shit like he always did, probably flipping through my stash of old comics. We were both low-key nerds. "Some would even say I'm a halfway-decent listener. If you want to get technical about it, I'm a killer best friend. So, if you decide you want to talk about what's going on in that huge noggin of yours, I'm…"

"You're what?" I asked after a moment of silence, looking

at the floor. "And what are you looking for, anyway? If it's *Deadpool vs. The Punisher*, I think it's on the dresser."

I gestured lazily in the direction opposite my closet, expecting to hear him clomp across my room any second. When he didn't, and still didn't say anything, I wearily lifted my head. "Man, what's…" I trailed off when I saw what he held.

"What the fuck are you thinking?"

My eyes bugged out at his anger. I'd only seen Chase pissed a handful of times, and only once had been at me. Sixth grade, over a stupid girl no less. But there was no mistaking the cold flash of fury in his eyes or the flexing of his fingers as they clenched around the open shoebox.

Fear hit my chest, followed immediately by confusion. Why in the hell was *he* pissed? He didn't even know Lily that well. If anything, he should be on *my* side, trying to help me find a way out from under this shitstorm.

I stared at him blankly, watching the vein in his temple pop…then realized what he'd assumed.

"Dude, no. That's not from a recruiter." I almost laughed at how wrong he was. How much easier would my life have been if it *had* been an illegal bribe? "That's not what that is."

"Oh yeah? Then what the hell is it? Because from where I'm standing, you've been freaking out about your parents being strapped for cash and now you're sitting on a fat wad of it stashed away in your closet. You realize this is your future you're messing with, right?"

"Damn, will you stop?" Getting up, I strode to my door. I looked both ways down the hall, making sure no one had heard his stupid theories, then closed it again. I grabbed the box from his hand and shoved it back on the top shelf. "Right motivation, wrong conclusion. I'm telling you, it's not from a recruiter."

Chase scowled and crossed his arms. Two seconds later, his hands were on his hips.

"Okay, then. What is it? Where did you get that money, and why are you hiding it?"

Exhaling, I nodded toward my bed, silently telling him to sit. In a way, I was glad this happened. If I had to go much longer keeping this bottled up, I would've gone insane.

When we were both sitting, him twirling a loose string from my comforter around his finger and me leaned against the headboard, I looked him straight in the eyes. "The money is from Lily's dad."

Unsurprisingly, his face twisted in confusion. Horror quickly followed.

"It's not as bad as it sounds. Or, damn, I hope not. You remember a few weeks ago I asked about her in gym?" Chase nodded slowly. "Well, the weekend before, she'd come in to the studio for a lesson. Not because she wanted to. Her dad made her because…" I cleared my throat. "It's not important why. The point is, he saw she wasn't into it. He travels a lot, and he figured the second he skipped town, she'd bail on the lessons. So he asked me to keep her interested."

Already, I saw the wheels turning in Chase's head, again drawing the wrong conclusions.

"Not like that…although, looking back, it could seem that way. It *was* the reason I started hanging out with her, initially, which now makes everything worse." I scrubbed a hand over my eyes. "Mr. Bailey paid me what it would've cost if he'd signed up for lessons, too, and all he asked was I be her partner and encourage her to stick with it. You know Ma needed the money. I figured this could help. But then…I don't know. We spent time together. And Lily? She's incredible, man. Funny and smart. Weird, too, but in a cute way. Quirky. She gets me like I can't even explain and has me so twisted up I can't see straight."

"And that's bad because…?"

I banged my skull against the headboard. "Because she doesn't know about the deal. She doesn't know her dad basically paid me to hang out with her."

Chase flinched. "Yeah, that's not good."

"No shit." I closed my eyes and hit my head against the wall a few more times, hoping it'd knock an answer loose. "Being honest is a big deal with her, and I've had two weeks to come clean and haven't. I've already blown it. Now we're together, and I know the second she finds out the truth, she'll be out the door."

Silence fell. Which, considering who my best friend was and the truth bomb I'd tossed at his feet, wasn't a good sign. Wary, I lifted my head, and he gave me a pensive look.

"I'm not gonna lie," he said, scratching his ear. "When you told me you were with Lily, I didn't get it. Not because she's not great. It's just, one minute you're claiming to be the next Dalai Lama, then the next, you're going out with Iron Stomach. It didn't make sense. But then I stopped and thought about it. Lily's cool, man. She's not like the usual girls you hook up with. And you, you're different with her. I'm just saying, if you tell her the truth, she might understand."

"That's the thing," I told him, frustrated. "She *is* different. She's too good for me. Flip the script, she never would've taken the money, and believe me, I've thought about giving it back. But my parents are struggling. After seeing the desperation in Ma's eyes tonight, I can't do that. Not when the studio's hanging by a thread, and not without another way to bring in extra cash." My breathing spiked, and my shoulders rose and fell with an almost desperate need for oxygen. I'd never felt more trapped in my life. "I also considered telling Lily about the deal, hoping she could see past the secrets and understand, but I can't do that, either. I shook her dad's hand and gave my word that I wouldn't. Honestly, though? It's more than that."

I sat up, and Chase stopped twirling the loose string around his finger.

"You say she might understand…but what if she doesn't? What if she thinks the only reason I'm with her now is because I was paid to be?"

My head started to pound, and it felt like a two-ton elephant was sitting on my chest. I stared at my dark blue comforter and quietly admitted, "I know I don't deserve her, but I've never felt this way before. If I tell her the truth, and she doesn't hear me out, or she doesn't understand, she'll bail. She'll get angry that I kept it from her and quit the lessons…quit *me*…and that'll be it."

I raised my eyes again. "But maybe…maybe if I wait another month, let the agreement run its course and get past the showcase, I can find another way to get my parents the money. And I can use the extra time to prove I genuinely care about her. That it's not just her dad or the money keeping us together."

Chase tightened his mouth in a wince. "I don't know, man. I get that you're in a tough spot, and I don't envy you. But I've got to say, I think waiting any longer is gonna bite you in the ass."

"You might be right," I acknowledged thickly. "But I'm praying like hell you're not."

Chapter Twenty-Two

LILY

Twinkle lights wrapped around a black-painted column reflected off hardwood like a spotlight. Even though the studio was relatively empty, and no one was here other than Marcus in the back office and Angéla at the front desk, it felt like a crowd was watching us rehearse. Waiting for me to mess up. Cheering when I didn't. It was the good kind of stressful *and* exciting—a strange combination that was quickly becoming addictive, fueling my adrenaline.

"Why don't we start again from the top?"

I blew out a breath and nodded. Mrs. Viktória smiled, then headed to the stereo system in the corner to start our music over. It wasn't the actual song we'd use for the performance—she'd yet to tell us what she'd chosen but was dangling it over our heads like a juicy carrot. We'd learn that crucial detail after we went through the choreography one more time. So far, we'd used a variety of stand-ins, "auditioning them" over the last week and a half, and I'd discovered whatever the choice, the rhythmic mix of drums and horns always spiked my energy.

As I took my place across from Stone, a bright pink poster over his shoulder caught my eye. The signs announcing the showcase followed me everywhere, as if I could possibly forget it was approaching like a freight train… or that the studio's livelihood seemed pinned to this one night going well.

It wasn't just the studio. The entire town was plastered with posters. Bulletin boards at grocery stores, front windows of restaurants, they were even in the cafeteria and on lockers at school, courtesy of Cameron, who was inviting everyone to watch her in the all-ladies burlesque-style routine. With each flier I passed, I reminded myself that it was for the greater good. What it wasn't good for, however, was my nerves.

Every time I imagined a packed auditorium, the "good kind of stress" transformed into a hint of the yucky.

The music started, "Muevete" by DLG, whisking away my quivery stomach as a smile broke free. It was impossible to hold onto fear when the familiar beat worked its way through my body. This was the first song I'd ever danced to with Stone. Almost four weeks ago, I'd walked through the doors prepared to throw the lesson and get my life back on track.

That day seemed like a lifetime ago.

"Are you ready?" he asked me now, his hand squeezing mine in time to the count.

I bobbed my head with the music, clearing it as I found the beat. When the only thing remaining was the exciting feel of his arms and the electric sound of the horns, I exhaled and said, "Let's do it."

Stone grinned…and then the world slipped away.

The first salsa basic transitioned into a cross-body lead, followed immediately by open breaks and a hook turn. After another basic, Stone wrapped me in a cradle, then rocked me back into a second series of the same steps, only this time trailed by a double turn.

As he spun me out, his eyebrows wiggling suggestively, I swallowed back a giddy laugh. The turns were my favorite part. I'd suspected with my gangly giraffe legs they'd be what tripped me up the most, but amazingly they weren't. Spinning around the dance floor in Stone's arms, watching his famous grin take over or his eyes turn molten with heat, made me feel pretty in a way I'd never felt before. Sure, I still stumbled at times and got dizzy. Occasionally, I'd take too long and lose the beat. But when I turned off my brain and truly let myself go, the turns were surprisingly fun.

Besides, those times when I *did* mess up, Stone was there, too, guiding me and believing in me anyway. And distracting me in the best way possible with those sexy Magic Mike hips.

Honestly, the entire routine was a blast. For the most part, we stuck to beginner moves, adding stylization when and where we could, making it our own, and other than sporadically stepping ahead of the beat, and once stepping on Stone's poor feet, I only really struggled with the short section of fast, intense, multiple spins toward the end.

Well, that and the final move, of course. But that was plain ridiculous.

As the third hammerlock turn came to an end, my chest grew tight. Knowing what was coming, my body started cringing away, like it could somehow protect me by revolt. Or, more accurately, like it could protect Stone.

The pretzel-like double turn signaled the ending of the choreography, and as I ducked under his sure, steady hands to complete the combination, my breathing spiked, and my own hands grew slick with sweat.

This was the part I loathed.

What made it worse was that I only had myself to blame. Calling attention to that World Championship ending at the barbecue had been a classic rookie mistake. Of course, Mrs. Viktória had added it to our routine, if for no other reason than to prove I could do it.

The problem was I *couldn't*. So far, I'd failed spectacularly. Every. Single. Time.

Stone's chocolate eyes locked on mine, making my pulse race as he spun me out, then sent me into a back rock. Squatting low, he held my right hand firmly in his left and nodded encouragingly.

"You've got it," he urged me on, the confidence in his voice making me want to believe he was right. That this time I *could* nail it.

I took a deep breath, then stepped up onto his rock-hard thigh with my right foot—

And kicked him square in the head with my left.

"Fu—" Biting back a curse, Stone dropped my hand to clutch his battered head, and I jumped to the ground, covering my mouth.

"I'm sorry!"

My apology was muffled, but I knew he understood because I'd been repeating the same phrase like a high-strung parrot ever since Mrs. Viktória first presented the crazy idea last Wednesday.

"I told you I can't do this."

Every stinking time I climbed over Stone's broad shoulders, I was so terrified of kicking him in the head... that half the time, it's exactly what I did. It was a horrible, embarrassing self-fulfilling prophecy I couldn't stop no matter how hard I tried.

How many times did a girl have to kick a guy in the face before he dumped her?

If it was less than twenty, I was living on borrowed time.

The few times I *hadn't* kicked my boyfriend of twelve whole days during the straddle hold, I'd gotten off balance when he pivoted me around for the final dip. That had led to me falling and clipping him in the throat while I went down. Not much better.

Twice I'd almost actually gotten it right, but both times were shaky at best, and they were done when we were only working on the one move, never as part of the whole routine. Today was our third session since Mrs. Viktória's announcement, our second Wednesday-night lesson, and Stone and his mom had developed their own parrotlike habit of saying I'd get it in time. That we had four more lessons to nail it.

All I heard was I had four more chances to kick my boyfriend in the head multiple times a night. And four more chances for him to finally have enough and give me the boot.

At the sharp *click* of heels, I spun to face Mrs. Viktória. Her smile was easy, full of understanding as she waved a hand in the air. "The ending will come, dear, do not fret. I have every confidence."

"That makes one of us," I replied, glancing back at Stone. As it was, the poor guy wasn't stoked about outing himself as a dancer in front of the town, and here he was dealing with girlfriend abuse. I winced, watching him rub his head, but he gave me a smile regardless, showing he still believed in me. Sweet, delusional man.

"Now, would you like to know the song I have chosen for your performance?"

My head snapped forward. If anything could knock me out of self-pity, it was that. Although she'd teased us ever since she'd taken over my lessons, she'd never given more than a few hints. I might not have been a natural dancer like Angéla, or a Channing Tatum doppelganger like Stone, but even I knew song choice was key. The right song could make or break a performance. Angéla had told me the same moves could be interpreted differently depending on a song's lyrics, its mood, and its theme.

Mrs. Viktória's green eyes grew wide with excitement. "You will be dancing to…" She paused dramatically, drawing out the suspense, and Stone beat a drumroll on his thighs… "A salsa remix of 'Shape of You'! The remix has the same lyrics as the Ed Sheeran version, but it's youthful and edgy, and also a bit *sexy*." She wiggled her shoulders playfully. "It'll be the perfect complement to the routine—and to the two hotties dancing it!"

I snorted. Loudly. I mean, I understood her wanting to hype us up for the showcase, and I could even see where, sure, a youthful, edgy song and dance would draw in a different clientele than the norm. Different clientele equaled fresh blood and new money pouring into Ilusiòn.

But I was hung up on one key word.

"*Sexy*?" I huffed a laugh, then fanned my face, blowing a puff of air up at my bangs. "Uh, yeah…I'm not gonna pull that off. I can barely pull off *cute*, and even that's a stretch. Youthful, hey, I've got that by age. Fun, eh, I can manage. Edgy is extremely doubtful, but catch me on a bad day, and maybe. But sexy?" I shook my head. "Mrs. Viktória, you've got the wrong girl."

The press of heat at my back and the hand on my hip put a stop to my rambling. "Trust me, Red," a voice said, low and rough against my ear. I inhaled the scent of wintergreen, and my stomach dipped. "You're sexy."

Stone tugged me around until I faced him, then he lifted my stubborn chin with his finger. "But that's in the eye of the beholder. What you need to focus on is fire. The inner desire to kick ass and take names. That's you to a T, pretty girl. You're fierce."

His grin was slow and deliberate, diffusing my rising jitters as more primal urges took hold. The guy was shameless. He could flirt the peanuts out of my M&M's and they'd still be delicious. But I was too far gone to care.

Quirking my lips, I poked his chest with a finger. "I see what you're doing, QB. You think by turning that unicorn-sneezing-rainbows smile on me I'm gonna get all twitterpated and forget to be nervous."

"My unicorn *what*?" The flirtatious grin transformed into a full-on smile with teeth and dimples and eyes all crinkly. Stone shook his head and pressed a chuckling kiss against my forehead. "Twitterpated? Damn, girl. My life was boring as hell before you came around, you know that?"

Warm breath coasted across my skin as he released a small, happy sigh, and in spite of my looming embarrassment—and the sheer certainty I'd look like a fool in front of half the town in my attempt to be *sexy*—I was filled to bursting with giddiness.

A throat delicately cleared behind me, and I blushed. Looking over my shoulder, I saw Mrs. Viktória fighting a smile. "We have fifteen minutes left for today's lesson," she said, shooting me a wink. "I think we should use that time to fine-tune the Cuban motion. It is vital to salsa, or any Latin dance, and I think it will help you find your inner siren."

"I'm not sure that's possible," I told her with a resigned sigh, "but I'm willing to try anything. Especially if it keeps me from kicking Stone in the head again today."

She laughed and clapped. "Excellent. Then let's move to the mirrors, shall we?"

Correction: I was willing to try anything that kept me from kicking Stone in the head *and* didn't involve watching myself in a mirror. I'd always been my own worst critic. I'd made an art form out of avoiding the huge shiny things mounted on the wall the last month, not wanting to pick apart my every movement, and I saw zero reason to stop the practice now.

Eyes wide with horror, I let Stone take my hand. Linking our fingers, he grazed his thumb over my palm, shooting delicious tingles up my arm, then led me to the shiny, reflective surfaces. Staring into the spotless glass, I ignored the flutters tightening my belly and avoided looking at myself by reading the words scrawled in black marker along the top: *Dance like no one is watching…because they're not. They're checking their phones.*

"Balance is key to the Cuban motion," Mrs. Viktória instructed, diving right in with the exercise. She hit play on the stereo, and the salsa remix of "Shape of You" began floating through the room. She lowered the volume, allowing us to get familiar with the beat while still listening to her direction.

"It is different from how we naturally move. If you didn't grow up in martial arts or dance, when you stop walking, both of your feet are flat on the floor. But we're looking for a step more like a horse waiting for his rider. Weight on one foot with the other poised to move."

Standing next to me, she demonstrated the step, meeting my eyes in the mirror.

"It's about rolling your feet, transferring weight. Crisscrossing your knees. The motion is hip, then foot, then weight, bending and straightening your knee. The hip rotating is what leads the movement, not the foot."

Sweat trickled down my spine while I tried to replicate the step, alternating my hips and knees. I felt ridiculous, like a graceless hack, straightening one knee while bending the other, moving one hip up and the other down. Talk about sexy. Here I'd been thinking I'd finally gotten a good grip on the basic move, only to find out I looked like a stiff, uncooked spaghetti noodle.

Stone must've seen my face, because suddenly he was standing beside me. "Can I make a suggestion?"

Wincing, I untucked my hair from behind my ear. "Uh, yeah. Of course."

Brow furrowed, he reached out and, holding my gaze, slipped my glasses from my face. The world instantly went blurry, but not enough that I couldn't still see the thoughtful look on his face. "Try this. Think of it as an extension of the exercise where you kept your eyes closed. Stop focusing so much on what you're doing wrong and feel the music. Trust your body to get it right. You know the steps."

It was on the tip of my tongue to argue that this was a *mirror* drill and I couldn't do it if I couldn't see—but, when I glanced at my reflection, I realized that wasn't true. I could still see my body. I could still see the movement of my leg and Mrs. Viktória watching with a pleased expression. What I *couldn't* see was every precise nuance, every tiny inflection. The view was distorted just enough to lose the sharp, unforgiving edges.

The music started over, and I mimicked Mrs. Viktória again, this time also trusting my body. As I gave in to the rhythm, the motion became more fluid. Without my glasses, it was as if the pressure was somehow off, and I sank further into the movement. And the further I sank, the more confident I became.

The song continued to weave its magic, and somewhere along the way, I forgot to be embarrassed. In truth, it could've been my blurry reflection, or the steps themselves, or knowing Stone was watching, but as I got more and more comfortable with the motion, a pink stain began warming my cheeks.

I had to admit, I felt…sensual.

"When you step, use the inside edge of your foot, then roll your weight. The heel simply kisses the floor, then you push off into the next step. Straighten your knee, and your hip rolls back. Yes! That's it! Beautiful!"

I grinned, starting to get into it now. My gaze trailed over my hazy reflected image. Feet to knee, knee to hip, hip to face, and back again. On the second journey up, I met my eyes and made a sassy face in the mirror.

"See?" Stone said, a slight chuckle in his words, and my gaze bounced to his. "Fierce."

A few minutes later, I was still grinning. Gathered around my lesson binder at a bistro table, the world clear once again, I dabbed my chest with a towel. My calves throbbed and there was a dull ache in my arches, but strangely enough, I liked the pain. I'd earned it.

"You have come very far, Lily," Mrs. Viktória praised. "I cannot wait to see the crowd's reaction! Obviously, I am excited about all the performances at the showcase, but I admit, I'm extra eager for this dance."

"Crazily, I'm getting a little excited, too," I admitted.

Oh, I was still terrified I'd fall flat on my face, kick the town's hero in his, or forget the steps the second the music started. But a part of me wanted to prove I could do it.

I scooted my chair back and wrapped the towel around my neck. "The girl who walked through those doors three and a half weeks ago never would've expected she'd be here now. Preparing to perform in front of an audience. Dancing the way I am." Stone squeezed my knee, and I shook my head in amazement. "I still haven't found a balance yet, but I must admit, adding a second lesson is paying off."

Stone's face fell at my words, and this time, I could've kicked *myself*.

Despite the extra lessons being my choice, Stone somehow felt responsible. Ever since he'd caught me in an anxious tizzy over my new schedule, he'd made it his mission to keep me stress-free—hosting study nights and driving to school so I could cram during the commute. Basically, doing the guy thing and trying to fix the problem.

The good news was I'd yet to miss an assignment or get anything less than an A. The bad was that I was nowhere near where I usually was by this point in the year. Between the two lessons a week and spending as much time as possible with Stone (for both dare and, ahem, more *personal* reasons), I was barely keeping up, while Cameron— confident, beautiful, cheer captain and dancer Cameron— was balancing life just fine.

Lack of sleep only compounded my problem. Who knew relationships caused insomnia? Staying up all night reliving kisses. Thinking about future ones to come. My favorite books never mentioned crush- or love-based insomnia, but it was *so* a thing.

My entire life had gone topsy-turvy to the point I barely recognized myself most days, but I didn't regret a single decision. Stone was incredible, and between him and Angéla and Sydney, my life was richer than it'd been in years. I didn't want to stop dancing. I continued to surprise myself on the floor and I was better than I'd ever imagined. More importantly, dance forced me to live in the moment. Turning off the white noise for two hours a week, even if it took away study time, was refreshing.

I just wanted to do all the above *and* kick Cameron's ass in the race for valedictorian. Was that too much to ask?

Hoping to lighten the mood, I said, "Of course, I'd be a

hot mess without my amazing partner. How lucky am I that you have bionic toes? Part of me still questions your sanity in asking to partner up, but it's too late now, I've called dibs. You're stuck with me, bucko."

Bumping his shoulder, I took a sip of ice-cold water, fully expecting his confident grin to emerge, or even the sneezing-unicorn one. Instead, I got the tight-lipped QB. Stone's eyes darted away as he took a long pull of his water, but I could've sworn I'd seen a flash of guilt.

I paused, recapping my bottle…then decided I'd imagined it.

Guilt was the furthest thing he should feel. If anything, he was the only reason I wasn't completely floundering. Even with the craziness—the nutty schedule, increased attention from our relationship, and fear of people watching me perform—my stress level was nonexistent compared to the start of the year. Dancing helped, but really, Stone was the difference. He was my calm. He lent me strength, and when I was with him, I didn't feel alone.

If he doubted his value, then it was on me to remind him.

Lucky for him, I planned on sticking around to do exactly that.

Chapter Twenty-Three

LILY

Okay, I understood Homecoming craziness now. Football was a whole different animal on home turf. The scent of popcorn, sweat, and cheap cologne still permeated the air, and the noise level remained off the charts, but there was something *electric* about watching the guys storm our own field, with a house full of their own fans—although, the extra zing could've been the glow of LED lights bouncing off my ginormous mum.

I bit back a smile as I adjusted the rope holding the eight-pound corsage around my neck.

I'd never been given a mum from a guy before. Mom and Dad had gotten me one in junior high, but that sweet little thing had nothing on this sucker. Rather than buy a ready-made version from a specialty shop, Mrs. Viktória had insisted on making it herself, and the result threatened to burn my retinas.

All I could say: the phrase "everything's bigger in Texas" existed for a reason.

The heart of my mum was a tiger's paw of blue and

white paper chrysanthemums, with an array of blue and white ribbons along with two black, sparkly boas trailing beneath. Some ribbons had dance shoe charms on them. Others had footballs. Still more had books. Two ribbons said Homecoming and Senior in glitter paint, and thanks to the LED bulbs illuminating the giant paw in the center, the entire thing was eye-catching, not to mention blinding.

But the two largest ribbons attracted the most attention.

Near the center of the arrangement, two silver ribbons held each of our names, one for Lily and one for Stone, in a huge, unmistakable font. Every time I walked, the *clang* of blinged-out cowbells assured everyone got a good, long gawk. And gawk they had. All. Day. Long.

From the moment I'd walked into school with cowbells clanging and lights a-glowing, eyes had been on me. When we'd gathered for afternoon assembly, I'd wager more students stared at me than they had the football team. Shock and confusion were the name of the game, as evidently there'd been a few people yet to hear Stone and I were together. Or, if they had, they hadn't believed it. Thanks to the monstrosity around my neck and the matching garter around his bicep, there was no denying it now, but strangely enough, the unwanted attention didn't bother me as much as I would've expected.

I wouldn't say it was *comfortable.* It wasn't like I suddenly hoped this would become my new normal, or my skin didn't prickle the tiniest bit, especially when the whispers became audible. But dread no longer twisted my stomach. The walls weren't closing in, and I didn't fear a looming anxiety attack. Dance lessons had helped me grow accustomed to the feel of eyes tracking me, and awesome friends who had my back certainly didn't hurt, either.

Sydney and Angéla had flanked me in the halls, and

we'd driven to the game together, too. Although Syd was working concessions, Angéla hadn't left my side all night… well, not until her bathroom break ten minutes ago. Right now, I was kicking myself for not joining her.

The sound system crackled, and I tensed on the bleachers. "On behalf of the faculty, staff, and student body of Brighton High, welcome, friends, to this year's Homecoming!" Ear-ringing cheers broke around me, and I discreetly scanned the crowd for Angéla. "Please join us in recognizing our elected court."

Fudge stick. Stretching my neck, I tried to see the alcove leading toward the bathrooms. Sadly, I wasn't made of rubber. Why did I have to have such a super bladder anyway? I knew I should've drank more water.

When the speakers crackled again, the announcer began calling out names. One guy and one girl, chosen to walk the length of the field together while students cheered and cell phones recorded. A pair was called from each class, freshman through junior, which left the two senior couples remaining.

"Mr. Chase Evan Winters, escorting Ms. Cameron Ann Montgomery."

Two girls, three levels down, turned in their seats to eye me up, then glance at the field before returning with their heads tilted in bewilderment. I met their stares evenly, twisting one of my sparkly ribbons around my finger. Hopefully, it was the only sign I was affected.

I couldn't blame them for being confused. I'd felt gangly and unattractive all my life. Even with Stone whispering that he thought I was beautiful and sexy, it was hard to believe, *especially* when I compared myself to the vision on the field.

Cameras flashed as Cameron strutted toward the risers on Chase's arm. In her skimpy cheer uniform, wearing a dainty tiara atop a pile of perfect waves and a princess sash draped across her curves, the bouquet of roses in her slender arms completed the perfect, glamorous picture.

I glanced at my simple shorts and tee, with long, skinny legs poking out from under my enormous mum. Glamorous, I was not.

At least she was walking with Chase. *That* was a boon. Stone had flat-out refused to escort her, and despite her attempts to force the issue, the advisor had rearranged the order.

"Mr. Ágoston Michael Torres, escorting Ms. Ashley Marie Thompson."

This time, the screams were deafening. People bobbed and weaved, holding up their phones to get the perfect shot of our local celebrity. I knew Stone hated every second those cell phones were trained on him…but that didn't stop me from whipping out my phone, too, and snapping a quick pic.

What? I was the girlfriend. I had rights.

Besides, this moment deserved to be recorded. It was one of the stereotypical experiences I'd always made fun of but now wanted to freeze-frame and remember. Stone had on his careful smile, still in his uniform sans helmet, with a princely sash draped across his jersey. His spiky black hair looked wet, and even from this distance, I could see the fire in his eyes. He was in beast mode, ready to get away from the extravagant display and back to the sport he loved.

In short, my man looked good. *Real* good.

Stone and Ashley joined the others on the risers, her on the bottom with the other girls, a mish-mash of fancy dresses and cheer uniforms among them, while he took the top with the guys, everyone in rented tuxes except for Chase and Stone.

It only took a second for him to find me in the stands,

and when his dark eyes trailed over my face, the tight smile softened. I sent him a subtle wink of encouragement, and he exhaled.

"It's time to announce this year's King and Queen of Homecoming. The students who you, the student body, have elected. To help crown our new royalty, please welcome back your previous monarchs, Ms. Erin Rains and Mr. Noah Ruckert!"

While various screamed versions of "Welcome Home," rose around me, my eyes narrowed in protective mode. Years had allowed Stone to master the calm, collected QB facade, but even from here I could see the storm raging beneath the cool surface. Being new to the Homecoming experience, I'd had no idea previous court members returned for tonight's reveal. If Stone knew, he'd clearly forgotten.

My hands clenched in my lap. We'd never discussed the story Aidan shared about the night Stone and Cameron broke up. How she'd cheated with Noah at a party. I hadn't seen the point in bringing up past hurts, and Stone wasn't always the most open person in the world. Regardless, Aidan had been right; you didn't walk away from that without it leaving a mark.

I shifted my gaze to Cameron, and even through my protective haze I could see the regret on her face. She clearly knew she'd made a mistake, which sucked, because Stone wasn't the kind of guy you got over. Now that I was finally paying attention to the rumor mill, I knew she wanted him back.

Unfortunately for her, the position of girlfriend had already been filled. He was *mine*.

"Brighton High, your king of Homecoming is…" The row of princes shifted on the riser, but there was no real mystery whose name would be called. Even so, I sat with my butt perched on the edge of the seat. "Stone Torres!"

I sprang to my feet along with the rest of the crowd. Feet pounded metal bleachers and shouts rent the air as Stone once again found me in the stands. For just a moment, his face shifted into his real smile, with a flash of those lethal dimples, and my heart fluttered in my chest.

He'd tried to play it off, but he'd wanted this. Approval meant a lot to him. As confident as he could be, at his core, Stone was just a guy who wanted to be loved and accepted.

Then Noah walked up, ruining everything.

With a condescending smirk, he handed over the new king sash, and Stone's expression turned lethal while he took it and draped it right over the old one. Next came a velvet cape Noah slid around Stone's broad shoulders, but when he went to place the crown on my man's head, Stone grabbed it from his hands. The look in his eyes clearly said *Back off*, and I held my breath, along with the rest of the crowd, wondering what would happen next.

Chase shifted forward. Cameron winced. But, with his eyes locked on me, Stone put the crown on his head and he smiled. For a fraction of a second, it was just the two of us in the crammed-full stadium. The literal king of the school, rising above the drama, and me, his brainy, dorky girlfriend, standing in awe. Life was so surreal sometimes.

"And now to announce your new queen."

The moment broke like a popped balloon, and I sighed, resigned to the inevitable result. It'd be nice, though, if a supernatural phenomenon struck or a miracle occurred. My self-esteem could really do without the hit of seeing my boyfriend and his ex being crowned together.

"Brighton High, please put your hands together for… Cameron Montgomery."

Eh. It'd been a long shot anyway.

Snorting under my breath, I watched as Cameron's hand flew to her face. Up and down the line of princesses, the other girls smiled and clapped delicately, looking about as thrilled as I was with the outcome, though probably for different reasons. The former queen helped Cameron exchange her dainty tiara for a bigger one, drape the new sash over her shoulders, and when the applause started to wane, held her hand as she stepped down and took three steps in front of the riser.

"Stone! The photographers need our picture."

Looking over her shoulder, she sent him a toothpaste-commercial-worthy smile—warm and open with a touch of familiarity, probably the same smile she'd given him when they were still together. My stomach roiled, and I followed her hopeful gaze to my boyfriend, who stood rooted on the top riser, visibly tense.

Sure enough, though, cameramen descended. With photographers now calling his name, too, Stone gave a small shake of his head and put on the old QB grin. He climbed down and took his place at Cameron's side, posing for the pictures while subtly shaking off the hand she kept trying to wrap around his arm.

Together they were flawless. Cameron looked like polished perfection, and Stone was a legend in the making. As cameras snapped, I could hear the crowd's thoughts swirling around me.

Wow. They make such *a cute couple.*

Why aren't they back together again?

And, my personal favorite. *What is he doing with Lily Bailey?*

No. I refused to let insecurity ruin my night. Sitting up straight, I raised my chin, feigning a confidence I didn't feel, and pushed away the toxic thoughts. If Stone had wanted to be with Cameron, he'd be with her. Right? *I* was the one wearing a mum with our names on it.

Nodding to myself, I looked away, ignoring the pointed stares as I stretched my back and tried to work some feeling into my lower body. The hard seats were making my butt go numb. As I wiggled and shifted, searching for a more comfortable position with a pasted-on smile, my eyes landed on Ms. Kat, my AP European history teacher, standing near the chain-link fence.

My faux grin dimmed at the edges. I'd finally turned in my research paper, and while the result hadn't been my best work, it had been good enough to get an A.

Unfortunately, Cameron had scored a touch higher.

On the field, the photographers dispersed. The court followed suit, but before slipping back to the locker room, Stone turned and found me one last time. Pride and adoration swelled within me, and I waved with a happy smile. He did one better, blowing me a kiss.

The girls in front of me gasped and whirled around as my face warmed, and Stone laughed, his eyes going crinkly. He darted back through the tunnel, and I floated on the bleacher.

In the grand scheme of things, how could I regret two points on a silly paper when I finally felt so alive?

I'd spent years striving to get perfect grades, eyes fixed solely on my goals, but Stone was right. This was senior year. What was wrong with slowing down and enjoying it? I didn't have to apply Early Action. Waiting until January for Regular Decision would not only let me include this semester's classes and activities on my transcript, but it'd give me time to get my grades where I wanted them. Plus, it would take some of the stress off *and* let me live a little.

This whole crazy adventure had started with Stone

setting out to prove high school was more than a stepping stone and me wanting to prove him wrong. But with one day left in our original timeline, I had to admit—forfeiting felt a lot like winning.

"Hey, hot stuff!"

Angéla's voice snapped me from my thoughts, and I searched the crowd to find her at the bottom of the bleachers, her tiny arms laden with food. She blew a puff of air at her bangs and hollered, "Missed me?"

"Oh, sorry, were you gone?" I teased back, earning a stuck-out tongue.

The crowd watched our exchange, along with Angéla's shuffling progress, with moderate amusement. Her slender arms somehow held two bags of popcorn, a serving of nachos, an order of fries, and a massive drink. The girl had an excellent future in waitressing if she wanted it.

When she reached our row, she successfully maneuvered around the scrawny guys with BHS slathered on their chests, then stopped next to me with a wide grin. The team stormed the field again, and the guy with the painted B jumped to his feet, bumping Angéla's arm and sending an explosion of popcorn into my lap. Her mouth fell open in a squawk.

Laughing, I scooped up a salty, buttery handful and shoved it in my mouth. "Yum."

She shook her head and took her seat with a grumble. "What's got you so giddy?" She waved her nachos at my face. "I saw that big old smile all the way from the concession stand."

I shrugged, realizing I *was* kind of giddy, despite the flash of insecurity. In fact, I felt like a weight had been lifted. "Nothing much. Just sitting here thinking life's pretty awesome. Great game, amazing friends, yummy snacks." I shoved a few more pieces of buttery goodness in my mouth, thinking about my mom. She would've loved this. "It doesn't get much better, does it?"

A bright smile bloomed on her face, and Angéla knocked her shoulder against mine. "Actually, it does." She handed over half the food haul, then reached into the pocket of her shorts to withdraw a bag of peanut M&M's. My heart did a squeeze.

"My hero," I exclaimed, snatching the treat.

Our silly laughter got lost in the sounds of the game.

Chapter Twenty-Four

STONE

Get ready.

Two words was all it took for my sister to taunt me. I smiled at my phone. Angéla had been here all day, doing the hair, nails, and makeup routine with Lily and Sydney for the dance. The trio had grown tight the last couple weeks—so much so that I was tempted to resort to playground politics and point out I'd seen Lily first. Not that I minded their friendship. I loved that they had each other and got along so well.

What I didn't love? Angéla hogging my girlfriend.

Returning the phone to my pocket, I blew out a breath. I needed to get my head on straight. I'd had a weird feeling since I woke up, like a premonition before a big matchup. It wasn't about Lily. Even without my sister's text, I knew she'd look incredible. No, this was about *me*.

Seeing Noah again last night messed with me. I'd shoved it aside for the game, but the second the clock had hit zero and the ref had blown the final whistle, the memories roared back. Every stupid smirk, every harsh whisper, every fucking screenshot. They were all there, in my head, reminding me I'd been replaceable. Interchangeable. Just another meathead holding a football and a springboard to popularity. Ma had given us the day off from the studio to get ready for the dance, but I'd shown up this morning anyway, helping with every class she'd had in the hopes they'd drown out the voices in my head. The whispers saying I'd fail my parents and that Ilusiòn would close. And the taunts promising that soon Lily would leave me, too.

As of today, our dare was over. So was the agreement with her dad. Lily had stuck with the lessons so, technically speaking, I'd fulfilled my part of the bargain. If I broke my word tonight and told Lily the truth, there wasn't much her old man could do about it. But *she* could. At the end of the day, promise or not, *good reason* or not, I'd kept a secret from Lily for a month. Confessing now would only push her away, especially without a backup plan in place that let me return her dad's money.

The showcase was just around the corner, and the day after it was over, rent was due. Unless a ton of new students enrolled between now and then, that would wipe out the rest of our savings and I'd have to give Ma the cash from Mr. Bailey I had hidden away. I swear to God, that damn shoebox haunted my dreams. It was all I saw when I walked in my room, and it'd gotten to the point where I avoided going in there at all other than to sleep. For two weeks I'd lain awake, staring at my closet and trying to think of a solution, any other solution, and a few nights ago, it finally came to me. An idea that could save Ilusiòn, long-term, *and* help cover the bills. The only problem was it required time and a level of patience I wasn't sure I had.

Opening my eyes to the solid oak door, I released a sigh and knocked. It did no good rehashing it on her doorstep.

Just for tonight, I wanted to forget that time was my enemy. I wanted to stop worrying about the studio or what tomorrow could bring and just hold Lily in my arms.

I need my girl.

Footsteps on the other side had me smiling for the first time today. I patted my left pocket, making sure the gift was there, and smoldered at the door as the lock turned. I didn't know if it was "unicorn" worthy, but hopefully it'd make her smile regardless.

A laugh built in my chest as the door opened. It died just as fast.

"Mr. Torres." Salt-and-pepper brows rose as Lily's dad stared like I'd presented a complicated math problem. "Can I help you?"

"Yes, sir." My jaw flexed, and I firmed up my voice. "I'm here to pick up Lily."

Blue eyes went cold. Mr. Bailey stepped back and appraised my suit, his mouth set in a disapproving line, and for a moment, I legit feared he'd slam the door in my face. Or worse, run upstairs and tell Lily about our deal. But he had as much to lose doing that as I did. Maybe more. He sniffed, then widened the door. "Come on in, then."

I stepped into the foyer, immediately noticing the quiet.

There was no music playing, no sound from a television. No idle conversation or echoed laughter. I couldn't remember the last time my house had been this quiet and it hadn't been the middle of the night. Weren't the girls here somewhere?

Wordlessly, I followed Mr. Bailey into the living room and found Nick and Sean already waiting. I lifted my chin in hello. As they nodded back, I took a short break from worrying about seeking approval to size up my sister's date.

Sean was on the soccer team. We'd never had a problem,

but the guy was spineless. It was no secret he'd had a thing for Angéla since we were freshmen, but he'd never made a move until now. He was a nice guy but way too shy. He'd let my sister lead him by the nose. She needed someone who'd support *and* challenge her.

As for Nick, he was cool, but we didn't hang in the same circles. He was smart, like Lily, Cameron, and Aidan. My IQ probably jumped a few points just standing next to him.

Looking away, I adjusted my pristine tie and studied the room instead.

Framed photos hung on the walls. A young Lily posed in all of them—with her parents in front of Cinderella Castle in one, near the Eiffel Tower in another. A collage of her entire life, up until three or four years ago, was painstakingly displayed on every surface, from the fireplace mantel to the expensive-looking coffee table to the grand piano in the corner.

In every picture, she looked happy. She was the spitting image of her mom, other than the blue eyes she'd inherited from her dad, and there was no denying they'd been close. All of them. I didn't understand how a guy who'd once been a family man could turn into an absentee parent, leaving his daughter alone for weeks at a time. Especially someone like Lily.

My jaw clenched, and I glanced at Mr. Bailey. He was already watching me.

A *creak* above our heads broke the stalemate. I lifted my eyes out of instinct…and suddenly forgot how to breathe.

A fallen angel stood at the top of the curved stairwell. In a black lace sleeveless dress that hit mid-thigh and three-inch red heels, Lily's legs were endless. They were the definition of temptation. With a plunging neckline that showed off her creamy skin, and her cinnamon hair in soft, loose curls, it almost hurt to look at her. She was that beautiful. But what stole my breath was the smile. It radiated joy and a confidence I hadn't yet seen in her. *That* was fucking sexy.

As Lily slowly descended the stairs, I tore my eyes away to look at her dad. I hoped to God the man never played poker. Every emotion was clear as day: Happiness. Pride. Grief. And overwhelming love. That was unmistakable. He might've forgotten how to show it, but damn, he felt it.

My mission was clear. For this to work, I had to win over Lily's dad. I didn't know if he thought I was playing games, taking advantage of the situation, or if he just didn't like me, but somehow, someway, I'd earn his respect.

"Stone." One word in that sweet-as-sugar voice had the stress of the last twenty-four hours melting away. Lily walked right up to me, her eyes never leaving mine, and I took her hand the second I could reach it.

"You're beautiful," I whispered.

I wanted to say more, but my throat felt tight. I also knew her dad was watching like a hawk, so I didn't kiss her lips like I wanted to. But I did kiss her hand.

Her skin was soft and smelled faintly of flowers on top of her usual citrus scent. Her three-inch heels put us at almost the same height, which let me look straight into her eyes as she blushed. "Thanks. You look amazing, too."

A cocky remark was on the tip of my tongue, but I held it back with a grin. This wasn't a moment for deflection. I brushed my thumb over the back of her hand, and the way she looked at me chased away the last of the shadows.

"I didn't realize you two knew each other that well."

Lily squeezed my hand, then turned to face her father. "Stone was brave enough to become my permanent partner at Ilusiòn," she told him, sliding me a smile. "Any guy who'd willingly withstand that abuse deserves my attention, don't you think?"

I glanced sideways at Mr. Bailey. His pinched face implied he didn't share his daughter's enthusiasm, and his narrowed eyes said he knew more about me being her partner than she did. Luckily, Lily noticed neither.

A throat cleared from above, and she winced. "Oops. We decided to take turns walking down so we could each have our moment." She shot me an amused look. "Your sister's idea."

"Obviously," I replied.

Sydney appeared next, my dramatic sister clearly in charge of playing things up. Lily's best friend had on an ocean-blue gown that cinched at the waist, then fell to her knees, and her blond hair was piled on her head. Nick met her at the landing, and whatever he whispered had her blushing something fierce.

Lily nudged me, and I glanced back to the top. Angéla smiled down at us in a beautiful gold dress that stood out against her dark hair...and clung to her body like Saran wrap. I groaned as I cut my eyes to Sean. Dude looked like he'd won the damn lottery. *Great.*

When she reached the bottom, Sean was still frozen where he stood. I shook my head.

"You stay up nights thinking of new ways to torture me, don't you?" I asked, and my sister responded with a radiant smile.

"You like?" she asked, twirling around. "Reminded me of Nova's dress in *Prom*. Only sexier." I groaned again, which made her laugh, and she thrust her phone in my hand. "Here. Ma's probably in the middle of a lesson, but she wouldn't let me leave this morning without promising to text her pictures of how everyone looks."

That statement set off a flurry of excitement. The other

girls handed over their phones, too, then they gathered in front of the marble fireplace while their dates snapped picture after picture. Angéla arranged them in various poses, and Lily smiled indulgently the whole time, but after the fifth photo, she sweetly asked, "Can we get some with our dates, too?"

"Oh, right." Angéla glanced at Sean and smiled. "Of course."

With slightly less enthusiasm than before, my sister waved him over, and I snapped a picture for Ma. When it was our turn, I held Lily close, trying to ignore the imposing man with his eyes targeted on my arm slung around her tiny waist. I held my breath and smiled for the camera.

Lily thumbed through the pictures on her phone and shook her head with a laugh.

"What?" I asked, peeking over her shoulder. I didn't see anything funny. We looked good together.

She grinned, then zoomed in on my face. "Hey there, QB," she whisper-teased, and I leaned in to study the picture. My eyes looked guarded, and my smile was stiff. It was an exact replica of most of my pictures.

"We have to take group shots," Angéla ordered, and each of the girls handed their phone over to Mr. Bailey. As he lined them on the coffee table, we paired up in couples.

Lily pressed up tight against me, and I slid my hand on her hip.

"This time, I want the real smile," she whispered, shooting me a look over her shoulder. Our lips almost brushed against each other, and as I held my breath, her gaze dropped to my mouth.

I rasped my thumb over the coarse lace of her dress. "Every smile with you is real," I whispered back, and when her liquid gaze lifted, it took everything I had not to kiss her.

"Everyone say, *Homecoming*," Mr. Bailey called out gruffly, and focusing on the girl in my arms, I smiled.

After another series of flashes, he held up his hand. "I'd like to take a couple with my own camera, if that's okay." Lily's soft lips parted, but she quickly nodded. Her dad shoved his hands in his pockets. "I used to be somewhat of a novice photographer. Haven't done it in years, though." He cleared his throat. "If you'll excuse me, I'll go grab my kit."

Lily watched him go with a slightly stunned expression, and I reached into my pocket for the velvet pouch. My guess was we didn't have a lot of time, but I wanted her to have this before we left. Squeezing her hip, I turned her toward me.

"I have something for you," I murmured, and her blue eyes sparkled.

"You do?" I nodded with a nervous smile. I hadn't given many gifts to girls before, other than Angéla, and truthfully, she'd picked out most of the others. This was one I'd had specially made. Lily bounced on her heels and asked excitedly, "Well, what is it?"

As she danced in place, I shook my head with a laugh, taking her hand and opening it. My stomach went into a bit of free fall tipping the velvet pouch, but when I slid the delicate silver chain into her palm, Lily gasped and stroked the small round pendant on the end.

Her voice was almost reverent when she asked, "What does it say?"

"*Chingona*," I told her uncertainly, and Angéla glanced at me. I cleared my throat. "It basically means badass in Spanish. A girl who marches to her own beat and makes her own path. Someone who's fearless and sexy." She lifted her eyes to mine, and I swallowed hard. "That's you, Lily. You're strong and you're fierce. There's nothing you can't do, and

I thought this could help you remember that."

Her lips trembled. My chest tightened in fear, sure that meant she hated it, and I rushed to say, "It's okay if you don't like it. You don't have to keep it. I know *badass* is a strange choice for a necklace. I can get you something else if you—"

Lily pressed her mouth against mine. The kiss was quick. One solid brush of lips before her dad returned. But even as I held myself back from deepening it, I couldn't let her go. I rested my forehead on hers, breathing in citrus and flowers, and stared into her beautiful eyes. This girl.

Beside us, my sister *aww*ed, and Sydney sighed. Lily laughed quietly.

"Put it on me?" she asked with a soft smile.

"Seriously, you don't have to wear it tonight. If it doesn't go with your dress—"

She put a finger over my mouth. "Please? I want to wear it. I love it."

"Yeah?" She nodded, looking at my mouth again as she slowly lowered her finger, and my hands clenched around her hips. I replied huskily, "As you wish," using one of Angéla's favorite movie quotes to speak for me.

Lily laughed as she twirled, holding up her hair so I could slide the delicate chain around her neck. I clasped it, letting my fingertips linger over the silky skin of her nape.

She shivered, and a slow smile curved my lips. I pressed a kiss against her skin, eliciting another shudder.

When I raised my head, Mr. Bailey was back. A storm raged in his eyes.

Chapter Twenty-Five

LILY

Brighton's gym glowed an eerie blue. Strings of glittering lights were tacked up near the ceiling, while swaths of white fabric were artfully draped on the wall, dressing up the place. The effect, admittedly, was kind of romantic. Unfortunately, fancy decorations and a kick-ass DJ couldn't disguise the lingering aroma of ratty socks and stale sweat.

Even so, it was the most spectacular dance I'd ever been to.

Technically, it was also the *only* dance I'd ever been to, but I doubted the memory of a hundred others could've topped this one. Stone looked incredible in his dark suit and red tie. He hadn't left my side since we arrived, holding my hand in the photo line, pressing kisses against my temple at our table, and twirling me around the crowded floor.

Yep, that's right. Lily Bailey was dancing in public.

Perhaps more noteworthy, so was Stone Torres.

Dancing to slow songs was one thing. Anyone could sway in place and fake rhythm. But fast songs didn't let you hide, especially once the gyrating crowd thinned out. Stone had once told me that people didn't want a "Mambo King" for their football captain, so when "Feel It Still" by Portugal The Man came on, I'd expected him to lead me back to our friends.

He shrugged when I glanced at our table. "The cat will be out of the bag soon enough," he said, swinging me back into his arms. I squealed, and his tense smile turned almost playful. "Besides, if I'm doing it right, no one will be looking at me anyway."

The line, while hot, set off a flutter of nerves in my stomach. I wasn't certain I wanted them staring at *me*, either. But then Stone put his hands on me, pulling me close as he swiveled his hips against mine, and I forgot all about our audience.

Thankfully, the room was dark. Other groups of dancers also kept people from gawking too much — and if they were, I was soon having too much fun to notice. Maybe it was the new charm around my neck, giving me an added boost of confidence. Tonight, I wanted to be fearless. I wanted to stop thinking so much and be the girl Stone saw when he looked at me. Even if just for a little while.

Song shifted into song, and I moved my body to the music. Before long, my dress was clinging to my back and sweat glistened on my arms. Stone slid his hand up my spine, threading his fingers through my damp hair, and when his teeth sank into his bottom lip, my stomach was a giant flutter. The lyrics to one of Mom's favorite songs and a sleepy Audrey Hepburn floated through my mind — I, too, could've danced all night.

Stone kept finding ways to work in moves from our routine. A turn here, a cross-body lead there. I was amazed at how easily they translated to mainstream music. My veins pulsed with adrenaline, and my smile felt permanently etched onto my face. For the first time in my life, I felt graceful. I felt lighter than air.

Honestly, I felt like a dancer.

I should've known the other shoe would drop.

It was toward the end of "Havana" by Camila Cabello, a sexy song that worked surprisingly well with salsa moves, that Stone shocked me again. He spun me out in a familiar move, sending me into a back rock, and my eyes widened as he squatted low.

A wave of anxiety rushed over me as he tugged my right hand as if to lead me into the dip I'd continued to fail at so spectacularly. I drew up short, shaking my head while I pleaded with my eyes.

I didn't want to fail again. Not here, not tonight. Not after I'd had so many wins.

The strong lines of Stone's face softened in understanding, and my heart gave a thump. Standing, he tugged my hand again, and this time I responded. The scent of wintergreen filled my head as he pulled me against his chest, hugging me close for a too-brief moment before he lowered me toward the floor, ending the song in a modified dip.

We hovered there, a heartbeat of silence stretched between us. His arms securely holding my weight, and our heavy breaths mingling. I ducked my head into his chest, inhaling harshly, and a warmth that had nothing to do with the press of bodies around us floated through me. The sensation spread, and as reality descended, my shoulders rocked with inexplicable laughter.

Stone's hold tightened, and after lifting us upright, he rested his forehead against mine, searching my eyes, his own lit with happiness.

"I'm trying to remember why I thought these years didn't

matter," I admitted somewhat breathlessly, and his chest expanded in an inhale.

Golden cheeks flushed from exertion lifted in a smile only *this side* of cocky. Sliding his hands up my arms, he skimmed his thumbs over my collarbone, dipping them in the hollow of my throat while an array of emotions flittered across his gorgeous face. Satisfaction, happiness, adoration… and what looked like a tiny hint of fear at the very end. It confused me, but then his eyes closed, and he brushed his lips against mine, and my thoughts scattered.

Stone's kisses made my head spin. We were in the middle of the dance floor, so I wasn't surprised when he didn't move to deepen it, choosing instead to keep it light and teasing, but it rocked me just the same. A jolt of desire tightened my core, shooting tingles of aftershocks racing across my skin. I didn't think I'd ever get used to the way he made me feel. Beautiful and wanted. Like a fierce *badass*.

Goose bumps spread down my arms, and he lifted his head. I opened my eyes, still a bit dazed, and said the first thing that popped into my mind.

"I need to go to the bathroom."

His eyebrows shot up, and I slapped a hand over my mouth.

"Okay then," he said, fighting a smile. "I'll wait here."

"No! Not like that," I rushed to explain, taking a step back. "Not like to *pee*…although, now that I think about it, I probably do have to go. We've been dancing for over an hour, and man, that punch really goes through you." My eyes widened in further distress, and I covered my hot cheeks with both hands. "Crap. What I *meant* is I need to go to the bathroom to freshen up. And clear my head. And stop talking. Did I mention I ramble when I'm nervous?"

The smile broke free as he closed the distance I'd put

between us. "I make you nervous?" he asked, his voice a low rumble.

I shook my head…then nodded helplessly. "It's more the way you make me *feel* that makes me nervous," I admitted, my nose scrunched.

Stone tucked a strand of hair behind my ear, then whispered across it, "And how do I make you feel?"

I shivered at the sensations that simple action incited, and my eyes fluttered to a close. "Beautiful," I whispered back, my heart starting to pound. "Like I never want you to stop kissing me. Like I don't necessarily want to *stop* at kissing, either."

Stone's sharp inhale made something low in my stomach clench, and I opened my eyes. "Like maybe getting sick that day was the best thing that could've happened to me," I added, placing my hand on his chest. "Because in the end, it brought me to you."

The muscles in his jaw flexed, and the look on his face was so intense, so vulnerable, he almost looked like he was in pain. "Lily…God, I want to make you feel those things, baby." He glided a thumb over the thundering pulse point in my neck, and the thick knot in his throat bobbed. "But… maybe not in the middle of a school dance."

He inhaled again, and his lips quirked in a rueful smile. Taking a step away, he said, "And not when I have to bring you home to your dad in an hour. Go. Freshen up. I'm, uh, I'm gonna go get some air."

The hungry look in his eyes made me smirk, and I couldn't help but preen a little. It was so crazy that I affected *him* as much as he affected *me*. Feeling strangely confident, I brushed up against him as I headed for the women's locker room, and when he groaned, I bit back a laugh.

Hips swaying more than usual, I walked across the room,

exchanging smiles with random classmates along the way. My black, lacy dress was a daring change of pace for me, as was the makeup. I'd asked Angéla and Sydney for help, wanting to step outside my usual comfort zone. Stone always seemed so sure about us, but tonight, I'd wanted to believe I belonged with him, too.

"Love your dress, Lily," Chloe Meyers said, gliding past too fast for me to return the compliment. Biting my bottom lip, I lifted my chin.

People knew my name. Strangers, or classmates who'd acted as such for years, had stopped to tell me hello or comment on my dress all night. I wasn't an idiot; I knew it was because I was with Stone. But I wasn't a ghost anymore.

It felt like I was coming up for air after three years of being underwater.

A happy thrill shot from the crown of my head to my exposed, red-painted toenails, strong enough to defy the hateful glare Cameron sent my way when our eyes clashed across the floor. I brushed my fingertip across the charm around my neck, shook off the unease, then ducked inside the locker room. A cloud of hairspray, perfume, and lingering bleach assaulted me, along with a complicated maze of gossiping girls and selfie piles that blocked my way to the stalls. By the time I did my business, scrunched my hair, and dabbed at runaway mascara, I'd overheard more about my classmates than I'd ever wished to learn. Strangely enough, it only made me happier.

Stepping back out into the gym, I took a deep breath of slightly fresher air and noticed a familiar form leaned against the stacked bleachers.

"Aidan, hey." A quick scan of the floor didn't reveal Stone, so I assumed he was still outside. I walked up in front of my tutee/friend and said, "You look nice tonight."

He sighed and adjusted his already loosened green-striped tie. "Thanks, but I hate these things. As soon as Brittany gets out of there, I'm taking this damn thing off and we're out."

I bit my tongue. According to one of the more *interesting* conversations I'd overheard inside the locker room, if Aidan played his cards right, he'd soon be taking off a lot more than his tie. I kept that tidbit to myself.

"But you look great," he told me with a friendly smile. "I saw you and Stone dancing. Wow. Maybe I should take lessons, too, huh? I'm usually happy if I don't make an ass of myself or step on my date's shoes."

Laughing, I rested my shoulder against the bleachers. "Between you and me, I've stepped on my fair share of toes, too. Luckily, Stone's feet are numb at this point, so he can't tell anymore."

Aidan chuckled, but his smile quickly turned pained. The air between us grew tense. "Lily, I owe you an apology." He released a breath, regret lining his face. "I was out of line in the library. I really meant to look out for you, but it was none of my business. Seeing the two of you together, it's obvious whatever tailspin he was in is over. You're good for each other. I never should've butted in."

Music swelled in the room, and I stepped closer to be heard. "You were being a friend. Yeah, it was a bit harsh, but it came from a good place."

Aidan smiled gratefully. "For what it's worth, you both look happy. In fact, I've never seen Stone like this before." I ducked my head with a grin, and he sighed. "Who the hell am I to give relationship advice, anyway? My love life's a train wreck."

"Oh, I don't know," I murmured with a secret smile. "Something tells me your luck might turn around sooner than you think."

A slow, curious grin curved his lips, and he leaned toward me. "Oh yeah? You been talking to Brittany?"

He wiggled his eyebrows playfully, wanting me to spill, and I laughed as I pushed him away. "Nuh-uh. My lips are sealed."

As Aidan dove at me again, he glanced over my shoulder. Whatever he saw had the smile falling instantly from his face. His eyes narrowed in confusion, then he looked at me and they blew wide.

"Hey, man." He backed away, hands lifted in the air, as Stone appeared by my side. "Just keeping your girl company while I waited for Brittany."

Stone stayed silent. He glared at his teammate, his arms folded and jaw set.

Aidan swallowed visibly. "Speaking of Brit, I should probably check on her. Yeah? She should have her phone on her." He tugged his phone out and waved it like evidence. "You two have fun. See you Monday, man."

He patted Stone's shoulder as he walked off, passing the locker room, and I watched him hustle away with a puzzled frown. Shifting my gaze to a sullen Stone, I tilted my head.

Weird.

"You know that was nothing, right?" I asked after an extended moment. A muscle in Stone's jaw flexed, and I placed a hand on his arm. "You're not…*jealous*…are you?" My eyes darted back and forth between his. "Because that'd be silly."

A group of girls was headed to the locker room, and to get out of their path, Stone stepped into me. I wrapped my arms around his waist, trying to meet his eyes, and he closed them as his shoulders slumped. My breathing hitched.

"Are you serious?" I buried my head in his neck, inhaling

his Ivory soap and wintergreen scent, and pressed my lips against his skin. A thrill danced down my spine when he shivered against me. "Stone, I realize you've been burned, but I promise, that's not gonna happen with me. You're the only one I want. You can trust me."

His chest expanded with an inhale, and he settled his hands at my hips. "I know I can," he told me roughly.

I raised my head and caught a hint of insecurity lingering in his eyes. I threaded my fingers through the soft hair at his neck, wanting to chase it away, and a small smile curved his mouth.

"Though, if anyone's silly in this relationship, it's you," he said, looking at me with an expression of wonder. "You still don't see how incredible you are." His thumbs rasped over the lace of my dress, and it was my turn to shiver. "I'll get through to you one day."

His dark chocolate gaze fell to my lips, where it lingered for a toe-curling beat. When it lifted, the last of the shadows were finally gone. He huffed a laugh. "Am I jealous, she asks? Damn straight, I am. *I* want to be the one making you laugh. You're *my* girl."

The exaggerated pout was so unexpected, so much like Angéla, that my head fell back in a laugh. Stone made a pleased sound in his throat. "God, that laugh," he murmured, gripping my hips tighter. "Do you have any idea how crazy I am about you?"

I shook my head, and he took my mouth in a searing kiss.

Shock had me freezing for a second. Stone hated spectacles. Making out in the open, next to the locker room where anyone could see? It would make a splash. But then he deepened the kiss, groaning as he slid his tongue against mine, and I forgot the world.

Chapter Twenty-Six

STONE

"I can't believe I'm doing this!"

Lily smiled from the driver's side of her car. The glow in her eyes and crazy tangle of hair dancing in the wind from the open windows momentarily distracted me from the lukewarm air-conditioning—not exactly hot but barely cool—and strange whistle that had been our morning's playlist. The radio itself was on the fritz, evidently having not worked for six months. I'd tried it anyway, after she'd insisted on driving, and a high-frequency buzz had emitted through the speakers.

"Silence lets me think," she'd said after I quickly shut it off. A sly grin had then twitched her lips. "But if you want music, I can always sing."

All I could say: it was a good thing I liked her so much. My girl had a voice that could make dogs cry.

Despite its lack of radio and air-conditioning, Lily clearly loved this car. Driving down back roads to the Lakefront, she smiled and hummed as horse pastures and open country surrounded us. Occasionally, she'd stroke the dash or flick the fuzzy purple dice I'd won for her at the festival, her eyes sparkling. This was *Debbie*. Her mom's pride and joy, and the one link they still had, other than dancing. Seeing Lily happy like this shifted the heavy weight that had been crushing my lungs all week.

"How does it feel being a delinquent?" I asked with a devilish smirk. Her musical laugh filled the car, and she tucked a strand of hair behind her ear, only for it to fly back out with the wind.

"Naughty and freeing at the same time," she replied, two adjectives I doubted existed in her vocabulary before she'd met me.

Although our one-month dare had expired, we'd extended it by silent agreement, both looking for ways to stretch past her comfort zone. Today's excursion was the biggest stretch yet. Honestly, I'd half expected her to use her veto.

Senior Skip Day was a rite of passage. Every year, the day after Columbus Day, the entire class met at the Lakefront for fun in the sun before senioritis hit and the pressure of college applications reigned. Report cards always went out the week before, which meant everyone knew where they stood, and while teachers were usually chill, there'd still be plenty of time to make up work before the end of the semester.

As expected, Lily's grades were awesome. If anyone could afford a day off, it was her.

The one glitch had been her dad, though not for the normal reasons. When she'd told him about the tradition and her plans to join in, he'd been all for it...up until I'd appeared to whisk her away, that is.

"Good," I told her, tapping my hand to an imaginary beat outside the car. The bright sun warmed my skin, pushing away worries of disapproving dads and replacing them with thoughts of Lily in a bikini. "I like giving you new experiences. I *especially* like making you—"

A loud squeal under the hood cut short the flirtation.

Wide, scared eyes flew to mine. Two seconds later, white smoke billowed through the vents. My first thought was the car was on fire. The second was to shut off the damn air-conditioning.

"Pull over," I ordered, trying and failing to calm the fear in my voice.

The squealing whistle had stopped when I shut off the air, but the smoke remained. Lily checked her mirrors then quickly tugged the wheel to the side. As soon as her foot tapped the break, I was out of the car.

"Pop the latch," I told her, my phone out to dial Gabriel's number. Moments like this, I wished I'd paid more attention when I used to hang at his shop. I slammed the passenger door shut and jogged around the front of the car.

"Stone!" The panic in Lily's voice snapped my eyes to hers, my hand on the hood.

Shaking, she waited for a semi to pass alongside us. Once it did, she staggered to meet me, her gaze clinging to mine. Fear and worry swirled behind her lenses.

With a fortifying breath, I popped the hood. The scent of burned rubber poured over us, and Lily grabbed hold of my arm. Coughing, I swiped at the air, clearing it away.

"She's gone," she stated brokenly. "Isn't she?"

I didn't know if she meant the car or her mom. Just then, probably both. Losing this car, losing *Debbie*, would be like losing her mom all over again. My eyes squeezed shut, wishing I could save her from this. Blindly, I grabbed for her, pulling her close and pressing my lips to her head.

"*¿Qué tal?*"

The familiar voice yanked me from my spiral. I glanced at my phone, realizing I must've hit call, and quickly put it to my ear. "Gabriel."

After a swift rundown of the situation, explaining how the smoke had dissipated once I'd opened the hood, my mechanic cousin said, "Yeah, doesn't sound like a fire. Have you checked the coolant?"

"You think it overheated?"

I leaned over to check and grunted under my breath. The cap was busted, cracked completely across the side and on top, almost broken in two. As for the coolant…

"Bone dry," I told him. "Totally empty. That would explain the burning smell."

Thanking Gabriel, I told him I'd call him later and clicked off. Staring at the engine, I made a plan, then closed the hood, steered Lily to the passenger side, and gently placed her in the car.

"Give me the keys, baby." I squatted on the side of the road, and her wet blue eyes held mine. They looked so lost. I took her hand, the one clutching her keys like a lifeline, and closed my fingers around it. "I'm gonna take care of it, okay? I need you to stay with me."

She nodded silently, and I reached over to buckle her in and press a kiss to her temple. Then I closed the door and blew out a breath, gripping my neck as I surveyed where we were. Luckily, we'd almost made it back to the main road. A gas station was about a mile ahead.

Once we got to the Shell station, I grabbed a gallon of prediluted antifreeze and a roll of duct tape. I also got a bag of peanut M&M's because I wasn't above bribing in a moment of crisis.

The sound of idling engines and country music drifted out of neighboring cars as I filled the coolant. Once that was done, I rigged the cap the best I could with duct tape to keep it from falling off. The sting of sweat burned my eyes, and I swiped a hand across my forehead. I'd done all I could. Closing the hood again, I cleaned my hands with a paper towel from the dispenser and chucked it in the overflowing bin.

The damn weight was back in my chest. This time for an entirely different reason. Knowing how much this was hurting her overshadowed my own selfish fears of her leaving me. Duct tape had stopped the bleeding, but the car was falling apart. This was only the tip of the iceberg, and I had a feeling she knew it, too.

Shoving my hand through my damp hair, I squeezed the tips in frustration. This was *not* how I'd imagined spending the day. I'd pictured Lily in a bikini, laughing in the water, and maybe stealing a kiss or two. Not sweltering in a humid car alongside the road. Feeling helpless to stop her pain.

I squared my shoulders with a sigh. I couldn't stop it completely, but I could damn sure let her know she wasn't alone.

I yanked open the driver's side door, and gratitude filled her eyes as she looked at me like Angéla did whenever she called me Captain.

"Is she fixed?"

The hope in her voice slayed me. I didn't have it in me to destroy that just yet, so I took her hand, gently kissed her fingertips, and placed our joined hands on the armrest. "It's not pretty, but it's holding. We'll go to AutoZone and I'll put in a replacement cap, okay?"

At this point, it was like putting lipstick on a pig, but at least it was an action step.

A half hour later, I had a replacement cap ordered, a potential diagnosis of leaking Freon along with who-knew-what-else happening under the hood, and a girl who owned a good chunk of my heart devastated in the front seat.

Lily turned when I slid back behind the wheel. Her hand clutched the charm I'd given her, and a heartbeat of silence stretched between us before she gave a quivery smile. "Stone, I wanted to thank you." I shifted in my seat to face her. "I've been sitting here thinking about what would've happened, or how I would've handled it, if I'd been alone today. But the thing is, I wasn't. You were there."

She licked her lips, then glanced out the windshield. "I struggle with anxiety. I know, shocking, right? But stress… it's usually a trigger for me, and over the last month"—she laughed softly and looked back with a wry smile—"let's just say I've had a lot of it. But somehow, in all that time, I haven't had a single attack. I've never felt out of control, and I haven't gotten sick again. Sure, I've had moments… short flares where I felt like I couldn't breathe, or the walls were closing in…but they went away as fast as they came, and it's because of *you*. You're my calm in the storm, Stone. Anxiety can't take root because you lend me your strength. You show me I'm not alone. I've spent three years having no idea how much I needed to feel like that." Her eyes filled again as she shook her head. "Something like today should've rocked me to my core, but it isn't, because you have my back."

"Baby, I'll always have your back. *Always*. Hearing you say I'm your calm…God, Lily, it makes me feel ten fucking feet tall because that's what you are for me, too." I shifted as close as the damn console allowed and cupped her face in my hand. "Which is why it terrifies me to think what could've happened if that had been a real fire. Or if I *hadn't* been with you."

Lily's chin trembled, and a tear fell down her cheek.

I brushed it away, wishing I didn't have to continue. But I couldn't sugarcoat the truth. As guilty as I felt for withholding the deal I'd made with her dad, *this* involved her safety. I had to speak up.

"What I did with the cap was a temporary fix, sweetheart, and we still don't know what's wrong with the A/C. Debbie has almost two hundred and twenty thousand miles on her. I get that she's a connection to your mom, and I know you're scared your dad will trade her in…" I stopped short of saying he should. "But you need to tell him what's going on. This is past the point of what you can handle on your own."

She took a ragged breath and slowly dragged her fingers under her eyes.

"You're right," she whispered, then cleared her throat. "I know you're right. I have to tell him, and—and I will." Her eyes begged me to understand. "Just not yet. Okay? I'll do it this weekend. We can do it together, if you want. But for today, could we focus on something else? Maybe skip the Lakefront, go get your truck, and just drive for a while?"

"Yeah, baby, we can do that." My hand hesitated around the key in the ignition, then, holding my breath, I flicked my wrist. When the engine turned over, I sent up a silent prayer of thanks. I took Lily's hand and said, "I'm all yours."

The day didn't go as planned, but it turned out to be one of the best of my life.

Instead of hitting the Lakefront, Lily and I grabbed lunch and went to a park. We walked nature trails. We lay on the grass and found shapes in the clouds. We fed ducks, talked about her mom, and arranged for Gabriel to check out her car again. It was the quietest, easiest, most relaxing day I'd ever spent. From total disaster to content calm in a few short hours. It simply confirmed what I already knew: Lily Bailey was one of a kind.

Lying on the grass, I couldn't help imagining how Cameron would've reacted in her place. She probably would've done an IG Live or story, in which she would've expected me to perform like a good boyfriend, coming off together like the world's most perfect couple. I couldn't think of a single date that hadn't been documented. Every nuance of our relationship had been online. If she hadn't been posting selfies or making duck faces at her phone, she'd been setting up and styling future posts. Nothing was real or spontaneous. Looking back, I have no idea why I stayed with her as long as I did. Being with Lily was like a breath of fresh air.

Unfortunately, as peaceful as our day at the park was, all good things came to an end.

Lily checked her watch and started squirming on the ground.

"Something wrong?" I asked.

"Not *wrong*," she said, sitting up. "But I do have to tutor Liam in an hour."

I pulled myself up, stretching the stiffness out of my back. "No problem." I started gathering the remains of our picnic lunch. "I've got film and weights anyway. While you tutor Liam, I'll hang in the gym, and then I can bring you home."

Returning to school on a skip day felt how I assumed breaking back into a prison would feel. My first stop was to see Coach.

Lily didn't know this, but after Homecoming, pictures of us at the dance had been posted online and a few of the more outspoken fans were speculating that I was no longer fully invested in the team. With gossip already swirling around town about my divided attention, the last thing I needed was him questioning me, too. Luckily, Coach didn't care about me missing class, though he did warn me not to do it again or he'd bench me. The other seniors would get the same talk, of course, but because I was team captain he held me to a higher standard. Then he waved me out of his office, and I went to hit the weights.

I was halfway through my final deadlift set when Aidan walked in.

"Hey, man." He looked nervous crossing the floor and took a seat on an open bench. "Got a second?"

"Yeah, sure." I set down the bar and snagged my towel, wiping my face as I stalled for time. It'd been over a week since Homecoming. We still hadn't talked about what had happened, but that was on me.

Aidan cleared his throat. "I wanted to explain about the other night. Lily and I, we were just talking. I wasn't hitting on your girl, man, I swear. She, uh…" He winced and stared at his lap. "She's my tutor. During our last session, I said some stupid shit, and I wanted to apologize."

My mouth opened, then closed. Honestly, I'd been the one who needed to explain. I'd acted like an idiot that night. Aidan wasn't Noah. He was a good friend who'd never hit on a girl I was dating. That didn't mean it was easy seeing them laughing and talking, though.

But what threw me was I had no idea Aidan did peer-tutoring. It wasn't like it mattered, he'd just always been the brain in our group. The smart jock. If any of us had our shit together, it was him.

Aidan's mouth lifted in a smirk. "You're surprised. That's on purpose. You remember those extra conditioning sessions with Coach?" he asked, and I nodded. "That's when I met with her."

I fell onto the opposite bench with a short laugh. "I'd wondered what that was about."

He kicked at the foam matting on the floor. "I was embarrassed. The guys make a big deal out of me being in the 'smart' classes, and I don't know, I guess I didn't want to shatter the illusion."

Aidan shrugged, playing off his admission, and I leaned forward with my elbows on my knees. "No illusions shattered, bro. You're still smart as hell. Even if you get help sometimes."

He met my gaze with a quick, grateful nod and glanced back at the floor. I cracked my neck, then flung my towel on the bench. Guess it was my turn to share.

"Listen, I'm glad you told me, but that night was on me. I've been dealing with some shit, and you caught me in the middle of it." With a sigh, I held out my hand and said, "I overreacted and I'm sorry. We cool?"

Aidan exhaled, looking relieved, and we shook hands. "Yeah, we're cool."

When I left the gym a half hour later, I felt lighter. The embarrassment over how I'd acted at Homecoming had been weighing on me, adding to the burden I already carried from everything else. Clearing the air made me eager to clear the rest, too.

Ilusiòn's showcase was in four days, which meant my day of reckoning was coming. My secret plan to save the studio was currently out of my hands, but I was trying to stay optimistic. Without it, I was back at square one, needing to tap into Mr. Bailey's money and without a long-term solution to help my family. As for the *other* plan, the one to save my relationship… I landed somewhere between cautiously hopeful and scared out of my skull.

One thing was for certain: there'd be no more delaying the truth.

Discovering how Lily felt about honesty, there was no excuse for me not coming clean at the carnival. Since I hadn't, I'd been living on borrowed time. Sure, I could argue that I'd had my reasons. My promise to her father the biggest. My worry about Ma and the studio another. But ultimately, fear was what kept me quiet. The possibility that once Lily learned the real reason I'd issued that dare she'd shut down, doubt how I truly felt about her, and bail.

My one hope was that by delaying the inevitable this past month, I'd somehow proven how much I really cared about her so that when I *did* confess, she'd give me a chance to make things right.

The hallway leading to the library was deserted. Lily's voice floated through the open door, sounding excited about fractions, of all things. She boggled my mind. Smiling, I stopped just outside the room, wanting to see her in action.

"Okay, so the first thing we do is rewrite each of the mixed numbers as improper fractions, right?" They sat at the only occupied table in the library. Lily was turned slightly away, facing the window, but I had a clear shot of the kid. "It's so much easier multiplying those. And what do we know about improper fractions?"

Her voice lilted in amusement, and the boy, who looked to be about ten, rolled his eyes. Still, he smiled as he answered, "They've got big heads."

"Yup," she said with a solemn nod. "They're jerks, and jerks love to multiply. Moral of the story, Liam? Don't be a jerk."

The kid laughed. "I won't." He grabbed his pencil to work the problem, and I noticed his left arm was bent at an awkward angle. Leaning against their table were two canes, each with a tripod base.

Lily sat back, watching Liam write his answer in his notebook. Her profile was soft with affection and happiness, and my chest physically hurt looking at her. Everything she did, she gave her whole heart and soul. She was incredible.

Liam narrowed his eyes, tongue stuck out in concentration. He flipped his pencil to erase what he'd written, then sat back with a frustrated frown, his gaze drifting across the room. It passed over me at the door— then immediately snapped back.

"Stone Torres." Awe underscored his voice, and I pushed away from the wall.

"That's me." I smiled as I walked into the room. Obviously, the kid was a football fan. "What are you two working on in here?"

"Math," he grumbled, and Lily nudged him with her elbow.

"Liam has a test tomorrow, but he only likes math when it has to do with sports or player stats," she confided in amusement. "You two have a lot in common. Liam's an athlete, too. He plays baseball for a challenger league and he's Brighton's number one fan. According to him, you're on track to decimate last year's completion record."

"Smart man," I replied, dragging an empty chair to their table. I spun it around and straddled it across from Liam. "My friend Brandon Taylor pitches for Fairfield Academy and volunteers as a buddy in the challenger league. Ever met him?"

Liam nodded excitedly. "Brandon's awesome. I wish they had a challenger league for football, because that's my favorite. Mom takes me to every Brighton game."

"Is that right?" An idea came to me, and I leaned in. "Well then, we should reward our biggest fan, don't you think? Tell you what. You study tonight and try your best on that test, and I'll see what we can do about getting you on the sidelines Friday night. We can use an assistant water boy, if you're interested."

Liam's eyes grew wide. "But you play the Morton Mustangs Friday. They're your biggest rival!"

"I'm aware," I replied, swallowing down a laugh. I shot Lily a wink. "But you'll have to study hard for that test, and your mom needs to see it. She's the one who's gonna tell Lily, and then I'll talk to Coach."

"You're on!"

The hero-worship on his face almost choked me up. So many people in our town idolized me. They admired me for my stats and revered me for how I handled the team. Most of the time I felt like one giant collection of expectations and idolizations. A caricature of myself. But with Liam, it was different. Sure, he'd looked impressed when I first walked in, but the hero-worship came later, for something I did *off* the field.

It made me feel like maybe I'd actually earned it.

Pride swelled in my chest, and I reached over, ruffling the kid's hair. Then I leaned in to see what he was working on. Algebra II and Advanced Math sucked, but I could handle fifth-grade fractions.

I gave a suggestion for the problem, and as Liam bent back over his schoolwork, eyes glowing with a newfound determination and his pencil ready, I glanced up to see Lily watching me with a soft, adoring expression.

Thank you, she mouthed with a gentle smile.

It was then that I knew.

I was in love with Lily Bailey.

Chapter Twenty-Seven

LILY

The setting sun cast a shimmering glow over downtown Cypress Lake as I studied Dad from the passenger side of his car. Tonight was "Family Night." The school board, in response to concerns about stress and our workload, had sprinkled six no-homework nights throughout the year in the hopes of creating free time for family bonding. This was the first one Dad was in town for, and he'd insisted on spending it with me at Ilusiòn.

Something was different with him. There was a new energy that hadn't existed before this last trip. The spark I'd seen in the guidance office was back in his eyes, blazing brighter than it had in three years. He'd been home for twelve whole days, with no talk of leaving again, and his office door had remained open since the night he'd arrived.

As cautiously optimistic as I was about the change, I was also terrified. So far, Dad hadn't noticed anything off with Debbie. He hadn't been home when Stone and I dropped her off yesterday morning, but I still had two more nights to get through until Gabriel picked her up Friday. He'd promised to run a full diagnostic and call me with the results, but with Dad's renewed presence, it'd take a miracle for him not to realize something was up before then.

It'd take an even bigger miracle to save my poor car.

Dad cleared his throat. "Is this your final lesson before the showcase?"

I shifted on the leather seat, tucking a leg beneath me. "Yep. Everything is pretty much set, we're just polishing choreography and working on our story."

"Story, huh?" He glanced at me. "Like acting?"

"In a way. Mrs. Viktória wants us to interpret the lyrics and apply them to our facial expressions and movements." I ducked my head, hoping the heavy fall of my hair hid my blush. "The song we're dancing to is about two people meeting, discovering they have a lot in common, and falling in love."

Actually, "Shape of You" was a bit more than that. It was overtly sexual, and the couple's relationship began with them having sex, but if I'd said that, I had a hunch Dad would've had a coronary and wrecked the car. He was acting protective enough as it was.

Still, he frowned at the windshield. "And you're dancing to this with Stone?"

I bit my lip to hide my smile. "Yes, Dad. He *is* my partner."

It was oddly cute, seeing him get all parental. I'd never really had a boyfriend for him to worry about before. When he'd surprised me by coming home early the day of Homecoming, I'd been so preoccupied getting ready I hadn't prepared him for meeting Stone. They'd met once at Ilusiòn, but he'd had no clue we'd started hanging out, or that we were now together. I could see how it'd come as a shock, returning home after spending so much time away and discovering your daughter was not only grown up, but she now had a love life.

Protectiveness aside, I would've thought he'd be happy with my choice in boyfriend. Ballroom lessons had been his idea, after all, and I was dating the teacher's son, which almost guaranteed I'd stick with it…as long as the showcase went well.

Dad harrumphed but said no more as he pulled into the parking lot.

When we walked inside, the chime on the door was swallowed by Christina Aguilera's powerful voice belting "Show Me How You Burlesque," which meant Cameron's group was wrapping up their samba routine. As much as I hated being impressed by anything having to do with Stone's ex and my academic rival, I couldn't help creeping closer to watch.

The five women were in their costumes, white button-down shirts, black shorts with fishnet stockings, and wide-brim hats slung low. As for the dance itself, I was mesmerized. Mrs. Viktória had outdone herself. While the moves were tasteful, they were also playfully sensual.

Despite being the bane of my existence, Cameron was a great dancer. She moved her body with style and grace, and she wasn't afraid to give herself over to the music, interpreting the seductive beats with the sway of her hips.

Part of me was envious; I'd love to look that confident. To *feel* that confident. But the truth was I'd come a long way in six weeks. In this tale, the gangly giraffe hadn't exactly turned into a swan, but I was a heck of a lot closer than I'd ever been in my life. I'd also somehow gotten the guy, and he liked me, lanky legs and all.

Across the room, the hero of the story, and one of the biggest reasons for my transformation, looked up from his textbook. When his eyes locked with mine, he smiled.

"Okay, ladies," Mrs. Viktória called, stealing my attention from her son. "That was beautiful. The air-conditioning will need to be turned down after that sexy performance!" She shimmied her shoulders, and the women in the routine laughed. "Now, I must start my next lesson, but please stay if you want to work on the variation we added to the middle. If not, I'll see you Saturday!"

With a happy cheer, the group broke apart, and most headed for the door. Only two dancers chose to stay, and not surprisingly, Cameron was one of them.

I had my doubts it was the call of samba that had her lingering—and not the chance to watch me and Stone— but either way, I mentally erased her half of the room. I didn't have the time or energy to worry about her motives. This was the final rehearsal before our very important, very *public* performance. I couldn't afford distractions.

As Mrs. Viktória strode toward the stereo system, Stone stood from the bistro table and closed his textbook. I motioned for Dad to take a seat, then sauntered toward my man.

"Get any studying in?" I asked with a sympathetic smile. Stone was spending his nights at the studio this week, coming in as soon as practice ended and staying until after closing, helping his mom and sister with anything that popped up. The stress was high leading up to the showcase, and the entire family was feeling it.

"Some," he replied with a tired smile. Dark smudges lined his eyes, and I reached up to touch them gently. Stone glanced at my dad, then took my hand. "How about you? Did you study for anatomy?"

"That test won't know what hit it," I replied, injecting my voice with false confidence. Science didn't come as easily to me as the other subjects, but I was as prepared as I'd ever be. Besides, he didn't need to add my stress to his already-toppling plate.

The bell-like tinkle of a music box rolled through the speakers, and Mrs. Viktória clapped. "My darlings!"

After I slipped off my glasses, Stone led me to the floor, and I snuck a quick glance at Dad, half expecting to find him on his phone. His hands were folded on the tabletop, his eyes focused and interested.

"You already know the dance. Tonight, I don't want you worried about steps. Instead, I want you to *feel*. Listen to the words of the song, and then become the characters. Let them live through you. Let them breathe. Okay?"

A flutter of nerves tightened my stomach as I nodded. Thus far, the totality of my acting experience amounted to me kicking my shoe across the room during the fourth-grade play and narrowly escaping knocking out the principal. Fortunately, my dance shoes had straps.

Even so, I glanced down to make sure they were buckled.

"This song is about the start of a new relationship," she instructed, circling us as the music continued. "The feelings you get when you first meet. The excitement. As the couple starts to dance, the man says it is like she is made just for him. They are meant to be."

Stone squeezed my hand, and my stomach fluttered for an entirely new reason.

At its heart, our song was about a man looking for love. While the initial spark came from physical attraction, it developed into something deeper. Something wonderfully unexpected. *That* didn't require acting.

We listened to the song several times, slowly bringing the couple to life. During each run-through, I became more and more like the girl—or she became more like me. Relaxing into the movement, adding more of a sway to my hips. It was freeing, taking on a new persona. It gave me that final push to let go and fully immerse myself in the choreography.

It didn't matter if *I* didn't feel confident in the movement; the girl in the song did. With her help, I nailed the sequence of fast, intense turns toward the end, and was even only slightly shaky on the dip.

Even better, I didn't kick Stone in the head.

The music drifted to a close, and a loud *whoop* rent the air. I laughed at Angéla as Stone carefully helped me back to my feet, and she, Mrs. Viktória, and Marcus, along with the other woman from the burlesque routine, all clapped and cheered. Even Dad pushed to his feet, wearing a huge, proud smile I felt in my chest.

Warmth radiated throughout my body, even as the air kicked on and goose bumps dotted my skin. The entire room felt lifted somehow. Like we were all in this together, and an unmistakable thread of hope and joy knitted us as one.

The only person not smiling, in fact, was Cameron.

Stone yanked me into his chest, breathing hard against my ear. "God, you're amazing."

"No, you are," I whispered fiercely, my heart racing as I looked over his shoulder at the mirror. A new message was scrawled in black marker across the top: *When you are in love, your heart dances to bachata.*

For the first time, Mrs. Viktória was wrong. It should've said salsa.

"Wonderful! Wow, wow, wow. My heart is overflowing!" My shoulders shook at the genuine, effervescent praise only Mrs. Viktória could pull off. "I cannot tell you how proud I am!"

Stone squeezed me one last time, then stepped away, and I bit my lip as I looked at his mother. "The ending was still a little shaky," I admitted, feeling the need to point out the obvious.

"Let it go, love." Mrs. Viktória walked up to me, her face soft with affection. "What have I told you? Forget the moves that already happened. Stop fretting the ones to come. Just dance, yes?"

I nodded, and she squeezed my shoulder affectionately. Then a strange gleam hit her green eyes and she turned to face the other side of the studio. The older blonde was already strolling to the leather sofa where she'd left her purse, apparently calling it a night, which left only one other student remaining. A certain brunette who now stood with her arms crossed and mouth pinched in a sour expression.

"Cameron," Mrs. Viktória called in a rather loud voice, "are you struggling with the changes to the choreography?"

Lips previously smashed together parted in surprise. "No?" The response came out like a question, and I bit back a smile as she bristled, shaking her thick brown hair over her shoulders. "I was just finishing up."

"Oh, good." Mrs. Viktória smiled warmly. "Then I will see you Saturday."

Cameron had effectively been dismissed.

She glanced at the ground, then raised her eyes and focused on Stone. "Think you can walk me out? I'd really like to talk to you."

"Nah," he said, grabbing a water from the table and uncapping it. "I think we've said all there is to say by now, don't you?"

He took a long gulp from the bottle, disregarding her as easily as his mom had, and Cameron's face tightened before her gaze shifted to me.

Eyes hard, she tilted her chin downward, clearly finding me lacking. But with no reason left to stay, she grabbed her duffel bag and shuffled out the door.

Mrs. Viktória turned and gave me a wink.

Angéla bounded across the floor. "Can we show her now?"

All thoughts of Cameron and the promise of retaliation I'd seen in her eyes flitted away at the pure excitement radiating from my friend's entire body. "Show me what?" I asked.

"We scoured through Ma's costume collection and found a few that would be *perfect* for you!" she exclaimed with a happy bounce. "They should fit, even with the height difference, and they're in the office now. I know you planned on wearing street clothes, but trust me, this'll be *so* much better."

She started to tug me away, and I dragged my feet, my hand flying to my chest. "Wait…are you serious?"

My wide eyes landed on Stone, and the quick flash of dimples told me he'd been in on it.

This was a big deal. For them and for me. Those dance costumes were Mrs. Viktória's pride and joy; she'd saved every single one, from every single performance her entire life. Angéla had once joked she loved the costumes more than her own children, and while anyone who knew the Torres family knew it wasn't true, it did show the care she put into them.

My thoughts drifted back to the park, when we were lying in the grass looking at clouds. I'd told Stone that more than anything, I wished Mom could watch our performance. After kissing my forehead, he'd told me she would be. Those words, spoken by an incredible guy in such a romantic, woodland setting, had made me feel like a fairy-tale princess.

If that were the case, then Mrs. Viktória was my Fairy Godmother.

Angéla tugged my hands again, dragging me to the front of the studio, and this time I went willingly. Mrs. Viktória led the way, pushing open the office door, but at the threshold, I glanced back, hoping to catch Stone's eyes again.

Unfortunately, he was preoccupied. He and Dad stood side by side on the gleaming hardwood, a wary look on Stone's face as he shoved his hands deep in his pockets. My smile dimmed. The two men in my life were at odds, but I hoped soon Dad would realize how amazing Stone was and how happy he made me. Then he'd drop the Protective Dad schtick, and everything would be perfect.

"Come on," Angéla scolded impatiently. With an indulgent grin, I let her tug me through the door into a world of pretty costumes.

Chapter Twenty-Eight

STONE

The moment the office door closed, Mr. Bailey lifted his chin toward the parking lot. "Let's take a walk."

I nodded tightly and blew out a breath, falling in step behind him.

This conversation had been a long time coming. Hell, it should've happened the night we made the agreement. He had no idea what kind of guy I was, outside of being the studio owner's son and someone who'd once made Lily smile. It made sense he'd question my motives now that I was dating his daughter. Especially considering how we started.

Night had descended when we pushed open the main door to Ilusiòn. The boutique shops were closed for the day, leaving only the lights outside the Mexican and Italian restaurants flanking the strip and the bakery a few stores down illuminated.

I followed Mr. Bailey around the corner, into a dim alcove that led to additional parking. As loose dirt crunched under my dance shoes, I realized this would make an excellent set-up for a thriller. Disapproving dad takes daughter's boyfriend out back into a dark alley. The script practically wrote itself.

...And Angéla's movie obsession had officially messed with my head.

Mr. Bailey stopped beside a large bench, but he didn't sit. Not wanting to appear weak, I didn't, either. The man already had a couple inches on me, and he handled negotiations for a living. Plus, he had the power to keep me away from Lily. I couldn't look like a pushover.

"Mr. Torres, I won't insult your intelligence by beating around the bush," he said, straight to the point. "When I hired you to dance with my daughter, I didn't mean for you to pretend to date her. It's clear to me that Lily is starting to care for you, and I think it's best for everyone if you cut ties after this weekend." His blue eyes sharpened on me. "You're confusing her."

My back teeth clicked. It was no secret he wasn't happy we were together, but this was ridiculous. I wasn't sure if it was *me* he thought so little of, or his daughter, but either way, it was an insult.

"Sir," I said carefully, trying not to show my anger. "I care about Lily, too. I'm not trying to confuse her. I just want to be with her."

Mr. Bailey stepped back, studying me from under thick eyebrows. "So you're not trying to mess with her head?" he asked point-blank, and I inhaled a sharp breath, gritting my teeth.

"No, sir. I don't play games. I don't like it when they're pulled on me, and I refuse to pull them on anyone else." I wanted to add that if he knew Lily at all, he'd realize she was a firecracker and smart as hell. I doubted *anyone* could get anything over on her. But, since I wanted the man to like me, I refrained.

"My relationship with Lily has nothing to do with our agreement or your money," I told him, wishing I could hand the damn stack over now and be done with it. "It might've started out that way, but six weeks is a long time, and like I said, I care about her. A lot."

My fingers flexed and fisted at my sides. As annoyed as I was for being questioned, I couldn't fault him for looking out for her. What he had to understand, though, was I wasn't going anywhere. I raised my chin and looked him in the eye. Mr. Bailey met my gaze, his chin lowered to look down on me, but after a few beats, he nodded curtly.

"I take it you haven't told her about our agreement?"

Despite my resolve to appear confident, I flinched.

"No," I admitted, the defensive anger leaving me in a rush. I scrubbed a weary hand over my face, then wrapped it around the base of my neck. "Even though I told you I wouldn't, I've wanted to. Tons of times." I glanced at him. "But I'm afraid she won't understand."

I almost told him my plan to confess this weekend but decided to keep that in my back pocket. The truth was, we were on the same side. We both wanted her happy. But if it was a choice between who'd come clean first—him or me—it was going to be me. I didn't want him getting any ideas of beating me to the punch.

With a heavy sigh, Mr. Bailey sat on the bench. Leaning forward, he set his elbows on his thighs and stared at the ground. The imposing statue of a man suddenly had the weight of the world square on his shoulders, and his face, usually stoic, was lined with worry.

I hesitated, then took a seat on the other end. As his chest rose and fell in a breath, I tapped my foot, feeling restless. I wanted to get back inside to Lily, but it felt wrong to leave. I still needed his approval. And the man looked wrecked.

"I'm afraid, too," he finally said, his quiet admission shocking my foot still. "I've screwed up so much with her. If her mother were here, she'd knock me over the head. I thought I was doing the right thing, but now..." He drifted off and sighed. "I couldn't handle it if my little girl got her heart broken because of a mistake I made."

Mr. Bailey raised his head, and his gaze pierced mine in the dark. "I'll back off and let Lily decide, but I'll be watching. I might be the world's worst dad at showing it, but I love that girl, and I'm awake and here now. I'll do whatever I can to keep her safe."

I nodded in understanding and swallowed down a lump of emotion. Lily was getting her dad back. Hell, I'd take a hundred suspicious looks if that was the result.

"We'll keep our agreement between us," he told me with a firm nod, pushing to his feet. Bonding time was over. I stood as well, and we walked side by side back to the studio with two words circling my brain—*for now*.

Chapter Twenty-Nine

LILY

Sydney whipped the car into her designated spot and shut off the engine, taking the blaring music with it. Blinking, I shook my head and wiggled my finger in my ear, adjusting to the sudden quiet. It was different, riding with my best friend rather than my boyfriend to school. For one thing, Sydney hadn't arrived at my door with Starbucks. For another, she'd insisted on playing the radio at ear-piercing decibels. She claimed it woke her up better than coffee.

While I *adamantly* disagreed, I had to admit—I wasn't tired anymore.

"Thanks again for the ride," I told her, grabbing my bag from my feet. "Stone said it was only today he needed to be here early. The game plan should be set now, so he can bring me tomorrow."

If for some reason he couldn't, I was tempted to take the bus. I loved Sydney to death, but I loved my sense of hearing, too.

"No problem," she said, throwing her keys into her purse

and popping open the door. "What are besties for?"

The words hit me in the heart, and I glanced over with a grateful smile.

Last night had been rough. Nightmares had plagued me, and I'd woken up with a lingering sense of unease. The mounting stress was getting to me. Worrying about the showcase, waiting to hear back about Debbie, having to confess the truth to Dad. Thank God he'd still been in bed when I snuck out this morning. While he didn't like it, it made sense for Stone to bring me to school, but if he'd seen Sydney in our driveway, he would've asked questions. After my long night, that might've tipped me over the edge.

With a sigh, I climbed out and tugged my schoolbag over my shoulders. I bumped the door with my hip, and when I looked up, Angéla was walking to meet us, her sweet face scrunched and her phone clutched in her hands.

Sydney joined me on the passenger side, and we exchanged a glance.

Usually, Angéla bounced through life, but today her steps were slow and awkward. I narrowed my eyes as she stopped a few feet away, then shifted her weight. "Are you okay?"

She winced. "Have either of you checked your phones this morning?"

"No," I replied, reaching in my pocket. Beside me, Sydney did the same. I held mine out, my thumbs unlocking the screen. "I'm guessing you mean like social media or something? What's going on?"

Admittedly, I was kind of a novice at the whole scene. Not having a ton of friends meant I didn't follow a lot of people, and I'd never gotten in the habit of posting random tidbits of my life online. Who'd have cared what I ate for breakfast, or what my weekend plans were? Sydney knew my schedule better than I did.

Angéla sighed. Her lips pressed into a tight, sad smile, and I staggered back at the emotion in her eyes. *Pity.*

My breathing spiked as the memories attached to that emotion rushed to the surface.

"I only just heard about it or I would've called you at home." Her gaze fell to her cell phone. "A rumor went viral on Snapchat. Supposedly Cameron…" She bit her lip, then started again. "Supposedly, Cameron overheard a conversation last night. Between my brother and your dad."

I swallowed thickly. "Oh yeah?" My thoughts tripped over the previous night's events. "Wait, what conversation? They didn't talk. Even if they had, Cameron left before we did."

"I don't know." Angéla shoved her phone in her pocket, then smoothed her hand down her jean-clad leg. "She says it happened near the parking lot? It's not like I believe any of it anyway." Her dark eyes widened, and a new emotion joined the one linked to so much pain. "Don't you believe it either, Lily. I'm telling you, Stone wouldn't do this. If he's not in love with you already, he's falling hard. Trust me, there's no way any of this is true."

"*What's* true?" I bit out, and heads across the lot whipped in our direction. I grabbed hold of the charm at my neck and struggled to take a deep breath. Lowering my voice, I asked, "What did Cameron say she overheard?"

I wasn't sure I wanted an answer. Stone and I hadn't exchanged the words, but even if Angéla was wrong, I knew how *I* felt. I loved him. A sense of foreboding whispered across me, telling me to get back in the car and beg Syd to take me home.

Angéla sighed, then stepped in front of me and put her hand on my shoulder. "She's saying your dad paid Stone to be with you…and that Ilusiòn got a bonus for putting you in the showcase."

For one, drawn-out moment, the entire world went still.

There were no cars pulling into the lot behind us. No classmates gathering in a small circle. No wind on my face, no sun in the sky. Just my soft-hearted friend staring into my eyes with sympathy, and the press of shocked pain resting on my sternum.

The blast of a car horn rocked me out of my trance, and I inhaled sharply, dragging air into my lungs. Then, I turned on shaky legs and started walking.

"Where are you going?"

Angéla fell into step beside me, and Sydney flanked my other side. Both girls had to practically push people out of our way.

"To the gym," I replied, my voice sounding odd and far away. "Practice should be over."

Although I didn't believe a word Cameron had posted, I wanted to hear that from Stone's lips. I needed to see his eyes go hard and hear him call her a liar. Then I could figure out how to respond.

The crowd followed us, and en route to the gym, I heard every whisper. Felt every stare. They were like tiny pinpricks of pain, each one stabbing and tugging me back to freshman year. Back to the days when I'd been pitied and ignored.

Hadn't I just been thinking that I'd *liked* the attention at Homecoming?

Hadn't I started walking the halls, finally feeling like I belonged?

The whispers of my classmates called me a fool. That was worse than being a ghost.

The metal door banged open and then stayed that way as I walked into the gym, followed by what felt like half the senior class. Syd and Angéla closed ranks on either side, and I picked up the pace, trying to outrun the panic building inside. I shoved it down, even as a wave of fear rolled over me. I needed to see Stone.

Luckily, halfway across the open floor, two familiar faces stepped out of the wing leading to the team gym. Stone and Chase were laughing, shoving each other as they ambled out, and the former's face lit up when he saw me.

"Hey there, pretty girl," he called, though his voice fell off as the crowd formed a loose circle around us. He glanced at our classmates in confusion, then dropped his bag. The sound echoed in the cavernous gym. "What's wrong?"

My already-racing heart picked up speed. "Is it true?"

Snickers erupted, and Stone shot our audience a menacing look. When he focused back on me, a slight hint of fear was in his eyes. The hairs on the back of my neck stood at attention.

"Is what true?" he asked.

"Did my dad…" I paused to inhale more air. "Pay you to be with me?"

My quiet voice belied the pit that had opened in my stomach. As my question was repeated in hushed whispers, Stone's entire body froze. Then his nostrils flared, and he turned on his best friend. Chase lifted his hands, stepping back with wide eyes.

Pain lanced my heart as their actions confirmed everything.

Angéla gasped, and wave after wave of agony crashed over me. The gnawing pit in my stomach stretched wide, tearing me open, and I wrapped my arms around my body as if I could hold myself together. As if I could stop the bleeding. Needles shot down my legs, and as my knees buckled, Stone lurched to grab me.

"Stay back!" I screeched, my yell bouncing off the shiny floor as I stumbled.

The crowd went silent, and Stone raised his hands.

"Lily, please." He went to touch me again and stopped short when I flinched. I clutched at my chest, needing more air, and he shoved his hand through his hair. "*Please.* Let me help you."

I shook my head, looking at the ceiling as I focused on my breathing. In through my nose, out through my mouth. Just like the guided meditations had taught. If I could've, I would've laughed at the irony. For the last month, Stone had been my calm. Now…now he was the storm.

As I struggled, a conversation I'd had with Aidan weeks ago came to mind. This had to be it. *This* was why Stone had asked about me in the gym long before we'd made our dare. He'd been gathering intel for his plan.

My vision went fuzzy at the edges, but I managed to drag in enough oxygen to ask the question tearing my heart in two. "Were you paid"—I paused for another ragged breath and looked him in the eye—"to kiss me, too?"

Horror washed over his face. "No! Of course not. It wasn't like that." With a curse, he grabbed my arms, ignoring my flinch. "I don't know how you found out, or what you heard, but it doesn't matter. *I* should've told you, from the beginning. But if you listen—"

His words fell into the void created by my hazy head and pounding heart.

A quick glance proved the crowd had moved closer, some now with their phones out. Ready and eager to capture my epic meltdown for posterity.

Tears pricked my eyes. As I sucked in a shallow breath, a surreal feeling came over me. One minute, I was in my body, and the next, it was like I'd detached from myself.

Everything was still happening, but to someone else, and I watched it play out in real time. I saw the people staring, saw them judging. I noticed Stone's mouth moving, the tendons in his neck popping out.

Get away. Before you lose control.

Knocking free of Stone's grasp, I slid my hands behind my neck and fumbled with the clasp of my necklace. "It was all a lie," I mumbled, talking to myself.

He shook his head anyway. "No. No, it wasn't. Baby, I'm telling you—"

"You were pretending," I interrupted, my voice breathy and winded as I fought with the chain. "The whole time. God, I...I thought you wanted me."

"I did!" Stone said fiercely, opening and closing his extended hands, clearly wanting to touch me but keeping his distance. "Baby, I *do* want you. Will you please just listen? Stop being so stubborn and let me explain."

A harsh laugh broke free. "Stubborn?" A final yank released the clasp of my necklace, ripping strands of hair from my scalp. I gathered it in my hand and threw it at him. "Don't you mean *fierce*?"

What an idiot I was. Believing a giraffe could become a swan. Or that the king of the school could ever want me.

The gathered crowd was a blur of faces, not one of them clear, but I knew what I would've seen if they had been. Pity and judgment. So much for fitting in.

Stone's hand clenched around the necklace, and I wanted to suggest he give it to his next charity case. But the oxygen wasn't there to speak. I was *seconds* away from losing control, and I couldn't let him—couldn't let our classmates—see me fall apart.

Turning on my heel, I fled.

Behind me, Sydney growled. Angéla told someone to

let me go. Stone, Chase, I didn't know. The crowd parted so I could run away with my tail between my legs, staying blissfully quiet as I pushed out the gym doors and sprinted back to the parking lot, panic chasing at my heels.

My breaths came faster and faster. Previous experience had taught me the symptoms would soon end, but I couldn't help wondering if I'd suffocate before then. My hands grappled with the latch to Sydney's door, and when it finally opened, I threw myself onto the back seat. Stretching out, arching my neck to find air.

The girls…they'll find me here.

That was my last coherent thought before darkness closed in.

Chapter Thirty

STONE

My shoulders hunched as I put my truck in park. Glancing up at Lily's house, the burgundy brick facade glared at me like a giant red stop sign. *Do not pass.*

I imagined the beast of a man living inside had even harsher words to say.

My grip tightened around the wheel. In all honesty, I could handle Mr. Bailey. It was his daughter I feared. Lily's face had haunted me all day, seeing her knees buckle and her screaming for me to stay back…then later, when she'd brokenly asked if I'd been paid to kiss her, too.

Swallowing back bile, I rested my head against the seat.

How did things get so screwed up? If we could've talked, if she would've let me explain, everything would be fine. Or if not fine, at least she wouldn't be believing the worst. Instead, I'd let her walk away. By the time I'd snapped out of it and pushed past her security guards—Angéla and Sydney—she'd been nowhere in sight.

When lunch rolled around and she was still missing, I'd

cornered my twin. Angéla could barely look at me, even after learning the truth, but she'd admitted Lily had gone home sick. It had taken her, Chase, Sydney, and Aidan to stop me from following her, and in the end, only two things had kept me from ditching.

Coach had warned me: skip again and I'd be benched. If that would've only affected me, I'd have said screw it and left. Let the town talk. But my future wasn't the only one on the line. The entire team was counting on me, and tomorrow's game was huge. Recruiters were watching.

The double-whammy came from Sydney, who'd venomously pointed out that Lily's dad had taken her to the hospital for tests, and now she was home and needed her rest. Evidently, panic attacks took a lot out of a person—and my girl had suffered a massive one. Because of me.

I slammed my hands against the wheel. The electric jolt that shot up my arm was nothing short of what I deserved. Fuck. I was supposed to be the one taking *away* Lily's stress, not making her sick. Hearing she'd spiraled so hard she passed out? *God.* It killed me.

Unable to ditch, and not giving a shit about classes, I did the only thing I could. Gossip had exploded after our showdown, but I'd chased the fires, putting them out left and right, starting right there in the gym with Angéla and Sydney— who was a fucking pit bull, by the way. Next time I got in a fight, I wanted that girl on my side. She was equal parts Emma Watson and Freddy Krueger. Smart and terrifying.

Jury was still out on if she or Angéla would forgive me, or if our classmates would believe facts over fiction. With Cameron's convenient disappearance midmorning, there was only so much I could do. The rumor mill was a runaway bitch, and once again, I was at the center of it. By now, I was used to it. Lily wasn't.

I glanced up at her window. The curtains were closed, the blinds shut. A vision of her cinnamon hair spread out like a halo on her pillow as tears glided down her swollen cheeks flashed in my mind, making my stomach roil.

Veto. Tell your mom I'm sorry.

I closed my eyes. I couldn't think about the text she'd sent me. Instead, I grabbed the cursed shoebox and climbed out of the truck. The weight was back in my chest, crushing my lungs, and as I hauled myself to the front door, sweat gathered at my hairline. Sticky drops slid down my spine, and the box trembled in my hand. My stomach was somewhere near my shoes.

What would she do when she answered? Turn me away? Slam the door in my face? My heart pounded so hard I was sure they could hear it inside. Blowing out a breath, I lifted my hand and rapped on the door.

I'd hoped to avoid a confrontation here. I'd swung by the library, just in case she'd shown up for tutoring, but she hadn't. Liam was there, though, and he'd brandished his aced math test like Harry Potter's wand. I'd fought through a smile for the kid, arranged for Ms. Joice to bring him to the sidelines tomorrow, then took off for my truck, planning to head here. Halfway to the lot, I'd gotten her text.

Faint footsteps had me flexing and curling my fingers. The door opened, and I wasn't surprised by who answered. Cold, hard eyes told me any ground I'd won last night had been decimated by Cameron's stunt, but I'd earn it back again. *After* I talked with his daughter.

I peered around Mr. Bailey's imposing frame, hoping to catch a flash of red.

"She's in her room." His gruff reply to my unspoken question had me leaning back, bracing my shoulders.

"Can I come in?"

"No." A vein pulsed in his neck, and he pulled the door closer, blocking my sightline. "Lily needs her space right now. She's hurting." The flash of anger quickly gave way to guilt as his deep voice cracked, and the steel band around my chest constricted. "I haven't seen her like this since..." He pressed his thin lips together. "Since her mother."

Damn, that hurt.

Closing my eyes, I took a deep breath as my arms physically ached to hold her. Blowing it back out, I tried again. "Mr. Bailey, that's why I'm here. I want to make it right. If you'll just let me in for a few minutes, I can tell her the truth and she'll see—"

"She already knows, Stone."

My mouth hovered open. Then I shook my head. "No. No, she doesn't. She wouldn't let me explain. She ran..."

Mr. Bailey grimaced. "Yeah, she tried icing me out, too. Sydney filled me in on what happened when I picked her up. I let her digest things for a few hours, but on the way home from the hospital, we talked." He glanced at the ground. "I told her everything."

I stared at him blankly. "So she knows it's not as bad as it sounded."

He huffed a breath and raised his eyes. "That ex of yours is a piece of work."

"Tell me about it," I muttered, scrubbing a hand across my mouth.

Okay, so Lily knew the truth. That was good, right? I mean, I'd wanted to be the one to tell her. I'd planned on looking into those big, beautiful eyes so she could look right back into mine and see for herself how I felt. That way she'd understand what we had was amazing, and it had jack-shit to do with money—even if it *had* been what brought us together.

Clearly, that plan was out the window. I needed to recalibrate.

On the plus side, she no longer thought the worst. She knew Cameron had lied, and everything else was a misunderstanding. But, if so, why hadn't she opened the door? Why wasn't she standing here, telling me this herself?

I glanced beyond Mr. Bailey's linebacker shoulders, trying to see into the living room. "You said you told her on the way home?"

"About two hours ago," he confirmed, watching me curiously. Which meant he saw the exact moment reality hit.

She knew before she'd texted.

It really was over. Lily knew the truth, and it didn't matter. She still didn't want me.

In a sick, morbid way, I was relieved. The world made sense again. I'd always known she was too good for me, and now, evidently, she'd realized it, too.

Woodenly, I lifted the box in my hand. "Here. Take it."

Mr. Bailey shot me a look that said he either expected a snake to pop out of the box or for me to crumble at his feet, but I was good. Numbness was setting in. With a sigh, he took the box and opened it, then raised his head in confusion.

"Count it," I told him, staring blankly at the brick wall. "It's all there."

Every dirty, tainted bill was in that box. Returning it sent me right back to where I'd been when this whole mess started six weeks ago, but that didn't matter. Not anymore.

"I don't understand. Lily told me about Ilusiòn's troubles. She guessed that was why you'd agreed to our deal."

I winced. Unexpected, the pain ripped through my protective shield of detachment, and the threat of tears burned my eyes. Lily got me. Probably better than anyone else ever had.

"It was," I said roughly, stepping back from the porch. "It was the *only* reason."

Backing up more, I shoved my shaking hands in my pockets and looked around. My shields were down, the numbness gone, and I was embarrassingly close to losing it on their front lawn.

Almost to myself, I said, "I thought it could help, but it's not worth it. Not like this." A lump lodged in my throat, and I struggled to swallow it down. "I should've never taken the money. It makes me sick. It was my *job* to be at the studio, and dancing with Lily..." I closed my eyes again as the pressure mounted behind my sinuses. "It changed my life."

I ducked my head, fighting the surge. Mr. Bailey embodied control. If I lost my shit in front of him, I could never look him in the eyes. But my feet felt glued to the damn ground. I couldn't walk away.

From the corner of my eye, I saw him shift his massive weight, and I clenched my jaw as cars passed behind me on the street. If he doubted my intentions again, or tried saying this was for the best, I swear, I was gonna lose it.

"You really care about her, don't you?"

"I'm in love with her," I admitted, gritting my teeth, tightening down, doing everything I could to resurrect my shield as guilt and pain and *what-if*s threatened to drown me where I stood. As the waves battered, a heavy hand fell on my shoulder.

"This is *my* fault," Mr. Bailey said. "I caused this. I was trying to look out for her, but all I did was hurt her more. Now I've hurt you, too."

His voice lost power, ending on a ragged whisper, and I lifted my head to see him staring with glazed eyes at the shoebox. His thick eyebrows were drawn together, and his mouth was pressed in a tight slash.

For a girl who believed she was weak, Lily had the power to bring strong men to their knees.

Her dad exhaled heavily. "Lily takes after my wife more than she knows. That wild, passionate streak comes from her." His lips lifted at the corners, and his face softened. "But with that stubbornness comes an incredible capacity to love."

My heart gave a pained thump, and blue eyes, so much like his daughter's, raised to meet mine. "She's hurting now. Embarrassed and licking her wounds. She hates it that she lost control in front of a crowd. My daughter thinks it makes her look weak." His face pinched, and his shoulders fell with a sigh. "*That*, she got from me. I've messed her up in many ways, it seems. She has no idea how strong she is, which is also on me. But if you're willing to tough it out and fight for her, I think she'll come around. Like I said, she's a hell of a lot like her mother."

A flame of hope kindled in my chest. Miniscule, really. Barely enough to roast a marshmallow. But I clung to it regardless.

Looking straight into her father's eyes, I made a promise to them both. "I'm not giving up."

In my pocket, my hand brushed against the necklace she'd thrown at me. Tugging it out, I asked, "Can you give this to her? You're right. She is stronger than she gives herself credit for, and if nothing else, I want her to remember that."

Stupidly, I'd assumed Mr. Bailey didn't know Spanish. Not everyone did. But from the amused quirk of his lips, I'd been mistaken.

"*Chingona*, huh?" He chuckled under his breath, then closed his hand around the charm. "I'll make sure she gets it."

We exchanged a look, one where, oddly enough, I felt

like we were on equal footing. It figured I'd win his approval the moment I stopped needing it. I shook my head at the irony and turned on my heel. Either way, it felt nice to have.

The walk to my truck strengthened my resolve. A text didn't count as closure. Until Lily looked me in the eyes and told me we were over, I would keep fighting. Yanking open my door, I glanced at the second-story window almost as an afterthought and watched the curtain drop.

Chapter Thirty-One

LILY

"I can't believe I let y'all talk me into this."

Shades of pink and purple lit the bleachers of Brighton stadium, giving the air a rose-gold glow. Sydney snorted and looped her arm around my elbow. "Yeah. Because a night staring at your bedroom walls sounds *so* much more appealing."

"No more hiding," Angéla chimed in from my other side, resting her head on my shoulder. If Sydney was my protector, Angéla was my gooey center. "Staying home means *she* wins."

There was no need to explain who *she* was.

It wasn't often that people surprised me, but as of this morning, color me astonished. Dad had wanted me to stay home again, but I'd refused. I'd already missed one test, I didn't want to fall further behind. I *had* relented on the anti-anxiety medicine, however; we were trying a different one this time, one that hopefully wouldn't give me headaches or nausea, but even so, it'd take several weeks to have an effect. I'd promised to call if I felt off, but with the blindside over, I'd figured I could handle school politics. When Sydney had pulled into the student lot, I'd been prepared for the stares. For the snickers, the smirks, and maybe even a dash of sympathy.

What I'd gotten was support.

Before we'd even stepped into the building, two girls had met us on the breezeway to tell me Cameron sucked. In the hall near the stairs, another girl had stopped to say she was looking forward to seeing me dance. She'd appeared genuine, too. At my locker, a group of passing guys had given me a thumbs-up, and then in government, another had asked where he could get my "You're Overreacting" tee with two science beakers on it. Not being snarky, either. Legit curious.

My world was in a state of flummox.

Cameron's attempt to alienate me and somehow win back Stone had turned on her. Miraculously so. While she wasn't suddenly persona non grata, her social standing had taken a severe hit. Evidently, while I'd been at the hospital getting pricked and prodded again, Stone had gotten to work. He'd spoken out, shot down rumors, and had set the record straight. If he'd come out swinging after Cameron had cheated in the spring, instead of hanging back and taking the blow, who knows what would've happened.

The fact he *hadn't* when it had only been his reputation on the line, and he'd done so now when it wasn't, wasn't lost on me. What I didn't know was what it meant. Or what I should do about it.

An icky feeling swam in my stomach, and I notched my head against Angéla's. "How can you even stand to sit with me right now? I'm leaving the studio high and dry. You should hate me."

"*Pshaw*," she countered, blowing a raspberry, then sat up so fast I almost got whiplash. "First of all, I'll always have your back, and secondly, we understand. I'm not gonna blow smoke up your butt and say it doesn't suck, because it does. Totally. You and my brother *kill* that routine, Lil, and it'd be a giant middle finger to the bitch if you danced. From the sound of it, almost the entire school is coming out, thanks to her stunt. They want to see this showcase Ma was supposedly paid to put you in, even if they know it was just another of Cameron's lies."

At that, my small smile twisted.

One good thing had come out of this mess. In a roundabout way, I'd still helped the studio. Ilusiòn's showcase should be packed, and with luck, those bodies would turn into paying students. Granted, half the expected crowd was coming for me, and they were going to be sadly disappointed, not to mention the fact that I was letting Mrs. Viktória down. I hated that more than anything. But there was no way I could handle the pressure. School was one thing, but being under a literal spotlight after yesterday's spectacle? Performing with all those eyes focused on me, wondering if it would happen again? No way. I just had to have faith that everyone who *did* come for me would stay and be blown away by the rest of the show.

Admittedly, though…a big piece of me still wanted to be a part of it. Never mind the pressure, twenty-four hours ago, I'd been as integral to the event as anyone, and it felt wrong not being there. It was strange how fast things could change.

"*But*," Angéla continued, pulling me from my downward spiral. "I get it. Ma gets it, too. More importantly, you dancing—or *not* dancing—has squat to do with our friendship. We're solid, you and me. Becas unite!"

She lifted our linked hands high, and I couldn't help grinning at her lovable enthusiasm.

Desperately needing further distraction, I surveyed the spirited stands. We were packed in, shoulder to shoulder, faces painted and signs waving. The cheer squad was out on the sidelines of the field, stretching in preparation for what should be a volatile matchup, and right at the center of the pile was Cameron. Her smile wasn't quite as vibrant as usual, her hair somehow less bouncy. Clearly, whatever she'd set out to prove yesterday had failed, and she'd lost more than she could've ever hoped to gain. But watching her now, I got a glimpse of the vulnerable girl behind the balls-to-the-wall, go-getter mask. Not enough to feel *sorry* for her—she'd made her bed and tried and succeeded in hurting me. But enough of a glimpse to help me remember she was also just a girl.

Beyond our rivalry, beyond our very different approaches to life, Cameron and I were the same. We both worked hard, we both pushed ourselves, and we both expected a lot out of our futures. Yet she was here tonight, despite the backlash of yesterday and in spite of the fact that she was taking the ACT tomorrow. It was the last chance to score big before Early Action.

When she'd mentioned it at our NHS meeting earlier this week, before the drama and probably in an attempt to make me nervous about the test, it'd been a toss-up on what was funnier—her reaction to me telling her I was content with my current score, *or* that I was no longer applying early to Harvard, either.

The thing was, the stress leading up to those tests wasn't worth it. Not when I'd already done well. In fact, *nothing* was worth making myself sick, especially not the future, a fact I'd only recently learned. Then again, maybe Cameron already knew that secret. She was here, after all, even with a test in the morning. Despite being a top contender for valedictorian, she'd never once stopped living her life. She was out enjoying it, not stuck in her room studying notecards and sharpening pencils.

It turned out, Stone was right. There was more to high school than grades. There was a whole lot to experience, too.

On the field, the cheer squad lifted a giant breakaway banner, and a pulse went through the stadium. Cypress Lake had turned out en masse to watch the biggest game of the season. According to Liam, Brighton and Morton took turns winning every other year, and technically, tonight should be Morton's. Unfortunately for the Mustangs, we had Stone at QB. Regardless of what those idiot announcers had been implying the past few weeks, I had no doubt the Tigers would emerge victorious.

A surge of blue and white uniforms flooded the end zone, and the crowd shot to their feet. I jumped up right along with them, heart pounding, as our classmates screamed at the top of their lungs. The team, huddled behind the banner, started bouncing, and from our seats, it was impossible to make out what they were chanting—but the passion in their voices, the steady rise of the tempo, and the frenzy of their feet had the entire arena going nuts. And when they ripped through the banner…everyone lost their minds.

"And now, your champion *Tigers*!"

Number five streaked across the field, and a stabbing pain hit my stomach. Sydney squeezed my hand in solidarity, and Angéla gently knocked her shoulder against me. Regardless of the ache, I reached into the side pocket of my bag, searching for my phone to snap a picture of the chaos that outshone Homecoming, then realized it wasn't there.

What the hell? Had it fallen out? Did I forget it at home?

Damn, talk about being in a head fog.

Three huge banners, emblazoned with *B*, *H*, and *S*, rippled in the air while guys in the cheer squad ran down the sideline. I followed their journey, the pain spreading to my chest, and a flash of blond hair caught my eye.

I gasped, which immediately brought Angéla's attention. I shook my head, waving away her concern. How could I explain what this meant to someone who didn't know him?

Liam's cheeks were so bright he looked like he'd swallowed one of the huge floodlights lighting the field. He was standing on the sidelines, bracing himself on his tripod canes as he handed a water to one of our players. Only recently did he transition out of a walker, and already he was talking about forearm canes, though that was probably a year or two away. Regardless, looking at him now, the word "disability" would never come to mind. Liam's energy, his incredible heart, were so big it was clear nothing kept him down.

So much of my life felt like a struggle. The race for valedictorian. My battle with anxiety. Missing my mom. Missing my dad. Watching Liam on a football field put everything in perspective. He'd have given anything to play the sport he loved, but he was equally thrilled serving water to his idols. Just being around them made him happy. Watching them play. Talking stats. Living vicariously. Liam understood what it meant to enjoy the moment.

The broken pieces of my heart clenched in unison, then sighed.

Stone had kept his promise.

God, I had to be a masochist. Why else would I willingly watch the guy I loved but could no longer touch? Seriously, being this close to Stone physically hurt. What made it worse was I wasn't just grieving the death of our relationship; I was grieving who I'd started to become when I was with him, too.

With Stone, I'd been an updated version of myself. A version that lived for the moment and was even starting to find her place. A bit of the old, sprinkled in with the new.

Now…now I didn't know who I was. My old patterns didn't fit. I wasn't the fearless girl from junior high, but I also wasn't the completely klutzy braniac, either. I wasn't Lily 1.0 *or* 2.0, and the two things that had given me any clarity and brought me back to life were gone—Stone, and through him, dance.

I couldn't lie. A part of me wanted to forget yesterday. I wanted to get up, rush the sideline, and pick up where Stone and I had left off. But embarrassment wasn't the only thing keeping me rooted in the stands. I was hurt, too.

The truth hadn't been as bad as Cameron claimed. So what? Stone still hadn't been honest with me. Lies of omission were as hurtful as direct deceit, maybe more so because he'd had *six weeks* to tell me about the agreement, and I'd practically begged him to let me in.

If he could hide something like that so easily, what else could he have hidden?

With my butt firmly planted on the bleacher, I watched Liam talk to the guys. His eyes went wide with enthusiasm at whatever they were saying, the team including him without question. Stone had given him this. The ache in my chest grew as Liam shuffled down the line and then stopped in front of number five.

Although he had his game face on, Stone bent to accept the water, turning sideways while he spoke with Liam. The boy tossed his head back in a laugh, and Stone ruffled his hair with a small smile—not the guarded QB grin I'd teased him about, but one that didn't quite engage his eyes, either. The broad line of his shoulders, enormous with the bulk of the pads, rose and fell with a breath, and despite the longing and sadness pushing in, threatening to tug me under…or maybe because of it…I wondered what he was thinking about.

Then, without warning, Stone was watching me, too.

My breath caught as the moment dragged on. The stadium and the crazy cheers fell away into silence. My vision blurred, but in Stone's dark eyes, I swore I saw love, along with regret. I so badly wanted to believe it but told myself it was probably a trick of the lights. However, whatever he saw shining in mine had his smile widening in degrees. His dimple flashed, and the barest hint of crinkle framed his chocolate eyes.

Overwhelmed, I grabbed for my necklace, needing the grounding of the charm to center me—only to remember I'd given it back.

A sensation like a cold wave washed over me, and I bowed my head. "I already miss him," I admitted, hoping the sounds of the crowd had carried away my broken whisper.

Beside me, Angéla sighed and rested her head against my arm.

Chapter Thirty-Two

LILY

When I walked in the house, the first thing I noticed was the quiet. The grandfather clock Mom had gotten on a trip to North Carolina a few years ago ticked in the corner, and the cool air-conditioning hummed overhead. Other than that, our house was silent. Disturbingly so. The lack of noise had become our new norm, but tonight, it played havoc on my nerves.

Tiptoeing down the hall, I prayed Dad was asleep. For some unknown reason, Debbie was parked in the driveway, right next to his silver Audi. That hadn't been the plan. Gabriel was supposed to run the diagnostic and then call with an estimate. If I couldn't swing it, I was going to pick her up next week.

Why had he dropped her off early, and without calling?

More importantly, what were the chances Dad hadn't noticed?

Holding my breath, I glanced inside his office, and when I found it empty, I exhaled in relief. "Thank you, Jesus," I whispered to the void.

"Good game?"

"Oh, crap!"

Heart in my throat, I spun around, cutting my eyes toward the darkened living room. The lamp on the far end table cast just enough light that I could see my father seated in the large, overstuffed chair, but not make out the expression on his face.

I forced a smile. "Uh, yeah. Tigers won."

Like an idiot, I wiggled awkward spirit fingers, but Dad didn't crack a smile. His broad shoulders rose and fell with a breath, his feet firmly planted on the ground, and I shoved my hands in my pockets to hide their nervous tremble.

Shifting my feet toward the stairwell, I feigned a yawn. "I think I'm gonna head on up to bed. It's been a long night."

When Dad remained motionless, giving no real indication he'd heard me, I bit the inside of my cheek and turned to leave. What little ground we'd won back since his return had been eaten away by his and Stone's agreement. While Dad had explained his reasoning, and I understood to an extent, I was still hurt and embarrassed. Not that I'd told him that. By this point, there was so much left unsaid between us, I didn't know where to begin.

I'd made it two whole steps when he called quietly, "Don't forget your phone."

Crap. I knew that would've been too easy.

Licking my lips, I spun back and casually strolled toward him, noticing how small my iPhone looked in his ginormous hand. It reminded me of the trips we used to take and how I'd slide my hand in his and instantly feel safe, regardless of how unfamiliar the area felt. Dad had always seemed larger than life, and once upon a time, he'd been my rock.

I came to a stop in front of him. "Thanks. It must've fallen out of my bag in the rush. You know Syd—always needs to be the first to arrive. If she's on time, she thinks she's late."

And now I was rambling. Never a good sign. Dad's eyes sharpened on me, and I held out my hand for the phone, hoping the shadows hid how it shook.

He handed it over, and with a heavy swallow, I slid it into my pocket. "Night," I offered weakly, and he nodded silently, not blinking once. Creepy.

Slowly, cautiously, I turned and managed to make it halfway through the doorway before he said, "I answered it for you while you were gone."

My feet froze on the carpet.

"About twenty minutes after you left, I heard it ringing. Darn thing was tucked under a throw pillow. No wonder you forgot it." When I looked over my shoulder, he had his hands steepled on his chin. My stomach clenched as sweat dotted my upper lip. "I don't know why I answered it. When I heard it ringing, I looked for it, and after finding it, my finger swiped across the screen on instinct. I didn't think you'd mind."

I shook my head, but I couldn't get my mouth to move. Standing in the living room, the lamp light was stronger across his face, so I saw the ever-so-slight pulsing tick in his jaw. I also saw when the careful, controlled mask finally slipped, giving way to intense disappointment swimming in his eyes.

"Twelve hundred dollars? Are you kidding me? I trust you to be responsible and *this* is how you repay me? Sneaking around behind my back and throwing away my money?" Dad shook his head with a look that said I'd let him down beyond belief. "Tell me, were you going to at least discuss the repairs with me *before* you agreed to them, or were you planning on hiding it like you did with the alternator?"

My mind raced to process all the information coming at me, and when I finally caught up, my eyes widened.

Dad huffed a breath. "Yeah, I know about that, too."

"*Gabriel*." The name came out sounding like a curse, which was exactly what I was doing to the mechanic in my head. "I can't believe he told you."

"Of course he did, Lily, you're a minor," he replied, scrubbing a hand over his face. "Don't go putting this on him. You're my daughter; *you* should've told me, but you didn't because you knew I wouldn't approve of sinking money into a car that's falling apart. Seventeen hundred dollars? My God, that's almost more than it's worth."

He pushed to his feet and started pacing the length of the sofa. "You should've come to me at the first sign of trouble. My God, with the kind of repairs it needs, do you know what could've happened if you'd been driving and something went wrong? There could've been an accident. You could've been hurt—or *worse*. I just don't understand. Why didn't you tell me what was going on?"

"Why didn't I tell you?" I repeated, my voice deceptively flat. Deceptive because the strangest sensation was churning under my skin.

Throughout Dad's monologue, my previously sluggish, anxious heartbeat had picked up speed. It was like every memory of him not being here rose up inside me. Putting work before me. Not wanting to talk about Mom. The whole mess with Stone. By the time he was done, blood *whooshed* in my ears.

"You want to know *why* I snuck around?" I asked, inching farther into the room. "You want to know *why* I didn't tell you what was going on?" A thrum of emotion now underscored my words, and my father's frantic pacing stilled, his frustration transforming into watchfulness.

A humorless laugh escaped my throat, punctuating the otherwise quiet room. "I didn't tell you, Dad, because *you're…never…here*!"

The sound of my scream bounced off every solid surface in the room. It was possibly the first loud noise the house had heard in years.

"How can I tell you anything," I screeched, "when you're never around to hear it? Why would I even *want* to tell you if I could? You've wanted to get rid of Debbie for years. Mom loved that car, and you want to throw her away!"

Dad looked at me like I'd lost my mind, or maybe like he no longer knew who I was. *Join the club.* "Because it's dangerous," he countered. "That car was old when your mother drove her. We were looking at replacing it before she got sick—she knew it was time to let it go—but that got shoved aside when bills started piling. Now it's even older."

A haunted look of pain filled his eyes, and I'm not gonna lie, it hurt. Seeing the old grief mixed with new guilt and shame, and knowing I'd caused it, stung. But it was too late to turn back the clock. This wound had festered long enough, and my skin itched with the need to release the toxins.

Crossing my arms, I repeated through gritted teeth, "Mom *loved* Debbie."

"Yes, she did," Dad agreed with a sad nod. "But honey, it's just a car."

Something inside me broke at those words.

"No," I sobbed. Three years of grief, loneliness, and fear shook my shoulders. "That's where you're wrong. It's the only part of her I have left."

With that, my chest caved in with the pressure. Two seconds later, strong arms were locked around me, and if I'd had the energy, I would've pushed him away. A voice inside screamed to punish him for all the times he'd pushed *me* away by traveling overseas or staying locked in his office. But I couldn't do it. Every muscle in my body felt like it was filled with sand, and ultimately, he was my dad. For better or worse, despite everything, he would always be my rock. If he still even wanted the job.

"Why?" I asked him—*begged* him—my head buried in his chest, my choked words muffled by the fabric of his polo. "Why did you leave me all alone?"

"Oh, sweet girl…" The pet name made my sobs stronger, and Dad tightened his arms around me. "I'm sorry. I'm so damn sorry."

I shook my head against his chest and clutched his shirt. For so long, I'd wanted to ask why I wasn't enough to keep him around. Why I'd lost *both* parents the day Mom died. But I'd been too scared to ask, terrified he'd shut me out completely.

"I've failed you," he whispered against my hair, holding me so tight it was almost painful. "This is on me. It's my fault. You did nothing wrong, sweet girl. I'm so sorry."

The whispered apologies became a litany through my tears, and he kept on holding me close, partially rocking me in his arms. I couldn't remember the last time my father had held me. Even at the funeral, my emotions had been locked away behind a steady numbness, and he'd been stoic, staying busy by taking care of everyone else. At the time, I'd had Sydney. But I hadn't realized how much I'd needed my dad to simply be there. To hold me and tell me we were going to be okay—even if he'd known we weren't.

When my gasps finally started to even out and my tears began to slow, Dad loosened his grip and tilted up my chin. Regret hung heavy in his eyes. "I'm ashamed of myself, Lily. I've made so many mistakes. You're right, I did leave you alone. I told myself you were independent and strong, and I kidded myself into believing you were living a teenager's dream, having the house to yourself. The truth is, I couldn't let you see the shell of a man I'd become."

Dad swallowed thickly as I wiped my eyes. "You always seemed like you had it together, and I let that be my excuse. I figured you didn't need me. I see now, we're more alike than I thought." My eyebrows furrowed, and he gave me a sad smile. "I kept everyone out—you especially—by traveling and working. You did it by studying and preparing for the future."

His words reminded me of something I'd once told Stone. How he'd hidden behind his QB smiles while I'd hidden behind my books. "Throwing myself into school was easier than focusing on how alone I felt."

Remorse flooded his face, and he cupped a hand over his mouth. I blinked blurry eyes, wondering where and when I'd lost my glasses, but I was too tired to search. Instead, I plopped onto the sofa, and Dad released a ragged breath as he sat on the soft cushion beside me.

"Unfortunately, it can seem easier to stay broken rather than deal with the emotions and let yourself heal," he murmured. "But I've let us both live in grief for too long, and I promise you, I'm going to do better. From here on out, it's you and me, kiddo. I'm not going anywhere."

Dad held my gaze, making sure I understood, and I nodded as a flutter of hope hit my chest. He didn't mean he'd never travel for work again, though I had a hunch the trips would be less frequent. He was talking about *us*.

My father was back.

"I know I don't deserve it," he said, his gruff voice cracking with emotion. "But do you think you can forgive me?"

Fresh tears sprang to my eyes, and I twisted my body to throw my arms around his neck. "I love you, Daddy."

"God...I love you, too, sweet girl."

Over the next hour, I became reacquainted with my dad, and in turn, he got to meet me. Not the polished versions we presented the world at large but the real us. The messy, hurting, confused, and grieving versions. We caught up on the last three years of each other's lives, opening up like we should've done all along, under the watchful gaze of our old family photos. Dad shared that he'd kept the grief away for the first year by losing himself in staying busy, but the loneliness always hit hardest at night. For a while now, he'd been wanting to cut back on the travel and be home more, but he'd felt stuck in a prison of his own making.

"Changing your course is hard," he said, smoothing my hair from my face. "But you're the most important thing in my life, Lily, and coming home to find you making yourself sick with stress was the wake-up call I needed."

"It was for me, too," I admitted, dropping my chin to my chest. My cheeks burned as I thought about my obstinate quest for valedictorian, followed by the past few roller-coaster weeks. "Dad, I feel like I don't know who I am anymore. Or what I want to do. Everything was meticulously planned out, but now, it's so messed up. What if—" I winced and looked away, scared to give voice to the thoughts that had been rattling inside my head this week. "What if Harvard's *not* right for me? Ms. Kat recommended a program for secondary education history teachers right here in Texas, and I'd love to be closer to you, and Sydney, and Angéla..." I stopped short of saying Stone, but it was still the truth. "What would Mom say if she knew I was second-guessing our plan?"

Dad made a choked noise that sounded a whole lot like a laugh, and I raised my head, eyebrows scrunched in confusion. "She'd say...thank God."

Huh?

He smiled and leaned against the cushion. "Sweetheart, Mom wanted you to be happy, and she loved that you wanted to share her college experience, but it tore her up thinking of you being so far from home." He shrugged a shoulder, like he wasn't currently challenging my entire worldview. "She wanted you close. After she got sick, she worried we'd drift apart if you went away to school."

His shoulders slumped, and I squeezed his arm before he could start apologizing again. His lips tightened, but he gave a curt nod and turned to look me in the eyes.

"The important thing is that you live *your* life, and not anybody else's. It's okay to share similar experiences with your mom and still follow your own path. Chase your own dreams. It doesn't mean you love her any less."

Hope wrangled with uncertainty, and I swallowed hard as we fell silent again. As I slid my knees up to my chest, my phone dug into my hip, and I pulled it out and tossed it on the coffee table. With my arms wrapped around my shins and my head rested against my father's solid arm, I took a breath and released some of the fear that had taken root in my heart.

After a minute, Dad's chest vibrated with a laugh. "Man, she would've gotten a kick out of you dancing, though." His eyes swung to mine. "Watching you at the studio the other night? I swear, it was like she was sitting right next to me."

"Yeah, I feel her there, too," I told him. "Kind of like she left behind a part of her spirit."

Sitting here with my dad, talking about Mom, I realized it wasn't just in the studio that I felt her, either. I felt her with us at Angéla's sleepover, I felt her at the game and bookstore, and I felt her with me here, the night of the dance. It used to be that the only way I felt connected to her anymore was when I drove Debbie, but the truth was, Mom wasn't in her old car. She was in my heart.

A smile twisted Dad's lips and he bumped my shoulder. "Did Viktória ever tell you Mom was scared of salsa?"

My jaw dropped, and I spun on my hip to face him.

Dad laughed at my sudden burst of energy. "Yup. As much as Isa loved watching others do the steps, she never felt confident enough to try the rhythmic styles. She would've loved seeing you do what she couldn't."

Warmth spread throughout my chest. Every time I thought of my mother's face, one word came to mind: fearless. She lived her life with passion and heart, right up until the very end. It was crazy to think I could've surpassed her in some way.

Dad cleared his throat. "She'd probably wonder why you're no longer dancing in the showcase."

My smile fell, and with a sigh, I tucked my legs up underneath me.

"Is it because of Stone?"

"He lied to me, Dad."

He raised an eyebrow and shot me a look. "By that logic, so did I."

"That's different," I said, fidgeting with the seam on the sofa. "I'm not dating you," I pointed out cheekily. "First, because that'd be gross, and second, because you're so dang old." He shot me a look, grumbling the word *old*, and I grinned. Then I blew out a breath and stared at the crisscross lines in the chenille cushion. "Stone kept that secret so easily. It makes me wonder what else he could have hidden."

Dad studied me, and I ducked my head, trying to hide behind my hair.

"You're scared," he said softly, but I still flinched. "You

love him…and love is terrifying."

I lifted my head in surprise, and he slid me a smile.

"It's wonderful, too, don't get me wrong. Best feeling in the world. But living with your heart outside your chest?" He hissed a breath. "Not easy. Love means letting someone else affect your happiness and trusting them to love you despite your ugly scars. But when they love you back?" Dad's voice wobbled, and I knew he was thinking of Mom. "It makes every terrifying second worth it."

I shook my head at the one flaw in his logic. "But Stone doesn't love me."

Dad smiled like he knew something I didn't. "Call it a hunch, but that boy is gone over you. Trust me." Stretching his arm across the back of the sofa, he put his hand on my shoulder and said, "Now tell me, what are you really scared of?"

A heavy weight settled in my chest, and I swallowed. "That I'm not enough."

The hand on my shoulder tensed, and I rested my chin on my knees. "I'm not saying this to hurt you, Dad, but you *left* me. I've been on my own for years. What if…what if it was guilt that kept Stone hanging around? What if he felt bad for taking the money, and being with me was some sort of penance? I can't take him back only for him to turn around and break my heart again when he gets tired of me and moves on. It's safer just to hold on to the memories than to put myself back out there."

Dad released a heavy sigh, then bent forward to kiss my head. "People can hurt us even when it's the last thing they want to do, kiddo. And hurt like that, from people we trust, it's hard to get over. But you don't have to forget to forgive. Most people deserve a second chance." He paused, then added a bit roughly, "Sometimes third and fourth chances, too."

My chin trembled as tears blurred my eyes. Again. At this rate, my body had to be close to dehydration. "Can we not talk about Stone anymore?" I asked quietly.

"One more thing," he said, "then we don't ever have to say his name again if you don't want."

As I raised my head and tightened my hold around my legs, Dad reached into his pocket. "Stone asked me to give this to you, and after consulting the internet, I think you should have it." In his palm was the necklace from Homecoming. "My Spanish isn't as good as it used to be, but I remember the fun words, and apparently, this one's been given a new meaning."

At his playful, knowing grin, I blushed, and Dad handed me the necklace.

"I've always been proud of you, Lily, but never as much as when I watched you on that dance floor the other night. You've changed over these last six weeks. There's a light inside you that's impossible to miss. The boy's right." He quirked an eyebrow. "You're a *badass*."

Shocked laughter burst from my lips, and the pleased smile on his face healed a few more of my broken pieces. Biting my lip, I brushed a fingertip over the charm. "I actually feel that way when I dance."

"Then why not do it tomorrow?" he asked. "Say the word and Viktória would jump to put you back in. Hell, words haven't yet been invented to describe how happy she'd be."

I laughed softly, imagining her reaction. "Yeah, she would. But what if I mess up? What if I see the crowd, freak out, and have another panic attack? On stage this time."

Dad pinned me with a look. "You can't escape life, Lily. Avoiding situations that can cause anxiety will only lead to other problems. It's best to deal with things head-on." His mouth, previously pinched with determination, softened with a self-deprecating smile. "Or so I've heard."

I returned his smile, then released a groan.

Blah. I hated when people used logic against me.

I threw my head back on the sofa and stared at the ceiling. Honestly, why *was* I fighting this so hard? Dad wanted me to dance. Angéla wanted me to dance. Mrs. Viktória definitely wanted me to dance. Hell, even *I* wanted me to dance.

If Stone were here, he would've called me out for being stubborn.

Dancing made me happy. When I was out there, doing my thing, I didn't fear the future and I wasn't trying to forget the past. I simply lived for the next step. Nibbling on my lip again, I admitted, "If I don't dance tomorrow, I'm scared I'll regret it."

Dad smiled, then grabbed my phone from the coffee table. "Then you know what you need to do."

Excitement swirled in my stomach. Opening my messages, I ignored the influx of unread texts from Stone and tapped Angéla's name. My feet bounced against the cushion as I typed.

Tell your mom I'm back in.

I quickly hit send, then stared at my phone, my feet tapping a nervous rhythm. Almost immediately, emoji faces exploded across the screen, along with a half dozen exclamation points, and I laughed as the worried niggles gave way to giddy butterflies.

Tilting my hand, I showed Dad Angéla's enthusiastic response, and he grinned, wrapping his arm around me. As I snuggled into his strong, comforting embrace, breathing in his familiar spicy aftershave, a few more broken pieces knit back together.

Chapter Thirty-Three

STONE

"*Under the spotlight, all the girls wanna fall in line.*"
Standing in the wings of Cypress Performing Arts Center while Cameron's crew performed their samba routine, I snuck a peek at the rows of cushioned seats beyond the curtain. Instantly, I regretted it. The place was packed. While a sold-out auditorium meant money for Ilusiòn, and with any luck, an influx of students, on a personal level? Total nightmare.

The huge stage left nowhere to hide. An array of blinding spotlights made sure of that. This wasn't Homecoming. There was no crowd to get lost in once I took the stage. Soon, the entire town, whether from their comfy in-house seats or virtually at home through social media, would know their quarterback was, in fact, a secret Twinkle Toes.

It didn't take a genius to guess what this week's drive-time gossip would be. For their sake, I hoped the DJs would at least be creative.

My gaze drifted across the tiered seating. Shadowed faces, some I recognized, others I didn't, swept by in a nauseating rush. In the first row, front and center, were the phys ed teachers for Cypress Elementary, Cypress Junior High, and Brighton High. I'd met with each of them over the last two weeks, armed with research and data from schools who'd implemented successful ballroom dance units into their programs. If all went right today, they'd be announcing plans for similar units in our own schools, taught by Ilusiòn instructors.

When I reached the fourth row, the tips of my ears flushed red. Holy hell. Coach hadn't been messing with me. He was actually here—and he'd brought what appeared to be half the team with him. *Awesome.*

"There!" Angéla's finger shot across my vision. I jerked back, having been almost punched in the face, and my sister rolled her eyes. "I told you she was here."

"Lily?"

She nodded with a smug smile, and I whipped my head around to follow where she'd pointed.

About three-quarters of the way down the second row, Mr. Bailey sat with his face buried in one of Ma's programs. Next to him were two empty seats.

My hand fisted in the curtain. When she'd texted Angéla last night, I'd immediately grabbed my phone, too, hoping she'd responded. I wasn't sure how many texts or calls it took to be a stalker, but I was damn close. I didn't care. Stopping meant giving up, or worse, letting Lily *think* I'd given up, and neither was an option. When I'd discovered my messages unanswered and unread, I won't lie, it crushed me. But I dusted myself off and focused on today. If Lily was dancing, so was I.

"Doesn't mean she'll give me a second chance," I murmured, glancing at Angéla.

Even so, it was a shot of adrenaline.

Ideally, Lily would've come backstage from the start, rather than sit in the theater for most of the showcase. We could've talked and cleared the air before our performance. But I could be patient. What I couldn't do was let her walk away again. Not without hearing me out.

Chase clapped me on the back. "Dude, you made a mistake, but you love the girl. You didn't set out to hurt her. Make her see that." He squeezed my shoulder, shoving me forward. "Fight for her, man."

"I'm planning on it," I said, knocking away his hand. I straightened my shirt, then messed with the buttons on my sleeves. "I just have to figure out how."

"Guys are useless," Angéla muttered under her breath, then looped her arm through mine. Tugging me farther into the wings, she said, "*Clearly*, this situation calls for an epic gesture. You need to sweep Lily off her feet. Seriously, have neither of you watched a rom-com?"

Backstage was a madhouse of costumed dancers, eager instructors, and a few family friends dressed in black who were helping as part of the crew. Chase ducked around Marcus and exaggerated a groan. "Angel, this might come as a shock, but not every situation can be solved by a movie reference."

"Oh, I beg to differ." She spun to face us and folded her arms with a smug little smile. "Seventeen years of data prove otherwise. It's simply a matter of finding the right one."

Narrowing her eyes, her foot tapped out a rhythm as she scrolled through her extensive mental collection of movie titles. Sighing, I pinched the bridge of my nose, while Chase shook his head. Roughly thirty seconds later, my sister snapped her fingers. "I got it! *Dirty Dancing*!"

Chase gave her serious side-eye, and I threw my hand in the air. "Uh, isn't that the one where the minister bans music? What do you want me to do, throw the town a prom?"

"*Ohmigod*, how did we share a womb?" Angéla smacked a hand to her forehead. "That's *Footloose*, dumbass," she informed me through gritted teeth. "*Dirty Dancing* is with Patrick Swayze and Jennifer Grey. You know, the one where Patrick says, 'nobody puts Baby in a corner'?"

She lifted her eyebrows and looked at me expectantly, but while I vaguely remembered the line and parts of the plot, I still didn't see where she was going with it. Mr. Bailey and I were on the same page now. He didn't hate me, there was no watermelon, and people weren't even sitting at tables out there.

"Seriously, useless," she muttered again. "Okay, follow me here. At the end of the movie, Patrick's character jumps onstage, grabs a mic, and tells everyone how he feels about her." She glanced between us, circling her hands in the air, like she was waiting for me to extol her awesomeness. "It's perfect."

I blinked at my sister, then hoofed it back to the curtain and made a stabbing motion at the packed house. "Have you seen how many people are out there? Your plan has her potentially rejecting me in front of the entire town."

And she wondered how we'd shared a womb.

Glancing back out at the crowd, I'd have wagered 50 percent already had their phones out. The second I walked on stage, that number would jump to a hundred. I wasn't being arrogant, either. People came today thanks to the drama from Cameron's stunt, and pouring my heart out à la Patrick Swayze would only feed the beast. *Especially* if Lily rejected me.

This wouldn't be like Cameron's betrayal last spring. Our relationship had been nothing but lust and ego. Sure, my pride had taken a hit, but in the end, that's all it was. I was in *love* with Lily. If she shot me down, I'd be devastated.

With a slow shake of my head, I turned away from the audience.

Chase and Angéla exchanged a look, then he asked, "Is she worth it?"

My response was immediate. "You know she is."

Angéla started eagerly bouncing on her toes, and I released a sigh. As annoying as my sister could be, she was a girl, which meant she understood a hell of a lot better than I did what *other* girls liked. If there was even a chance this could work—that Lily would take me back—it meant I had to try.

My shoulders slumped, and I laughed softly as I gave in to the inevitable. Angéla clapped her hands excitedly.

"Good," Chase said, rocking back on his heels. "Because she's here."

Smiling, he looked to his right and lifted his chin in greeting, then thumped my shoulder before heading onstage to introduce the next routine. I rubbed a hand over the back of my neck and stared at the scuffed ground, psyching myself up to face her.

For forty-eight hours, all I'd wanted was for us to breathe the same air. I'd wanted to lose myself in Lily's blue eyes and tell her I loved her. Now that I could, nerves were locking down my muscles and fear was spiking my blood. My jaw flexed in time with the music.

Drawing in a deep, calming breath, I turned around prepared to grovel—and exhaled in an explosive rush. "*Damn.*"

Lily always looked incredible. Jeans, snarky-ass tees, crazy skirts, or purple sassy underwear, I'd take her any way I could have her. But put her in a dress, and the girl absolutely slayed me. Every time.

The scarlet dress was sleeveless and had a deep, plunging neckline, leaving the pale skin of her throat exposed. The fit was tight, molding to the curve of her hips, and loose tendrils of flashy red sequins skimmed across her thighs as she hesitantly walked toward me, her teeth biting into her plump lower lip. Between the short hem and nude dance heels, her legs looked endless, and it was a toss-up what I wanted to do more—drag her back to my truck or show her off as mine. The wary look in her eyes said neither would be accepted.

"This was Ma's?" I asked Angéla roughly, conflicted over my body's reaction.

My sister snorted. "Relax, Romeo. She never wore it."

Thank God.

Shoving my hands in the pockets of my dance slacks, banking on it keeping me from pulling Lily into my arms, I covered the distance between us. Sydney, who'd walked in with her, frowned.

Turning to Lily, she asked, "Want me to stay?"

She shook her head with a small smile. "Nah, go sit with Dad. He'll probably need you to hold his hand. I think he's nervous enough for the both of us."

Sydney carefully put her arms around Lily's neck, dodging the artful mess of curls piled on her head, and gave her a hug. "Break a leg, Lil. And make sure those shoes are buckled tight."

Laughing, Lily shoved her away, and Sydney blew an air-kiss. Then, with a smile for Angéla and conflicted grimace for me, she waltzed back down the darkened hallway leading to the auditorium. Lily twisted back to face us, her fingertips fidgeting with a row of sequins.

I cleared my throat. "You look amazing."

Her sweet smile seemed pained as she said, "Thanks.

You do, too."

Those pretty eyes swept over the outfit I'd eventually approved of—black dance slacks and a black, long-sleeved button-down with the top two undone. When Lily's gaze paused on the exposed skin at my throat, a slight blush brightened her cheeks.

My lips twitched, but I withheld a gloating smile. Inwardly, though, I did a fist pump.

Marcus walked up and smiled broadly at Lily. "You look great, kid." While she ducked her head, smiling awkwardly at the compliment, he consulted his clipboard. "Okay, you two are up next. Once Mary and Dale finish their waltz and Chase does his thing, Viktória wants to say a few words, so she'll be the one to introduce you. The two of you will close us out."

As Lily began sharing the raving comments she'd overheard in the audience during the show, I tuned in to the music pouring from the stage. Mrs. Mary and her husband were dancing to "Come Away with Me" by Norah Jones, and they'd just entered the soft instrumental section near the end.

We only had about a minute left to talk.

How could I win her back in sixty seconds? How could I possibly make her understand how much she meant to me—how sorry I was—in less than a commercial break? And how could I even try with Marcus hoarding in on my precious time?

Frustrated, I opened my mouth to urge him along when another crew member called his name.

"Better take care of that," he muttered, looking suddenly harried. "Good luck, guys."

While Lily mumbled her thanks, I quickly reached for her hand. Shockingly, she let me take it, and a cautious spark of optimism rippled through me. A spark that grew into an inferno when her right hand closed around the pendant at her throat.

She was wearing my necklace again. That had to mean something. Right?

Raising my eyes, I solemnly asked, "Are we okay?"

Lily's gaze darted over my face. "Yeah, Stone, we're good."

Relief hit fast and hard, and my heart started to race. Other than that she loved me, it was all I wanted to hear, and I was tempted to tug her against me and never let go. However, I sensed a *but* coming.

She looked away, but not before I saw the flash of hurt in her eyes. "We're good as dance partners," she clarified, and any hope I'd built overnight shattered like Ma's old china.

Out in the auditorium, the crowd cheered, and Mrs. Mary and Mr. Dale jogged past in a blur of elated smiles and muted squeals. As Chase went out to vamp, Ma skipped over to where we stood, Lily wincing at the ground, and me unable to look away from her face, afraid we'd never be this close again.

"Ah, Lily, you look ravishing in red. Like an enchanting rosebud—or maybe a spicy pepper, eh?" Ma wiggled her eyebrows, not picking up on the tension between us...or ignoring it completely. "Everybody ready?"

Lily forced a tight smile, and I nodded distractedly, wishing I could slow down time. Ma headed for the stage, and as I watched her go, Angéla stepped in my sightline with a hand on her hip and a fiery expression. *Epic*, she mouthed.

I swallowed. "Ma, wait!" Dropping Lily's hand, I turned to where my mom had stopped in the wings. "You think I can take the mic for a second?"

A look of curiosity crossed my mother's face, but as

always, I had her full support. "Of course, love. They would love to hear from you. Most are here for you two anyway," she said with a teasing smile. "Just let me introduce you."

The dying applause from Chase's antics swelled again as Ma glided across the stage. Lily tilted her head, watching me from beneath her eyelashes. I huffed a laugh as she pursed her lips.

Yeah, good luck guessing what I'm up to, Red. I can't believe it myself.

"Such lovely friends here today," Ma said warmly, her voice carrying through the room. "We at Ilusiòn are so grateful you have chosen to spend your morning with us. It is a joy and a privilege to share dance with the community that I love. Before I release you to the delicious hors d'oeuvres and desserts The Baking Room has so generously provided, we're excited to show you one last routine. This couple is very special to me—I think to many of you, too—and one of them wishes to speak before they perform. As I'm not above a little nepotism, I agreed!"

Ma laughed joyously, and the crowd joined in, the rise of excited murmurs implying several had snuck a peek at their programs. An assumption confirmed when she said, "Won't you please join me in welcoming the lovely Lily Bailey and her partner, my son, Ágoston 'Stone' Torres!"

Whistles, claps, and even a few catcalls—definitely from my teammates—erupted beyond the curtain, and with a tight smile I held out my hand, hoping Lily would take it. When her palm slid against mine, the pressure in my chest eased a fraction. I started leading her to the stage, but when we reached my sister, Lily tugged back on my hand.

"Wait." Biting her lip, and with a quick glance toward the beckoning stage, she slipped off her glasses and handed them to Angéla. She wrinkled her nose. "Can't hurt, right?"

I gave her a small smile, then continued forward, eventually leaving her where the spotlight wasn't focused.

Here went nothing.

Or, well, everything.

Projecting confidence I didn't feel, I strolled to my mother and accepted the mic with a quick kiss to her cheek. Ma beamed at me before stepping back.

Damn. The audience had multiplied during the short walk from backstage. Though I knew that wasn't possible, my anxiety didn't care. Swallowing hard, I glanced to where Chase and Angéla were standing in the wings. My best friend nodded in solidarity, then slid his arm around my sister's shoulder. A look of surprise—and something else—washed over her face before it went carefully blank, and she sent me a thumbs-up.

"Most of you are probably surprised I'm up here." The spotlight centered on me, and I squinted in response. *Thanks, Dad.* "You're used to me wearing cleats, not dance shoes." I kicked up a foot, and as everyone chuckled, I forced my shoulders to relax. Focusing on the control booth, I imagined I was speaking to an empty room. "For those of you who didn't catch it, my mom owns Ilusiòn. Over the last thirteen years, she's done a lot for this town. The studio has provided space for several school dances, her students have entertained you at countless festivals, and hundreds of you have walked through her door for lessons."

The side curtain rustled, and I peeked over to see Ma standing next to Angéla. Looking at her, I said, "Dance has the power to change your life. It gives confidence, and through it, you learn teamwork, focus, and discipline. It's also a great way to stay fit. Tons of athletes include dance in their training, right along with weightlifting and cardio, because it adds flexibility and coordination. Personally, I can attest it relieves tension before and after an intense game."

Ma clasped her hands against her chest, her eyes soft and grateful. I smiled, then turned my attention to Lily. "Dance also introduced me to someone incredibly special."

Although she was still in shadow, I felt her surprise. I held a long, nerve-wracking breath, praying like hell I wasn't about to make this worse, then exhaled into the mic.

"I've accomplished a lot in my life. Most of you have witnessed it. But for the first time ever, I'm standing in front of you scared to death—and not just because I hate public speaking, either." While people laughed in support, my gaze, now adjusted to the bright lights, skimmed across the second row. Mr. Bailey and Sydney were leaning forward, lips parted and eyes wide. "I'm scared because I screwed up. I hurt someone I care about, and while it feels like I'm standing up here naked right now, she needs to hear my apology. And she deserves to hear it in front of all of you."

Sydney's mouth twitched in an approving smile, the equivalent of a three-minute cheer for her. My confidence grew, and my frantic grip on the mic eased.

"Over the last six weeks, Lily Bailey has taught me a lot, which is funny, because I was *supposed* to be teaching her. See, we had this deal…a dare, really. She'd take a few lessons, and I'd show her how to live in the moment. Instead, she taught me to stop fearing the future."

Somewhere, a phone rang. An agitated chorus of *shhh!* rang out, and I laughed, a soft chuckle of breath, as it was quickly silenced. Turning back to my partner, I watched as Lily raised her fingers to her lips, her beautiful eyes full of wonder.

"The future scared me because I didn't have the answers yet. To tell you the truth, I still don't. But I was so afraid of one day failing, letting down all of you, that I gave up on dreaming. I set my life on cruise control and went through the motions. But Lily…she saw right through me."

Glancing back at the spellbound audience, I had a feeling my speech was taking longer than Ma had expected, but thankfully, I was almost done. Just a bit more groveling to do.

"Lily taught me about hard work and determination. About how to let someone in—*really* in, enough to see the parts that aren't perfect. Most of all, she's taught me I can't hide everything behind a smile." I winced. "I do that. My frustrations, my insecurities, and the days I just don't want to deal, I hide it all behind an easy smile. She calls it my QB grin." I shot her a look, and she shook her head, a small, awestruck smile on her lips. "But the thing is, with her, I don't need to be the carefree guy at the top of the world. When she looks at me, she doesn't see football or expectations. She just sees me. Flawed and real, and, according to *her* anyway, a bit cocky."

"More than a bit," she called out, her raised voice playful, and as the crowd laughed, a second spotlight turned on, illuminating her pretty face. Tears were in her eyes, and I took a couple steps until I stood in front of her. Blocking the harsh glare of the lights.

"Red, there's a million reasons why you deserve someone better than me," I told her. "But I'm hoping none of them matter more than the fact that I'm in love with you."

Lily's mouth tumbled open, and a surge of murmurs and *aww*s rose from the auditorium, along with telltale flashes of cell phones. A tear escaped, gliding down her smooth cheek, and I took her hand in mine.

"I love you," I repeated, the relief of finally saying it almost leaving me weak. "I love how clumsy you are. I love how weird your outfits are and how you can't carry a tune to save your life. I love how passionately loyal you are and how hard you make me laugh. You're driven and focused, and you make me want to reach higher, do better. It kills me I ever made you doubt that." Sliding my fingers through hers, I squeezed and said, "Lily, you once told me you were looking for where you belonged, but see, I already know where that is. It's with me. Following me on the dance floor, but inevitably leading me everywhere else."

Delighted laughter sprang from her lips. Like always, it sent my heart racing, and a sense of invincibility washed over me. Her eyes glided over my face in wonder, and as she released my hand to slide it up my chest, the whispers of witnesses and the creak of seats drifted away.

Her gaze locked on mine, and I saw the truth before she spoke it. "I'm in love with you, too."

Lily's soft whisper, amplified by the microphone, carried across the room, and the auditorium exploded in cheers. My hands trembled as I scooped her up and buried my face in her hair, breathing in her sweet, citrus scent.

A deep voice, sounding a hell of a lot like Aidan's, shouted, "Kiss her, bro!" and Lily laughed, wrapping her arms around me.

The microphone slipped from my hand, and Ma's amused voice rose above the applause. "Well, it is good they are performing a dance of love, yes?"

I groaned at the attempted segue, but Lily giggled, pulling back to smile at me. A rosy glow lit her cheeks, and with the love and happiness shining in her eyes, my world clicked back into place.

Ma smiled indulgently. "Are you ready *now*?" she asked, and I glanced at my girl.

A confident grin curved Lily's lips, and she grabbed hold of the pendant at her throat. "Let's do this."

Falling into position across from her was as natural as breathing, and with no secrets between us, I felt like I could slay dragons. What still terrified me, though, was dancing in front of a packed auditorium. It was ridiculous and dumb, worrying about their judgment, but I'd lived most of my life seeking validation. It was hard to flip it off like a switch.

I gazed out at the crowd, imagining their reactions, and Lily squeezed my hand.

"Hey, no one else matters, right? It's just you and me and the music." Those were the words I'd told *her* during our first lesson together, and a smile broke across my face as she repeated them. Blue eyes twinkled as she added, "Just keep your eyes on me, QB."

The music started…and we danced.

Epilogue

STONE

The heady scent of charred meat made my stomach rumble in time with the heavy salsa rhythm currently floating in the air. Leaning my back against a column on my porch, I popped the top of a Dr Pepper and chugged. After a long day with huge wins, there was only one thing that sounded better than a cold drink, good food, and a chance to breathe easy for the first time in six weeks, and Lily was already on her way.

To call today a success would be severely underselling it. The buzzing crowd had barely dispersed from the auditorium—leaving behind a mile-long list of interested new students—when Ma had called for a celebratory barbecue. That had been before I'd even introduced her to the phys ed teachers, too. As expected, they'd loved every minute of the showcase, in particular the youthful energy Ma had infused in her routines, and they'd been eager to discuss introducing dance to their schools. Surprise had filled Ma's wide eyes when she turned to me, followed quickly by gratitude, and I'd had to tamp down the overwhelming rush of pride.

Turned out, I'd found a way to help my parents after all.

After twenty minutes of trying to drag her away, we'd ended up leaving her at the auditorium gushing with the teachers over ideas, so we could get home and start the grill. After a quick change, I'd helped Dad prep the meat while Angéla took over decorations and Chase made a run to the store. An hour later, the music was on, the place was set, and the grill was fired up. Now I just needed my girl.

Damn, it felt good knowing she was mine again. Just thinking it had my knees going weak with relief, and my T-shirt snagged on the brick at my back. Two days without Lily had been two days too long, and I was determined never to go through that again. If I did screw up in the future—and let's face it, I probably would—I definitely wouldn't make such a mess of it.

This experience taught me I needed her. Lily centered me. When those big blue eyes were locked on mine, my rough edges smoothed away. Lily made me feel like I was more than football, that I could do anything. She got me. Plain and simple.

Across the backyard, Angéla caught my eye, and I lifted my soda in gratitude. The days of teasing my sister about her Hollywood obsession were over. Today proved epic gestures were legit. I owed my relationship to her…well, and to Patrick Swayze.

A *beep beep* had me turning around, hoping to see my favorite redhead walking through the back door. Instead, I saw my favorite pint-sized Hungarian whirlwind. That worked, too.

"My handsome boy!" Ma beamed a megawatt smile as she cut a line toward me, navigating patio furniture. Throwing her arms wide, she slung them around my waist and declared, "You take such good care of me."

She squeezed me tight and glanced up with green eyes liquid with love and hope. The hope was a nice change of pace.

"You happy, Ma?" I asked, hugging her back.

"Yes, my darling. So happy. The teachers and I made plans for the programs, wait till you hear! And then Marcus suggested a teen class at the studio for all the fresh new faces." Her excitement was palpable as she bounced on her toes. "A whole new generation is going to fall in love with dance!"

My throat squeezed with emotion. "That's awesome, Ma," I told her, hugging her a little tighter. Seeing the worry erased from her eyes and knowing I'd made it happen? Right then, I wondered if it was possible to be *too* happy.

Then, she ruined it by smacking me upside the head.

"*Sh*— Crap! What the hell was that for?"

"That, my darling, is for not listening," she replied with a knowing twist of her lips. "Don't think I didn't notice you butted in. I didn't want you worried. This was our problem. You are the child, and I want you focused on school."

Rubbing my head—don't let her size fool you; the woman packs a serious wallop—I considered stating the obvious. We were in the position we were now, Ilusiòn saved, *because* I didn't listen. But, before I could stick my foot in even further, she continued with a determined lift to her chin. "Just because you ended up right doesn't mean *I* was wrong."

I bit back a laugh at her logic. My mom was a lot of things: vivacious, loving, passionate, and most of all, stubborn as hell. When she believed she was right, there was no arguing with her. That was fine by me. I'd take slightly annoyed but hopeful over lost and depressed any day.

Besides, Ma also had a gooey center.

Wrapping an arm around her shoulders, I tugged her close and pressed a kiss against her hair. "Love you, Ma." I waited until she slumped against me with a happy, forgiving sigh, then whispered, "Even when you're wrong."

At her gasp of mock-outrage I laughed and jostled her against me. "Listen, you do everything for us, and I know how much the studio means to you. This was my turn to step up. I wasn't about to sit back and let it go without helping." Her eyes went soft again, and I had to add, "After all, I inherited my stubbornness from *you*."

With that, I pushed off the brick column and danced away with a grin, turning back at the door to send her a wink. The humor in her eyes said we were good, and more than that, we were set. My gut told me Ilusiòn would be just fine after today, and my gut was never wrong.

Inside the kitchen, I headed straight for the basket of apples on the counter, needing a snack to hold me over until that meat was ready, only to freeze when the chime of the doorbell echoed off the tile.

Twenty steps had me at the front door. "Mr. Bailey," I greeted with a polite head bob, my eyes locked on his daughter. "Glad you could join us."

Lily smiled shyly, love radiating from her eyes. I was tempted to take the covered tray in her hands, give it to her dad, and drag her to my room. Instead I took it from her and lifted it to my nose. "Mmm. Brownies."

She huffed. "How on earth did you guess that?"

"Red, I don't have time to explain the intricacies of the male stomach to you," I replied, earning a snort from her dad. I widened the door and waved them through. "But rest assured, when it comes to food, I know my stuff. Especially if it involves chocolate."

Lily rolled her eyes but gave me the smile I was looking for, then wrapped her hand around my arm. Mr. Bailey glanced at our connection for a full beat before bringing his eyes to mine and giving me an approving nod. Another piece clicked into place.

I led them through the house and back outside where Dad immediately handed Mr. Bailey a beer and Ma started reminiscing about his days at the studio. I wished Lily could have had both her parents here, and a part of me wondered if Mrs. Bailey would've approved of me, too. I had to hope she would if she knew how much I loved her daughter.

After setting the brownies on the table, I threaded my fingers through Lily's and tugged her over to our love seat. As we sat down, the memories of our stolen night on these cushions washed over me, urging me to make new, fresh memories—and soon.

"Dad and I had a good talk on the way over here," she murmured, turning to face me while sliding a leg under her. "During Thanksgiving break, we're gonna take a long-overdue family vacation. Go tour a few Texas colleges before applications are due."

"Oh yeah?" I was so busy watching the way the slight breeze lifted her cinnamon hair that it took a few heartbeats for her words to sink in. Once they did, my spine snapped straight. "Wait. Do you mean…?"

Lily nodded and tucked a chunk of hair behind her ear. "Harvard is an amazing school," she told me, "but I recently realized it's not where my heart is anymore."

"It's not?" I asked, scooting across the cushion until our thighs were flush and my hand was curved around her blushing cheek. She bit the corner of her lip and shook her head.

"There's no way Boston can duplicate a Cypress Lake

churro," she replied seriously. I shot her a look, and she grinned. "Plus, Texas schools have a lot to offer. The commute will be easy, and I'll be close to Dad, which will be good. We have a lot of repairing to do."

I nodded sagely, then brushed my thumb across her jaw. "Are those the only reasons?"

"N-no," she whispered, goose bumps prickling across her skin. "You, uh, might have something to do with it, too."

Our gazes locked, and that same sense of peace and connection I felt the night of our first kiss rushed over me. What did I do to get this lucky? "You know, maybe my family should take a college trip, too," I said, sliding my hand down to the soft skin of her throat. I followed the movement with my gaze, realizing it was *my* turn to feel shy. "I, uh, think I finally figured out what I want to do."

"You mean like in college?" she asked, and I looked into her eyes as I nodded. "Stone, that's great! But what did I miss in the last two days? Did something happen?"

"Liam happened," I admitted, remembering how it had felt out on the field. As heartbroken as I'd been missing Lily, seeing the love of the game in his eyes had woken something up inside me. "That kid…I know you know this, but *damn* is he awesome. He's fearless and strong, and all he wants to do is play football. It got me thinking about other kids, kids who love sports but for some reason find they can't play."

I raised my eyes to hers, nervous as to what she'd think of my idea. "I want to be a physical therapist and help children like that. Help kids like Liam accomplish their goals. Or get as close as humanly possible."

Admiration lit her expressive blue eyes, washing over me like a balm. "Stone, you'd be incredible at that."

I kissed her nose. "*You're* incredible," I tossed back, hearing even as I did how cheesy it was. Ask me if I gave

a damn. Lily's lips twisted like she didn't believe me, and
I leaned my forehead against hers. "Red, I don't think you
realize how much you've changed me. For the first time in
my life, I have a sense of direction. A plan for the future
instead of a giant question mark. I'm happier than I ever
thought I could be, and it's because of you."

The self-deprecating smirk transformed into a happy
grin, and when I returned it, Lily's gaze fell to my lips. Desire
tightened my stomach as her warm breath coasted across
my chin, and I leaned in, brushing my mouth across hers.

…And got slapped on the back of my head.

"Shit!" Turning around, I glared at my twin and asked,
"What is with the women in this family knocking me around
today?"

"There are parents afoot," Angéla shot back happily,
setting down a loaded tray of cheese, lettuce, tomato, and
other fixins for burgers. "Keep it PG, Romeo."

She winked at Lily, who blushed an even prettier shade
of pink than before and pushed to her feet. "Here, let me
help you get things ready."

The heated look she sent my way said we'd definitely
be picking this back up later—when annoying sisters and
parental figures weren't around—and then she took off for
the overflowing table. One minute she was on the move…
stepping over my feet and the coffee table to get across me…
and the next, she was falling through the air.

It was like déjà vu from the stairwell.

Without thought I stood and clenched my hands around
her waist, tugging her back against my chest and saving her
from face-planting onto the deck.

Angéla gasped, Lily groaned, and before I could stop it,
a chuckle escaped my throat.

"Someone order a white knight?" I teased against her ear,

enjoying the excuse to hold her close, even as the previous heat in her eyes was doused with embarrassed annoyance.

"One of these days, QB, I'm gonna be the one saving *you*," she huffed, letting me guide her back to her feet. Once she was firmly planted, I set my hands on either side of her pretty face and looked square in the eyes I loved so much.

"You already did, Red. You already did."

Acknowledgments

In the entirety of this roller-coaster author life, there are two things that fill me with equal parts joy and terror: the slow, constant blink of the cursor at the start of a new novel...and the bittersweet request from my editor for Acknowledgments. The first symbolizes endless possibilities, countless stories to tell and twists to explore, and the impossible task of choosing one. The second represents all the incredible people who helped a particular story come to life — and the truly scary prospect of accidentally leaving someone out. If I do that now, please know that it is simply my homeschooling mama brain at fault, and that I appreciate each and every person who speaks encouragement, assistance, and love into my life. I'm so very blessed!

Eyes on Me is my eleventh published novel to date. That's mindboggling to write. What makes it even more incredible is that I'm still working with the same editor who kicked off my dream. Stacy Abrams, I adore you. Completely, wholeheartedly, and with so much gratitude and joy that I can barely stand it. Thank you for putting up with my tome-length comments during editing and my overthinking ways, and for being my calm in this business. Also, a huge shout out to Judi Lauren. Thank you so much for your hard work and eagle eye, and for loving Stone as much as I do!

Entangled Publishing is an incredible family and that

supportive, dynamic energy is 100 percent because of our fearless leader, Liz Pelletier. Liz, you've always been in my corner, cheering me on, but you took it beyond with this book. Thank you for helping me find Lily and Stone's story, and for your sweet patience with all my questions. So much love and gratitude to Hannah Lindsey, who is such a pleasure to work with that I've officially requested her for life! All my thanks to the staff who work so tirelessly behind the scenes, helping me shine: Heather Ricco, Jessica Turner, Katie Clapsadl, Curtis Svehlak, Meredith Johnson, Debbie Suzuki, and Melanie Smith. I don't know what I did to deserve working with such an amazing company, but I'll never stop being grateful.

A huge shout-out to my foreign rights agent, Rebecca Mancini at Rights Mix, for being so gracious and awesome. You'll never know how much it means to see my words written in different languages and being able to show my daughters that dreams come true and this world is smaller than we think. The written word binds us together. What a beautiful thing for them to learn!

I had the most amazing alpha readers ever with this book, and *Eyes on Me* would not exist without Staci Murden, Ashley Bodette, Moriah Chavis, and Megan Wilson. These incredible women read each chapter as I wrote it, giving me their thoughts and insights, their love and gentle guidance, and with each cheer and every nudge, this story took shape. Lily and Stone live and breathe because of you, and words don't exist to describe my gratitude. You helped me believe in this book, your words encouraged me, and you made it better than I could've ever hoped for. Thank you, friends!

As always, thank you to my author twin, Cindi Madsen, for always being my listening ear and sounding board. Also, all much love to Wendy Higgins, Katie McGarry, Amalie

Howard, Angie Frazier, and Suzanne Young for all the hand-holding, support, and laughs along the way.

Flirt Squad, you rock! Thank you for always believing in me and all your support. I know you waited a long time to meet Stone…I hope he was worth it!

Holly, Viktória, Emanuele, John, Dimitri, and the entire staff at Fred Astaire Dance Studio Champions—thank you for inspiring me! Also, thank you for bringing dance into my marriage. Weddings and date nights will never be the same. Viktória, thank you for being such a feisty dynamo that *needed* and *deserved* to be immortalized in fiction. I hope I did you justice! Holly, thank you not only for being such a wonderful teacher, but for all the wonderful advice and suggestions for this story. You women are my heroes!

My husband is more than my rock; he's my best friend, my critique partner, my sanity, and my heart. Gregg, I love you more than life itself. Thank you for constantly showing me that romance is real and that love is worth fighting for. Also, thanks for all the football info! I worked in Drew Brees for you (hehe). SHMILY!!

Jordan and Cali, my two beautiful girls…thank you for inspiring me. You are both such gifted writers and you push me to be better, too. I love how enthusiastic you are about the written word, and I cherish all our discussions about the books on our shelves. Teaching you every day is my greatest privilege, and being your mom is my greatest honor.

Finally, thank *you*, fabulous reader. There are so many options out there, so that you chose to read my words means everything. I hope I entertained you for a short while. Thank you for every email, every review, every tweet, and every post you write. I save them all and pull them back out when I get stuck or need encouragement. Thank you for making my dreams a reality. I'm humbled. To God be the glory.

LOVED *EYES ON ME?*

Then you won't want to miss
Rachel Harris's hilarious and heart-melting
time-travel trilogy!

Read on for an excerpt from

MY SUPER SWEET
SIXTEENTH
CENTURY

Available now wherever books
and ebooks are sold.

I am alone in Florence.

A quick check to my watch confirms I have an hour before I need to be back at the hotel, and I plan to enjoy it.

A couple of guys zip by me on bikes as I turn down a side street, wandering and exploring, following the crowd and my internal navigation system. I end up at an outdoor market and slow my natural stride to match the lazy pace of the other patrons. Stalls are bursting at the seams with leather jackets, purses, and belts, and I make a mental shopping list of all the goodies I plan to come back and buy. At an outdoor delicatessen, a young boy working behind the counter offers me a sample of biscotti, and it literally melts in my mouth.

The street sign for the Via Sant'Antonino is ahead, and even though it's only been fifteen minutes, I decide to head back to the hotel. It's probably best not to push Dad to the limit on the very first day. Plus, if I come back early, maybe he'll give me a get-out-of-jail-free card on that *family* dinner later.

Fat chance, but hey, it's worth a shot.

I round the corner, and a dark army-green tent catches my eye, its front flaps fluttering in the breeze. It seems odd—a tent in the middle of the street—but I continue past until two older women walk by and I hear the word *gypsy* over the clanging of church bells.

My ears perk up, and I stop. Maybe it's Victor Hugo's influence—Esmeralda, the badass gypsy in *The Hunchback of Notre Dame,* is my favorite character in the novel so far—or the whole When in Rome—er, Florence—mentality, but I decide to be wild for once.

In forty-five minutes, I'll be having lunch and finalizing plans for a lavish, extravagant, overpriced, stupid, *unwanted* birthday gala where I'll be forced under a microscope for all the world to criticize. I want—no, *need*—to do something just for me.

Something private and very, very un-Cat-like.

I pull back the flap and enter the gypsy's tent.

Inside, it's dim, with only a few lit candles illuminating the space. The flap closes behind me, but for the effect, it may as well be a steel door—the outside noise is completely muffled. I take a step, and gravel crunches under my sandals, sounding all the louder in this spooky setup.

I've officially walked into the Twilight Zone.

"Hello?"

I stretch my hand out and feel a ledge. Opening my eyes wide, I struggle to read the framed sign perched atop some sort of intricate shelving system. It says to place any bags or belongings on the top shelf, and to take off my shoes and slide them into the tray provided.

I really don't get how Steve Madden gladiators will interfere with a psychic reading, but whatever. I'm being wild.

Tiptoeing farther inside, following the trail of dotted candlelight, I continue to be amazed at how large the space seems. It's a freaking tent, and not even a big one at that, yet I feel as though I could walk forever. One side is completely lined with shelves, and from the flickering flames of the candles, I can see rows of teacups, labeled vials, unlit candles, crystal balls, and stacks of cards.

As I drift toward the back of the tent, the smell of patchouli incense tickles my nose, and I see a small card table with a black silk sheath draped over it. Resting in the middle is a large sapphire-colored candle, its flame a spotlight on the woman sitting behind it.

Her entire face is covered by purple veils; only her eyes

are visible.

Creeptastic.

"What answers do you seek?"

I jump. Not because I didn't see her mouth move or the fact that she spoke English. But her voice is not at all what I expected. It's youthful, cautious, and...Russian?

I lean closer to get a better look, but all I can see is the layers of veils covering her head and mouth. And those eyes. Even from this slight distance, they are hypnotic. A combination of ancient wisdom and sparkling humor, as if she's peering into my mind and laughing at what's inside. My scalp tingles, and a shiver of unease dances down my spine, but I refuse to leave. I've already come this far.

The woman, or I guess I should say girl, lifts an eyebrow, and it disappears behind a veil. I realize she is waiting for an answer, but for the life of me, I can't remember the question. I blink a few times and rack my brain, my eyes never straying from hers.

"You fancy a reading, *tatcho*?"

Her blunt question and flat, tired voice shake me out of my trance and remind me this isn't real. If it wasn't for the occasional funny beep of tiny foreign cars, this could totally be happening in some back room in West Hollywood. Not that I believe any of this hocus-pocus stuff, anyway. The only destiny I believe in is the one I can control. So I shrug and say, "Yeah, whatever you usually do, I guess."

The gypsy flicks her wrist, causing dozens of bracelets to *clank* in unison, and motions to the chair opposite her. She continues to stare at me from behind the table, her head slightly tilted, her hazel eyes narrowed. Finally she nods and walks over to one of the shelves, her layers of bright, multicolored chiffon skirts swishing around her feet. She picks up a teacup.

I wonder if I should mention that I don't really dig tea. "What is your name?"

Part of me is tempted to tell her if she were a real psychic she'd know it already, but somehow I doubt that'll go over too well. "Cat."

She pauses mid-sit and lifts her head. "Cat?"

Her disbelieving tone irks me. I straighten my shoulders, put on my usual mask of aloofness, and say, "Caterina. You need a last name, too?"

Although I can't be sure, I think I hear her snort from behind the veil, which just annoys me even more. It's impossible to get a handle on this girl. The gypsy shakes her head and begins preparing the tea, and I pretend to relax back in my seat. A nervous energy buzzes through my veins. Maybe this wasn't the best idea I've ever had.

Holding the pearl teacup by its delicate handle, the gypsy pours hot water from a kettle on a nearby hot plate, and then stirs in a heaping spoonful of tea leaves from a tin. Neither of us speaks while the tea steeps. She just sits across from me, her eyes boring into mine. I try to glance around the tent but continue to be drawn back to her gaze, like she exudes some type of magnetic force field. Eventually my eyes grow accustomed to the dark, and I'm able to see hers more clearly. They are strangely beautiful, like a luminous marble, amber colored with specks of russet, jade, and charcoal.

It's spooky. But I'm completely transfixed.

The spell is broken when she reaches for the cup. She blows on it, holds it out, and says, "You are right handed, so you must take this cup with your left. As you drink, relax and clear your mind. Try not to think. If something does continue to come to mind, however, hold onto it. Meditate on it. Make sure to leave a small amount of tea at the bottom of your cup and try not to consume too many of the leaves. When you're done, hand it back to me."

There seem to be an awful lot of rules just to drink some tea and make up a fake fortune, but I'll go with it. I take a sip. The tea is hot, and the floating leaves are icky and tickle my mouth, but I drink. I try to keep my mind clear like she said, but for some annoying reason, Jenna keeps popping in. Visions of her laughing and constantly trying to give me a hug assault me, then are replaced with equally disturbing ones of my mother. Fuzzy snapshot images from when she was actually around and then clearer, sharper ones from the big screen. Despite my every attempt to do or think otherwise, my mother continues to appear.

In my effort to stop the movie playing in my head and push away all the chaotic emotions those two women bring, I nearly drink the entire cup of tea. Luckily, I catch myself and hand it back. Definitely want to avoid incurring any gypsy wrath. I wipe my mouth and pretend not to be eager to hear her response.

Okay, so maybe I'm the tiniest bit superstitious.

She swirls my cup three times, then dumps the last bit of the tea into the saucer. She keeps the cup overturned for a few seconds before flipping it back over and peering inside.

I tap my fingers on the table and ask, "See anything good?"

The gypsy nods. "*Arvah*. I see a tent."

"A tent? You mean, like the one we're in?"

She nods again. "A *tsera*—a tent—is a symbol for adventure. You may find yourself doing something completely different soon. Perhaps travel is in your future."

Hmm. A tent like the one we're in and traveling in my future. Pretty convenient, considering I'm a tourist. Aloud I say, "Adventure, huh? Like emancipating myself and relocating permanently to Florence?"

She lifts an eyebrow, and I wave her off. "Kidding, obviously."

I get up from the table and realize the tent has gotten smaller. No, that's silly; my eyes must have adjusted to the dim lighting. Either that, or this chick has some seriously freaky tea.

I walk back to my bag at the front of the tent and hear her fall in step behind me. As I stretch to reach into the front pouch to get my wallet, I twist around. "How much for the, uh, session?"

The gypsy's eyes grow wide, and her brows disappear behind the veil again. I look down, expecting to find a tarantula or some other crazy creepy-crawly to justify her being so freaked, and see the small tattoo on my right hip exposed. I drop my arms and yank down my shirt.

She bolts toward me, staring intently at the cute top now covering my body art. "May I?" she asks hesitantly.

I bite my lip and think. I never show anyone my tattoo. Considering my age, getting one wasn't exactly legal, especially since I didn't have Dad's permission. But more than that, it's personal.

A reminder.

But the girl seems so fascinated, and it's not like I have to share its meaning or anything. If she's a real psychic, she'll know. Very slowly, I lift the hem of my shirt to uncover my upper right hip. Her fingers flex as if she intends to brush them over my stomach, and I flinch. Gingerly, she draws them back.

"The painted pear."

The gypsy's voluminous outfit of veils tickles my arm. We're the same height, so I have no problem looking into her eyes. The skin around them crinkles, and if I thought she looked intense before, it was nothing compared to this enthrallment. She's practically humming. I lower my shirt again and say, "Uh, yeah. It's from my favorite Renaissance painting. *Madonna and Child with Apples and Pears*?"

I'm normally not one to turn my statements into questions, but the girl is kind of freaking me out.

She nods and then claps her hands, and I get the distinct impression that I'm missing something. "The *ambrol*. The Renaissance. *Misto!*"

A muscle in my eyelid starts to twitch as I slowly follow her to the back of the tent where she's flitting about. I know I should probably just leave, but I can't stop watching the scene playing out before me. It's as if someone flipped a switch—all reserved gypsy mannerisms have completely been thrown out the window. Or in this case, out the tent flap.

The girl twirls and dances over to a shelf containing rows and rows of unlit candles. "It is time," she says, darting a glance back toward me, a Cheshire cat smile on her face. "I have waited years for this *divano*."

She runs her fingers across the orange candles, then the white, and hesitates over the yellow before landing on the purple and nodding. She grabs a bejeweled jug and motions me back to the table with a wag of her head.

"Please, stay but a moment more." Her smile withers when I hesitate with one hand on my bag. "There will be no charge."

If living in LA has taught me anything, it's that nothing is ever free. I check my watch. It's one thirty. It'll take me twenty minutes to get back to the hotel from here, which means I have ten minutes, tops.

But I'm intrigued.

I walk to the table and sit on the edge of my seat. The girl's smile returns, and she sets her supplies down. "You may call me Reyna," she says in a noticeably thicker accent as she carves *Caterina* onto one side of the candle. I want to tell her it's Cat—my self-involved mother may have named me after her, but only Dad's allowed to utter my given name—but what's the point? This will all be over in a few minutes, and I'll never see this girl again.

Reyna writes something else on the other side, but I can't make it out in the candlelight. Then she picks up the sparkly jug and pours what appears to be oil onto the candle before setting it down on a mirror and lighting the wick. I jump at the sudden burst of light. The dancing flame, along with the reflected glow, causes elongated shadows to fall across the table. Strange shapes appear within the inky outlines, and I struggle to convince myself it's just my overactive imagination rearing its ugly head again.

I have definitely seen one too many movies.

Staring into the flames, Reyna chants, "Powers that be, powers of three, let Caterina's destiny be all that I see."

She repeats it two more times before grabbing my hands and closing her eyes.

Nothing happens, and I assume whatever voodoo stuff she tried to do failed. Surprise, surprise. I go to get up, and then the table begins to shake.

Reyna's cool fingers snake up and grasp my wrists.

I try to wrench them away, but Reyna's grip tightens as she pulls me forward and throws her head back.

Suddenly the flame snuffs out and the room goes black.

Every sense I have goes on red alert as I try to remember any of the moves from the self-defense class Dad made me take. I can see the headline now: Daughter of Hollywood Murdered by Nutcase Gypsy.

She frees my wrists, and I cradle them to my chest even though they don't hurt. A queasy feeling churns in my stomach. My skin prickles, and there is a subtle yet undeniable roar in my ears.

I sense Reyna moving around in the dark, and my muscles clench, ready to bolt. She strikes a match, and a spark ignites. When the large candle is relit, Reyna is standing over me, eyes glittering. I spring from my chair, my hand at my throat.

"Dude, are you trying to give me a heart attack?"

Reyna ignores my gasps for air and nails me with an eerie stare. "Caterina, a great adventure is in store for you. Be sure to keep your mind open to the lessons ahead."

She nods toward the front of the tent, almost dismissively. I stand there disbelieving—and to be honest, more than a little frazzled—waiting for more. Surely she's going to explain what all *that* was about.

Or not. Instead of giving any semblance of an explanation for the creepy parlor trick I just witnessed, Reyna just continues to stand there smiling, bouncing on her toes.

Okay, then.

With a shake of my head, I move to the front of the tent. "Well, thanks. For the free reading. That was…interesting."

I grab my bag and slip my feet into my sandals. As I slide my sunglasses on, I keep waiting for her to say something, anything, but she remains silent.

This chick is two French fries short of a Happy Meal.

I stop just inside the tent, a hand on the front flap, to look at her one last time. Even from this distance, Reyna's eyes visibly dance with emotion. I give a stilted wave, and she nods again, but as I turn around, she whispers, "*Latcho Drom*, Caterina."

With chill bumps racing down my spine, I pull back the flap and step outside.

My first thought as I take in my surroundings, squinting

at the bright sunlight permeating my shades, is that I must've been in the tent for a lot longer than thirty minutes. My next thought is that Italians are crazy.

The street is inexplicably filled with reenactors, dressed as if they're at a Renaissance festival and taking their jobs way too seriously.

I stand there blinking, watching a donkey-drawn cart full of produce roll past me down the narrow road. The clattering of the cart's wheels on the cobblestones echoes off the buildings, and all of a sudden, I am hit with the powerful stench of animal feces.

Lovely. Definitely time to head back to the hotel.

Stepping away from the tent, I feel soft fabric brush across my leg. Absently, I look down and freeze.

I'm wearing a flowing golden gown.

What the heck?

Flipping my sunglasses onto my head, I whirl back around to interrogate Reyna, but instead of the tent I just stepped out of, I see a goat. A freaking goat. Both the tent and Reyna are gone.

What was in that gypsy tea?

Mystified, I think back to the last half hour and try to make sense of what's happened. All around me, people are dressed in similar period outfits, without a single badly dressed tourist in the bunch. The buildings look the same but cleaner, and somehow everything seems brighter, the colors sharper. There are no rumbling engines to drown out voices or the rasping *click* of cicadas.

I wander absently down the road, past reenactors hawking food from makeshift stalls, searching for any type of reflective surface to look into—perhaps a sideview mirror of a car or a shiny window—but the *polizia* must have cleared the streets for the weird reenactment. Maybe it's a national holiday. How that explains my wardrobe change, however, is completely beyond me.

I spin around, disoriented, and my backpack slaps hard across my back.

Normalcy.

I'm not crazy. I have my backpack, my white-knuckled grip on sanity. I stoop down and tear into it, grateful it's loaded with so much crap. I unzip my makeup case and pull out my compact. When I glimpse my reflection, I do a double take.

The first thing I notice is that my zit is gone.

Hallelujah for small miracles!

Then I notice the scrubbed face. Every lick of makeup that I painstakingly applied a few hours ago is gone. I like to think of the face as just another canvas to paint on, and right now, mine is completely blank. It's like I'm auditioning for a Neutrogena commercial. Tilting the mirror farther and sliding off my shades, I see my hair is twisted on top of my head in a braided crown, a vibrant red ribbon threaded through it. Definitely not the way I fixed it — I stopped doing ribbons in kindergarten.

Maybe I'm dreaming.

I pinch myself. Hard. "Freakin' A!"

Nope, not a dream.

Enrapt in the enigma that is suddenly my life, I rub my arm and stare at my backpack, the one thing that still makes sense. I don't hear the man dressed like a crazed Shakespearean fanatic until he is standing right in front of me. He touches my hand and looks at me with concern. "Signorina D'Angeli?"

My spine tenses, and my teeth clench, but I paste on a sunny smile. Someone was bound to recognize me or see the resemblance eventually. I yank my hand back and open my mouth to inform him he's wrong—that I'm not my mother—but out comes, *"Vi sbagliate."*

Holy crap!

Do I know what I said? I think for a moment and realize I do. I'd said, *"You are mistaken."*

Since when do I know Italian?

He gives me a puzzled look and motions with his cane toward a carriage that is sitting on the side of the narrow road. I look at the people traipsing about and realize I've become the center of attention—as if *I'm* the weird one!

My worst nightmare is coming true, standing in the middle of their scrutiny with no place to hide. Having one parent in front of the camera and the other behind it, you'd think I'd relish the attention. Or at least be used to it.

I hear their muffled whispers and understand every Italian word. Every witty comment made at my expense.

It's like my brain is automatically translating.

I bunch the soft fabric of the dress in my hand and then reach up to feel the ribbon in my hair. I lightly skim my fingers over my chin and feel my lack of zit. I take in the costumes of the crowd, the stench of the animals, and the Italian I can now speak and understand. And suddenly it hits me.

Reyna must have pulled some kind of gypsy mojo.

Maybe this is one of those nifty "change your life" magic scenarios like in the movies. I mean, mostly I'm still expecting to blink and be right back in the midst of overpriced, gaudy tourism, but for now, the gypsy-time-warp explanation is infinitely better than thinking I've lost my mind. As I decide to go with that option, I feel my frantic tension melt away.

The growing crowd seems to notice my change in demeanor and begins shooting one another amused looks, but I don't care anymore. A smile stretches across my face. Evidently I was wrong earlier; Reyna *is* a psychic mind reader, because if this is her special brand of bibbity-bobbity-boo, than she made my exact daydream from earlier in the courtyard come to life.

The long gold gown, the braided hair, the Italian merchant's daughter, the time period. I am in Renaissance Florence.

I stare dumbly at the ground, the words and reality sinking in. *I'm in Renaissance Florence!*

**IF YOU ENJOYED THIS EXCERPT, PICK UP
MY SUPER SWEET SIXTEEN CENTURY
WHEREVER BOOKS AND EBOOKS ARE SOLD.**

A SEXY, WITTY NOVEL THAT WILL REMIND YOU

Life loves a good curveball...

whatever
LIFE
throws
AT YOU

by Julie Cross

Seventeen-year-old Annie Lucas's life is completely upended the moment her dad returns to the major leagues as the new pitching coach for the Kansas City Royals. Now she's living in Missouri (too cold), attending an all-girls school (no boys), and navigating the strange world of professional sports. But Annie has dreams of her own—most of which involve placing first at every track meet...and one starring the Royals' super-hot rookie pitcher.

But nineteen-year-old Jason Brody is completely, utterly, and totally off-limits. Besides, her dad would kill them both several times over. Not to mention Brody has something of a past, and his fan club is filled with C-cupped models, not smart-mouthed high school "brats" who can run the pants off every player on the team. Annie has enough on her plate without taking their friendship to the next level. The last thing she should be doing is falling in love.

But baseball isn't just a game. It's life. And sometimes, it can break your heart...

EASY A MEETS *THE CARRIE DIARIES* IN THIS
EDGY, CONTEMPORARY NEW RELEASE

ASK
ME
ANYTHING

by Molly E. Lee

I should've kept my mouth shut.

But Wilmot Academy's been living in the Dark Ages when it comes to sex ed, and someone had to take matters into their own hands. So *maybe* I told Dean, the smartest person in my coding class—and the hottest guy I've ever seen—that I was starting an innocent fashion blog. And *maybe* instead, I had him help me create a totally anonymous, totally untraceable blog where teens can come to get real, honest, nothing-is-off-limits sex advice.

The only problem? I totally don't know what I'm talking about.

Now not only is the school administration trying to shut me down, they've forced Dean to try to uncover who I am. If he discovers my secret, I'll lose him forever. And thousands of teens who need real advice won't have anyone to turn to.

Ask me anything…except how to make things right.

A TAUT, FAST-PACED THRILLER FROM VICTORIA SCOTT

we told six lies

by Victoria Scott

Remember how many lies we told, Molly? It's enough to make my head spin. You were wild when I met you, and I was mad for you. But then something happened. And now you're gone.

But don't worry. I'll find you. I just need to sift through the story of us to get to where you might be. I've got places to look, and a list of names.

The police have a list of names, too. See now? There's another lie. There is only one person they're really looking at, Molly.

And that's yours truly.

entangled teen

an imprint of Entangled Publishing LLC